Bookishly Ever After

Mia Page is a British author who got obsessed with *The West Wing* and somehow ended up spending ten years in Washington, DC, three of them working at the loveliest bookshop.

MIA PAGE

BOOKISHLY EVER AFTER

avon.

Published by AVON
A division of HarperCollins*Publishers*
1 London Bridge Street
London SE1 9GF

www.harpercollins.co.uk

HarperCollins*Publishers*
Macken House
39/40 Mayor Street Upper
Dublin 1, D01 C9W8
Ireland

A Paperback Original 2024
24 25 26 27 28 LBC 6 5 4 3 2

First published in Great Britain by HarperCollins*Publishers* 2024

Copyright © Claire Handscombe 2024

Claire Handscombe asserts the moral right to be identified as the author of this work.

A catalogue copy of this book is available from the British Library.

ISBN: 978-0-00-858734-5

Set in Birka at HarperCollins*Publishers* India
Printed and bound in the United States

For Allison Blake, forever the Elinor to my Marianne

Lexi Austen's New Year's Resolutions

- *Employ a manager so I don't have to be in the bookshop 24/7 and can have an actual life.*
- *Find the one decent guy in Washington DC (there must be one, right? Surely?) and make him my boyfriend. If that means going back on the apps, then okay, fine, whatever.*
- *Finally read* Mansfield Park *so I can properly call myself an Austen Completist. No point having my surname and being possibly (?) related to Jane if I haven't even read all her books.*

Chapter One

The date isn't going well.

Not that Lexi is surprised. Do they ever go well, really?

It started going wrong when she arrived at the bar, red-faced and sweating a little under her thick winter coat, and – horror of horrors in this town full of overachievers – four minutes late. And when the guy – Chad, Tom, Randy, whatever this one is called – finally stops talking about himself, his day, his commute, his Very Important Job, his choice of drink, Lexi's lateness is the first thing he chooses to comment on. Obliquely, of course. So that it doesn't seem rude. But he and Lexi both know better.

'Busy day?' he asks.

Lexi opens her mouth to defend herself, but she already knows from those two words and the slightly disparaging tone in which they're uttered exactly how this conversation is going to go.

'Actually, yes,' she says, after a deep breath and an internal count to ten. 'My days are all busy.'

Chad/Tom/Randy does the quizzical eyebrow thing people always do when she says things like this, i.e. when she says anything that implies that owning a bookshop is not all sunshine and puppy dogs, perching on high stools at artisanal coffee shops with a paperback open in front of her.

Lexi catches the bartender's eye to order what has become an emergency daiquiri.

'My meeting with my accountant overran,' she tells Chad/Tom/Randy, which, while it's true, is not the reason she's late. The reason she's late is that Layla – one of her favourite customers – was looking for a new thriller to take on holiday, and what was she supposed to do? Just leave her there to browse with no help or guidance, when Lexi knew a book that is perfect for her had just arrived, in long-awaited paperback?

'Cause that's a hard pass.

And then, when she started chatting about her latest five-star read, was Lexi supposed to hold her hand up, interrupt her, and say, 'I'm terribly sorry, but I have to stop talking to you about books because I'm meeting some random dude from one of the useless apps and it'll probably turn out to be a giant waste of everybody's time, but I'm going to choose to prioritise him over you right now?'

Again, no.

You might be surmising from all of this that perhaps Lexi isn't giving Chad or Tom or Randy a fair chance. Perhaps she's misread his tone, and he isn't being patronising at all, and she is just letting the nine thousand other dates she's had with DC dudes and their overinflated egos colour this experience, and Chad or Tom or Randy doesn't deserve it.

Well, maybe.

But also, maybe not.

'Accountant?' he repeats, and she hears it, the surprise in his voice, and then witnesses him trying to catch himself. 'I guess there's more to running a bookstore than sitting around reading all day.'

Lexi loves her job, but if there's anything about it that she doesn't love, it is, in fact, that she barely has time to read anymore, artisanal coffee shops or not. Honestly, it's a shock that she has time to shower some days. But if you're not working in politics, or – at bare minimum – in a politics-adjacent NGO, you might as well be sitting at home twiddling your thumbs as far as most men in Washington are concerned.

This dating charade is clearly a waste of time. She has known this since date 837 – since date 8, if she's honest with herself – and the last thing she has to spare is time.

Lexi takes a sip of her strawberry daiquiri, a long breath, then another sip. She'd be lying if she claimed she wasn't tempted to walk out. But this is a really good daiquiri, and she's more than earned it.

'Yes,' she tells him. 'There's managing a team schedule and paying bills and keeping customers happy and pitching publishers for events and keeping an eye on social media and balancing the chequebook and writing press releases and adding things up over and over to make the numbers make sense. For example.'

Chad or Tom or Randy has the decency to look sheepish, at least, which is how she knows she'd gauged his tone correctly. That he really was assuming owning a bookshop is a walk in the park, that maybe she'd have loads of free time to do his laundry and cook for him while he's out doing the more important thing of lobbying Congress for some vaguely unethical deal or schmoozing with someone who might be able to get him a job at the White House in the next administration.

Still, maybe she should let the drink work its magic. Maybe she should give him the benefit of the doubt. And maybe, if this wasn't her nine thousandth date with limited to zero prospects, she would have.

But she's tired.

You know, from all the sitting around reading books she pays herself millions of dollars to do.

So she asks Chad or Tom or Randy about his job, so that she can zone out and drink her daiquiri and make a graceful exit after a few polite comments. It's not walking out, exactly. But it's as close to it as she can manage.

And on the way home, she deletes the apps.

Chapter Two

When Lexi inherited her grandmother's bookshop, there was never any question that she was going to move to DC to run it. Selling it didn't once cross her mind. Her grandmother had intuited this, which was why she'd passed it on to her in the first place.

After all, what self-respecting bookworm with the last name Austen wouldn't want to have their own bookshop?

Light streaming through the window, creating a patch of sun for the resident cat to nap in, and casting a dappled pattern on the bookshelves. Handsome dads helping their little ones sound out newly learned words. Groups of teenagers clutching their milkshakes and debating the relative merits of dystopian trilogies. And Lexi's favourite thing of all: customers who aren't quite sure what they want and trust her with their next read, leaving the shop with arms full of books that perfectly fit their tastes: an unputdownable story of dysfunctional families, an experimental book of poetry, nonfiction to help them better understand the history of their city.

Who wouldn't want that?

But it turns out that owning a bookshop isn't just about a love of reading. It isn't even just about loving people, including in their less pleasant moments. Both of those things, Lexi can do: one of them without any effort whatsoever, the other painstakingly learned through thirty-two years of existing in the world.

But, maths: this, she cannot do.

And it also turns out that owning a bookshop involves a lot of maths.

'Uh-oh.' Natalie, Lexi's events manager, takes one look at her face as she sets down her fresh cup of tea.

Lexi mentally congratulates herself, not for the first time, at having successfully trained an American to make tea the way God intended, with properly boiled water and a splash of milk, using a kettle and not – shudder – a microwave.

'You okay? You have your *this-isn't-adding-up* face on.'

Lexi forces a smile. She knows it's not necessarily professional to air her worries to her colleagues – her employees – but she's only human, and she needs a sounding board. A decade or so older than Lexi, Natalie was the first person she took on six years ago who wasn't already working with her grandmother, and she's been with her through the ups and downs, the excitement of trending on TikTok and the despair of quiet January Mondays with close to zero sales. Lexi knows she can trust Natalie to keep things confidential.

'I really want to give everyone a pay rise. Goodness knows you all deserve it after everything you've all done to keep us open for the last few years. And I know it's three months away, but I've got to think about extra stock for Independent Bookstore Day. Plus the mural needs a fresh lick of paint . . .'

'Okay, Lexi,' Natalie says, shaking her head and swishing her long black hair in her high ponytail. 'Breathe.'

Lexi obediently inhales the steam from her tea and counts to ten. In the short-lived silence, Natalie tries to change the subject.

'How was the date last night?'

'Awful. More of the *isn't it nice to own a bookshop, you must have lots of time to read* rubbish.'

Natalie winces on Lexi's behalf. She knows being patronised is one of her red flags. 'Ouch.'

'Yeah. I'm starting to think I should give up on this whole dating thing. It's exhausting.' While Natalie is clearly still thinking about how to respond, Lexi returns to her original source of stress.

'Anyway, we've got to find some money to up our marketing. We're haemorrhaging customers to Sam Dickens.'

For almost thirty years, Lexi's grandmother's shop happily coexisted with the bookstore around the corner and its overly curmudgeonly owner, Arthur. Second Reading was a higgledy-piggledy shop crammed with used books shoved into every corner – health and safety seemingly be damned.

But then came 2020, and everyone had to do what they could to survive. Second Reading was sold to the highest bidder, and that highest bidder was Sam Dickens, and Sam Dickens had Ideas.

'I mean, would it have killed him to pivot to literally any other direction? People who love old books love expensive fountain pens. And jigsaw puzzles. And maps! Sometimes they love artisanal beer, too.'

Natalie nods. 'Locally crafted, to further support small business.'

'Exactly. It would have been perfect. But no. It had to be new books.'

Natalie knows this drill. This isn't the first time she and Lexi have had this conversation. It's not even the fifth, or the tenth. She recites the next line from Lexi's usual monologue.

'It had to be new books, taking up more and more of the shop so that now it looks like the second-hand stuff is just an afterthought, tucked away in a forgotten corner. New books are our brand. Not his brand.'

The thing is, though, Lexi isn't just incensed as a shop owner. She's also incensed as a reader, a browser, an engaged member of the community on Capitol Hill. Like so many others in the neighbourhood, she loved Second Reading for a certain kind of experience. For serendipitous finds and the smell of old books. For the slight hit of adrenaline that comes with wondering if a crammed bookshelf is going to collapse onto her head, delivering her the perfect read the way that Isaac Newton's apple delivered him world-changing inspiration.

In short, for the different vibe.

And, as a bookshop owner, she'd loved that this shop posed no direct threat to hers. In fact, when a customer urgently needed an older book that Pemberley Books didn't have in stock, she would have no qualms about sending them up the street.

Not anymore.

Now, it's war.

After Sam bought the shop a couple of years ago, he rebranded it, giving it the slightly pretentious if appropriately punny name of Great Expectations, and slowly edging out the mess and the serendipity, turning it gradually into a shiny corporate shell of a bookstore with lots of space and hard edges, all the personality of a Barnes and Noble meets all the charm of an Apple Store. Lexi isn't the only one who hates that. There have been protests. Sam doesn't care, though. He just wants to make money. Capitalism over community, profits over people. Bottom line over books.

At least, Lexi assumes so. Sam had seemed so reasonable when he'd come to introduce himself back when he took over Second Reading. Not overly friendly, but perfectly willing to stick to the unwritten laws of bookselling on the Hill. But as she's watched him gradually transform the previously beloved institution into something soulless, she's had to question her previous judgement.

'You know,' Natalie says, and here, flicking a strand of her long black hair over her shoulder, she deviates unexpectedly from the script. 'I can't help noticing he is very good-looking. And I'll bet *he* knows there's more to running a bookshop than sitting around reading.'

And then, as if she and Lexi weren't in the middle of a conversation, Natalie walks away, closes the door, and leaves Lexi furiously tapping the end of her pencil on a notepad, aghast at what Natalie is suggesting. Sam is everything that is wrong with the book world, and quite possibly the world more generally. It doesn't matter how good-looking he is. She'd never be *that* desperate.

Chapter Three

It's 9 p.m. by the time Lexi is stumbling home to the town house she shares with Erin, the childhood friend she reconnected with when she moved to DC six years ago. It's been dark for hours, but she doesn't feel unsafe walking on Capitol Hill. The neighbourhood is sleepy at night; truth be told, it feels sleepy most of the time except at weekends, when residents wander around Eastern Market with handcrafted lattes in hand, browsing handmade jewellery, fresh bread, and watercolours of DC, mingling with tourists on the stretch of 7th Street that's free of cars on Saturdays and Sundays.

At 9 p.m. on a Thursday night, kids are tucked up in bed, and if political interns are out partying, they're doing that in other, hipper parts of DC, like the Wharf or Union Market. Older staffers are no doubt working late, in the name of impressing a boss and moving up that all-important power ladder.

Lexi isn't much of a political type herself. She landed here somewhat randomly when her grandmother passed away and left her the bookshop – in addition to the curvier build and the Irish pale skin, freckles, and red hair she'd inherited from her at birth. She'd never lived in the US since she was unexpectedly and prematurely born here thirty-two years ago, and it seemed like a good opportunity to discover her American roots and honour her grandmother's memory.

It's not like life was going brilliantly in London. Lexi was treading water in temporary admin jobs while she figured out what she actually wanted to do with her life, feeling increasingly left behind by her university friends as they moved higher up the ladder in the banking and management consultancy jobs they'd sworn they were only taking for a couple of years to build up some savings before they moved on to some worthier cause. And while it was lovely to cuddle her baby niece, it seemed like, with new motherhood, her sister didn't have as much room for Lexi in her life anymore. The opportunity for a new start couldn't have come at a better time, along with the realisation that yes, of course! Books. Books were what she was meant to do with her life. They had always been her refuge, through the loneliness of her childhood and the grief of losing her dad to cancer in her teens and then her mum to a senseless car crash not long afterwards. She'd just never thought of books as a potential career.

Up until the move to DC, her US citizenship had been a little theoretical, something she hid at school so she wouldn't be bullied for being different, and then, in adulthood, something she wheeled out at parties and work awaydays when she needed a fun fact about herself, but nothing more meaningful than that. But when she showed up here, DC set about winning her over as it had in her summertime visits as a child, with its elegant monuments and its pastel row houses and the smell of ambition in the air, which, despite herself, she's always found very attractive. And now it's six years later, and Lexi can't imagine living anywhere else.

She can't imagine living *with* anyone else other than Erin, either. It had seemed like a miracle to find on social media that her childhood friend was living in DC. When Erin had left London – so long ago, on the cusp of the new millennium –

she and Lexi had kept in touch for a while, but the time difference and Erin's new, busy life and, later, the demands of secondary school, had widened the distance between them until it seemed unbridgeable by Instant Messenger.

Bumping into Erin again in this newer version of cyberspace was another sign that Lexi should embrace the move to America for the bookseller life, one of the biggest points in the 'pro' column of her list, the one that tipped her over the edge. Of course she *wanted* it, but there was also the matter of leaving behind her baby niece and her university friends, in particular her forever crush Scott. Yes, he had a new girlfriend, but Lexi was forever hopeful he'd eventually realise that none of these other women were right for him. She's grateful now that her new life meant moving on. She hadn't quite realised how exhausting the pining had been.

'Hey,' Erin calls from the kitchen as Lexi dumps her bag heavily on the floor and flops onto the sofa.

'Hey yourself,' Lexi says. 'Good day?'

'Another day at the coalface of American democracy. So, by definition, yes.'

'But in actual practice?'

Erin throws a tea towel on the table and perches on an armrest next to Lexi. She pulls a face. 'Same old spreadsheets. Same old annoying coworkers.'

Lexi's heard some good stories about Erin's job and the nerds who work for the Federal government. She's heard about the colleague who's always trying to recruit people into the legging-selling business. She's heard about the guy whose desk is so overrun with plants you can barely find his face among the foliage. She's heard about the days, a decade ago, when Erin had to put in night shifts around report time, babysitting the printer, refilling paper and ink as necessary while it churned out line after line of reportable expenses. And she's also mildly afraid of all the maths that goes on there.

In contrast, running a bookshop seems like a picnic.

'You?' Erin asks.

'Same lovely books. Same lovely coworkers.' It's been a good day: she brings to mind the deep, warm laugh of Marcus, whose job it is to unpack all the boxes and scan them into the inventory in the office next to hers, and who loves nothing more than a good dad joke. A chat she had with Hazel about *Clara Reads Proust*, a short novel she's just finished and can't wait to press into the hands of everyone who likes books about books. Elijah and Tessa running around the shop, filming TikToks, bringing energy and vigour and a little chaos in their wake. 'We're rearranging our romance section, making more space for it. Considering whether to experiment with shelving them by trope: enemies to lovers, friends to lovers, only one bed, that kind of thing.'

'But don't some romance novels have more than one trope? Like, can't friends take a road trip and find there's only one bed and mayhem ensues?'

Lexi has recently read a book with that exact plot point. 'Yeah, that's one of the things that makes it tricky. Not as tricky as real-life romance, though.'

'Uh-oh.' Erin searches Lexi's face, clearly figuring out if this is the beginning of a long conversation. 'Should I boil some water for tea?'

'Nah,' Lexi replies. 'There's nothing to say, really. Except that I've given up. There are officially no good men left in DC.'

'I'll boil some water,' Erin says. After all this time living with Lexi, she knows when a conversation is likely to escalate into a moment that calls for tea. From the kitchen, Erin calls out, 'I don't think that's true, though. What about that guy you went on a couple of dates with just before Christmas?'

Lexi shakes her head. 'Not DC. The suburbs. Arlington. And it took forever to get to his house, remember? The Blue Line was single tracking, so I took an Uber along with everyone else dating people across the river and the traffic cost me an arm and a leg in surge fees.'

'But he was otherwise nice?'

'Yeah, I liked him a lot. But it was never going to work.'

Lexi braces herself. She knows what's coming along with the tea that Erin is handing her: the lecture about her pickiness. *But, come on. There's always* something. *Even when you think you've met someone, they turn out to have a five-year plan to move back to Texas, or to be so busy with grad school and networking that they can barely squeeze you into their diary, or to be so obsessed with work that they can't talk about anything else and can't stop checking their phone for important emails.*

'Do you think maybe—?'

Lexi shakes her head to cut Erin off. 'No. The guy before the Arlington guy wanted to lecture me about Brexit and got very annoyed when I turned out to know more about it than he did. The one before *that* was very disappointed that I hadn't gone to Oxford or Cambridge.' She switches into her terrible impersonation of an American accent, whiny and nasal and not at all flattering. '*What, like, you mean you didn't even apply? Why would a person not even apply?*'

'I'm sorry,' Erin says. 'You're right. Dating sucks. Remember the guy I went on a date with before John? The one who

15

dropped as many acronyms into the conversation as he could? I swear it was just to see if I could keep up with all the government talk and if I was DC enough and important enough.'

'Which you totally are.'

'That's right. And even if I wasn't—'

'That's no measure of your worth as a person,' Lexi says. 'Or your intelligence and ambition.'

'Exactly.'

Erin and Lexi have had a version of this conversation many times over the years, though less so now that Erin has John, who works on the Hill but doesn't brag about it, who doesn't use acronyms without checking first that everyone knows what they mean, who seems open to whatever life throws at him, regardless of what his largely theoretical five-year plan might say.

'So I guess if I'm going to stay in DC, I'm just going to have to resign myself to being single forever.' Not that she had much luck in London, either. But then, as her sister was forever pointing out, she only did ever have eyes for Scott the Unattainable.

'Not necessarily,' Erin says. Ever the one to look on the bright side. 'You never know who might be just around the corner.'

'Hmm.' Lexi sips the last of her tea, unconvinced. It doesn't matter if there's no one around the corner. Living here is worth it. The bookshop is worth it. She hopes so, anyway.

Chapter Four

Lexi is at the till counting change before the shop opens when there's a knock on the door loud enough to startle her. She looks up, and the hairs on her arms respond before her brain kicks in. Because it's Sam Dickens standing there. And the thing about Sam is that Natalie was right: he's also very handsome. Green eyes that crinkle in the corners and fool you into thinking he is kind; a ridiculously chiselled jawline that would be more appropriate for an actor than a bookstore owner in DC, a city which, famously, has all the egos of Hollywood with none of the charisma or looks. Tallish, but not so tall as to be intimidating or tempt you to make terrible jokes about what the weather's like up there. Far too good looking for a ruthless businessman.

Part of Lexi is tempted to let him stand there for a while, but he's carrying a couple of boxes, and it seems unreasonably mean to make him wait in the freezing January temperatures. Not that he doesn't deserve it, necessarily, but you never can be too careful around people who think all's fair in love and business.

After unlocking the door, she lets him in.

'Samuel!' she cries, her voice full of sarcastic surprise. Playful banter is how Lexi masks her dislike of him. 'How delightful. To what do I owe the pleasure?'

He rolls his eyes at her. 'I know you have the last name and all, but do you *have* to talk like a Jane Austen novel?'

Lexi frowns at him. If she really were a Jane Austen character, and not just someone who randomly shares her last name, she'd have a witty comeback. But this isn't Derbyshire in the 1800s. It's a Tuesday morning on Capitol Hill, and she is rendered speechless by irritation and that damned chiselled jawline.

'Anyway,' he says, while she's still trying to think of something clever and cutting. 'These boxes were delivered to us, but they're addressed to you.'

She stands on tiptoes to peer at the top of one of the boxes. Not that she doesn't believe him, of course. She just wants to make sure he isn't pranking her. An orange publisher label peeks out.

'New books from Penguin Random House?'

She doesn't say the next part out loud, but she thinks it so hard that he must be able to hear it. *I guess I can see why they made that mistake. Since you never used to order new books.*

'Look,' he says, ignoring her pointed observation. 'If this isn't a good time, I can take them back and you can come get them at your convenience.'

Lexi realises that she's being a bit mean. This is an uncharacteristically kind and helpful thing he's doing for her, even if he doesn't seem happy about it, and the last thing she wants to do in this bitter cold is traipse up the road and round the corner and lug the boxes back to her own shop when they're already here to start with. Meanwhile, she's punishing him by making him stand in her doorway with two heavy boxes, probably determined not to let on that his arms are giving way. She's enjoying the punishment, but still.

'It's really nice of you to bring them over,' she tells him, grudgingly but meaning it.

'Yeah. I didn't want them cluttering up my hallway.'

'Understood.' She swallows a *sorry* that was forming at the back of her throat and opens the door wider. 'You can leave them here,' she says, pointing at the corner.

'I can take them down to your storeroom,' he offers, unexpectedly. 'Really. It's no trouble.'

Obviously, he wants to snoop. But it's five minutes till opening time and Lexi still hasn't finished counting the till float; she's behind because of the interruption. The less lugging of books, the better for her increasingly creaky back, and besides, what's the worst thing he can see down there? Boxes of new releases to finish shelving today? It's not like what's coming out is a surprise. All he'd need to do is open a copy of *Publishers Weekly*.

'Thank you,' she says, with as much grace as she can summon. 'That would be great, actually.'

He nods, in lieu of a smile, and makes his way downstairs. One of the boxes has caught on his coat, and it's ridden up. Lexi tries not to notice his shapely bottom as he walks down the stairs. She is unsuccessful.

On her way into the shop that morning, Lexi had had a text from Debbie. 'So sorry to say, but I have flu.' She knows it's bad if it's going to stop Debbie coming into work. She is a keep-calm-and-carry-on type, conscientious to the Nth degree, a perfectionist in everything – she trains the staff in pristine gift wrapping, sends out reminders to dust shelves, figures out the rota. Really, she'd be a perfect manager, if

Lexi could afford to pay her for it. Debbie has worked at Pemberley Books since it belonged to Lexi's grandmother, when her twins went off to college and she was looking for something meaningful to fill her days with. Lexi would trust her implicitly to run things like a well-oiled machine. She could go off to brunch or have a lie-in, guilt-free, or even – imagine! – a holiday, knowing everything is taken care of. The thought makes her practically giddy. But sadly, the reality of those figures means she can't afford to give anyone that particular promotion.

Without Debbie, Lexi will be on the shop floor today, jumping in to help Tessa at the till when it gets busy, and otherwise wandering around offering help to browsing customers, taking special orders, and straightening out the books on the display table, which inevitably become a little skew-whiff as the day goes on. Lexi loves being on the shop floor – another reason to hire a manager. It's not just about having the breathing room for time off and visits to London to hang out with her sister and family, Chloe and Peter at their almost unbearably cute ages of six and four. She also, when she's here, doesn't want to be squirrelled away in her office. She wants to be out where the people are, where the book action is.

So she's thankful for the excuse to do that today, and she's glad to be working with Tessa, the only other British bookseller at Pemberley Books. Lexi loves having her around to commiserate about cultural miscommunication, the lack of decent tea, and craving mince pies at Christmastime. *Is it just me*, they sometimes say to each other, *or . . . ? Or is it weird that they rake away leaves as soon as they fall in autumn, depriving us of the pleasure of stepping in big crunchy piles* of them? Or is it impossible to get used to dates being written backwards? Or is it funny when Americans suddenly care about actual football because they're doing well in the World Cup?

It's Tuesday, Book Release Day, so Lexi fetches the pre-orders from the storeroom downstairs – a couple of armfuls of them. There's a special place in her heart for customers who pre-order: who take heed of their favourite authors when they tell them that they're genuinely helpful for building buzz, or who are nerdy enough to want the signed book or the bookmark or the occasional mug that rewards a pre-order. She's just arranging the books on the pick-up shelf when Shelley, one of her favourite customers, pushes open the door.

'I've got your pre-order of the new Tia Williams,' Lexi tells her. She anticipates excitement. It seems as if every Instagram account, every roundup for February reads, and every book podcast she listens to has been raving about this book. Lexi loved *Seven Days in June*, her previous book, so she's excited too, even if she isn't quite sure when she'll get a chance to read it.

'Oh,' Shelley says, shuffling from foot to foot. 'Thanks. That's great.' But there's something forced in the *thanks*.

'Did you not want it anymore?'

'Oh, no, I do. I can gift it to my friend for her birthday. She'll love it!' Again with the forced enthusiasm, the forced exclamation mark in her voice.

Lexi isn't sure she wants to delve. But, unusually, she does. 'Do you already have it?'

'Yeah.'

'But it just came out this morning.'

'I was really desperate to read it. Great Expectations had it out early. I'm sorry. I'll still buy this copy,' she adds quickly.

'Okay.' Lexi scans the book before Shelley changes her mind, puts it in a bag, and hands it over. 'He shouldn't have had it on the shelves before publication day. But that's not your problem.' She's trying to keep smiling, to not communicate the seething anger she feels. The battle between Sam and her isn't her customers' fault, and they aren't going to keep coming if they feel scolded. But her fists clench by her sides despite herself. Shelley shuffles away, down into the lower floor to browse her favourite genres and hide her mortification.

'I can't believe it happened again,' Tessa says.

'Again?'

'Oh yeah. This isn't the first time.'

If Sam has been paying any attention to Pemberley's social media – and Lexi knows that he does – he will have noticed that this is a book that her staff and customers are excited about. That they are, in fact, putting on an event for the author to come and speak and sign books. This was no accident. This was an act of war.

Chapter Five

You might be forgiven for thinking that the last thing a bookshop owner wants to do on an evening off is hang out in another bookshop. But that's if you don't take into consideration that people go into bookselling because they are insufferable bookish nerds, and there's nowhere they'd rather be than in a bookshop, any bookshop, at all times.

Besides, it's Galentine's Day – the annual American celebration of friendship – and coming to Kramers was Erin's idea. Lexi wasn't going to argue: it's not only a bookshop, it's a restaurant too, so what's not to love?

'Cheers,' Erin says, raising her glass of Malbec to clink with Lexi's. 'Here's to . . . how many years of friendship?'

'Too many to count,' Lexi replies, but she's already adding them up in her head. Erin's dad was seconded to London when she was eight, and for a couple of years she and Lexi were in class together, dressed in the same dark grey skirts and V-neck burgundy jumpers, their striped ties neatly around their necks. They played their violins next to each other in the school orchestra and browsed through the library shelves together and kicked a football around at weekends. And then Erin went back to America, and for the rest of her school life Lexi never found another friend quite like her.

'We were eight, and now we're thirty-two,' Erin helpfully supplies. 'So twenty-four?'

'I feel old.'

'We *are* old, that's why.'

But being old also means having lots of shared memories. It's six years now since Lexi moved to DC and bumped into Erin in the wine aisle of the Trader Joe's on 14th Street. Six years of karaoke nights and trivia nights and brunching around DC. Six years of arguing about the relative merits of new books versus the classics. Six years of Thanksgivings with Erin's big noisy family, arguing over the pros and cons of different types of cranberry sauce and eating so much sweet potato casserole she thought she might explode. (Lexi had been highly sceptical of eating a dish topped with marshmallows as part of the main course, but she's long since rescinded that scepticism. Faced with that level of deliciousness, she really had no choice.)

'This place is genius,' Erin says, raising her glass of Malbec, the two of them having already polished off a bottle with their dinner. 'I could live here. Sleep over there, under that table. I mean, books and food. What more do you need?'

'Literally nothing,' Lexi agrees, as they get up and head to browse the shelves.

They start at one edge of the bookshop, making their way gradually through the shop, picking up books and handing them to each other.

'Here,' Lexi says, passing the latest Katherine Center to Erin. 'Read this. Then read all of her books. I love her.'

'But wouldn't you prefer I bought her books at your shop?'

Lexi shrugs. The wine has gone to her head. 'Sure. But we're here now, and you've got it in your hand. Strike when the iron's hot, and all that.' The unspoken thing: Lexi and Erin don't browse bookshops together as much as they used to, and Erin doesn't pop into Pemberley Books as much as she once did. Life is busy for both of them these days. And then, of course, there's John. More and more, Lexi finds herself alone in the flat, wishing Erin was home to process her days with, to bounce ideas off, to have the same old tired but comforting argument about what Erin sees as Lexi's obsession with new books when there are so many good ones not just from the eighteenth and nineteenth centuries, but from, say, five or ten years ago.

Nobody, except her sister, knows Lexi better than Erin does – because of their shared history and because Erin is the kind of person who takes the time to really listen, and also because she's lived in the UK and can help Lexi bridge the cultural divide that comes up more than she might have expected six years in. Lexi had initially struggled to make friends in the US. She'd been burned a few times by effusive, enthusiastic women who said they loved her and hugged her generously and made grand proclamations about how they really must hang out but then never seemed to be available. It made her ache, sometimes, for her gang of university friends back in London who made no such proclamations, because they weren't needed. Friendship seems less fraught, somehow, in England. But thanks to Erin, Lexi has been included in a big group of friends who meet up for karaoke and trivia nights and Jazz in the Garden. She isn't lonely anymore.

Lexi knows she can rely on Erin. And so in turn, Lexi tries her best to be supportive of Erin's relationship with John, to not remark on Erin's frequent absences. But her heart pinches increasingly often at mentions of him. And sometimes, at 3 a.m., Lexi feels all over again like the ten-year-old who lost her best friend overnight and never quite recovered.

Erin looks at the colourful spines of the other Katherine Centers lined up on the shelf, a paper rainbow. 'Should I buy all of them?'

'Yes,' Lexi insists. 'You absolutely should.'

'Browsing tipsy is fun,' Erin says, scooping them all up and making a pile in her hands.

'Agreed. Especially if it means you buy the books I tell you to buy.'

'Well, you're the book expert,' Erin says. 'It's only fair.'

And that right there? That is one of the best things about owning a bookshop. Putting the right books in the right hands – and people taking your advice because they know you know what you're talking about. There's nothing Lexi would rather do with her life than that.

Chapter Six

Lexi loves being in the shop when it's buzzing with people: young women recommending romance novels to each other, or book club members chatting to Marcus or Hazel about the group's next read, or a publisher rep flicking through the catalogue with Megan, her fashionably bespectacled and endlessly enthusiastic book buyer, helping pick the titles that are likely to sell well at Pemberley Books. That's the beauty of an independent bookshop: curation, tailor-made to the tastes of its owner and staff, yes, but also to the needs of the neighbourhood, both for work and for play.

But Lexi also loves it when everyone else has gone home and the shop is sleeping, and it's just her, Pippin purring in her lap, as she sets sales goals or sends out press releases or analyses bestseller lists. She has an office tucked away from the sales floor, but when she's alone, she unfolds an events table and puts herself smack bang in the middle of all the books, inhaling them, remembering what this life that's chosen her is all about. She puts on music; she sings. This is her kingdom, this little part of DC, this place where she feels at home after never quite fitting in anywhere for most of her life. This place that, since her childhood visits to her grandmother, has felt like taking off uncomfortable shoes and putting her feet in warm padded slippers.

Lexi doesn't know if her grandmother always intended

to leave the bookshop to her, or if it's a decision she made later in life. There was a letter left to her with it: *I can't think of anyone more able, or more enthusiastic, to run my beloved bookstore and take care of Pippin. I know you'll do a fabulous job. Have fun with it; redecorate; change the name and the book selection if you want to; adapt it as you want and need to. The shop is yours now. I entrust it to you.*

Lexi was so grateful for her grandmother's confidence in her, and especially for her generosity in blessing Lexi's adapting of it: without it, she might have been tempted to leave everything as it was in homage to her, and that would have quickly grown stale. She repainted the walls in colourful shades, with accents of pink and green and yellow. On the front window, she added a decal of an Austen quote: *I declare after all that there is no enjoyment like reading!* And then, when customers round the corner to push open the door, they find the second half: *How much sooner one tires of anything than of a book!* And yes, as many smartasses have pointed out to her, that's a quote by the vile Caroline Bingley, who doesn't even like books, but even a broken clock, et cetera. It's also a whole lot more welcoming than that other great Austen quote (which Lexi secretly agrees with): *The person, be it gentleman or lady, who has not pleasure in a great novel, must be intolerably stupid.*

Tonight, she's just written *Independent Bookstore Day* at the top of a sheet of paper and underlined it in various colours when her phone lights up with a text from her older sister, Stephanie.

Any hot dates tonight?

Alas, no, and by hiding out in the shop on Valentine's Day, Lexi had been hoping to forget about what day it is, about the lack of any romantic prospects in her life. It's starting to get lonely in Singleville; she winces internally with every wedding picture, anniversary dinner, and ultrasound image on her Instagram feed. Honestly, sometimes Lexi has wondered if she should start going to church, since that seems to be the place to meet men, and not just any men – the kind who are ready to commit. It has certainly worked for Imani and Catherine and Sofia – Erin's friends who've slowly become Lexi's friends, too.

On the occasional night off, when she's not meeting her friends for karaoke, it's depressing to text around and find that nobody's free because they're with their other halves, cooking chicken casserole or whatever it is that married couples do on a Wednesday night in February. She doesn't even know *how* to cook chicken casserole without a HelloFresh recipe. And if they're not cooking together, they're off having Instagram-worthy adventures or lying on a beach somewhere. She hasn't been on holiday in ages and she tells herself that it's because work is too busy, and yes, it's true, work *is* busy, but also, who would she go with?

She's got the bookshop, though, and that's what Lexi pours her heart and energy and frustration into. The bookshop is all she needs. It's fine. She's fine.

Except it's not entirely fine, is it? Without even looking at the latest figures, she knows sales are continuing to slow. She can feel the amount of customer buzz in the shop and she knows it's less than it used to be. She knows she's missed out on some author events lately, that they've gone to Great Expectations instead, and so have all the social media posts and all the sales that come with an event: the book itself, so the author can sign it, but then all the incidentals, because while you're in a bookshop, you might as well pick up the latest Amor Towles and a couple of birthday cards.

Sam is getting too good at this game. He has to be stopped, by any possible means. Profit margins in bookshops are paper-thin as it is, and he's eating into hers. Pemberley Books is Lexi's whole life now; it's a community hub on the Hill, a well-known bookshop people travel to because of the book clubs, the thoughtful curation of hardback new releases, the growing romance section, the fun and sassy cards. She can't afford to lose the shop, and neither, she hopes, can bibliophiles in and around DC. They survived a pandemic, for Pete's sake. All of them worked so hard, under less than ideal conditions: the masks, the policing of the door so that only a certain number of people could come in at once, the driving around town delivering books to local residents who'd ordered online. And of course the ambient stress, the fear, the uncertainty of it all. Still, they showed up; they gave their all.

The shop has survived, and in some ways, thrived, through all of that, even if the same could not be said of her and her staff. They're exhausted; they're less resilient than they used to be. They deserve pay rises and bonuses, not the threat of closure. Lexi has tried all the obvious things to gain the upper hand over Sam, all the things that are within the realm of fair and sometimes not-quite-fair competition. She has designed a new range of tote bags and mugs that, not-so-subtly, call Pemberley Books 'Capitol Hill's bookshop'. After Sam brought in his reward scheme for loyal customers, she revamped hers to make it more attractive. When he has sales, she has them too, and she offers five per cent more discount than he does. All of these things feel slightly dirty and a little desperate, and often counterproductive. But she can't let him gain the upper hand. Tonight, as Lexi works, she's sitting by the classics, within sight of the shelf of gorgeous Penguin clothbounds. They look so aesthetically pleasing, all of them the same height, each with its own distinct colour and pattern. Even *Pride and Prejudice* looks pretty, despite the questionable choice of brownish yellow for its cover.

Ah, *Pride and Prejudice*. The book that taught all of us the universally acknowledged truth that if you hate someone at first, you'll probably end up marrying them. But that, admittedly, was before dating apps.

No hot dates, she texts her sister. *Not a single Mr Darcy in sight.*

Lexi can almost feel Stephanie's eyeroll. Since the dawn of time, she has been trying to get Lexi to be 'realistic', to not expect fireworks. To settle, in other words – just like Stephanie has, though, of course, Lexi would never say that out loud. Stephanie's husband, Chris, is perfectly nice . . . but that's exactly the problem, isn't it? Who wants to upend their life for *perfectly nice*?

Lexi doesn't want to settle. She's seen not only Stephanie but also too many of her friends do that. If a man is going to interrupt Lexi's life, upset its delicate balance, he's going to have to be special. And if settling for nothing less means she'll be sad and lonely for the rest of her life . . . well – okay, maybe she'll reconsider.

But not now.

Not yet.

She's not giving up. There's still plenty of time.

There's really nobody in your life who's arrogant and annoying? Surely arrogant and annoying is the whole brand for DC men.

Stephanie isn't wrong about that. DC men – the transplants, anyway – come to the town wanting to fix the world and quite possibly rule it; in the meantime, they bask in the reflected glory of the congressman or senator or worthy cause they work for. They all wear suits, and it's hard to be ugly in a suit. But they're all basically the same: they're not interested in anyone who can't help them get ahead in some way.

Lexi reluctantly has to admit that there is one man who doesn't quite fit that mould. Arrogant and annoying: yes. But not *quite* the same as the rest of them. His life isn't built around politics. It's built, like hers, around books.

It's just a shame that he's her competitor, and not a potential suitor.

A competitor who needs to be stopped, distracted, thrown off his game.

It is suddenly very clear what the plan is. Lexi will make Sam fall in love with her. She'll turn to her maybe-relative Jane Austen for inspiration. There's no risk of her falling in love with him, because she'll keep her head screwed on and remember that despite his good looks, he is first and foremost an enemy that must be vanquished. And thanks to the distraction, he will be.

~~Independent Bookstore Day~~
Lexi Austen's plan to woo Sam Dickens:

- *Drop a handkerchief in front of him*
- *Take a turn about the park*
- *Give a piano recital (learn to play first??)*
- *Take him out dancing*
- *~~Push him into a lake~~*

Chapter Seven

Erin and John have been pretty serious for a while now, so Lexi should probably have expected this. It's Valentine's Day, after all, and men, she has found in her shambolic dating life, are often not very imaginative. But Lexi was wrapped up in her own lightbulb moment – her newfound plan to woo Sam, for the good of her bookshop – and it didn't occur to her to think that tonight could be anything other than an average if overpriced and over-pink date for Erin and John.

But when she hears Erin's excited voice from outside the front door as she fumbles for her keys, she knows.

Erin has her back to the door when Lexi walks in, and she tries to creep up the steps without her noticing. She wants to give Erin privacy for this phone call; she also wants time to process, to rearrange her features into excitement and sort through her feelings until she can mostly just be happy for Erin. It's what Erin deserves; it's what friendship is; and Lexi knows that unselfish celebration is what Erin would do for her.

But it's hard, because this is also the end of an era. Erin will move out, and Lexi will have to trawl the internet for a new flatmate. She'll be confronted with the fact that she's in her thirties and still flat-sharing with randoms. That everyone else around her is growing up, getting married, moving on, but despite her very responsible and slightly stressful job, Lexi is stuck in a post-student state. And also that somehow she is failing to do that most basic of things: to find someone to share her life with. Yes, as established, DC dating sucks, but somehow other people manage to succeed at it.

Lexi tiptoes to the staircase, but it's too late: Erin's noticed her. Lexi does her best to match her brightest grin; her facial muscles feel like they're responding, but she can't be totally sure. Lexi wiggles her own ring finger at Erin with widened, inquisitive eyes, and Erin, still speaking nods and shows off her own finger, dazzling with a brand-new ring, diamond with sapphires. Lexi tries, unsuccessfully, to stop her heart from dropping.

'Listen, Mom,' Erin says, finally managing to get a word in edgeways. 'I'll call you back later, okay?'

Erin throws her phone onto the sofa and runs over to hug Lexi. Lexi squeezes her tight.

'Finally!' she says into her hair. 'It's about time.'

It's actually only been six months, so this is a bit of a running joke. But Erin and John are both really serious about their Christian faith, and when you're saving yourself for marriage, and you've been waiting more than thirty years, you do things fast.

'Tell me everything,' Lexi says, and Erin does.

The proposal at sunset on the wide marble steps of the Lincoln Memorial, the delightful surprise of it all, the tentative plans they're making for the wedding.

'And of course, you'll be my maid of honour, right?'

'Of course.' Lexi nods with all the enthusiasm she can muster, her auburn hair bouncing on her shoulders. 'I'd never forgive you otherwise.'

'I know I'm supposed to plan some fancy way to ask you, and maybe I'll do that later and you can act surprised?'

'Of course!'

Six years into living here, Lexi still hasn't got used to the pageantry of American wedding prep: professional headshots to announce an engagement, wedding showers and bachelorette parties, and the rituals of asking friends to be bridesmaids with all kinds of creative and elaborate plans, from a succession of posters *Love-Actually*-style, to a gift with a card inside, to (shudder) hollowed-out books containing a piece of jewellery and a letter. It's probably the Brit in her, but spontaneous, understated but heartfelt questions are more her thing.

She's just thrilled to be asked, thrilled about the friendship it represents, and thrilled to have an Important Job on the day so that she won't feel like a spare part.

It won't matter at all that she's still single. It'll be utterly irrelevant.

'And of course, you can bring a plus-one if you like.'

Ah. Maybe not so irrelevant.

But that's okay. How long can it possibly take to woo Sam with the time-honoured tricks of Jane Austen? She can definitely do it by then. Two birds, one stone: she won't be a loner, and he, seeing her all dressed up as a bridesmaid, will only be further distracted.

She doesn't have time to prevaricate among the petunias. It's time to put the Jane Austen Experiment into action.

Chapter Eight

Wednesday night is karaoke night, and nothing gets in the way of that. Not even engagements and weddings. At least not yet.

'C'mon,' Lexi tells Erin. 'It'll be good for you. You're about to disappear into the tunnel of wedmin doom for the next year. You're going to need to have some fun.' *And so will I*, she adds mentally. She'll need the distraction from her impending loneliness.

Erin looks up from the kitchen table, from her newly acquired pile of bride-themed magazines. 'I'm sorry, but did you just refer to my wedding as a tunnel of doom?'

'No.' Lexi shakes her head vigorously, to underline her point. She refrains from telling Erin that her wedding does, in fact, spell doom for *her*. She knows she's going to have to do a whole lot of refraining over the next year. Erin is Lexi's friend – her *best* friend, even; certainly her oldest friend – and she loves her. But still, everything is changing – it smarts a little. 'Not to your wedding, of course not. But to all the stuff that goes with it. Planning is hard. And I'll help you, I promise. You know I love a good list. But only if *you* promise to take Wednesdays off for karaoke.'

'I can't promise every—'

Lexi puts her hand on her hip, the universal sign of being both Displeased and Serious, and Seriously Displeased.

Erin holds up her hands in defeat. 'Fine.'

But Lexi can't help wondering if, instead of *Grease* duets with Erin, she'll have to resort to 'All By Myself' more often than not.

Across the city at Muzette, Lexi is a couple of drinks in, which is her sweet spot for both singing and talking. Or, as the karaoke gang sometimes call it, never shutting up.

'I want to sing something about having a plan,' she tells them, proving their point.

Sofia, Imani and Catherine exchange looks. They're wondering, probably, if they should ask what she's talking about. They're deciding, probably, all things considered, not to. But Lexi is two drinks in, so she's going to tell them anyway.

'I've got a plan,' she announces, unnecessarily.

'Fine,' Imani says. 'I'll bite. Would you like to tell us what? Because, call me perceptive, but I sense that maybe you do.'

If Lexi weren't two drinks in, she'd play coy. Instead, she blurts, 'Enemies to lovers.'

The blank looks warn Lexi that she's going to have to explain. Maybe bring a few copies of *Beach Read* or *The Hating Game* to hand out next time, for everyone's education.

'All the best love stories start out with people who hate each other.'

Erin fiddles with her engagement ring. 'Sometimes they start with people who are friends,' she says quietly.

Lexi looks at her; it's possible she even glares. She will not be deterred in this moment.

'Do you have any particular enemy in mind?' Imani asks. She's clearly determined not to drag this out, which is a shame, because Lexi had a whole plan to make them guess.

She's a little sad that they haven't already. It's not like she's never complained about this particular nemesis.

'Sam. The bookshop guy. He's just so . . . so . . .'

'So?'

'So annoyingly *good-looking*. I bet half his sales are down to how good-looking he is. And that's just not fair, you know? It's pretty privilege. Isn't this supposed to be a meritocracy?'

'The book world, you mean?'

'No. I mean, yes. But—' She waves her drink around, a few drops jumping out and hitting her in the face. A total waste of a perfectly good daiquiri. 'This. America.'

'Honey,' Sofia says, 'I don't know who's been telling you lies about the 'American Dream', but it's been dead a long time.'

Lexi knows this, of course. She knows there's no such thing as a level playing field. But that's not, in this moment, the point. She crosses her arms and wrinkles her brow like a stroppy teenager. At work, she has to be responsible. She has to be people's boss. She has to make sure she can pay them, make sure they feel appreciated, make sure they are given tasks where they can thrive. But when she comes to karaoke with her friends, she gets to act her age. Or, possibly, significantly less than her age. It's a welcome release valve. Sometimes she thinks she might entirely lose the plot without it.

'Here,' Catherine says, throwing the folder of song choices at Lexi, open to the page featuring Gnash's 'I hate u, I love u'.

Lexi reads through the lyrics and shakes her head. 'It's too sad. And besides, this song implies he's got someone else, and as far as I know he hasn't.'

'You want us to find a song that matches your exact situation?' Erin asks, in a tone of voice that suggests that is very unreasonable. She tends to use that tone with Lexi a lot, especially when Lexi is two drinks in. 'Rival business owner, inconveniently attractive, very annoying, *You've Got Mail* style?'

'Exactly,' Lexi says, satisfied.

'Wait,' Imani says. 'We *are* talking about Sam Dickens, right? The Sam Dickens with the ruthless businessman of a father? The one who swallows up smaller companies and puts others out of business?'

'Well,' Lexi says. 'Yes. I've heard that too. But you can't hold people responsible for who their parents are.'

'Maybe.' Imani's tone of voice suggests there's no *maybe* about it. That in fact she definitely disagrees. 'But I also heard he's making his way around town breaking hearts left and right. Stay clear of him, girl. You're better than that.'

'Yeah,' Sofia agrees. 'He ghosted my roommate. And her coworker, too.'

Lexi didn't know this about Sam, but through the fog of her now-third drink (don't judge, she wouldn't be such a lightweight if she weren't so tired from working *all the time*), it somehow doesn't surprise her. 'You're probably right.'

Sofia looks at Imani and Imani looks at Erin and Erin looks at Catherine and Catherine looks at Sofia. They wait. They all know a *but* is coming.

'But that's the genius of the plan.' Lexi is shaking her drink again, and it's splashing everywhere. Erin gently removes it from her fingers. 'I'm not going to fall in love with him. He's going to fall in love with *me*. Which will throw him off his game. And enable me to get the upper hand back in the bookshop wars.'

'Umm—' Imani begins.

Catherine cuts her off. 'There seem to be multiple problems with this plan.'

'Like what?'

'Well, for a start, it's not super ethical.'

'He's done plenty of not-exactly-ethical things in the bookshop wars.'

'Two wrongs—' Sofia starts.

'Multiple wrongs, actually,' Lexi corrects her.

'And then there's the small matter of your heart,' Erin says. 'How are you going to make sure that *you're* not the one who's distracted and thrown off her game? How are you going to protect your heart from getting broken?'

'Because I'm going into it with my eyes wide open. My guard will be up the whole time. Besides, he might be good-looking, but he's a terrible human. That ought to be enough to prevent any shenanigans.'

Lexi's friends exchange looks. They are, for once, seemingly rendered speechless. 'Fine,' Lexi says, before they get another chance to talk her out of her flawless plan. 'I'll sing "I hate u, I love u" if that's what everyone really wants.'

It feels to Lexi like a very long wait until she gets the catharsis of belting out the lyrics. Love and hate: you wouldn't think it would be so hard to tell the difference between them. You wouldn't think they could coexist so easily. But the more she sings, the more she wonders how much she *actually* hates Sam. Whether in fact the hatred she *thinks* she feels is really envy at his business sense and success. The unfairness of his good looks is another question entirely.

Chapter Nine

Spring in DC is delightful. There's the cherry blossoms, of course, but also: say what you like about the kind of people who can afford to live near the Capitol, but they know how to garden. Lexi tries to stop and look, and sometimes takes an Instagram-worthy photo or two but, more often, a mind picture to carry her through the day. On her way to work, there's this one tree with a branch that sticks out beyond the garden it's planted in, and for the couple of weeks that it's in bloom, she likes to pause and breathe in its sweet scent. Sometimes, if she's preoccupied and she rushes past without remembering, she makes herself go back and do it. It's so ephemeral, and one day she'll walk past the tree and the blossom will be gone. So she wants to make the most of it while she can.

In London, spring is different, a different set of flowers at slightly different times, grey skies, a lot more rain, and if you really want to wear skirts, you'd better pair them with tights. Here in DC in mid-March, the clocks have already gone back to allow for lighter evenings, and it's almost time for regular leg shaving. Few things make Lexi happier than the start of Birkenstock season and her soft, bare legs exposed to the sunshine.

Few things, that is except soft, bare legs exposed to the sunshine and a latte in her hand from Peregrine. Her number-one piece of advice for people who want tips for opening a bookstore is this: be near good coffee. (And, ideally, also near a bar with a great happy hour, because tipsy customers are among the best customers: the most fun, the most open-minded. A bookworm's resolve to read what they have at home before buying anything new is flimsy at the best of times; give them a margarita, and they've forgotten they ever made that particular resolution. They'll also let you talk them into trying a new genre, or a book that's just beyond their comfort zone – a love story without a guaranteed happy ending or a memoir by a politician they don't know much about. And sometimes, they'll drag their Happy Hour friend into the shop with them, a friend who says they're not much of a reader, but Lexi puts *The Idea of You* in their hand and the next week they're back for recommendations, hooked for life, exclaiming: 'I didn't know books could do this!'

They know Lexi well in Peregrine; the baristas know to start making her a latte as soon as they see her out of the corner of their eye. You can't put a price on that, especially given that she is normally running late. Not because she's lazy, but because she always thinks she can get more done in any given amount of time than she actually can. She forgets to factor in things like a two-minute chat to with Erin on the way out of the door, or getting halfway down 2nd Street before she remembers she needs to turn around and go back to smell the blossom.

Today, though, Lexi doesn't just grab her coffee from the bar where it is waiting for her and immediately run. Today, she lingers, pretending to be in the midst of an existential crisis about how many packets of sugar she wants (actual answer: none). What she's interested in is the table at the very back, and the people sitting at it that she clocked as soon as she came in: a pretty blonde delicately wiping her eyes with the edge of her sleeve, and opposite her, the back of a head that Lexi recognises all too well. They're speaking too quietly for Lexi to hear over the gurgles of the coffee machine and the customers placing their orders. What's happening is pretty obvious, but she can't help being nosy: she'd like the details. She'd like to know how it factors into her plan.

Just as Lexi is wondering how much longer she can get away with standing there eavesdropping, the girl stands up abruptly, swings her Kate Spade handbag onto her shoulder, and bumps Lexi's arm in her rush to get out of there. She doesn't apologise, and Lexi doesn't mind: she's been there, in that bubble of post-dumping grief, and she knows it's all but impossible to be aware of anything other than the deep ache in the pit of your stomach. The thought of ever going through that again makes her shudder.

Back at the table, Sam has his head in his hands. He's running his fingers through his hair, trying no doubt to shake the mortification of it all. For a brief second, Lexi feels sorry for him. She'd assumed he'd be callous, unfeeling, but he seems genuinely upset.

Before she can stop herself, she slides into the wooden chair opposite him.

'Hey,' she says softly.

Sam lifts his head, looks at Lexi, and breathes out heavily through his nose. He closes his eyes briefly, like he might open them again and find her gone. But, undeterred, she's still here.

'I guess you heard all that?'

Sadly, she did not. 'I saw enough to fill in the blanks. You okay?'

'Yeah.' He shakes his head, which makes the messaging a little mixed, a little confusing. 'Better off without her, you know?'

Lexi wonders, not for the first time, why so many men seem to resort to this kind of bravado. It's okay to say you're gutted something didn't work out. One day, when she's got money to burn, she'll take out an ad in the *New York Times* to raise awareness of this fact.

'Let me guess,' she says. 'She was crazy?'

He knows Lexi is baiting him, so he doesn't go there.

'No, not crazy. Just . . .'

'Wanted some commitment?'

He looks at her, right into her blue eyes, like *how did you know*, like it's any kind of mystery. 'Yeah.' He sounds defeated.

'And not handsome enough to tempt you, I guess?'

It's a dig, but it's also a test. Does he know what Lexi is quoting? Does he realise she's accusing him of being the worse kind of romantic villain: Mr Darcy before his transformation?

'Okay, Miss Austen. For your information, she's plenty handsome enough to tempt me.'

Lexi is pleasantly surprised but also irritated that he got it so easily. She knows it's not pretty, but a part of her wanted the jolt of adrenaline that comes with feeling superior for a second. But if she wants that, she is going to have to resort to some obscure line from *Mansfield Park*.

'You just – wouldn't want to dance with her?'

'Oh, we've danced. We've done plenty of other stuff too.'

Lexi tries not to picture it. She tries not to let certain images flash through her mind. Those piercing eyes, his shirt off, his arms around her . . .

'Anyway,' he says. 'Don't you have a bookshop to run? I heard there's growing competition in the neighbourhood. You wouldn't want to let them get ahead of you because you were distracted by a good-looking guy in a coffee shop.'

'That's an excellent point. My latte and I will go take over the world now.'

She's aiming for a smile, and she thinks she sees a shadow of one. Does Sam deserve her sympathy, her efforts at cheering him up? Did she just want to disarm him? Or was it just morbid curiosity that made her sit down opposite him? Lexi isn't sure, but she's surprised at her own reaction, at how much she wanted to put an arm around him, at the jostling of emotions inside her: anger at a man hurting what seemed to be a perfectly good woman for the mortal crime of wanting to define a relationship, yes, of course. But, also, wanting so desperately, plan or no plan, to know his backstory, the particular reason for his own particular fear of commitment, his moving from woman to woman. Sadness at his own sadness. Which doesn't feel much like an enemies thing.

But as long as he runs Great Expectations, enemies is all they can be. Because if they're not enemies, what are they? They're certainly not friends. It's too early to think about this; she hasn't even finished her coffee yet.

Chapter Ten

Barely an hour later, Sam is in her shop with a box.

'Penguin Random House really needs to get its act together,' he says, huffing a little as he leans the box on the counter, nodding at Elijah behind the till, presumably to signal approval of his nerdy T-shirt. Star Trek, maybe? Lexi isn't quite sure.

On the other side of the bookshop, Lexi is rearranging greeting cards, tidying up their racks, filling in gaps with new arrivals. As far as she's concerned, PRH can keep making this mistake if it gives Sam a reason to come and see her and a chance for her to put her plan in practice. And while she doesn't have a handkerchief to drop – she's pretty sure she doesn't even own a handkerchief, and nor does anyone under the age of seventy – she *can* drop one of the greeting cards she has in her hand. Perhaps the one that says *There's nothing sexier than a reader*. It thwacks onto the floor with much less elegance than a handkerchief, but needs must.

'I'll grab that,' he says.

There's no need for him to; she could just as easily do it herself. It's not as if she's carrying a heavy stack of hardbacks. But she lets him. This is all part of the plan. For the few seconds he's down on the ground, she enjoys being above him. She feels as if she's in control. Maybe that was part of the handkerchief thing in Jane Austen's day, when women had so little power.

From above him, she notices, too, as he stands, the length of his eyelashes, the particular shade of his green eyes. Her stomach lurches, not unpleasantly.

'Thank you,' she says, her fingers brushing his. Has she done it on purpose? It's unclear even to Lexi. But she holds his gaze a fraction of a second longer than necessary, and that – that is definitely on purpose. Because who wouldn't want to look into those eyes for as long as is polite, and potentially a little longer?

'You're welcome,' he says, and she thinks she notices a hint of pink in his cheeks. 'Should I take the box downstairs?'

Lexi should say no. She should say, *Don't worry about it, it was nice of you to even bring it over*. But she remembers the pleasant view when he last walked down her stairs.

'If that's okay?' she says, with a faint bat of her own eyelashes.

This time, with no coat, she's hoping the boxes will catch on his T-shirt instead, show off his abs and perhaps some dark hair pointing down from his belly button.

No such luck, sadly.

While Sam is downstairs, Lexi idly picks up her trusty bookshop notebook from behind the till and has a flick through. If she wants to give her booksellers a pay rise, or even just a surprise mid-year bonus to show them how much she values them, and, as a side benefit, help instil additional loyalty so that they aren't tempted to look elsewhere, then Independent Bookstore Day is her best bet.

The American Booksellers Association does great work pushing the day, publicising it on social media, providing exclusive merch to sell, and helping booksellers workshop ideas. At Pemberley Books, they decorate; they have flash sales and giveaways; they give out stickers for their customers to proudly wear as they wander around Eastern Market buying fresh pastries or DC themed mugs. Inevitably, because Capitol Hill is basically a village, they'll bump into someone they know and the sticker will spark a conversation, and then their ex-colleague or their daughter's friend's dad will find themselves in the shop, keen for their own sticker and their own opportunity for some community-based virtue signalling.

That's the theory, anyway, and Lexi has to admit that it works pretty well. Independent Bookstore Day is always their biggest sales day outside of what Americans call the holiday season – those glorious weeks after Thanksgiving that kick off with Small Business Saturday and culminate in frantic last-minute shopping on Christmas Eve. On Independent Bookstore Day, the community turns out in force and Bookstagrammers fill their feeds with pictures of their book hauls and of Pippin, her grandmother's tortoiseshell cat. Lexi usually manages to wrangle him into wearing a sparkly silver bow tie for the occasion. He's always a crowd-pleaser, but never more so than when he's all dressed up, even if a bow tie is all she can manage without getting scratched. It's such a shame; Lexi has all kinds of ideas about literary disguises for him. Independent Bookstore Day isn't as big a deal for second-hand bookshops, though, and so this is the first year Lexi might potentially have to share it with someone: Sam.

If pressed, she'd admit that she's not good at sharing the limelight; she's a sort-of only child with a sister much older than her who moved out before Lexie hit her teens, and the kind of person who loves a fuss to be made of her – surprise cakes at restaurants complete with sparklers and singing waiters, that kind of thing. It makes her beam with joy and pride when customers tell her how much they love the shop, and on Independent Bookstore Day that happens a lot. Her cheeks ache from smiling for a solid week afterwards. It's a feeling that keeps her going all year, through the doldrums of dark Januarys and stiflingly hot but just as quiet Augusts, when she inevitably wonders, like clockwork, if she's going to make it, if all this hard work is worth it. On Independent Bookstore Day, Lexi knows she's in the right place, knows it deep in her gut. And she knows, too, that she's doing her grandmother proud.

And then, of course, there's the practicality of the day. It's important for filling the coffers, for shifting books that have been taking up valuable shelf space for far too long through the judicious use of discount codes and two-for-one offers, for impressing publishing industry insiders with innovative ideas so that they will then be more inclined to send Pemberley Books their most interesting or most fun or most lucrative authors for in-store events.

Needless to say, Lexi has no intention of sharing any of these perks with anyone, let alone her nemesis.

She has three options: she could bare her teeth – her uneven, slightly-yellowed-through-too-much-tea-drinking teeth – and warn Sam. She could hope he doesn't know what a big deal Independent Bookstore Day is. Or she could sweetly offer to cooperate and play nicely together.

And, let's face it: Sam's not going to be particularly threatened by her British teeth, and she grudgingly admits that he's a good businessman, in the same way that selling books as a loss leader as a way to get customers hooked on your relentless, all-encompassing website is good business; if all you care about is getting insanely rich and you don't mind the repercussions on the publishing industry, authors, and other bookshops (whose closure is in fact part of your business model). So there's precisely zero chance that he doesn't know about Independent Bookstore Day. Lexi is sure that, like her, he reads every word of the ABA's marketing emails.

So that leaves Lexi with the third option. The only option, in truth, which works with the plan to woo him.

Cooperation.

Ugh.

Fine.

'Listen,' she tells Sam as he reaches for the door handle on his way out to sell new books that people could buy at Pemberley Books instead. 'We should talk.'

He turns his head to face her. She can't read his expression, but if she had to guess – maybe playful? 'Really?'

'Yes.'

He lets go of the door handle, spins his body around, and walks to the counter. He leans his hands there. Lexi tries not to notice his elegant fingers or think about the things they could do. *Focus,* she tells herself. *Remember the time he did a flash sale on the day you were celebrating the bookshop's sixtieth birthday. Remember the books he's put out before publication day because he doesn't care about following the rules. Remember the times you've seen some of your favourite customers furtively scurry into his shop when they didn't know you could see them. Imagine those fingers covered in papercuts, which surely, despite the heroic display of box carrying just now, is what he deserves.*

'About anything in particular?'

Ugh, seriously. What kind of question is that? Does he think Lexi wants to idly chat about the weather over a cup of coffee? *Focus*, she tells herself again.

'IBD,' she tells him. Is the use of the initials a test to see how much he knows? Maybe.

Sam raises an eyebrow, which does not help his cause. Lexi has always been jealous of people who can do that. 'Irritable bowel . . . disease?'

Lexi tries not to smile, but it's hard. There's mischief in his eyes, and it sparkles.

'Independent Bookstore Day,' she corrects.

'Ah.' He leaves a pause, waiting maybe for his joke to land. It's a good one, actually – and appropriate, since the stress of Independent Bookstore Day actually does mess with Lexi's digestive system every year. Not something she intends to bring up with Sam, though. 'I've got to run now.'

She tries not to picture him running. His shapely legs in too-tight shorts. A sheen of sweat on his forehead and upper lip. She swallows hard.

'You run too?'

She pictures their meeting like a high-powered *West Wing* scene: the two of them running around the tidal basin, with the marble dome of the Jefferson Memorial looming imposingly ahead of them. Him, too out of breath to refute her brilliant ideas and incontrovertible argument that he should leave the fun events to her, forever. Because, of course, in this scenario, even though she only runs short distances as an occasional stress-buster, she's fitter than he is.

'It's a figure of speech, Alexandra.'

Her breath catches. Why does her full name sound so good on his tongue and his lips?

He tilts his head and looks at her, like he's trying to figure her out. Like he's going to ask her a thousand questions. 'Let's grab a coffee sometime soon, and maybe a walk in Lincoln Park? And talk IBD?'

He does air quotes around IBD and Lexi can't tell if it's because he's making fun of the acronym, or because he thinks it's an excuse to talk about other stuff. She hopes, for the sake of the plan, that it's the latter, that he thinks she's finding ways to be around him because she likes him.

She nods, trying to be nonchalant. Grabbing a coffee at Peregrine and walking around Lincoln Park gives her mild PTSD: in the spring of 2020, her entire social life and more than a few terrible dates consisted of doing just that. When Lexi can't sleep, she closes her eyes and counts its trees in her mind's eye: *that's* how well she knows it now.

'Ping me,' he says, and then he's gone.

Chapter Eleven

Lexi is bending down to tie up her laces for a quick run around Lincoln Park when Erin comes down the stairs with a pile of wedding magazines, ready to make an evening of flicking through them in front of Netflix.

'Stress run?' she asks, knowing full well Lexi isn't a fan of exercise for its own sake.

'Yeah.'

For about half a second, Lexi considers telling her about the frustration of increasingly feeling alone, of being the only silent one at brunch while all her friends share tales of proposals and dates, of scrolling through Instagram, her breath hitching every couple of seconds with each engagement ring or perfectly choreographed young family in matching sweatshirts. But Erin is part of those Instagram pictures now, part of the reason for that hitching of breath, and Lexi doesn't want to rain on her parade, to imply anything less than full-throated support and excitement for her.

Instead, she veers onto another, subject of frustration.

'Sam,' she says simply.

'Yeah,' Erin says. 'About that. How's this going to work, exactly?'

Lexi unties and reties her shoes, thinking about how to respond. Thinking about how much to divulge, aware that it sounds perhaps a little bit bonkers.

'I'm taking a leaf out of Jane Austen's book,' she says. 'Piano recitals, balls, a turn about the park, that kind of thing.'

'You'll be waiting a while for the next inaugural ball,' Erin points out, ever mindful of this kind of detail.

'It doesn't need to be so literal,' Lexi replies, though she has to admit she wouldn't hate something with a presidential flavour. January 2025 is a long way off, though. 'Any party will do, really.'

'And he'll take your hand to dance and hate will turn to love and then he'll let you have bookselling on the Hill all to yourself?'

Lexi has tied and untied each shoe three times now and stretched the limits of plausibility for being down near the ground, avoiding Erin's eye. She stands up and faces her.

'Something like that,' she says, in response to her sceptical tone. 'I admit I'm fuzzy on the detail.'

'Please be careful,' Erin says. 'I don't want to see you get hurt.'

'It's fine. If the rumours about him are true, he's probably got a heart of stone.'

'It's not him I'm worried about, though.'

'I'm fine. I've got the bookshop.'

Erin opens her mouth to say something, then closes it again. But it's too late; Lexi's seen.

'What?'

'It's the bookshop that's landed you in this trouble to start with.'

It's Lexi's turn to go quiet. 'Yeah,' she says eventually, before she heads out the door towards the park.

The scents of the beginning of spring linger in the air, roses and daffodils in well-manicured gardens, magnolia blossoms starting to coat the pavement. Lexi gathers more speed than usual as she runs down 4th Street and turns onto East Capitol, the sandstone and marble-domed monument to American democracy behind her at one end, the park ahead. She focuses on her breathing and on the satisfaction of expending the excess energy she seems to have in her limbs whenever she thinks about Sam. He's hot; he's funny; she also must not allow herself to be too distracted by either his hotness or his funniness, because that is not part of the plan. It's a delicate needle to thread. Hence this run, to clear her head.

Breathe.

Breathe.

Lexi dodges a little girl on a bike, a scooter left lying on the red pavement, a family posting a letter into the blue mailbox on the corner of 6th Street. She waves at a regular customer, browsing one of the many Little Free Libraries for some free reading to add to the expensive hardbacks he can always be counted on to buy from her at 10 a.m. on publication day. She remembers to appreciate the un-British blue sky, the sun on her face, the hint of warmth to come. But still, underneath it all, she can't completely shake the Sam thing, the mental equivalent of restless leg syndrome that seems to be the result of seeing him, thinking about him, or planning anything involving him.

Out of breath at the traffic lights before the park, she leans her palms on her thighs and tries to steady her lungs, her body, her emotions. The lights turn red, green, yellow, red, and she's raising her head to ready herself to cross into the park when she's suddenly aware of warmth, her body reacting to something before her mind has fully processed it.

'Hi,' Sam says next to her, breathing hard too.

'Hi,' Lexi says, sounding as unsurprised and unfazed as she can. Which isn't very.

She has the excuse of the changing of the traffic light; it's time to start moving. It makes no sense to stop and talk, not when the seconds are ticking down on the pedestrian Go sign. It certainly makes no sense to look at him in his shorts and be further distracted by his legs.

She takes off running – *breathe, breathe* – and so does he, the two of them, breathing hard next to each other, falling into step with each other, sweating next to each other; a choreography of sorts as she picks up speed and he matches her.

At the Emancipation statue, they separate. Lexi veers left; Sam veers right. But, from across the patch of grass, she keeps him in her peripheral vision and runs, runs, runs, always keeping slightly ahead of him. Which seems like a great metaphor for her life, until, at the other end of the park, the stitch she's been trying to ignore slows her down, then stops her.

Sam takes the corner opposite Lexi and comes to a standstill next to her.

'You okay?'

'Yeah. Just a stitch.'

Humiliating.

'Okay,' he says, but he doesn't leave. They stand, breathing hard, sweating, next to each other. 'You sure you're okay?' he asks again, maybe just to fill the awkward silence.

'Yeah.'

The silence between them stretches some more, like they both want to say something but can't quite face it.

'Okay,' Sam says again eventually. 'So long as you're sure.'

Lexi nods, her stitch already receding as she massages her side. 'I'm sure,' she says. But she actually isn't really all that sure about anything.

Lexi has barely walked through the bookshop door after her shower when her phone vibrates in her pocket. It is, of all things, an email from Sam. Very forward, considering *she* was the one supposed to contact *him*.

So when should we have our bowel disease meeting?

This started funny but has become less and less so. Lexi loves Independent Bookstore Day (in case that somehow wasn't clear) and while it's okay for her to make jokes about the abbreviation, it somehow doesn't feel like anyone else should get to. The bookstore world is like a family, fiercely protective of its own, and there are certain in-jokes only insiders get to make. And while it's technically true that Sam is part of the family now, he's more like a brand-new stepbrother who still needs to earn the right to make fun of the rest of the siblings.

Lexi looks up from her phone just as Natalie swerves away to avoid collision. The staff are used to keeping their wits about them: Lexi's mind is always half on something else, so it's wise to be ready to jump out of the way. Unless, of course, she's recommending books to a customer: in that scenario, wild horses couldn't drag her off, let alone distract her.

I'm sure you're very busy and important, she writes back, *so you can name the time.*

They need to spend time together for the plan to work, and they really do need to talk strategy so that they don't tread on each other's toes. Mostly so Sam doesn't tread on Lexi's. She's not as fussed about *his* extremities staying intact.

Coffee and a walk mid-morning? Let's say 10 tomorrow?

Okay, first of all, 10 a.m. is not mid-morning. Lexi has barely got going by then. But Americans love to get up early so they can 'work out', as they call it, and generally feel virtuous about life. From what Lexi saw of Sam's six-pack the other day when he was carrying boxes, he's no exception. She generally finds morning people to be among the most irritating, so that checks out. Why is starting work at 7 a.m. considered somehow more virtuous than finishing at 10 p.m.? Maybe it's petty not to let Sam even have this tiny victory, but well, Lexi is feeling pretty petty.

11 a.m. and you've got yourself a deal.

Fine.

Chapter Twelve

Even though Lexi is on time to meet him (a supernatural achievement), Sam is waiting for her outside Peregrine with a dog leash on his wrist and two drinks in his hand.

He nods to her in greeting. 'I got you a latte,' he says, handing over the coffee. His skin grazes hers, which has no impact on her whatsoever, not even a small spark of electricity that is probably just static.

'Thank you,' she says automatically, but on the inside, she's irritated. 'How did you know it's what I wanted?'

He shrugs. 'A latte is the perfect drink from here. I've tried them all and analysed them. You don't want to obscure the espresso with too many other flavours. A latte takes the edge off the bitterness but lets the espresso shine.'

She wants to tell him that just because it's *his* favourite, that doesn't mean it's objectively better, let alone what *she* wants. But the annoying fact is, she can't argue with his logic, because lattes are always what she gets, without putting anywhere near that much thought into it. 'Okay,' she says eventually.

'Oscar wants to get going,' he says, and she looks down and sees his dog. It's the kind that even Lexi, avowed cat person, can't resist, a little fluffy one, what her dad used to call a ball of wool on legs and what other people call a labradoodle.

'Oscar is a great dog name.'

'Right? I think so too.' Sam smiles, a proud dog dad. 'It's our routine when he comes to visit, Peregrine and a walk in Lincoln Park. He knows he gets to run around with his dog friends when we get there.'

'You know,' Lexi tells him, 'I really had you down as more of an Alsatian kind of guy. Or maybe a Rottweiler owner.'

Something about Sam loving this adorable ball of fluff makes her reconsider him as a person. Which would be fine, if she was planning to fall for him. But she's not, so she'll just have to file it under Interesting Things She Would Write in Her Diary if She Had Time to Write a Diary.

'I'm full of surprises,' he says. It's playful; it's maybe a little arrogant, too.

'Oh yeah?' She has this ridiculous urge to take his hand, to show him she is full of surprises too. To be fair, she is a little light-headed. This coffee is the first thing that's gone into Lexi's stomach since her first-thing-in-the-morning cup of tea. It's been crazy at the bookshop, back-to-back meetings with Megan and Debbie about socks and mugs and notebooks and Tessa about the social media and the new accountant Lexi is hoping will solve her mathematical woes.

To be honest, this walk is the last thing Lexi has time for today. She should be brainstorming actual Independent Bookstore Day ideas with her staff, rather than a rival bookstore owner, plan or no plan. But she didn't want to get judged for being flaky, so here they are.

Oscar runs around the patch of the park designated for dogs, his leash still dangling because he took off excitedly before Sam had a chance to remove it. Sam's explained that it's Oscar's first day in DC, a visit while his parents are out of the country, and he seems thrilled to be back in Lincoln Park. No trace of 2020-related PTSD for this guy.

Lexi clears her throat, determined to get back on track with the business talk. 'So . . . Independent Bookstore Day. What are your plans?'

Sam sips at his coffee. Lexi is fully aware of what he's doing: the pause for dramatic effect. 'What's in it for me to divulge that?'

'We should work together. We're friendly bookstores, right?'

He raises an eyebrow, like *since when?* Lexi thought she'd been better at concealing her irritation. She should know herself better by now.

'How do I know you're not just going to steal my ideas?' he asks, with what Lexi has come to recognise as playfulness.

Lexi is incensed. 'Excuse me. I have ideas of my own. I don't need to steal yours.'

'Really?' Sam licks latte foam off his lip, but she catches his smirk anyway. 'And what are these ideas?'

Lexi opens her mouth and nothing comes out. She really should have thought this through better.

'Ha!' he says. 'See? You don't want to tell me either!'

'We might . . . decorate with balloons?' she blurts, wanting to prove him wrong, even though he isn't, exactly. Balloons? So lame. Why did she have to go and say that?

Oscar trots over to them, his leash still dangling. Maybe he wants to go home? Maybe this conversation can be over now? Lexi will retreat back to her cosy bookshop and Sam will retreat back to his corporate one and they shall never need to speak again of this misguided attempt to work together.

Sam bends down to scratch Oscar's ears, and Lexi spies an empty bench and heads towards it, ready to slump there in defeat and wave Sam off back down the street while she sits sulking for a little bit.

But as she takes a step forward, so does Oscar, and her feet get tangled around his leash, and then, bam! Ground, meet Lexi; Lexi, meet ground.

Excellent.

Very dignified.

Also, owww. Painful.

Lexi must have hit her head because everything looks a little blurry all of a sudden. Including Sam, and the pattern on his shirt.

Wait, was there a pattern there before? Or did she throw coffee at him on her way down?

Lexi wants to die.

'You okay?' He sounds like he's underwater.

'Yeah,' she says. 'Yeah. Fine. Sorry about your shirt. I promise I wasn't trying to destroy it just because it has your shop's logo on it.' While she's down on the ground, she's kind of hoping it will swallow her up.

He looks down, registering the coffee impact for seemingly the first time. 'Don't worry about my shirt. I'm more concerned about you right now.'

'I'm fine,' she says again, but it comes out funny. Also, Lexi is still on the ground. And did he say he was concerned about her? That doesn't sound like the Sam she knows. Except she doesn't know him, not really. She can't stop looking at the swirl on his T-shirt. It looks like chocolate, which makes her want to lick it.

'Here,' he says, reaching out his arm. 'Take my hand.'

'Why?'

Oscar snuffles at Lexi. Maybe he's concerned about her, too.

Sam frowns. 'So you can stand up?'

All of a sudden, this makes sense. Lexi can't live down on the ground of Lincoln Park forever, after all. 'Right. Right.' She grabs onto him. 'Your hand is soft,' she tells him.

This makes Sam laugh, for some reason.

'You're supposed to say thank you when someone pays you a compliment,' she says.

'Thank you,' he says, smiling, and shaking his head like he's despairing at her. 'And you're supposed to use my hand to pull yourself up.'

'Right,' Lexi says again. She'd been so busy trying not to stroke his hand that she'd forgotten about the standing-up part.

Oscar looks at her expectantly. She hoists herself up, landing on Sam's shoulder with a thud.

He doesn't complain. 'Good job,' he says instead, and Lexi feels a little prickly at being patronised but also too tired to put up a fight. 'Can you sit?'

'But I just stood up.' Lexi's confusion could be coming from anywhere: the pain in her head, the swirly pattern on Sam's top, or the feeling of his hand on hers.

Sam looks like he's trying not to laugh. Lexi is enjoying how nice his face looks, so she forgets to be annoyed.

'On the bench,' he says. 'I want to check you're okay.'

'I'm fine,' she tells him again, because he must not have heard the first couple of times.

'Well then, I guess that clears it up.' Sam rolls his eyes. 'Where does it hurt?'

It feels like general pain all over, so Lexi pats around her head until she locates the source of it, at the back. 'Here,' she tells him.

'Okay. I'm going to drive you home, and we're going to put some ice on it, okay? Then you're going to lie down and take it easy for the rest of the day.'

This seems unnecessary. 'I'm fine,' she repeats. 'Thank you, though.'

'Humour me, okay?'

A petulant part of Lexi wants to say, *Why? Why should I? You're my mortal enemy.* But even if he's trying to make her do something she doesn't want to do, it seems like he is at least being nice about it. So she refrains.

'You really don't have to drive me, though. I live, like, two blocks that way.' Lexi points in the vague direction of the town house she shares with Erin.

Sam looks suspicious. 'Like, actually two blocks? Or are you exaggerating because you just want to get rid of me?'

'I would never . . .' Lexi must have hit her head hard, because she was about to say she would never want to get rid of him. Which is ridiculous. Things at the bookshop would be a lot less stressful if they got rid of him, for a start. 'I would never exaggerate,' she says instead.

'What, like never ever in a million years?'

He is baiting her.

'I see what you did there,' she says, making sure he knows she knows. 'It's three and a half blocks. I'll be okay. But also, I have to get back to work.'

Sam shakes his head, and touches Lexi's arm to get her to look at him. (It feels nice. Warm.) 'Look at me,' he says, when it doesn't work.

She doesn't want to. He's her mortal enemy. But something in his voice makes her do what he asks. And she has to admit his eyes are nice. Like emeralds, or like ocean depths.

'Your eyes are very green,' she tells him.

'Thank you?' He sounds like he's not sure if this is a compliment. Which is a good thing. Keeping your enemies close may be good, but keeping them on their toes is even better.

'I know what you're doing,' Lexi says. 'You're just trying to make me go home so I can't do any bookshop work and you can put me out of business.'

'Okay, first of all, I'm not trying to put you out of business.'

'You're not?'

He shakes his head and she opens her mouth to argue further, but he bulldozes past her. 'And I'm not going to fight about that with you right now.'

Good: an argument to look forward to. Lexi can start planning her witty ripostes in advance. Always helpful when you get the chance to do that.

'But, secondly, you're hurt, and I want to make sure you're okay.'

Lexi narrows her eyes, which somehow intensifies her headache. 'You're being a good guy,' she says, like a revelation. She feels herself grinning. Her head feels heavy. She rests it on his shoulder, which feels much better. It's nice. She could close her eyes and—

'I'm doing the thing that any decent person would do in this scenario,' he says softly, his breath brushing her face.

'You're not a decent person, though.' She says it before she remembers that bantering isn't really a thing in the US, not really a form of flirting or even expressing friendship. She says it, also, not totally sure if she means it. Because Lexi thought she hated him, but everything is suddenly blurry and confusing.

'You hit your head pretty hard, so I'm ging to assume you don't know what you're saying.' She can hear a smile in his voice somehow. She wishes she could turn her head to look at him, but everything hurts. 'Your eyes are open, though, right?'

'Yes,' she lies.

'And you'd never lie in a million years, right?'

Lexi forces her eyes open. The light hurts them a little. 'Not in a hundred billion years.'

'Good.' Sam's voice vibrates through Lexi's bones, like they're one person. It's nice. She could get used to it.

But wait, no. Mortal enemies! Bad thoughts!

Chapter Thirteen

It takes longer than you might think to walk three and a half blocks. Especially when the person you're with has a firm grip of you, his arm around your waist, while his laughably small dog trots along beside you, and possibly you're walking a little slower than strictly necessary because you're enjoying his warm hand a little bit too much and you don't want him to let go.

'Is anyone home in the daytime at your place? To look after you?'

Lexi finds herself wishing she could say no. Probably not just for his company? No, she'd have to have hit her head pretty hard to think that. Probably it's just so that he'd have to stay with her, losing a valuable day of plotting his takeover of DC's literary world, which would mean the plan was working. But Erin works from home most days – her government job is one of the few where the powers that be took note of their workers' preferences to come into the office once or twice a month and thought, *Okay, we'll push it to once or twice a week, but otherwise we'll let these nerds be.* Not, of course, that Sam would stay anyway. That would be ridiculous.

'Yeah. My roommate.'

'And she's a good roommate? Not, like, some random stranger from Craigslist?'

Lexi laughs, and it resonates through her skull and throbs a little, but it's worth it. 'Craigslist? What is this, 2009?'

'Maybe she's also a time traveller? You gotta watch out for these random roommates.'

Lexi shakes her head to reassure Sam, which also hurts. She has to learn to stay still. 'She's not a random. I actually know her from growing up in London together and we reconnected when I moved to DC. Plus, she has this whole posse of church friends who can be activated at the push of a button.'

Sam stops walking abruptly. 'The actual push of an actual button?'

'No.'

'Okay, good. Because I gotta say, that would seem a little . . .'

'Cultish?'

Sam nods.

'Yeah, no. I think it's like an internal message board where you sell things and give stuff away and organise meals for families who've just welcomed a new baby. Stuff like that.'

'An internal message board? Like Craigslist?' He's messing with her, she is pretty sure.

'You're obsessed with Craigslist today.'

'Apparently yes, today I am.'

'I suppose there are worse things to be obsessed with.'

'Like what?'

Lexi can see her house from here. There's probably not time to go into everything she suddenly wants to talk to Sam about. She'd give anything, though, to know what his obsessions are. Good, bad, indifferent. But especially the bad ones. It would make the plan so much easier to put into action.

'Money?' she prods. 'Sex? Drugs? Success at all costs?'

Sam's arm around her loosens, like Lexi has hit a nerve. She can't decide whether it's a good or a bad thing.

'When is it actually obsession, though?' he asks. 'And when is it just healthy focus?'

'An excellent question.'

They let that indeed excellent question hang in the air for the next half block.

'Well,' Lexi says, somewhat regretfully, wishing there was a way to keep leaning into Sam's touch, keep walking together like this, skirting dangerous topics forever, or at least for several more hours. 'This is it.'

'The yellow house? I love this one.'

Lexi smiles, but her stomach tightens at the thought of having to leave this adorable home when Erin gets married. 'Thank you. We love it.'

She fumbles for her keys in her faded Sally Rooney tote bag. Not for the first time, she wishes she could be one of those people who always put their keys in the same bit of the bag so that they can always find them at a moment's notice. Every Black Friday, like clockwork, she buys a new bag with many compartments, precisely so she can trick herself into becoming one of those people. But somehow, she always ends up grabbing one of the tote bags in her tote bag of tote bags and her keys end up at the bottom among a general debris of lipsticks, tissues, review copies of books, crumpled-up receipts, and the hand sanitiser she will probably carry around for the rest of her life.

'Should we maybe just knock on the door?' An eminently sensible suggestion from Sam, but Lexi feels oddly affronted.

'You don't trust me to find my keys?'

'I just . . .' He seems to be weighing his words carefully. 'I think it might be easier, that's all.' And then he can't resist it. He has to go there. 'Someday, we'll have a conversation about always putting your keys in the same place so that you can easily find them.'

She narrows her eyes and turns her head to do her best approximation of a glare.

'But you've thought of that already, of course.'

Right at that moment, her hand happens upon her key. She waves it at Sam in triumph.

'You just prefer the slight adventure of never quite knowing how long it's going to take you to find it.' A reasonable deduction.

'Shut up,' Lexi says, but not as forcefully as she'd like, because Sam is taking the key out of her hand and his fingers clasping hers feel good. And soft. And soothing, somehow. It's nice to be looked after, even by her mortal enemy.

It's taken Lexi so long to find her keys, though, that Erin has heard the voices outside and come to see what the commotion is about. And, horror of horrors, Lexi and Sam have not yet disentangled. So the first thing Erin sees when she opens the door is that Lexi is literally joined at the hip to her nemesis. Lexi can see in Erin's face that she's struggling to process what's happening.

'I banged my head,' she tells her quickly, before anyone says anything regrettable.

'I'm concerned about signs of concussion,' Sam adds. 'She's saying crazy things about how I'm her mortal enemy and I want to destroy her bookshop.'

Did Lexi say those things? If so, she can assume she's fine. Those aren't the words of a confused person. They might, however, be the words of a person whose so-flimsy-it-barely-exists filter has been knocked out of place by said bump on the head.

'I'm Sam, by the way,' he says, holding out his hand.

'Hi. I'm Erin.' She duly shakes, and Lexi thanks her lucky stars that Erin doesn't respond that of course she knows exactly who Sam is because they discuss him several times per day and that Lexi was correct about his being quite irritatingly handsome.

'I assume I'm a household name around here.'

Ah. So he's read through her anyway. She wishes she could think him arrogant for this assumption, but it's hard to come to that conclusion when in fact he is entirely correct.

'Something like that,' Erin says diplomatically. 'Anyway, come in.' She crouches, noticing Oscar and scratching him behind the ears. 'And who do we have here?'

'This is Oscar,' Sam says. 'Arguably, all of this is his fault.'

'He tripped me up with his leash,' Lexi explains.

Oscar wags his tail both happily and obliviously.

'Is it okay if he comes in too? I can tie him up outside if not.'

Lexi tries not to show it, but she's becoming more impressed by Sam with every moment that goes by. Truth be told, she is neutral on dogs (though she'd never admit this in a place like DC), but not always the biggest fans of dog owners, who seem to assume everyone will be okay with their pet jumping and licking, in the same way that new parents assume everyone will think their baby is cute. In Lexi's experience, it's best not to take either of those things for granted.

'Sure,' Erin says, picking up Oscar, who seems delighted

71

by the attention. It's true that Lexi and Sam neglected him a little as he dutifully trotted along beside them. To be honest, Lexi had kind of forgotten about him altogether. She blames the concussion that she may or may not have. It's definitely not because she was distracted by Sam's arm around her waist or his soft fingers on hers.

Lexi is barely through the door when she collapses on the sofa. Sitting is good.

'How are you feeling?' Erin asks her.

'Fine. It's fine. I'm fine. He thinks I need to take the day off and sit around at home, but only because he's plotting my downfall.'

Sam sticks his tongue out at her. This should be an affront, but now Lexi can't stop staring at his mouth.

'Point well argued,' Lexi notes sarcastically.

'I can take it from here,' Erin tells Sam. 'If you need to go back to your plan of world domination.'

'You're sure? I can stay if it's easier.' He shuffles on his feet, seeming reluctant to go.

'I'm sure. Thank you for delivering her safely back.'

Erin puts Oscar down, and he immediately jumps onto Lexi's lap, looking as if he's deciding whether he is going to lick her face. She really hopes he doesn't.

'Need me to leave the therapy dog here with you?'

It's a sweet offer, and one she knows dog owners don't make lightly. 'You'd really do that?'

'Sure.'

Lexi is suspicious, though. 'Wait a minute. Are you punishing him because this is all his fault?'

'Ha. You got me.'

She squeezes Oscar tighter. 'I forgive you,' she tells him.

'Don't listen to Daddy.' And that is how she knows she is, if not concussed, then seriously damaged. Lexi doesn't believe in referring to humans as relatives of animals.

'It's okay,' she tells Sam, turning down his generous offer. 'You've done more than enough. Just don't think that this gets you out of Independent Bookstore Day planning.'

Sam looks at Erin; Erin looks at Sam. 'Yeah,' he says. 'I think she's probably fine.'

They laugh, a little gang of two. Lexi doesn't like it. Erin is meant to be on *her* side.

'Call me if you need anything, okay?' Sam says, and this makes up for it a little.

'You mean at the shop? I don't have your personal number.'

He grabs his phone to punch in Lexi's number and give her a missed call, and Erin catches her eye and mouths, *Smooth.* Like all of this was a plot to get Sam's contact details and insert herself further into his life. As if.

'Okay,' Sam says, bending over Lexi to pick up Oscar. His breath on her face is comforting and energising at the same time, if that is even possible.

'Get some ice on the back of your head ASAP,' Sam calls from the hallway.

'On it,' Erin says, heading to the freezer to grab a packet of cold peas. She wraps it in a tea towel and hands it to Lexi. 'Sorry I'm not a hot dude leaning over you tenderly as I do this,' she says, helping Lexi to arrange herself so that the peas become a pillow.

'What's that supposed to mean?' Lexi, of course, knows exactly what it's supposed to mean. But she's lost all powers of debate.

'Oh, nothing. Just – this all reminds me a lot of Marianne Dashwood.'

'Marianne who had Willoughby carry her home after she twisted her ankle in the rain and fell in love with him even though he quite clearly wasn't The One? *That* Marianne Dashwood?'

'Precisely. She was obsessed with him and blind to truth and logic, if I remember correctly.' Erin looks at Lexi over the top of her glasses as if to underline the point she's just made.

'I'm not obsessed,' Lexi says. 'Or blind. And I still hate him. He was just steadying me and making sure I was okay.' She can hear a hint of petulant adolescence in her own voice and she doesn't like it.

'Uh-huh,' Erin says, nodding. 'Let me ask you one thing, though. What did he smell like?'

'Coffee. Fresh laundry. And— Wait. This is a trap, isn't it?'

'I wouldn't call it that, exactly. A test, maybe. Which I'm sad to say you've just failed.'

Lexi sticks her tongue out at her roommate. 'Not fair. I'm concussed. You shouldn't be mean to me right now.'

'You're concussed, yet you can remember the exact combination of scents that make up Sam.'

'I'm just observant, that's all. Anyway, don't you have work to do?'

Erin shrugs. Safeguarding democracy can obviously wait. 'It's a quiet day. I'll warm up some soup for you, okay? And then we can make a list of all the reasons why it'd be a bad idea for you to further pursue this plan of yours.'

Lexi is starting to regret how much she tells Erin.

Lexi Austen's plan to woo Sam Dickens:

- *Drop a handkerchief (greeting card) in front of him* ✔
- *Take a turn about the park* ✔
- *Bonus swoon into his arms* ✔
- *Give a piano recital (learn to play first??)*
- *Take him out dancing*

Chapter Fourteen

Aside from handing her a book, the only sure-fire way to keep Lexi still and not thinking about work is to put her in front of a TV adaptation of a Jane Austen novel, preferably *Pride and Prejudice*. The BBC adaptation from the Nineties has always been Lexi's comfort blanket, the thing she reaches for when she gets her yearly flu, which isn't really flu but just a bad cold. She knows she's on the mend when she's well enough to read, but for those first couple of days, she needs Jennifer Ehle and she needs Colin Firth.

Today, though, because of Erin's Dashwood references, Lexi is craving *Sense and Sensibility*. You can't beat the 1995 adaptation: it might be a bit worn and old-looking, but it's also like reuniting with old friends: Emma Thompson, Kate Winslet, Alan Rickman, Hugh Grant. Colin Firth is a grave omission, of course, but that only means she'll have to watch *Pride and Prejudice* next to complete the set. Not exactly a hardship.

Lexi must be at least a little concussed, though, because images of Sam keep popping up in her head. At the ball scenes, she imagines dancing with him, his warm hand in hers, even though she's never been to a ball and she's pretty sure Sam wouldn't even countenance it. And then, of course, there's the scene with Marianne and the ankle, Dashwood and his gallantry. Lexi remembers how kind and gentle Sam was with her yesterday, the reassuring warmth of his arm around her waist, the genuine concern in his very green eyes, which may or may not have featured in her dreams last night.

If Erin didn't want Lexi thinking about Sam, she probably shouldn't have encouraged the *Sense and Sensibility* movie. But then, catch 22: Erin also knows as well as Lexi does that with anything she loved less, she would have just been on her phone, half working, not really resting. With a beloved old favourite, Lexi can rest her eyes and let the dialogue wash over her, and then, right when she knows a good bit is coming up, pop an eye open for a couple of minutes. This is why it's the perfect sick day activity: minimum effort, maximum reward.

And it's fine that Lexi's mind drifts from time to time, because this is a film she knows so well. It's fine that it drifts to Sam and his warm hand, Sam and his green eyes, Sam and his weirdly analytical coffee habits. She needs to be truly invested if this plan is going to work. If he's going to fall in love with her, she needs to convincingly act as if she's not repulsed by him. She's just getting into character; that's all. She's just doing what it takes to save her bookshop.

When Sam first bought the shop, it seemed like Great Expectations would continue to coexist peacefully with Pemberley Books. He seemed kind and cordial, and assured Lexi that even once the refit was complete, his bookshop would have a completely different vibe to hers. He was going to focus on nonfiction: biographies, history, politics. The Serious Stuff that Serious People in DC want to read, or least feel like they *have* to read, in order to keep up with conversations at dinner parties or impress their bosses on the Hill or research for their appearances on MSNBC and Pod Save America. He planned to host events along those lines, too: live recordings of podcasts, conversations between thinkers on the economy and immigration and voting rights.

Pemberley Books, of course, also sells these kinds of books and also hosts these kinds of events. There's no getting away from them in DC, and especially in this particular part of DC, where the most politically engaged, most powerful, and most influential people congregate at work and after-work receptions and happy hours. Where people passionate about specific issues or democracy in general assemble to march and wave banners and voice that passion. So it would be crazy to have a bookshop on Capitol Hill and *not* cater to them. Lexi's grandmother did, and Lexi always has, too.

But it's not where her own interests lie, or those of the majority of her staff. They love poetry, and literary fiction, and beautifully written memoirs, and thrillers to keep them turning pages when they'd otherwise be tempted to doomscroll through social media. They need humour and romance – *so much* romance. Their section is expanding year by year as they make room for a genre that's growing in popularity. Whoever came up with the idea of rebranding it with bright colours and cartoon covers deserves a medal, or at least a hefty commission. Pemberley Books has a book club devoted to the genre, and that book club is the most fun one they have: even when Lexi is stuck in her cave doing admin, she can tell that from the giggles that drift into her office, and from the crumbs on the floor and the empty glasses afterwards.

And then there are the families who come to pick up books. Lexi's shop is homely; it's a nice place to hang out with squishy, if slightly worse-for-wear sofas. Sam's bookshop is all hard edges and shiny surfaces, a Serious Place for Serious

People, a slightly hushed atmosphere as befits his Cathedral of Learning.

It's not that those Serious People aren't welcome at Pemberley Books. Everybody is. But Lexi does see why they might want a different experience, even if it's a joyless, soul-destroying one.

So, at first, it was okay. But then . . . plot twist. Sam started stocking fiction. The bestsellers only: okay, fine. Lexi personally doesn't think that's what indie bookshops are for: they're for championing hidden gems, tailoring recommendations to each individual customer, their interests and needs, and gently challenging them to go slightly beyond their comfort zone. They're not just for picking up the season's buzziest books. But Lexi can also see that the Serious People may want to pick up the latest Maggie O'Farrell or Colson Whitehead while they're at the bookshop anyway for Bill Gates's Serious Thoughts On Whatever.

The thing is, though: Lexi can see it coming a mile off. Because once you start stocking bestselling fiction, where do you draw the line? She's bracing for the day when he decides that the top 10 isn't enough, and maybe he should go with the top 50, and maybe some paperbacks, and why not arrange them in sections of some kind? And then what if the Serious Literary Authors decide to go to him for their events? Pemberley Books love those, too. Lexi wants those readers to come to them – the actual enthusiasts, not the people who cynically decide to throw in some fiction to help their bottom line.

So she'd better hope that this plan of hers will work and that Sam's being in love with her will throw him off his game. As for Lexi, books are in her bones and the shop is embedded deep in her muscle memory. She knows what she's doing, can do it standing on her head, though, of course, it's much more fun to do it properly engaged. She remembers her mum knitting while watching TV and having a conversation. When Lexi's tried it, she's been quick to discover that what she needs is a silent room and every ounce of concentration she can summon. And *that* is the difference between an amateur and an expert. The difference, in other words, between Sam and her.

But also, even if Lexi does end up slightly distracted, she has an incredible staff: passionate, knowledgeable, engaged with the book world. Case in point: while she's here at home with frozen peas on her head, watching *Sense and Sensibility* and daydreaming about knocking Sam off his game with a little judicious snogging – just to get into character, you understand – she knows she doesn't need to worry about the shop. Does she worry anyway? Of course. It's her personality to worry, it's her job to worry, it's a tribute to her grandmother to worry. But she doesn't *need* to. Her team sells, wraps, advises, recommends, tidies, shelves, curates, returns, dusts. They know what to do, the new staff are trained by Debbie, and Debbie is faultless. Lexi doesn't plan on getting distracted any more than she planned on spending today on the sofa with Alan Rickman and Hugh Grant. But if that's what needs to happen, in the name of commercial competition, she is covered.

It's all going according to plan. Or it will be just as soon as her head stops hurting and the room stops spinning quite as much. As soon as Lexi is able to stop thinking about snogging Sam.

Chapter Fifteen

First things first, as soon as Lexi feels like herself again: a piano recital.

Can Lexi play? Well, no, not exactly, but in the words of a young musician from one of the most beloved Christmas films of all time, that is nothing but a 'tiny, insignificant detail'. As we all know from that film, all you have to do is spend a few weeks learning to play a solo well enough for a school concert, and you can win over the love of your life.

Not that Sam is *that* – he's just an enemy Lexi is trying to distract – but it's still worth a try.

Does Lexi have time to learn? Questionable. Half-hour lessons: fine. That seems like it should be doable, especially if, say, the lessons are at Music on the Hill, a short walk from the bookshop. But then, rumour has it that lessons aren't enough, and you also have to practise. Lexi isn't sure how she is meant to fit that into her routine. She also isn't sure what to do about the other tiny insignificant detail: she doesn't have a piano. She's hoping Music on the Hill can help with that. Do they have practice rooms, too?

This brilliant plan is getting more complicated by the minute. But, of course, as Lexi well knows, nothing worth doing is ever simple, right? Running a bookshop is certainly no picnic, and yet here she is, still standing, after all the complications of the last few years. Logistical challenges have never been enough to faze her.

A couple of days later, Lexi is pushing open the door to the adorable music shop, which has become a bit of an institution in the neighbourhood over the last decade or so.

'Hi,' says the man behind the till. 'What can I help you with?'

'I'd like to learn the piano,' she tells him. 'But I don't have a piano. Or any idea where to start.'

'Ah,' he says, pushing his glasses up his nose. 'Well, that's okay. You came to the right place.'

In her peripheral vision, Lexi is aware of someone flicking through stacks of sheet music, browsing. One day, she'll be able to do that, choose whatever music she feels like playing. But, for now, she assumes it's textbooks all the way.

The music shop man talks Lexi through different options for teachers and she has a brief flash of a daydream, because falling in love with her piano teacher seems like the stuff of romance novels. But then she snaps back to attention, because that is *so* not the point. She's doing this so that Sam will fall in love with *her*, have his head turned by the distraction.

Which is why, when the man browsing the sheet music clears his throat and (cue the slow-mo) she turns to look at him, she nearly jumps out of her skin.

Sam.

'I can teach you,' he says.

'You?' Lexi is still processing his being here at all, and now here he is with this surprising offer.

A smile twitches at his lips. 'Sure. Why not?'

'I didn't know you played.'

'Of course you didn't. Why would you know that?'

It feels like an accusation. Like she hasn't taken the time to get to know him. Or like she's assumed he wasn't deep and sensitive enough to have hobbies beyond world domination. To be fair, the accusation isn't completely unfounded. In Lexi's head, Sam is a two-dimensional villain, if admittedly a good-looking one who smells nice. But when exactly is she supposed to have had a chat with him about piano playing?

'Sam's one of our regulars,' the music man says.

That's the kind of place Capitol Hill is. A place with regulars. A place where the baristas at Peregrine know your order, where you bump into your friends at the bookshop, where you jog past a local author who, like you, is also running with earphones in, and you both point at your ears and say 'Taylor Swift' in unison.

'We keep trying to recruit him as a teacher. He's brilliant. Too busy with his bookstore, though, apparently.'

'Hey.' Lexi nudges Sam. 'That seems like a good idea. Why don't you go into the piano teaching business instead?'

His eyes darken. Lexi was mostly kidding. But it seems like she's inexplicably made him sad, and she feels it as a punch to the gut.

'Why don't I,' he mutters.

Back home in England, Lexi would have said *sorry* by now. But in the US, she's had the apology habit trained out of her, and besides, she isn't entirely sure what she's done wrong.

Back behind his counter, the music man looks from Lexi to Sam and Sam to Lexi. He isn't sure what's happening either.

'Because you're a very good bookseller,' Lexi says, wanting to redeem herself and clear the air of the weird awkwardness.

'I'm a very good pianist, too,' Sam says, levelling his eyes with Lexi's. He says it with authority and conviction, and Lexi has no reason not to believe him. Still, is it weird? Did it get weird in here? 'Anyway, the offer's there if you want it.'

'I'll definitely think about it.'

This isn't just a line. Lexi *will* definitely think about it. She'll think about them squeezing next to each other on the piano stool, legs and butts touching. She'll think about him taking her hands and placing them on the right keys, making sure her fingers are neither too stiff nor too relaxed, with just the right amount of tension in them. She'll think about his breath on her neck as he leans in to point to a line of music. She will *definitely* think about it. For the purpose of the plan, of course.

'You can use my piano to practise, too, if you want,' he adds, yanking Lexi out of her daydreams. Her cheeks are warm and flushed; it's all those thoughts of fingers and hands and what, exactly, they can do.

She shakes her head to erase those thoughts and narrows her eyes at him. 'Why are you being so nice to me?'

The man behind the counter coughs and finds something to do in the back room.

'To throw you off your game,' Sam says, holding Lexi's gaze as her cheeks continue to burn. 'While you're busy learning your scales, I'll be taking over the literary world.'

'Ah. That figures.'

There's a smile in his eyes if not exactly on his lips, as if he's willing Lexi to think he's at least partly joking. But could it be that he has a plan, too?

'Well,' she says, not biting, 'I appreciate the offer.'

The thing is, though: how can she wow him with her sudden brilliance at piano playing if he's seen her learning and practising? Jane Austen's heroines didn't learn from the heroes. They learned from their governesses. But Lexi doesn't have one of those. She has limited time, and limited funds, and no access to Julie Andrews.

On the other hand, if Sam teaches her, maybe she can wow him with her innate skills and incredible ability to learn. Who knows, maybe she has hidden musical talents – hidden even to her and her primary school recorder teacher.

'How much do you charge?'

Sam laughs. 'Pay me in books.'

That's ridiculous on a number of levels. Like Lexi, Sam can get books at the wholesale discount. And like her, he gets dozens of advance review copies for free. He must have an ulterior motive, which is exactly why she probably shouldn't do it. But, just think: she'd get to snoop around his apartment, find some clues to help her get ahead in the bookshop competition. *That* is obviously why she's interested. She's certainly not curious about his bedroom. Or his bed. Obviously not. It's weird that she's even thinking about not thinking about that, to be honest. What does his bed have to do with anything? What is *wrong* with her? Is she still concussed?

Ugh, she needs to lie down.

Alone.

In a dark room.

And think about her choices. Definitely not anything else.

Chapter Sixteen

When Lexi grabs her phone off her bedside table the next day, there are fifty-six text notifications.

This time, it's Catherine's turn for an announcement: she started dating Drew a few weeks before Erin started dating John, so, of course, it stands to reason that her engagement wouldn't be too far behind. But still, the news kicks her in the stomach even as she starts humming *Another one bites the dust*. Already, Lexi feels herself drifting, unable to take part in some conversations, biting her lip to keep cynical comments from slipping out.

These friends have been her lifeline for years now; she was so grateful to finally find them. What if it all falls apart? Looking for friends in DC is every bit as soul-destroying as the dating apps, and for all the same reasons: the busyness, the ambition, the fact that it feels like, when you first meet someone, they are sizing you up for your potential usefulness to their career. Or you might find someone you really click with, but then it turns out they live across the river, in the suburbs, not in DC at all. She's tried the expat groups; she's tried the alumni clubs. And it's fine, it's all fine for surface-level conversation, for companionship, even for fun. But what Lexi longs for is to be known, to be understood, to be part of in-jokes and to share history with someone. None of that is possible in an instant. The thought of starting again makes her a little queasy.

She hopes they'll all stay friends after Erin gets married. But what if they don't? Living with Erin means that Lexi automatically knows what's going on, gets included in everything, despite being the lone singleton in the group, and despite not being into the church thing. But when that is gone, then what?

What if Erin takes John to Thanksgiving, and she doesn't get to go?

What if this changes everything?

What if DC loses its sense of home?

It hasn't taken Lexi long to spiral into despair over this one announcement, but the spiral is, nevertheless, complete. She needs a distraction from all these emotions, and a plan to defeat Sam's evil genius is just the thing.

As the agreed day for Lexi's first piano lesson has approached, she has found herself interested, curious, wanting to learn. Excited about having something in her life that is – whisper it – unrelated to books. Excited, too, about putting this Sam Plan of hers into action. Sure, the turn about the park wasn't exactly a roaring success, but who can resist a piano recital?

Sam lives in Navy Yard, of course, in a soulless building, lured away from the community and the pastel houses of Capitol Hill by such mindless pleasures as a rooftop pool and an amazing view of historic buildings. Lexi follows someone into the lobby – they obviously didn't think she looked like a parcel thief or a serial killer, which, on balance, is probably a compliment. She takes the lift up to his floor – the seventh – and long before she's outside the door to apartment 732, she can hear him play, his fingers dancing on the keys.

Something inside her melts. Lexi hates herself for being so predictable.

She must have walked faster than she usually does, for no particular reason, and she's early, so she stands outside his door, listening, barely breathing. He might not play with such abandon when she's in there. This feels like a stolen moment, delicious, like a childhood midnight snack.

At four o'clock exactly, she takes a deep breath and rings the bell. He stops abruptly, and she regrets not waiting a minute or two for him to end the piece. She hears footsteps, and forces herself to breathe like a normal person.

'I didn't expect you to be on time,' Sam says, by way of greeting, pulling the door open and stepping back to let Lexi in. He's wearing grey fluffy slippers, which she didn't expect, in the same way that she didn't expect his family pet to be a labradoodle. She takes the hint and removes her shoes, grateful for her very recent pedicure and her sexy bright red toenails. If toenails can be sexy, that is. Feet are kind of weird, right? Let's be real.

'That's a little unfair,' Lexi tells him, even though the jab at her lack of punctuality is anything *but* unfair. It's actually a miracle she's arrived on time, never mind early. Especially in the middle of the day, with a thousand things going on at the shop. Still, Sam's never *personally* experienced her lateness. It doesn't feel like he's earned the right to tease her about it.

'Your reputation precedes you,' he says, and yeah, okay. Lexi doesn't know who's been going round complaining about her inability to be on time, but that's only because it could be just about anyone she's ever met. So, fair enough.

'Cute slippers,' she says in retaliation, and to change the subject away from her flaws.

Sam looks down at them as though he's never seen them before. 'Thank you,' he says, apparently deciding that Lexi is sincere. And truly, there's nothing wrong with his slippers. He just didn't strike Lexi as the slippers type.

She stands awkwardly in the middle of the room and does a quick spin with her eyes. Another unexpected thing: he lives in a studio apartment. Obviously, booksellers don't tend to be swimming in cash – nobody goes into the book business to get rich, with the possible exception of He Who Shall Not Be Named. Hopefully not for the glamour either, or they'd be sorely disappointed. But something about Sam screams money, and so does the Google search Lexi has done: he's the third Samuel Leonard (Leonard!) Dickens, of the Dickens media empire. It seems odd that he couldn't spring for a one-bedroom flat, at least.

Lexi's eyes, inevitably, are drawn to Sam's sofa, which is also his bed. It's right there. She could literally jump and land on it. Maybe they could dispense with the whole piano lessons thing and just go straight there? It seems like the more direct route.

But no! No. She doesn't actually want to, like, *do* anything with him. Because Samuel Leonard Dickens is totally unsuitable. Standing in front of him, thinking about how soft his hair looks, Lexi had almost forgotten this crucial point.

He gestures towards the sink. 'First things first,' he says. 'Wash your hands.'

She almost laughs; she bites her lip just in time to stop herself. Which is just as well, because Sam confirms he's serious with a stern nod. Fair enough. Lexi washes her hands before touching books, and people have been known to laugh at her for that, too.

'I'm very clean,' she tells him. It seems important to clarify that.

'Nevertheless.'

Lexi bites her lip again, because who says *nevertheless* in conversation?

'Okay.'

His soap smells of honey and milk, and she immediately recognises it from that time he scooped her off the ground, his unexpectedly soft hand on hers.

'Why do you want to learn?' he asks, Lexi's back still to him as she diligently counts to twenty seconds as we have all so recently been taught to do.

'I love that question.' She is stalling. She doesn't know what to say. So she takes another page out of Jane Austen's many books. 'I suppose I want to be an "accomplished young lady".' She hopes the air quotes she uses will make it sound a little less weird.

Sam laughs, through his nose. 'You really do live inside a novel, don't you?'

'Best place to be.' Speaking of which, she does another quick spin. She can't help noticing something else: *where are the books?* And then she says it out loud. 'Where are your books?'

He picks up an e-reader from his dining table and holds it at eye level. Lexi almost has a heart attack.

'Relax,' he tells her. 'It's a Kobo.'

Another trick she has developed since 2020: Lexi breathes in, holds it, breathes out. Slowly. How can a bookstore owner have no respect for the actual printed word? Lexi spends most of her time looking at, touching, smelling books. Her superpower is that she can tell the difference between a

British paperback and an American one by scent alone. And then there's the best thing about American paperbacks: those matte, scratchy covers, rough to the touch. She's been known to read British books in their US editions – *Never Let Me Go*, for example – simply for the feel of their covers.

Lexi knows she's, well, *special*. But that specialness is why she has built her life around a bookstore. She's wondering now if falling in love with a soulless rival is really all it's cracked up to be.

Not that she's falling in love. Not with Sam. Just, like, hypothetically.

The shock must still be written on Lexi's face, because Sam continues to justify himself. 'A book is about the content. I just don't think the format is that important. It's the words inside that matter. Don't you agree?'

She opens her mouth, goldfish-like, and closes it again.

'I'm teasing,' he says. 'I know you don't agree.'

'I bet you dog-ear pages too,' she remarks. She says it with so much vehemence that a tiny bit of spit escapes with the *p* of pages.

He's kind enough not to point it out, or to wipe his arm, where it's landed. She's dying anyway, though.

He shrugs, as if none of this is calculated, as if he doesn't know exactly what he's doing to her. 'Sure. When I read galleys or whatever.'

Lexi is tempted to turn on her heel, to leave here and now. She's heard enough. 'You know that's worse than not washing your hands before touching a piano, right?'

Sam shakes his head. 'If you say so.'

Lexi narrows her eyes at him, scowling.

'You're going to kill me with your bare hands, aren't you?'

'I was considering it,' she says. 'Yes.'

'You should learn some piano first. Use me before you dispose of me.'

She has a brief flash of how, exactly, she'd like to use him.

No, no. This won't do.

'What, and leave my DNA on your piano?'

'Ah, yes. I see the flaw. Maybe you'd better not kill me today.'

'I'll try to restrain myself.'

'That's very magnanimous of you,' he says. He points at the piano stool. 'Sit.'

'You're very bossy today.'

'I'm the teacher. You're going to have to get used to doing what I say.'

'Fine. In this one particular situation.'

She can actually think of a couple of other situations where she might be okay with it, but she keeps those thoughts to herself.

With Lexi on the stool, he pushes her closer to it, like she weighs nothing. Which she definitely doesn't. His breath grazes the back of her neck. She braces herself so that she doesn't shiver.

'Sit up,' he tells her.

She thought she already was. Clearly her posture needs some work. She straightens her shoulders and her back.

'Can you find middle C?'

She really wants to be able to say yes. She really wishes she had any idea what he is talking about. Lexi was always a good student at school, the one perpetually with her hand up. It feels disconcerting to be so clueless.

She shakes her head sadly. 'Sorry.'

'There's no need to apologise.'

'I know. But I'm British. It's what we do in these kind of situations.'

'And what kind of situations would those be?'

Lexi shrugs. There is no way she can define what is happening right now.

Sam is standing at the end of the piano, looking down at her, waiting for a response.

'I want to be good at this,' she tells him.

'You're a beginner,' he reminds her, smiling. 'By definition, you're not going to be good at it yet. That's kind of the whole deal.'

'I feel vulnerable,' Lexi confesses. She didn't mean to say it out loud. But him: standing above her, the expert. Her: sitting here, waiting to be taught. Entirely at his mercy.

'I'll be gentle,' he says. His tone is kind. There's no hint of mockery in it. Lexi is taken aback by that. She swallows, hard.

'Thank you,' she says. 'I appreciate that.'

'Now, let's find middle C.'

Sam shows Lexi how all along the keyboard there are groups of notes, patterns that repeat themselves, with two black ones and then three, over and over. That the first white one in each grouping is a C. That the fourth one of those Cs is the middle one. She pushes it down. It makes no sound.

'You have to press it a little harder,' he says. 'You won't break it, I promise. Try it with your thumb.'

She looks up at him. It's making her weirdly nervous, him up there.

'Would you feel better if I sat down?'

She's thankful he's read her thoughts, even if it's a little odd.

'Yeah, maybe.'

Lexi doesn't know why she's so nervous. Maybe it's the bed in the corner. Maybe it's all the talk of finding things and how to touch them. She shuffles along the piano stool. These things are easily big enough for two.

He could grab a chair, of course. That might be more . . . appropriate? But he takes the hint and sits next to her, their sides touching. Heat travels up Lexi's leg. She feels herself flush.

Concentrate, she tells herself.

'May I?' Sam asks, his hand hovering over hers.

'Of course.'

He takes her thumb, and presses middle C with it. She feels it now, the pressure that's needed. And also, her thumb is on fire. Who *is* this guy? What are these superpowers?

Middle C echoes out. Lexi feels triumphant. She feels, too, like she wants to lean her full weight against Sam and close her eyes while he plays the piano. But that's not technically why she's here.

With her other fingers, she presses down on the next keys. 'I'm going to guess these are D, E, F, G?'

'You're a fast learner.'

'Thank you.' She turns to him. He smiles, and she mirrors it. 'And the black keys?'

'Those are half tones. C sharp comes between C and D.'

'Makes sense,' she says, even though she's not sure it does. She's not sure her brain is capable of taking in much information right now. She runs her fingers along each black key. 'This is so basic, isn't it? You must think I'm a total idiot.'

'You're a beginner,' he says again. 'It's okay to not know things.'

'Still, though. I bet most people don't get to adult life not knowing how to read music.'

'You'd be surprised.'

'Thank you for taking the time to rescue me from my ignorance,' she says.

'You're welcome,' Sam says, not unkindly.

'So what comes after G? Is it H?'

He laughs. He clearly can only take so much. 'No. Back to A.'

'Wouldn't it make more sense to start with A?' This all seems unnecessarily complicated.

'I know it seems that way now. But . . .'

He plays from middle C to E, and his thumb goes under the bridge made by his fingers and all the way through to B and to what Lexi assumes is the next C, his hands moving back towards her. She watches his fingers doing this so naturally and once again has to restrain her overactive brain from thinking about what else those fingers might be able to do.

'Do you know what that is? The thing I just played?'

'A . . . scale?' Lexi isn't sure where that came from. She's glad, though, that she voiced this sensible thought, rather than anything else going on in her brain.

Clearly, neither does Sam. 'You do know something.'

'Hey.' She punches his arm playfully.

'Ouch,' he says, rubbing it, though there's no way it hurts. 'So C major is the most straightforward scale, because it doesn't have any sharps or flats. No black keys. That's why we start there. Whereas other scales . . .'

Both Sam's hands fly on the piano. Lexi watches his fingers land on white keys and black keys, in a logical, progressive order, making the same kind of pattern that sounds somehow different each time.

'Huh,' she says.

'Those are all scales, too. They're just more complicated.' He turns his head to face her. 'You look scared, but there's no need to be. You don't need to worry about most of those for a long time yet.'

'Okay.'

The idea of a long time feels both scary and enjoyable. A long time of coming here, into this flat, being taught by Sam. She forgets, when she's in this room, that they're mortal enemies. Sam seems to forget it, too. His tone is gentler, kinder, more patient, even if he can't resist the odd acerbic dig.

'All right,' he says. 'So notes can last different amounts of time, right?'

Lexi nods. That much, even her beginner's brain can comprehend.

Sam grabs a book from the top of the piano. He opens it, bends back the spine. 'It has to lie flat,' he says, by way of explanation. He can guess how Lexi feels about bent spines. And then, unexpectedly: 'Sorry.' Just as unexpectedly, she finds herself forgiving him.

He points to a note on the page. 'See that there? That's what we call a quarter note. Though I think your people call it a crotchet, for reasons unknown to anyone else.'

'You know,' she says, 'none of this makes a lot of sense. We start with a C, not an A. And we start with a quarter note, not a whole note. This must be killing you, with your love of logic.'

Sam frowns. 'It has its own internal logic.'

'Okay.'

Telling Sam that something he loves lacks logic is obviously sensitive. Lexi has touched a nerve. But like the pro he is, he rises above it. And she has to admit, he's good at this teaching lark. Things make sense the way he explains them.

By the end of the first lessons, Lexi has played an entire line of music, which feels like a minor victory.

'Thank you,' she tells him. 'I feel more accomplished already.'

'You're welcome.' Sam looks at Lexi full in the face, and she forces herself to hold his gaze. 'I hope spending half an hour with me wasn't too unbearable.'

'No,' she tells him, surprising herself a little too. 'Not at all. It was . . . nice. You're a good teacher.'

Sam nods, like he already knew this, but it's nice to be told nonetheless. 'Thank you.'

'Ever considered doing this full-time instead of running a bookstore on Capitol Hill just metres away from mine?'

'Get out,' he says, but he's smiling. And Lexi finds that she is too.

Chapter Seventeen

Nothing makes Lexi feel as good as being in the bookshop with her staff and her customers. It's the best therapy. Even tucked away in her office, away from the shop floor, there are memories. A *Nevertheless She Persisted* cross-stitch that Erin made for her unironically when she officially signed the deeds to the bookshop, which in 2020 seemed to mock her but then gave her the strength and determination to keep fighting when it seemed impossible to even imagine survival. A photo of her grandmother smiling at her, reminding her of good times together in the shop and of her full confidence in Lexi, even when Lexi doesn't feel like she deserves it.

And a few footsteps from the office, a little girl around nine or ten is curled up on the bookshop sofa, reading. Lexi can't quite tell what – but she's transported back to her own childhood – to the safety of books after Erin left and she found herself often alone, which was preferable to being with so-called friends who'd make fun of her red hair and mock her with their terrible atempts at American accents when she came back from her summers in DC with a slight twang and the odd change in her vocabulary. The bookshop is her safe place, and she loves that it's a safe place for others too.

Any thoughts on Independent Bookstore Day?

The text from Sam lights up Lexi's phone. She's ordered

balloons and extra chalk pens to decorate the board outside. She's booked in the decorators to give the mural outside a fresh lick of paint. She's dug out notes from previous years and looked through what now feel like tired old ideas. But otherwise, all she really had are endless pieces of paper with IBD 2024 written at the top, and meaningless doodles below.

Lots of thoughts, she types back.

Cool. Want to meet about it? Maybe we'll have a stationary meeting this time. Less dangerous.

Lol, she types, with an eyeroll emoji, but her actual face is smiling.

Lexi is two minutes late to Peregrine, and Sam is already seated with two lattes when she gets there, at the back of the coffee shop under the oversized old map of DC. She sort of loves that Sam knows her order and pre-empted it. He notices, and he remembers. This is a good sign for his levels of smittenness, and therefore of distraction.

'Let's hope none of my regulars see me,' she says, by way of a greeting. 'They'll wonder what competing bookstore owners have to talk about.'

'I think most people think that all booksellers are friends,' he says. He takes a sip of his latte and runs his tongue slowly across his top lip to catch the stray foam. And, presumably, to get her attention. She forces herself to look away.

'Poor deluded customers,' she says, laughing.

'Indeed.'

'So,' Sam says. 'Have you had a moment to think beyond balloons?'

'Of course.'

'Let's hear it.'

Lexi thinks on her feet. 'Well, if we're going to compete, we should actually *compete*.'

Sam wiggles his eyebrows. 'What did you have in mind?'

'I was hoping you'd have some ideas, too.' She hopes he doesn't notice that she is stalling.

'Okay, Miss Austen.'

She takes a sip of her coffee and waits for Sam's contribution.

'Miss Austen,' he says. 'That's a great name for a bookshop owner.'

'So is Dickens. Is he any relation of yours?'

'Not that I know of. What about you?'

'I don't know. Maybe very distantly. We call her Cousin Jane in my family.'

'And how does she feel about that?'

Lexi rolls her eyes and laughs. 'Still, what are the odds? Both of us with names of classic authors . . .'

'Maybe that's our IBD competition. You try to sell as much Austen as possible; I try and sell as much Dickens as possible.'

'That's too easy,' she says. 'Nobody cares about Dickens anymore. No offence.'

'Really?'

'Fine, maybe some people do. But Austen is fashionable in a way that Dickens isn't. He's a dusty old read for middle-aged men.'

'Sounds like you're onto a winner, then. But to make it more interesting – we count how much money we make rather than the number of books sold.'

Great Expectations still has a room of second-hand books,

and the occasional first edition. He could wipe the floor with her. And counting it this way also means that she can't do mega discounts, which is her primary way of selling a lot of books fast.

Sam jumps on her hesitancy. 'If nobody cares about Dickens anymore, what have you got to lose?'

Lexi has backed herself into a corner. 'Fair.' She's also pretty confident that Jane beats Charles hands down.

'All right,' Sam says. 'It's a deal.'

'Smart, witty and fun versus serious and worthy. Seems very appropriate.'

'For our bookshops.'

'Sure, but also for us.' Lexi has finished her latte, which is unfortunate, since well-timed sips make for great punctuation in conversation. 'So what are the stakes here?'

'Stakes?' Lexi is surprised that Sam seems so surprised.

'Yeah, as in what do I get if I win?'

'Grudging respect and admiration.'

'I mean, I assume that's a given. But what else?'

He scratches his chin, considering this. 'If I win, you have to come and work a shift in my shop.'

'Fine.' Lexi doesn't want Sam anywhere near her staff and places he could snoop around, so she can't reciprocate. She thinks about her making-Sam-fall-in-love-with-her list, how this is a golden opportunity to strike something else off it. 'But if I win, you have to come to a dance class with me.'

'A dance class?'

'There's going to be salsa dancing at Erin's wedding. I want to be prepared.' This is blatant fabrication, but will do nicely as an excuse. 'I need a partner to practise with.'

'Fine. I'm not going to lose anyway, so I have nothing

to worry about.' But he can bluff all he likes: Lexi saw the nervous look cross his face.

'Exactly,' Lexi says, and when she puts down her cup and walks out, her mind is already whirring with Austen themes for IBD.

Chapter Eighteen

The last Saturday day in April dawns bright and cheerful, and the adrenaline is already pumping in Lexi's veins when she wakes up. It's her favourite day: better than birthdays, better than Christmas. Independent Bookstore Day. The competition with Sam is just one aspect of what will make the day fun. Not to mention beating him.

Arriving at the bookshop half an hour before opening, she notes approvingly that there's already a queue of eager customers, both regulars and DC bookshop hoppers who know that if they make it to four or more independents today, they'll be entered into a draw to win a pile of novels in the genre of their choice. Balloons float above the chalkboard outside. Indoors, Megan and Natalie busy themselves with laying out cupcakes and plastic champagne flutes for buck's fizz. Debbie puts final touches to the Austen-themed displays. Marcus re-acquaints himself with the till system; usually, he's a behind-the-scenes guy, keeping books flowing onto shelves, but today everybody is out on the shop floor. Hazel, her tidy silver bob newly trimmed, wipes down the counter area, making sure everything is pristine. It won't take long before everything descends into happy chaos, but it's good to start a day like this in some semblance of order, at least.

'It sort of surprises me that we haven't leaned in harder to the Austen theme before,' Lexi hears Natalie say on her way past to the kitchen for a fortifying cup of tea.

'An old hang-up from my schooldays,' Lexi tells her 'I was desperate to blend in. And with the red hair and the American passport . . . the Austen thing was one thing too many that set me apart. I guess I've always felt a bit squiffy about it because of that.' A vague nod to her famous potential-relative in the name of her bookshop is one thing; leaning in totally is another. But today, because of the competition with Sam, she'll do what it takes.

Soon, it's 10 a.m., and shoppers are streaming in. Lexi assumes her position at the info desk in the nerve centre of her bookshop, and absorbs the vibes. Here, she'll hand out rewards for the best chalk drawing on the pavement outside the shop. She'll dole out raffle prizes in the form of bookmarks and stickers and tote bags and gift vouchers. And, in the meantime, she watches as customers mill around, checking out the new displays made in preparation for today: a shelf of books that feature bookshops, a table of notebooks with anti-capitalist slogans, a stack of Jane Austen paperbacks – each one with a raffle ticket included as added incentive to purchase a classic you've been meaning to get to almost as long as you've been alive.

Lexi manages to stave off the need for a lunchbreak by snacking on the cupcakes that arrive from Baked and Wired at regular intervals. But by 2 p.m., she is gasping for some caffeine, and dying to know how it's going round the corner with Sam's shop.

'I'm doing a coffee run,' she tells Megan and Elijah behind

the till on her way out, to cover her tracks. A coffee run on a Saturday can take ages. Nobody will need to know that she'll be popping into Great Expectations as part of that while she's out. 'Place your orders now.'

Outside Sam's shop, a boy dressed in some approximation of Victorian clothes sings 'You've Got to Pick a Pocket or Two', and another boy dressed similarly runs behind people, exaggeratedly peering into handbags. A third paces up and down with a sandwich board, letting people know about Charles Dickens First Editions in the shop. Lexi has to hand it to Sam: this is genius, even if the cockney accents leave a lot to be desired. She won't go inside and give him the satisfaction of telling him so, though.

She doesn't have to. As if a mere thought has conjured him, Sam materialises next to her. 'Come to spy, I see?'

'Merely curious,' Lexi replies.

'I see. How's it going at Pemberley?'

'Really well,' she says. She doesn't have the figures yet, but she knows buzz when she sees it. 'No need for gimmicks.'

'I see.' Sam is smiling, though. He knows even without Lexi owning up that she is impressed. And while period dress and re-enactment isn't really Lexi's thing, she's still gutted that she didn't think of it herself.

Still, by the end of the day, the Pemberley tills are empty of change and full to the brim of credit card receipts. It's been the best and busiest day the shop has seen in quite some time, better even than last Christmas Eve. Maybe, just maybe, the buck's fizz which later on was replaced by straight bubbles had something to do with that. Tipsy browsing being, after all, the best browsing.

Chapter Nineteen

'I promised I'd come dancing,' Sam says. 'I never said I'd do it without complaining.'

'Noted,' Lexi says. She's still smugly enjoying her victory in the Austen/Dickens competition as they travel up on the Red Line to Friendship Heights. She's also, if she's honest, very much enjoying the idea of being legitimately allowed to hold hands with Sam, touch him, be up close to him. She can see how in the age of her maybe-ancestor, with all its etiquette and firm boundaries, the prospect would be thrilling. It's been too busy lately for a second piano lesson; they need to get back to them.

In the dance hall, they hang close to the wall while they wait for proceedings to start. Lexi would normally find someone to chat with at this point, establish within seconds that she owns Pemberley Books, maybe recommend a book or two. But Sam's usual easy-going openness isn't on display today. He seems to want to be invisible. Lexi humours him; she's not a monster.

The dance instructor, a petite woman with her brown hair thrown up in a messy bun, claps her hands. 'Okay,' she says. 'It's time to partner up, everyone.'

Lexi bites her lip to hide a smile. The reason she is here, in this dance class, is precisely for this reason: that it's time to partner up. And for once she is not the one left over, having to dance with seventy-five-year-old Marjorie.

Within fifteen seconds, Sam has stood on her foot. 'Sorry,' he says, sounding genuinely stricken.

'It's okay.' She smiles, attempting to put him at ease. It hurt, a little, but that's not the point. The point is, he's here, despite his misgivings. Holding her hands, brushing her bare arms, being up close and personal. She doesn't even mind that he hasn't dressed up. She just hopes he's appreciating her slightly-lower-cut-than-necessary dress.

As the class progresses, Lexi loses track of the number of times he stands on her foot, or, for that matter, that she stands on his because he hasn't moved in time. So much for the sexiness of dancing, of touching, of his hands on her waist. She isn't even sure she's that attracted to him right now – not because he's bad at this; that, in itself, is endearing – but because he's increasingly grumpy about it. Embarrassed, probably, which is entirely understandable – but the grumpiness is no fun for either of them. In those Jane Austen adaptations, they always make it look so easy. Maybe she would have been better off dancing with Marjorie after all.

'It's okay not to be good at something, you know,' Lexi says as they make their way to the metro, warmth in her voice despite her growing impatience at his sullenness. She bumps his shoulder with hers. 'Especially the first time you try.'

He shrugs. She waits. 'I don't like it.'

'Dancing?'

'Yes, I mean no, not specifically. I don't like not being good at something.'

'It's an uncomfortable feeling,' she says. 'I get it. But isn't it worth it, to learn something new and stretch yourself?'

He shrugs again. Lexi didn't have him down as a shrugger. There's something boyish about it. It should be unattractive, but . . . well, it isn't.

'I mean, like, how about when you took over the bookshop? That must have been a stretch.'

'I was good at it,' he says. 'I am good at it. I learned the basics of business from my dad – it was drilled into us. And the people stuff, I can do that pretty well too. It was just learning about the book trade that I needed to do, and retaining information is one of my skills. So . . .'

'You dad must have taught you well.' Lexi keeps her voice neutral, encouraging even. Trying not to betray just what he thinks of the head of Dickens Media.

'Not as well as he wishes,' Sam says, with bitterness in his voice. 'That's for sure.'

'You didn't want to go into business with him?'

'No,' he says. 'I wanted to be a pianist. But that wasn't deemed an acceptable ambition. Business is the only thing that matters in our family. Already by being a bookseller I'm testing the outer limits of that. It's not exactly the most profitable business in the world.'

'You wanted to be a pianist?'

'Is that so surprising?'

Lexi shakes her head. 'No. Apart from your terrible sense of rhythm, that is.'

'That's different,' he says, the sullenness back in his voice. 'Moving your feet and your whole body is very different to a feel for rhythm when you play the piano.'

'I know. I was teasing.'

They step onto the Metro escalator, one behind another, which buys them an excuse for a couple of minutes of silence and gives Lexi a moment to process. As they stand on the platform, she's grateful for the eleven-minute wait until the next Red Line train.

'Has your dad made peace with you not working with him now?'

'Not really, no.'

There's a forcefulness and a weight in his words that makes Lexi take notice.

'Do you get on okay with him otherwise?'

Sam snorts. 'His business is his whole life. He doesn't know how to have a relationship outside of it. He barely knows how to have a conversation that isn't about it. And when I finally got up the courage to tell him that it wasn't for me, it was like the biggest slap in the face to him. He's never recovered from it, and neither has our relationship.'

This seems almost unbearably sad to Lexi. 'Maybe if he saw your bookshop and how successful it is . . .' She bites her lip to keep from adding the next part – how successfully it's threatening other businesses, just like his dad's business does.

'Nah,' he says. 'I've given up.'

'That's sad,' Lexi says.

'Can you believe it's another seven minutes till this Metro shows up?'

Lexi laughs, although she knows a change of subject

when she hears one. 'Yes. It's always like this. There'd be riots in the street if this happened in London.'

'I thought the British were too polite for riots?'

'You might be right there. There's a reason we've never had a socialist revolution like the French.'

Lexi takes the hint and allows the change in subject. For the rest of the wait and the metro ride, they talk cultural differences and whether socialism is or isn't a bad thing and why Americans are so afraid of free healthcare. But before she gets off at Metro Center to switch to the Blue Line she throws out one last line.

'I wish my dad was still alive. I'd do anything to keep up my relationship with him if he was.'

As the metro doors shut, the look Sam gives Lexi is heartbreaking – a mixture of sadness and regret. Lexi carries it all the way home.

Lexi Austen's Discoveries about Sam Dickens

- *Beautiful piano player*
- *No patience for DC metro*
- *He's learned his ruthless business skills from his dad*
- *He also desperately doesn't want to be his dad*
- *He's less secure than he seems*
- *Terrible rhythm*
- *Worse hand-eye coordination*
- *Very, very green eyes*

Chapter Twenty

Lexi shows up eager and early to her second piano lesson, just like she always did on the first and second and sometimes third day of school, before the apathy and the drudge and the realities of homework started to sink in. She's always been an eager kind of learner. She liked the predictability of school: she worked hard; she got good grades. It bugged her when people who barely did any work somehow aced their way to an A. She liked predictable outcomes; she liked the seeming fairness of it. One of the hardest things about grieving her mum was that it knocked all the energy out of her; she made it through finals at university in a daze, but all her get up and go had got up and gone, and did not return for several years.

Now, she works hard; her bookshop, until recently, has been successful. When that equation is off, something feels viscerally, frustratingly wrong. It took her an embarrassingly long time to understand privilege, to understand that sometimes people get to skip stages in the hard-work-equals-success equation because of something they lucked into, like being born straight and white and relatively wealthy, and even more embarrassingly long to realise that her own equation has a lot of that privilege behind it, the world seemingly designed for her, a right-handed, able-bodied, straight white woman from a nice middle-class family. But still, that hopefulness of the first day of school has stayed with her; that hope that she's going to learn something new, eventually be good at something new.

Lexi is contemplating how to knock on Sam's door with both hands full when he opens it; he must have anticipated her arrival. It's early: the only way they could fit in the lesson today was to meet before work. Lexi isn't usually a fan of 8 a.m., but, weirdly, the thought of seeing Sam had her out of bed after only a couple of pushes of the snooze button and a few minutes of Instagram scrolling. It must be the after-effects of that concussion a couple of months ago; she isn't sure how else to explain what is happening to her.

'I brought you coffee,' she tells him, because miraculously, she got up early enough to swing by Peregrine on the way to Sam's. Alli had to do a double take: she's never seen Lexi before 10 a.m.

Sam runs his hand through his still-damp hair: he's probably been to the gym already today. Lexi tries not to think about that, his shallow, rapid breathing, his biceps popping as he lifts weights. She's betting he's strong. She's not the lightest, but she'd be willing to bet the year's shop takings on his being able to lift her up and fling her onto his sofa bed.

Is it hot in here? she finds herself wondering. Because her face feels hot, and so does her inside leg.

'Thank you,' he says, his fingers grazing hers as he takes his latte from Lexi. 'That's very thoughtful of you.'

'Yes, well. Don't get used to it.' Lexi isn't sure the banter will land well with an American. 'I got it extra hot, so it would survive the journey,' she adds.

'Ah, yes. The long schlep from Capitol Hill to Navy Yard.'

'It *is* a long schlep. Metaphorically speaking. I crossed cultural and political divides for you.'

The words just hang there. Maybe he didn't notice their implication?

'For me?' He definitely did notice. 'That is truly touching.'

'For my piano lesson, I mean. I'm very dedicated to my craft.'

Sam nods thoughtfully. 'Ah.'

He takes a sip of his coffee, foam attaching itself to his upper lip. Lexi has an almost irresistible urge to wipe it off with her thumb, but she manages to get it under control and respect his personal space. She doesn't usually want to get this close to people before 10 a.m., but, again: let's blame the concussion. Or maybe the coffee, since she drank most of hers on the way over. Did she read somewhere that caffeine is an aphrodisiac? Because now that Lexi is inside the flat, fully exposed to Sam's enthusiastic air conditioning, with the sofa bed he could so easily fling her onto, she's definitely still feeling hot.

'I appreciate the sacrifice of your long hike,' Sam says, playing along. 'Or at least my piano does.'

Technically, it's him and his piano making the sacrifice and doing Lexi a favour, but this doesn't seem like the time to quibble.

Sam sits his latte on top of the piano. Lexi looks at him askance. 'Is that allowed?'

He nods gravely, in recognition of her excellent point. 'You're right. Probably not. I wouldn't want to set a bad example.' Then he nods again, towards the piano stool.

Lexi sets her bag down and does as she's told. She's going

to have to get used to his bossing her around. She wishes she could say she hated it.

At the end of the lesson, during which Lexi has learned about the different clefs and the way you read music differently depending on if you're playing it with your right hand or your left hand, Sam looks at her like he wants to say something. The silence stretches out and she starts to feel squirmy.

'Are you heading to the shop now?' she asks, for something to say more than anything else.

'Yeah,' he replies. 'Sure. Why not.'

'You don't sound very sure.'

'I have admin to do, and sometimes I do it from home. But there's no reason I can't do it from there.'

Lexi likes to hide in her cave in the shop for her admin, knowing that just beyond the wall, children are reading with their parents, Pippin is wandering around, and Megan or Debbie or Hazel are putting just the right books in just the right hands. It grounds her. It reminds her why she's doing the chasing of bills, the arguing with the internet provider, the organising of rotas. She doesn't know exactly what motivates Sam, because it doesn't seem to be that, exactly. He's a mystery to her, still.

'Want to walk together?'

He raises an eyebrow. 'People will talk.'

Lexi laughs. What a ridiculous idea that anyone would think anything was going on between these two bitter rivals. 'Let them,' she says.

'Okay.'

Sam picks up his keys and his backpack, which is ready and waiting at the door. If it had been the other way round, Lexi would have needed at least ten minutes of faffing. First of all, she wouldn't have been able to find her keys, even though there's a hook just by the door perfect for hanging them when she gets in. She does this six or seven times out of ten, but you can guarantee that the times when she doesn't do it are the times when she's in a rush to leave. It's the kind of thing her mum used to shake her head at her for; now it's Erin who shakes *her* head. Then she'd scramble around gathering her notebooks, her Post-it Notes, her highlighter pen. As Erin has pointed out many times, it would be much easier to just leave all of that at the office in the shop. But Lexi always intends to do more work at home, even if she does mostly end up flopping on the sofa, exhausted, chatting to Erin or catching up on Netflix's latest must-watch or, if she really wants to feel virtuous, reading an advance review copy of a book for an upcoming event.

What nobody tells you about owning a bookstore is you end up reading less than ever, despite all that increased access to early and free or cheap material, and despite being around people whose enthusiasm for books is infectious. Lexi finds herself saying, *That sounds great, I'll have to read it soon* far more times per day than she ever has, and actually doing it less and less. If she's perfectly honest, the reason she wants to hire a manager she can entrust with the day-to-day running of the shop isn't just so she can have a life, see her friends more and be more present for them, and maybe even fit in some dating on the side. It's also so that she can have time to read again. She misses the lazy Sundays she used to have in bed with a cup of tea and a good novel, emerging from a happy ending well into the evening, simultaneously wondering where the day had gone and feeling deeply satisfied with how she had spent it.

She used to read purely because she loved it. And also because it made her feel connected to her grandma. They always talked about books when she was alive; she always wanted to know what Lexi was reading, what she thought about it. Her guilty pleasures were Jilly Cooper and Mary Higgins Clark, but she loved to sink into literary fiction and poetry, too.

But then, books became more than a passion for Lexi: they became connected to the dopamine hit of Instagram likes and growing follower counts – a performative hobby rather than a private one, and she knows there's no way to put the proverbial genie back into that particular bottle. And then, owning a bookstore: well, that's a whole other thing, because now books are tied up with mundane things like paying her rent and keeping on top of electricity bills, with managing staffing issues, with choosing healthcare plans, with competing with Sam, and with the darker aspects of late-stage capitalism. So when Lexi wants a break and she picks up a book . . . it doesn't quite feel like a break. And the shameful fact is that sometimes she resents the shop just a little bit for that.

Outside, it's roasting. The summer humidity that will frizz up her wavy hair hasn't quite kicked in yet, but it's a very warm spring day – the kind of day that back home people complain about because it's 'too hot'. And because Lexi is British, and because she is feeling suddenly awkward at being outside, in public, with Sam, this seems like an appropriate way to break the silence.

'I love this weather,' she tells him.

'Say what you like about the British,' he says, 'but you guys certainly know how to appreciate the sun.'

'Well, yeah. We have to. I've been here six years, but shaving my legs in early April is still a novelty. And yeah, it's a pain. But I love the feeling of soft legs and a dress.'

Sam makes a sound like he is being strangled.

'You okay there?'

'Yup.' He nods energetically. 'Sure. Absolutely.'

Another pause, and Lexi has already used the weather as a topic to defuse the awkwardness. So now what?

They walk in silence along I street, the cars on the busy South Capitol Street behind them rescuing them from hearing themselves not speaking. But as the traffic noise recedes, Lexi scrambles to think of a question. It's going to be a long twenty-minute walk otherwise.

'So do you like living in Navy Yard?'

'Here we go,' Sam says, under his breath, and then, louder, 'I do. I love living in Navy Yard. I love living in a new-build apartment. I love the rooftop. I love the pool.'

It's Lexi's turn to make a strangled noise. She hopes he interprets that as jealousy and not as her trying not to think about his body in tiny Speedos. (He's obviously too cool to wear Speedos. It just makes for better imagination games.)

He mirrors Lexi's question back to her. 'You okay there?'

She thinks about mirroring his answer – *yup, sure, absolutely* – but that seems a little . . . much.

'Yep. Totally fine.'

'And let me guess. You love Capitol Hill? Just love it? Wouldn't dream of living anywhere else?'

He's not wrong, of course. And yet for some reason

117

it annoys Lexi that he finds her so easy to read. No pun intended.

'Obviously.'

She can almost feel him rolling his eyes beside her.

'I love the sense of community there. I love that Alli knows my name and my coffee order. I love walking to work. I love bumping into my regular customers at Trader Joe's.' She pauses, waits for a response. 'I guess it's not as great if you have things to hide, though. Or people to avoid.' It comes out pointedly, and that's the way Lexi meant it to. She's poking the beast, seeing if she can solve the mystery of who Sam is, really.

'I don't have anything to hide,' he says. 'I just don't like everyone up in my business.'

'And ex-girlfriends all over the place?'

Lexi's hand flies to her mouth. She hadn't meant to say that, shocks even herself with that response. What's more shocking, though, is Sam's reaction: he laughs.

'Something like that,' he says.

'Doesn't it bother you?'

She's timed her question right, or wrong, depending on how you look at it. Because they're at a crossing now, waiting for the little man to turn white (not green, like back home), and so they're stopped, still, and it's easier for them to look at each other. He can't just brush off her question.

The silence stretches as they wait. Lexi starts to wonder if he's heard her, so she nudges him with her shoulder, and he looks at her.

His eyes, unexpectedly, are sad.

'It bothers me a lot, actually,' he says.

Lexi wants to say, *Then maybe stop breaking up with people? Or at least stop dating people till you're ready to commit?* But

118

the sadness in his eyes stops her. Bickering and sparring and bantering are one thing. They're fun; they're an adrenaline rush. But hurting him, kicking him while he's so obviously down, while he's letting himself be vulnerable . . . well, that's something else altogether.

Once upon a time, she might have wanted to hurt him, just a little, for the stress he's caused and the fact he's taken away the pleasure she once had at being the undisputed Book Queen of Capitol Hill. But then she remembers his kindness in looking after her, the softness of his touch as he guides her fingers on the piano keyboard, the laughter in his voice when he finds her Briticisms amusing. It's not that she forgives him, exactly. But she's less into the idea of hurting him.

'Then—' She's been wondering how to phrase the question without sounding accusing and mean, but it turns out she doesn't need to. A one-word prompt is all Sam needs.

'I just can't seem to make it work. I can't seem to make myself want it enough. Since—'

He stops abruptly and stands still, like he can't open up and walk at the same time.

Lexi tries to prompt him. 'Since . . . ?'

She sees his shrug in her peripheral vision. This is all she's getting from him today. But it's enough. Enough to convince her that he's not an asshole or a two-dimensional villain in some terribly written sitcom, that instead he has a complicated backstory and maybe even hidden depths.

Lexi lets the silence hang a little bit longer, just in case. Sometimes silence is all it takes for someone to open up, or, in her case, to start babbling incoherently. Babbling incoherently isn't really Sam's thing, though.

But when he does start talking again, he changes the subject abruptly.

'So what have you been reading lately?'

This is smart, Lexi notes approvingly. If there's anything that can distract her, throw her off the scent of a juicy conversational titbit, it's asking her about books. She's aware of the tactic, but she figures she'll have plenty of other opportunities to get him to open up. There's something about Sam at the piano: he becomes a softer, more open person. The closer they get to Capitol Hill and to parting ways on the corner of 7th Street and Pennsylvania Avenue, the straighter he stands, becoming a shrewd businessman again.

Which is why Lexi wonders if she should tell him the truth about her current reading material. She worries it might open up the kind of can of worms that's inappropriate between business rivals before 10 a.m. on a Wednesday morning.

'*The Hating Game*,' she tells him anyway. 'It's a romance novel.'

Lexi doesn't read a lot of backlist – books published more than a year ago. It's part of her job to always read forward, to know what's coming up in the immediate future of publishing, which authors would make for great event guests, what books they're going to be recommending to their customers this season. And it's not just her *job*. She loves to know, to talk buzzy books with her staff and with other industry insiders. Six years in, there's still nothing quite like the thrill of an advance copy of a book she's been excited about since she saw the deal announced in *Publishers Weekly*. But when Lexi is in a reading slump, or when she needs a comfort read, she likes to return to her tried-and-tested favourites. Classics, or *Bridget Jones's Diary*, or *One Day*, or *The Idea Of You*. Or something really hot and fun, like a well-written romance.

'What's it about?' he asks. 'I mean, love, I assume. Enemies to lovers?'

'I'm impressed that you know the terminology.'

She intended it as a compliment, or at least as grudging admiration, but her tone comes down harder on the grudge than the admiration.

'I'm a professional,' he says. 'It's my job to know these things.'

'To know romance?'

'To have an understanding of the book world as a whole.'

'Okay, fair.'

'So what's it about?'

'It's about two rivals in the publishing industry who hate each other. Only it turns out that what they thought was hate is actually latent simmering sexual tension.'

'Wow,' Sam says, and it's not as sarcastic as Lexi might have expected. 'What made you want to read that?'

He's timed his question just right, almost as if in retaliation. They're at another crossing, the one right before they go their separate ways to their separate, warring bookshops.

Sam turns his face towards Lexi, and without thinking about it, she turns to face him too. Her face is burning up; she can feel it. It's not the springtime warmth, and it's not sunburn – thank you, sunscreen-laden moisturiser. It's heat more powerful than either of those things.

'I couldn't possibly say,' Lexi replies eventually, a hint of flirtation wrapped in self-protectiveness.

Sam chortles, through his nose. 'I didn't think so,' he says. 'This is where I leave you. Have a great day!'

And off he walks, apparently unfazed.

Lexi watches him, forgetting to turn left, forgetting to cross the road. Remembering vaguely that she'd once upon a time vowed to distract him while she remained unbothered. That seems unlikely now.

Chapter Twenty-One

After a couple of piano lessons, it has become clearer to Lexi that a recital is a little way off for her, let alone one where she will wow Sam enough for the plan she has in mind. So when Erin unexpectedly can't use tickets she has to see Yo-Yo Ma at the Kennedy Center, she jumps at the chance to take them off her hands.

It doesn't have to be Lexi doing the playing for the music to work its magic. Music itself is enough, and the grandeur of the Kennedy Center adds to the romance of any occasion, with its pristine red carpets, its high ceilings, its feeling of space, its crystal chandeliers hanging down like giants' earrings.

She isn't surprised when Sam replies the instant she texts him about the tickets. The concert has been sold out for months.

'Really, thanks for this,' he says as she gets off the red minivan shuttle from the metro. He, of course, is already waiting at the Hall of Flags entrance, wearing a navy-blue suit, smarter and tidier than she's ever seen him. The Kennedy Center is the kind of place that makes you want to dress up. Lexi is wearing black sparkly shoes with a small heel and her trusty little black dress, V-necked with just a hint of decolletage. 'It's the hottest ticket in town.'

'Hotter than the White House Correspondents' Dinner?' It's just a couple of weeks till the great, the good, and the not-so-good of the news media and selected Hollywood stars descend on the capital to hear the president and a professional comedian make jokes at their own and opponents' expense.

'Hotter to *me*,' Sam clarifies.

As am I, Lexi wants to joke, but she isn't sure they're there yet.

As they watch, Lexi almost forgets who's sitting next to her. She's mesmerised by Yo-Yo Ma and his piano accompanist, the soaring melodies, the subtlety of their playing, the movement of their fingers. She only *almost* forgets, though, because there's a force field of warmth between her and Sam. She'd love to watch him watching, to see the reactions in his green eyes, to see what he's like when he's fully, completely focused. She'd love to take his hand, to lean her head on his shoulder. But she doesn't want to interrupt his moment, and anyway, it's too soon for that, and she hopes the *almost touching* of it will be as sexy and attractive to him as it is to her.

His eyes are shining when he turns to her at intermission, and with a hand on the small of her back, he leads Lexi to pick up their bubbly rosé and stand on the terrace. This is one of her favourite places in DC, walking among the fountains, below quotes by JFK on the importance of the arts.

'He's quite something, isn't he?' she says.

'Yes.' Sam raises his glass, and Lexi clinks it with hers. 'To many more evenings like this,' he says.

Lexi isn't sure if it's that or the wine that makes her cheeks feel pink.

Standing in the warm April air, drinking their drinks, they chat easily about nothing of great consequence. DC, music, books.

'Fifteen minutes is never long enough for a drink at intermission,' Lexi says. 'I have to down it so quickly and I get tipsy.'

Sam looks at her, and she wonders if he's considering taking advantage of her tipsiness. But in this, at least, he is a gentleman.

'Do you think music is better when you're tipsy?' she asks him.

'I think a lot of things are better when you're tipsy.'

Lexi thinks about Galentine's Day at Kramers with Erin. 'That's true. Browsing in a bookshop, for example. It lowers your inhibitions. You're more likely to just go for it and buy the book.' And then, because of the tipsiness, she keeps talking. 'I think Tipsy Browsing would make a great bookshop name, actually. One with wine, obviously.'

'I like it,' Sam says. 'But you can't be an Austen and not have that feature somehow, right?'

'Yeah.'

'Families, right?'

'Yeah. Speaking of . . .' Lexi takes a deep breath and a final sip of her wine for bravery, and also because the end-of-intermission bell has just gone. 'Have you spoken to your dad lately?'

'Actually, yes. I mean, once. And we talked about inconsequential niceties for a few minutes, and neither of us slammed the phone down mid-sentence.' Sam scrutinises the bottom of his champagne flute. 'There's a long way to go still. And I need to see that he's changed, which I guess will only come with time. But yes. I wanted to say thank you, actually.' He looks up and meets her eye. 'Shall we?'

Lexi nods, and takes his arm with hers. 'I'm really glad. Thanks for telling me. And thanks for coming with me tonight.'

'You're welcome,' he says, and bends down to kiss her cheek. It burns, but in the best way.

Chapter Twenty-Two

By week five of the piano lessons, Lexi and Sam are in something of a routine. On Wednesday mornings, 8 a.m., always somehow miraculously on time, she's outside Sam's door. Every week, he asks if she's found somewhere to practise. And every week she's forced to admit that, no, somehow a week has gone by and she hasn't had five minutes to think about it. So she's studying music theory and how to read notes. But she's not really getting any better, as such. Even Lexi, with her limited knowledge, is aware that practising is a big part of the whole learning-to-play-an-instrument thing. But let's face it: in Jane Austen's day, women had nothing to do *but* sit around playing the piano. It's maybe easier to be accomplished when you're not running your own business while being distracted by one of its existential threats.

The thing is, learning to play the piano is less and less the point of these sessions. The point, increasingly, is to get close to Sam. And that . . . well, *that* is working. They walk to their respective shops after the lesson and they talk about all kinds of things: what they're reading, the latest DC gossip, which politicians and journalists they've seen in their bookshops or in line at Peregrine. Never specifics about work, because that veers too close to sleeping with the enemy territory. And she doesn't want to think about sleeping with the enemy, or that sofa bed in his flat.

So Lexi knows more about Sam's life now. She knows that he's the middle of three boys, and the only one not to go into the family business. That his mum, dad, and brothers all still live in New York City. That, like so many New Yorkers, he believes it to be unequivocally the best city, if not in the world, then at least in North America. Everything, apparently, is better there. Especially the coffee.

'So,' she tells him on their walk back to the Hill that May morning. She's stopped walking, and she waits for him to stop, too. 'I've listened patiently to a lot of these rants about NYC. I've smiled and I've nodded. And I've put up with it. But I will not have you slandering the good name of Peregrine.' She lists for him all the regional competitions they've won over the years – a region, which, incidentally, includes New York. She lists the national awards. Then she crosses her arms and waits for an apology.

'Fine. I conceded that Peregrine is acceptable.'

Acceptable! Huh! Last time Lexi went back to London for a visit she went from coffee shop to coffee shop, convinced that in the year of our Lord 2023 surely there had to be something better than Costa. And, to be fair, there *were* places better than Costa. But none of those places could hold a candle to Peregrine. She spent half the plane journey back to DC daydreaming about her next latte.

'It's delicious, is what it is,' she protests.

'Okay, yes, fine. But name another good coffee shop in DC.'

Lexi counts them off on her hands as she names them. 'Pitango. Cameo. The Wydown. And the Cuban coffee at Colada Shop is To. Die. For.'

Sam sighs.

'See? No reason to move back to New York, ever.'

'Except for all the other reasons.'

'Name one.'

Sam pretends to think, to count them on his hands. Then he chooses one. 'The theatre.'

Lexi has to admit that Broadway is incredible. But how often does a bookshop owner have both the time and the money to go to the theatre? Let's say six times per year, tops. And she can easily find six shows per year at the Kennedy Center that she wants to see. Nothing, to her mind, beats the grandeur of the Kennedy Center. Out on the terrace, she likes to pretend she's an extra on the set of *The West Wing* as she sips her bubbles and looks out over the river, up to the cathedral, high on a faraway hill, or to the Jefferson Memorial, that temple to American independence, greatness, and liberty. You don't get views like that from the door of a New York theatre.

'No, but there is the history in the theatres themselves. Ask any actor where they'd rather perform. You can bet your bottom dollar they're not going to say DC.'

Lexi watched enough interviews back in the heyday of her obsession with *The West Wing* to know that's probably true. The guy who played Josh Lyman was always talking nostalgically about biking through the city with his girlfriend on the handlebars. She imagined him taking her to dates at cheap places that seemed French and therefore fancy because of their red-and-white-checked tablecloths. And the thing is, you can't argue with nostalgia. Maybe *that's* why so many actors love New York. It's where they headed, bright-eyed and full of hope, to make their dreams come true. And now that their dreams *have* come true, they feel disloyal when they go anywhere elsewhere. It would be like leaving the love of their life, the person they've built their whole lives with, had children with, been through the ups and downs with, weathered a pandemic and an insurrection with, won awards and lost awards with, for a hot young thing on a whim. And some – okay, many – of them would rather do that than leave New York. Because the difference is that New York is still hot.

And Lexi gets it, in a way, because that sense of loyalty is what she feels about DC. She and her sister would fly over every summer as unaccompanied minors, their tickets and passports in a pouch on a lanyard around their necks, the flight attendants making a huge fuss of them. And then they'd land at Dulles and their grandmother would be there to welcome them, her arms already out and open for a hug, smelling of cinnamon from the apple pie she'd just finished baking. On the drive from the Virginia suburbs into DC, Lexi would listen happily to the hum of the conversation between her sister and her grandmother up front as she'd look out at the city, imagining herself in a film with orchestral music swelling behind her. They'd pass the Washington Monument, tall, reaching into the clouds, pointing up to infinity. The Kennedy Center, bright and confident beside the river. The imposing lions at the entrance to the Arlington Memorial Bridge, guarding the entrance to the capital. It was pure magic to her, and it made her feel part of something bigger, made her feel like her American passport really meant something, that it wasn't just her ticket to a shorter queue at arrivals than the one her sister had to go through. Once, because of delays, they landed after dark, and the lit-up monuments on the drive in made her gasp. It was magical. A film set.

And then, as if all of that wasn't enough: the bookshop! Lexi would spend hours on the sofa there, people watching, a precocious child, equal parts sweet and vaguely irritating. If she'd known then that this place of wonders in this magical city would be hers someday, she would have been insufferable. Her sister would try to coax her away to museums, and she'd sometimes succeed, because who doesn't want a chance to gaze at the inauguration gowns of a dozen first ladies? But mostly, Lexi would hang out at the shop, tidying displays, shelving books, learning where a novel goes when its author has two surnames. She'd read books cover to cover and then recommend them to the nearest child even vaguely her age. And then when her grandmother was finally done for the day, they'd go home and eat dinner and bake actual brownies, the chocolate smell filling the town house with blue walls and a red door on East Capitol Street.

It's no surprise Lexi loves DC and defends it fearlessly from such baseless accusations as its being inferior to New York. Not to be dramatic, but it feels a little like an attack on her when someone badmouths the place. Or perhaps to be a little dramatic, since that is also part of who she is.

'So if you love New York so much,' she says to Sam now, 'how come you're not living there?'

There's a pause, and for one glorious moment Lexi thinks she's won. But alas . . .

'I met someone,' Sam says, like that explains everything. But then he realises it doesn't, so he elaborates. 'A woman. Fell head over heels in love with her. She was from here, and she was always trying to get me to move. We'd settled on Philadelphia as a compromise, because it's easy to get to both places from there, but then she sent me an article about how the bookshop was up for sale and said, *Hey, you're always talking about wanting to do this. How about now?*'

Lexi parks her questions about that part for later. Sam has always struck her as an opportunist, not a lifelong dreamer, and certainly not someone who's always dreamed of owning a bookshop.

'That was all it took?'

He laughs. 'No. It took a lot of persuading on her part.' Lexi tries not to think about what that persuading might have looked like. 'And a lot of meetings with the bank. And a few arguments with my dad, who wasn't okay with my not being in the family business. But eventually, I did it. And now here I am.'

'But you're not together anymore?'

'No.' Lexi is surprised not to hear any bitterness in his voice – only sadness. 'A few months after I moved here it became apparent that she wasn't so much in love with me as she was with my family connections and the money she thought I had because of them. Which I don't.'

This is a lot to take in. Lexi has so many questions. Like, *how* did it become apparent? What happened? Who is this woman and how could she be so callous? And, most of all, has Lexi finally hit upon his villain origin story?

Lexi's pulse is racing. She realises she's furious at this woman for uprooting him from his beloved New York and then breaking his heart. Although she is surprised to realise that part of her is also grateful that she brought him here.

'That's why I need the bookshop to be a success,' he says, meeting Lexi's eyes. 'Otherwise, it's all been for nothing.'

Dagger: heart. For the briefest of seconds, Lexi is tempted to surrender in the Great Bookshop Wars. But then she remembers all the reasons her bookshop matters to her. The reasons *she* needs it to be a success.

Nice try, she thinks, but she's not callous enough to say it, even as a joke.

'That sounds hard,' she says instead, holding eye contact. 'I'm sorry.'

'Thanks.' And then, as is so often the case with him, the moment is over as quickly as it came. 'Anyway, speaking of which.' They're standing on their 7th and Penn corner now, and he gestures in the direction of Great Expectations. 'I better get going.'

'Yeah, me too.' She pauses to think of the right thing to say, and definitely not because she's thinking about what it might be like to kiss him, right here on this street corner. 'Thank you for telling me all that.'

Sam's voice modulates back to the softer tone it takes on when they're in his apartment and it feels like he and Lexi are friends. 'You're a good listener – you know that?'

Lexi did not, in fact, know that. She gets called a chatterbox a lot. But having to be careful what she says around him leaves more room.

'Thank you,' she tells him, still not breaking eye contact.

And then, unexpectedly, he opens up his arms, inviting her in for a hug, and just as unexpectedly, she doesn't hesitate. He smells of clean clothes and cedar and possibly old books. Lexi could stay there forever. They fit just right, her head under his chin. It feels natural, like home. Like belonging.

'Have a good day,' she says. She wants him to have an

excellent day, not just a happy one or an easy one, but a productive and lucrative one. She wants him to feel like it's all been worth it.

She just doesn't know what that means for her yet.

Or her shop.

Or her heart.

Chapter Twenty-Three

When Lexi walks into the shop that Wednesday morning, it's obvious that Tessa and Hazel are deep in discussion. The furrowed brows and crossed arms tell her that this isn't the usual chit-chat about books. Lexi knows they're not arguing; they get on well, and Hazel especially is not confrontational. She's the kind of person Rudyard Kipling was no doubt thinking of when he wrote 'If': the kind of person who can keep their head when all around are losing theirs. Sensible haircut, kind voice, secret recipe for the world's best lemon drizzle cake, which she brings into work on special occasions and sometimes just because. Tessa loves Hazel, even asking for early shifts specifically so they can work together. When Lexi walks in, smiles replace the frowns in the kind of falsely breezy way that suggests they didn't realise that she had seen their postures through the door.

'Morning,' they say cheerfully from behind the counter. People working in customer service know to do this regardless of what's on their minds.

Lexi worries, briefly, that her betrayal is all over her face – that she's been spending time with their arch-rival, the threat to the bookshop, the threat to all their jobs – and not only that, but actually enjoying it. Struggling, if she's entirely honest, to pull herself away. So Lexi can't really blame them for their secrets; she has plenty of her own.

She heads down to the office, past the shelves of advance review copies begging to be added to the already overwhelming piles of them she has at home. A few of the titles on the spines call out to her. *Later*, she whispers in their direction. *I'm coming back for you.*

She's just gathering herself at her desk, flipping on her computer and bracing herself for the usual onslaught of emails, when someone knocks.

Nobody ever knocks. Lexi's staff flit in and out with abandon, to feed the cat, or grab a book or run an idea past her, or, if they have been sufficiently trained and they want to earn some brownie points, to bring her a cup of tea. She likes it that way; she never wants to be the hidden-away boss, inaccessible and mysterious and slightly scary. Which is why it's been worrying her somewhat that Tessa and Hazel seemed to be hiding something from her. She's worried not just what the thing itself might be, but also about why they felt they couldn't tell her, and what it says about their relationship with her and about her as a boss.

Lexi closes the door tight only when she really needs to focus and her break in concentration is going to result in disaster, like faulty maths or booking two prominent authors for events on the same night. Her staff know not to bother her then, but otherwise, if the door is ajar, as it is now, they know they can come in whenever.

So a knock is unusual, and she braces herself for more weirdness. The entire day has been unusual so far, starting with a hug, of all things, from Sam, of all people.

'Come in,' Lexi says, and she isn't surprised to see Tessa there.

'Hi,' she says, shuffling her weight from one foot to the other. 'Can I talk to you about something?'

It's nice to have someone around who is softer about how she phrases things. Americans are more direct than Tessa and Lexi – and than most Brits Lexi knows. They don't *ask if they can ask a question*; they go ahead and ask it. They don't pad emails with platitudes about hoping you're well and not worrying about it if it's too much trouble. It's a bit jarring; as a Brit, Lexi often feels like she's being told off. Even emails from friends end with a cold *Best*, and nobody feels the need to punctuate texts with two kisses, or any kisses at all. Lexi has to admit, though, that directness does have its advantages. There's a lot less passive-aggressiveness around and at least you usually know where you stand.

'Of course you can,' Lexi tells Tessa. 'Tea?'

'No, thank you,' she says, unusually. 'I'm okay. It's just a quick thing.'

Pippin stirs in his basket. He'd no doubt like it if Lexi and Tessa kept their voices down so he can proceed with his nap. Like most cats, he assumes that the place where he eats and sleeps is his domain, and the humans are the intruders. Every night, he no doubt thinks to himself: *Finally! They've got the message and left me to my kingdom*. And then, when they all turn up again the next day, he's grumpy about it. But by lunchtime, when they've fed him and he's readjusted, he's remembered he likes them, and he allows himself to be snuggled, petted, and occasionally manhandled by an overenthusiastic child.

Tessa starts pulling at the sleeves of her cardigan. She's nervous. This can't be good. She's not resigning, is she?

She can't be. Aside from all her work on social media and marketing, which is worth its weight in e-comm orders, she is one of Lexi's best booksellers. She makes no secret of the fact that she loves this job.

'Is everything okay?' Lexi asks, tentatively.

'Yes. No. Not really.' Tessa sighs, composes herself. 'My landlord is putting up my rent.'

Lexi sees immediately where this is going. 'Ah.'

'And I'm trying to make the maths work.' Lexi notes approvingly the *s* on the end of *maths*. 'But I'm just not sure that it can.'

Lexi, being British, knows how to read into this indirectness. 'You need a pay rise.'

'Ideally, yes.' Tessa can't quite meet Lexi's gaze. 'And maybe more hours?'

'More hours can always be arranged.'

There's always someone on holiday or off sick; there are always extra tasks to be picked up here and there, organising displays, running book clubs, starting a new account on whatever the social media *du jour* happens to be just in case *this* one is the hot new thing, the one that takes off, the one where Pemberley Books goes viral.

'A pay rise, though . . . well, I've actually been trying to work this out, for all of you. You've all worked so hard these last few years.'

Tessa nods and pulls at her sleeves some more. 'Can I just ask how likely do you think it is, really? It's just, I've been digging into my savings, and there's almost nothing left.'

Lexi doesn't want to have to say that all she can afford, if she can afford anything, is an extra fifty cents, or maybe, if she really pushes it, an extra dollar an hour. She doubts that will make much of a dent in Tessa's overall needs. She wishes, not for the first or fifth or twenty-seventh time, that the publishing industry wasn't like this, with everyone getting squeezed at every level: booksellers, editors, almost all the authors except for the very lucky ones. Everything, everyone is operating on paper-thin margins, except for the CEOs of the big publishing companies who can pick out pretty much any yacht they want to. It shouldn't be like this: bookselling is a skill, and one that brings joy to millions of people. It deserves to be recognised as such, not just with nice words, but with actual action. And, let's be honest, actual dollars.

'I want to help,' Lexi says. 'I don't want to lose you. Give me a day or two to figure it out, okay?'

Tessa nods again, and swallows hard. Lexi gets the distinct impression that if she attempts to form any words, she'll cry, and that she's trying to avoid that at all costs. Pippin opens an eye, like even he's deciding if he should break his no-snuggles-before-lunchtime rule.

'I'll make you some tea,' Lexi tells her, and this time she's not giving Tessa the option to decline. 'Go and take a few minutes in the staffroom if you like.'

She nods again and leaves, and as the tea brews, so does Lexi. It was all going so well before Sam showed up with his stupid green eyes and his stupidly well-thought-out business plan. It's clear on all the graphs that Lexi's accountant shows her that growth has massively slowed these last couple of years, and there's no denying that that's in part Sam's fault. You can make all the arguments you want about how more bookshops equals more readers coming to shop in the neighbourhood, but the maths is fairly simple. They're not going to buy twice as many new books. When it was used books versus new books, that was different: different markets, different needs, different ways of shopping. But if a customer is looking for a copy of the buzzy new hardback, they're only going to buy it in one of two places now. And the buzzy new hardbacks are often the books with the highest profit margins. Pemberley Books can't afford to lose half their buzzy new hardback sales to Great Expectations. Not if they want to grow. And not if they want to keep their best staff.

Lexi is furious on Tessa's behalf because she's more than deserving of the pay rise she needs, as are all her staff. And she's furious on her own behalf, because losing booksellers is both sad personally and costly professionally. Experienced booksellers with years of insider knowledge are often better at recommending books, better at convincing customers to leave the shop with five books instead of three. Customers know whose recommendations they gel with, and they often come in especially for that bookseller. All of that is lost when you start again from scratch with a new person. Plus there's the time and cost involved in training a new member of staff, the inevitable mistakes they're going to make with the pernickety point-of-sales system.

She's furious on behalf of everyone in the publishing industry, too, because smart, engaged, passionate readers like Tessa are exactly who they need, who they should be doing their utmost to keep. And she's furious on behalf of the undervalued, under-the-radar authors she champions. An enthusiastic bookseller can make all the difference to them.

And all of this fury, Lexi heaps on Sam. Is all of it his fault? Maybe not all of it. Lexi can't very well hold him responsible for the decades-old structural issues. But in this particular instance, she *is* holding him responsible. If the takings line on the graph had continued to follow the trajectory it had been on, she could have given everyone a two dollar per hour pay rise this year, and maybe even a mid-year bonus, too. She could have employed a store manager to give herself room to breathe, room to date, room to sleep. Room to actually practise the piano so she can do the recital and win the heart of . . . the guy she's currently furious at? (Maybe she hasn't quite thought this through.)

Instead of which, here she is, trying and failing to crunch numbers. She thinks she can find fifty cents per hour for Tessa, but she also knows that is going to eat at her until she can afford to do it for everyone else, too. And it's probably not even going to help Tessa that much.

Ugh. Stupid, stupid Sam, and his stupid, stupid green eyes, and the stupid, stupid distraction of him. Lexi needs to get a grip and fight for her shop. Fight for her staff. And try to wrest her heart back from the deep well it's fallen into.

Chapter Twenty-Four

Tomorrow as usual? Sam texts Lexi that night. She makes the mistake of swiping the message, which means he'll see she's seen it, and it will be weird not to reply. But she doesn't want to reply. She's fuming.

It's not like everything was perfect, or even easy, before Sam showed up and changed the direction of the shop. But it was a little less difficult. If they worked hard on a pre-order campaign or an author event, they saw results. People are willing to work hard when they see results. But when, staff meeting after staff meeting, they can tell their boss is trying her hardest to put a positive spin on disappointing news, Lexi can sense the atmosphere in the room shifting. So now there's no pay rise *and* there's not even the gratification from witnessing the fruits of hard work. Lexi feels like she's letting her team down, and she hates that. Her staff deserve better, and frankly so does she, and so does the shop, for its many years of loyal service to Capitol Hill.

In her text app, Lexi types and then deletes, types and then deletes. She takes a perverse kind of pleasure in torturing Sam with appearing and disappearing and reappearing dots on his phone. And sure, maybe he's not watching them. But it's 11 p.m. on a weeknight and so, like any self-respecting millennial, he is most likely lying in bed and staring at his phone. Because what else is there to do at 11 p.m. on a weeknight? Certainly not sleep. Not when there's all this anxiety to not-quite-process.

The piano lessons are fun and she's making progress, albeit only in the tiny increments that are possible when you don't have anywhere to practise. There are practice rooms across the city in Dupont Circle, but it takes forty-five minutes to get there and forty-five minutes to get back, and that's before she's done any actual playing. She doesn't have that kind of time. Because she's working every hour she can. Because she has to, thanks to Sam.

?, he types, after a while. Succinct and to the point. He could just as easily have written *WTF*, so Lexi appreciates the restraint.

The question she's turning over, the reason for the appearing, disappearing, and reappearing dots is, does she want him to know she is angry? Clearly, a big part of her does. But the more sensible part of her knows that open warfare is not the answer. The last thing she needs is him amping up his game, working even harder to compete with her, overlapping more and more of his stock with hers. If he knows about enemies to lovers, there's no telling what else he's been covertly researching. Like, for example, how much the romance genre has been propping up the industry in recent years especially. And yeah, sure, it doesn't totally jibe with his customer base, whereas Lexi and her staff have worked hard at curating and growing their romance section. They've got their loyal local customers, of course. But the out-of-town visitors, the casual browsers, they don't know the nuances. The end-of-year lists of best bookshops in DC, the mid-year City Paper poll: they all say Pemberley Books is a great general bookshop with a strong romance section, lots of fun events, booksellers who can knowledgeably and enthusiastically advise on every genre; that Great Expectations is especially good for non-fiction. If that balance changes, they'll be in trouble. Lexi isn't sure who D:Ream thought they were kidding when they sang that things could only get better; it's always, and especially in this case, possible for them to get much worse.

All in all, Lexi supposes she had better be nice to Sam. Return to the previous state of affairs: surface politeness underpinned by quietly seething rage. It's harder, though, now that Sam is a fully realised person to her and not a caricature of a villain, now that she knows a little of his past. Now that she knows how thoughtful and kind he can be. Now that she's seen his gorgeous eyes up close. But she can do it. She is almost sure she can do it.

I'm getting self-conscious about my lack of progress, she types, a warning of her cooling enthusiasm and her cryptic lack of responses just now.

You're doing great, he types back immediately, and then, before she can stop herself, she's flirting.

I bet you say that to all the girls.

Now it's Lexi's turn to watch the dots appear and disappear as she stares at the too-bright light of the screen in her dark bedroom.

I don't let the other girls touch my piano.

Damn it, that's a good line. Lexi is smiling. She's also a little warm between her legs. He has won this particular battle.

You say all the right things. 8 a.m.?

Sure. Looking forward to it. And to my latte.

Chapter Twenty-Five

Just for that, Lexi considers not taking Sam the latte, but that's a level of petty she can't quite bring herself to stoop to. Plus, she's going to Peregrine for herself anyway. It really is no skin off her nose to get two lattes instead of one.

'I see you in the morning a lot more than I used to,' Alli says when she takes Lexi's order. 'And always with the two lattes. Very mysterious.' She smiles and wiggles her eyebrows, signalling that Lexi should feel free to tell her what's going on. But that would require Lexi knowing what's going on. And, quite frankly, at this point in time, she has no idea. What had once seemed like such a no-brainer of a plan to make Sam fall in love with her so that he'd be distracted and less of a threat seems fuzzy now at best.

'Early-morning piano lesson,' she tells Alli. 'On a mission to be accomplished.'

'Ah.'

She looks so disappointed that Lexi can't help throwing her another crumb. 'With a very hot piano teacher.'

'Ah,' Alli says again, noticeably brighter. 'Extra hot like the milk, right?'

'Exactly.'

And that is Exhibit A of why Lexi loves this coffee shop,

and why you'll never be able to convince her that there's a better one in New York, or really anywhere in the world.

* * *

Sam buzzes Lexi into his building, and his door is ajar when she makes it to his floor. It feels weird to walk in without knocking, but she does it anyway, with her elbow, then nudges the door open further. She slips off her shoes in the entryway, noting again that she approves of Sam's cleanliness, as evidenced by his no-shoes-in-the-house rule.

Not a particularly sexy thought.

Not that sexiness is why she's here.

She's here to preserve the peace or at least prevent further escalation of the war. It's a bonkers idea that sex could have anything to do with it, not when she's so angry with Sam. Mr Darcy would never behave the way he has, sabotaging something so important to Lizzy . . .

. . . Aside from the happiness of her sister.

Never mind. Scratch that.

'Hi,' Sam says from the piano stool. By this point, Lexi is well and truly flustered, and he can probably see it in her face. 'You're looking a little pink today.'

Yup. There it is.

'It's warm outside.'

Lexi says a brief prayer of thanks to the weather gods for the excuse of the rapidly warming DC weather. (She'll probably take it back in August as sweat streams down her back on the way to the shop.)

'Mmm hmm.' Sam looks amused, like he doesn't quite believe her. He holds out his hand for the coffee, and, as always, their hands graze, and, as always, it feels like electricity.

Lexi thinks again of Mr Darcy, this time in the 2005 film, stretching out his hand after helping Elizabeth into the carriage, like he's felt that electricity too.

What a moment.

It's probably a stretch to compare this to that.

And anyway, Lexi is angry. She is trying very hard to remember this.

Today, Sam is wearing shorts and a green T-shirt the exact colour of his eyes. His hair is still damp from his post-gym shower. Again. He really must be strong enough by now. Definitely strong enough to—

Nope.

'So you were tempted to sleep in this morning and not come see me?'

'Your piano.' Lexi wants to make that very clear. To Sam, to herself. These piano skills he's teaching her will come in very useful when she finds herself a suitable guy. Because Sam definitely isn't the one, she tells herself, as he walks over to the table to grab a pencil for marking up her piano book and she notices, not for the first or second or twelfth time, how shapely his legs are, how well defined his bum is.

He definitely isn't the one, she tells herself, as he stands next to her, watching her play a C major scale with both hands, saying 'good, good, that looks really good' with a note of pride in his voice that she can't decide is for her as the learner or himself as the teacher.

He definitely isn't the one, she tells herself, as he leans over to turn the page while she plays and he feels his breath on the back of her neck as everything she knows about notes and scales threaten to flee from her brain.

'All right,' he says, way too soon. 'That's your half-hour.'

It didn't feel like half an hour. 'Really? That was quick.'

'Time flies, I guess. When you're having . . .'

In her head, Lexi is begging him to finish that sentence. To finish it quick before her brain does it for both of them. She looks up at him, into his enlarged pupils.

'Fun,' he says eventually, his voice catching a little, after way too long a pause. 'I'm glad you came today. I enjoy teaching you.'

'Thank you,' she says, her polite, good-girl upbringing kicking in. 'You're a good teacher.'

She doesn't move, because she suddenly doesn't trust herself. He doesn't move, either. She sits there, looking up at him, and his eyes, and his mouth, and thinking, *This is a dangerous moment. I'm only here to keep the peace, not to fall in love with him. He's not an appropriate love interest. We all know this: my friends, me, him, probably.* He's probably just trying to distract her. She knows this. And still, she can't quite rip her eyes away from him.

'Thank you,' he says. 'You're a great learner.'

Lexi has never known anyone to say *thank you* in a tone that says, *Come to bed.* But neither of them moves. They're frozen in place.

'So why didn't you want to come?' he asks, softly. 'Really.'

Lexi contemplates several responses before she alights on the truth. 'Because I'm mad at you.'

'Oh?' He seems surprised. And, to be fair to him, she has not been acting like someone who is mad at him. She has been acting like someone who is in the tight grip of an all-consuming crush. 'Why is that?'

'For the same reason I've always been mad at you.'

It's easier, from down on the piano stool, below his eye level, to throw accusations at him. But Lexi knows they'll have more force if she stands up. So she does. And then immediately feels awkward and sits back down again.

'One of my booksellers asked me for a pay rise yesterday. She deserves it, too. They all do. But I can't afford it. You know why?' The anger doesn't feel quite so visceral now. There are other emotions crowding it out. But Lexi is determined to access it.

Sam puts his hands out in front of him, in a *beats me* posture, and Lexi instantly has no trouble accessing her anger. Playing dumb, on top of everything else? Come *on*.

'Because of you, Sam. Because of you and your stupid shop.'

'Hey, c'mon. That's not fair.'

But she's on a roll now. 'Your stupid, soulless, Apple Store of a bookshop in a part of town that doesn't need one because it already has mine.'

Her voice is well and truly raised now. She hopes the neighbours are enjoying the entertainment. How did they get from that electric moment, when it felt like they might be about to kiss, to this, so fast?

'Ouch.'

She feels that *ouch* in her own gut, too.

'Well,' he says slowly, calmly, evenly. 'Maybe some people need a store that's not all cats and romance novels.'

She definitely felt *that* in her gut.

'If those people exist, I don't want to know them. Who doesn't like cats and romance novels?'

And then she braces, because what if it's him? What if he's the one who doesn't like those things? Then they could never be friends. Not that it matters. Not that it matters at all, because who wants to be friends with *him?*

'Anyway,' she tells him. 'My shop is so much more than that, and you know it, too.'

He is silent, breathing hard, hungry-looking. Hungry, Lexi assumes, for a fight. But she's already said way too much.

'Anyway, I should go.'

'Okay.'

Lexi pushes the stool back, scraping it across the floor in a way that sets her teeth on edge. Sam hasn't moved and now they're standing awkwardly close, and she has to get past him to pick up her bag. He doesn't move, though. He doesn't cede ground. So now she's going to have to make a big show of going round the other way, awkwardly walking around the piano stool. She breathes in, walks around, gets her bag.

'Thanks for the lessons,' she says as her parting words.

'You're welcome,' he says, still calm, still even. Somehow, the fact that he's still perfectly polite is even more infuriating. 'I've enjoyed them.'

This seems more than polite. This seems . . . like he means it? 'What?'

He smiles. 'You heard me.'

'I mean, yes. I heard you. But—'

'The feeling of hate isn't mutual, is what I'm saying.'

'I don't . . .' She can't quite say it, that she doesn't hate him either, that she's been very focused on trying to hate him, but it's been impossible. She's frustrated. She's cornered. And he's standing there, all green-eyed and handsome.

So she does the only logical thing.

She stands on tiptoes and kisses him.

She hadn't meant to. She wasn't prepared. It takes her by surprise, and it's just a peck. And then she's mortified, because he doesn't respond. So she takes a step towards the door, ready to get the heck out of there.

Chapter Twenty-Six

As Lexi reaches for the door handle, she feels a hand land on her free arm.

'No you don't,' Sam says.

'What?'

'You don't get to do that.'

'Do what?' Lexi's brain is panic and confusion, fight-or-flight adrenaline pulsing through her limbs.

'Kiss me and then run away like nothing happened. Or like something did happen and now you're scared.'

'I'm not scared,' Lexi says, which is among the Top Ten lies she's ever told, ranking slightly below talking her niece Chloe off the ledge when she was ready to stop believing in Father Christmas. She looks down at where his hand is gripping her arm, sending waves of heat through her entire body. He lets go.

'It's okay to be scared,' Sam says, in his piano teacher voice, soft and patient. 'I'm pretty scared too.'

In any other circumstances, Lexi would laugh, because this is preposterous: she's the least scary person she knows. It doesn't feel like a laughing kind of moment, though.

'I'm not scary,' she says.

Now it's his turn to find the humour. So maybe it is a laughing kind of moment after all. 'You're terrifying,' he replies. 'You protect that bookshop like a mama bear.'

'It's important to me.'

'Of course it is. And it should be. I'm just saying – I never quite know when a roar is going to erupt. Or when I'm going to get injured.'

'You're not going to get injured.' *Your bookstore might, though,* she wants to add, but it feels like the wrong kind of moment for that, too.

'Oh,' he says, 'but I really might.' And he puts his hand over his heart.

'Oh,' she repeats, a different kind of *oh,* one of realisation and maybe a little fear of her own. 'But I thought—'

'You surprised me just then,' he says. 'I didn't expect a kiss. You caught me off guard. That's why it wasn't exactly my best work. Now, with your permission, I'd like to try again.'

He sounds like a character from one of Lexi's favourite novels. It doesn't exactly hurt his cause.

'Permission granted,' she tells him. This time, it doesn't take her by surprise. This time she gets to hold her breath and hear her own heart thumping in anticipation.

Sam pushes a strand of hair behind her ear, almost as if he needs a few seconds to compose himself. Then he cups her chin and looks into her eyes. Connection feels like too weak a word for what's happening. It's like their souls are syncing up. A shiver runs down Lexi's back. This moment feels solemn, a before-and-after kind of moment, a nothing-was-ever-the-same-again moment. And in this moment, she has almost forgotten about their bookshop and their rivalry, about Sam's inferior love of books, his lack of respect for fiction. Lexi knows what they say about getting together with someone who turns out not to have any books at home: that you should run. But he has an e-reader, so it's fine. And this moment feels somehow bigger than all of that. Like a shifting of the stars. Like whatever their souls are made of, Lexi's and Sam's are the same.

He closes his eyes, and she follows suit. She focuses on steadying her breathing. His lips land gently on hers, and there's the static of them. They nudge hers open. Lexi wants the teasing, the *before* moment, to last. To notice the transition of her life into its second act. His lips linger on hers, and she tastes him. And then, suddenly, she doesn't want to hang back on the edge of act two anymore. She breathes in his saltiness, his oakwood-scented shampoo. She lets him lead, tease her lips with his, her tongue with his, and then she takes over, ravenous, desperate. All of her fury is channelled into this kiss, along with every bit of passion she's ever felt for a book, for a character, for her bookshop, every bit of energy.

Lexi becomes aware that they're both moaning, animal sounds at the back of their throats; they've moved from tenderness to arousal to desperation terrifyingly fast, and she should stop it. She thinks she has a meeting with her account— Does she have a meeting with her accountant? Sod the meeting with her accountant.

She nudges Sam's knee with hers, hoping he'll get it, hoping he'll move them over to the sofa, to the bed. She doesn't even mind if he doesn't fling her, if they both kind of collapse.

Instead, though, it seems like she's broken the spell. Sam pulls back, a little, just enough for Lexi to be able to see the desire in his eyes.

'Should we slow down?' He asks it regretfully, sadly, like he wishes he didn't have to be a good boy about it.

'No,' Lexi tells him, because she has no desire to be a good girl. Even though part of her acknowledges that, in fact, yes, maybe they should slow down. That she should take five minutes to sort and sift through her feelings before they do something that it might be difficult for her, for them both, to recover from. She looks over at the bed. It's calling to them; she can almost hear it.

'I might need to slow down,' he says, still breathing hard.

'Okay.'

'It's not that I don't want to,' he says, sounding as disappointed as she feels. 'It's that maybe I want to a little bit too much.'

'That sounds like just the right amount of wanting.'

'I don't want to mess this up.' He sounds almost sad.

'I'm confident you'll do a good job.' Lexi thinks of all the broken hearts that litter the streets of DC. If he didn't know what he was doing, there wouldn't be so many women out there struggling to get over him. Not that she wants to think about those other women right now.

'No,' he says. 'Not that. Us.'

What is it about that word: *us*? It runs down Lexi's back in the form of another shiver.

'Oh.'

She can't exactly say, screw *us*. I just really want to be with you right now. Honestly, she doesn't know if there's an *us* to speak of. And right now, her body is telling her that she doesn't care.

But Lexi knows herself better than that, and she knows too that now is not the time to be callous, because hers isn't the only heart at stake here.

Sam kisses her again, more gently, this time, like he's trying to shift gears back down from fourth all the way to first. She follows his lead. It's a *goodbye for now but we'll pick this up later* kind of kiss. And she very much wants to pick it up later.

'Let me take you out for dinner sometime soon?' he says. 'Do this right?' He cups her chin again, mirroring the beginning of this surreal moment.

Lexi doesn't really know what to say, so she goes with the obvious.

'Sure. That would be nice.'

Not as nice as that bed looks, but there's plenty of time for that. She hopes so, at least.

Chapter Twenty-Seven

Needless to say, Lexi is really quite flustered when she gets to the shop. She pushes the door to open it instead of pulling it, despite having opened the door thousands of times over the last three decades, and she finds her accountant waiting downstairs on the sofa, a pile of books next to him. She's fifteen minutes late: in America, this is practically unforgivable. It's a very punctual culture: she has had friends text her to let her know that they are going to be three minutes late. Three minutes! Surely that's on time? If you asked her, Lexi would tell you that everything within ten minutes is on time. Maybe it's a British thing; maybe it's just a Lexi thing. Fifteen minutes is pushing it, though, even for Lexi, even for Brits. Still, her accountant knows her well by now, so he's probably not surprised. He'd probably settled in for the duration with the pile of books.

'I'm sorry,' she tells him, by means of a greeting. 'I lost track of time.' That's close enough to the truth, right? She's not exactly going to tell him that she was snogging her business rival.

'No problem,' he says graciously, standing and flashing his perfect white American teeth at her. 'I've been perusing your thriller section. This really is a great bookstore.'

'Thank you.' Lexi ignores the word *bookstore* and chooses to bask in the compliment. It's not so much that *bookstore* is an American word; rather, that it makes her think of big corporate places that are not exactly soulless – since no place with books can ever be entirely soulless – but certainly devoid of the character and personal touches and community spirit of a shop like Pemberley Books. *Shop* has much more of a cosy feel, a friendly neighbourhood vibe. Plus, it reminds everyone that its owner is British, which for some reason she's never fully understood makes them think she and her shop are both quaint and sophisticated.

She also ignores the unspoken undertone to her accountant's question. *Nice bookstore you have there. It would be a shame if anything happened to it.* But, of course, that's why the accountant is here: to make sure that nothing *does* happen to it. So he's also letting Lexi know how much she needs him, and that she'd better pay attention to what he says.

Then again, it's also possible that she is overthinking a basic compliment. But in her defence, her head is all over the place right now.

'Shall we?' She gestures towards the cave office. She wonders if Pippin is in a prematurely cuddly mood today. She sort of feels like she could use the comfort.

Lexi isn't sure where this sense of foreboding has come from. Maybe her accountant's demeanour – he doesn't have the tall, confident posture of someone about to deliver good news. Or maybe a delayed panic response to what just happened with Sam. She has barely had a minute and a half by herself since he left her at the corner where he turns right and she turns left. She hasn't had a single second to process a single thing about that kiss. Good idea? Bad idea? Idea that is potentially extremely detrimental to her business? Who knows. But, either way, Lexi suspects that snogging your biggest business rival is not exactly Accountant-Approved Behaviour. She hopes she's not blushing, but she knows that hope is probably futile.

When they walk into Lexi's office, Pippin opens an eye and then curls up tighter, clearly in *do-not-disturb* mode. So he will obviously be no help whatsoever.

This is a closed-door situation. Lexi hates those.

'Sit, sit,' she says, seeing he is carrying a bottle of water and suppressing her urge to offer tea. It doesn't matter how long she lives here, it will never be normal to start a meeting without a cup of something hot and soothing. She could really do with one herself, if she's honest. But it'll just put off the inevitable, delay the start of this meeting even further, and risk irritating the accountant.

Even at the best of times, Lexi hates accountant meetings. The numbers give her a headache – firstly because she's never been a maths girl, and secondly because they tend to unearth problems she didn't know she had, problems that will now require solutions.

She looks longingly at the kettle.

The accountant clears his throat and opens up some folders.

'First,' he says, 'the good news.'

This is unexpected. 'Glad to hear there is some.'

He doesn't laugh. Blood instantly freezes in Lexi's veins.

'Your sales continue to increase month after month, year after year. Whatever you're doing with marketing, it's working.'

She makes a mental note to thank Tessa profusely when she delivers news of her tiny pay increase.

'It's stock management, too,' she tells him. Keeping an eye

on fluctuating publisher discounts and using their space for books that will actually sell are crucial to the bottom line. Her book buyer Megan deserves a pay rise, too.

'Yes.' He clears his throat again. Pippin shifts, irritated, or maybe sensing a change in the vibe. Maybe feeling protective. It's impossible to tell what goes on in that feline head of his. 'The bad news is, the increase in costs is fast catching up.'

He passes Lexi the graph of the shop's takings, which shows the increase in their sales flattening since Sam opened his store. But there's another line on the graph, and it's their expenses. That line is definitely not flat. In fact, it's fast catching up to the sales line.

'I want to stress that this isn't anything you're doing wrong. I know there isn't a lot of fat left to trim. It's just – inflation, all that.' He waves his hand around, gesturing, Lexi supposes, at the general state of the world. She nods, her throat constricting. He points to both lines, emphasising their angles. 'For the next three months, we need to work really hard at both increasing sales and decreasing costs.'

He says 'we', but he means Lexi. Lexi and her team, who have already been working flat out to do both of those things.

She nods. 'So no pay rises.'

'Raises are completely out of the question,' he says.

Lexi knows that Tessa isn't the only one with money issues. Inflation is nipping at everyone's nose. If she's not careful, her staff are going to start looking elsewhere for jobs. She looks around for a paper bag to breathe into, but alas: nothing.

The accountant talks her through some other details about bills, but it's as if she's underwater. Everything is blurry and faint. The fluffy feelings of an hour ago are well and truly gone, swept under these numbers and their scary realities and by the feeling that she's letting her grandmother down. Her grandmother, who weathered so many ups and downs of economics and managed to keep the shop thriving.

Lexi isn't sure even a cup of tea will fix this.

'Thank you,' she says, shaking his hand when he leaves, but she's never meant it less. 'I'll be in touch.'

'Anything you need,' he says. He seems to get it, though – of course – he can't possibly understand just how much this bookshop means to Lexi, to the neighbourhood. 'If you need to bounce some ideas off me, you're welcome to shoot me an email.'

'Thank you,' she says again. 'I appreciate it.'

But, secretly, she hopes the door will hit him hard on the way out.

Chapter Twenty-Eight

It's a miracle that Lexi gets anything done at work today, what with the twin distractions of bad news from her accountant and that frankly very hot kiss from Sam. At any given moment, it's anybody's guess whether she's going to jump up and down in glee or collapse into a puddle of tears.

Well, not exactly *anybody's*, since nobody else can know about any of it. Hopefully, she'll figure out a way through the financial crisis and they'll never have to know. As for the other thing . . . they'll have to find out one day, like when they get married in the bookshop, not that Lexi has thought about that for one second. But for now, it's all about professionalism.

It's hard sometimes, retaining that veneer, being the boss of women old enough to be her mum, women with maternal instincts who, in any other situation, she would happily adopt as her surrogate aunts. That's why she likes to have her nails done and carry Kate Spade handbags – for the air of being a grown-up. It's how she justifies them, anyway: she deserves the treats for all her hard work *and* they help her feel like the boss she is. Win-win.

So she doesn't get that much done. She drinks a lot of cups of tea. She tries not to wonder why all of this comes so easily to Sam when she can't seem to get it together. She contacts the local radio station to see if they'll give her a deal on some ads. She brainstorms new book clubs they could start, to broaden the reach of the shop and increase its footfall. Book clubs are worth their weight in gold: firstly, for the good vibes. On harder days, seeing a group laugh and someone passionately advocate for a book they're maybe the only person to have liked warms the cockles of Lexi's stressed-out heart. But also, secondly, and more cynically, for the money. Pemberley book clubs don't require that their members buy their books at the shop, because Lexi isn't an idiot: she knows that not everyone can afford to regularly buy hardbacks at full price from an independent bookshop, no matter how much they deplore the space-faring habits of a certain billionaire. But once they're in the shop and they've been plied with wine to get conversation going and lower book-buying inhibitions, their best intentions to be sensible with money start to weaken. They take recommendations from each other and from Debbie or Megan or Natalie; they linger by the display of book-themed socks; they let themselves believe that this, *this*, will be the month they finally get organised and it will all be thanks to *this* specific notebook and *these* specific pens. Book clubs bring joy, and they bring dollars. Again: win-win.

Pemberley Books has a romance book club, a thriller book club, a memoir book club, a lit fic book club. What they don't have, yet: a social justice book club, a kids' book club, a book club that focuses on backlist: the stuff that isn't brand new, that's faded from Instagram, that isn't on three-for-two deals in chain bookstores. Publishing gets very excited about all things shiny and new and forgets pretty quickly about those older books. But normal readers don't, especially when they have people like Lexi to remind them. For a while, she ran a classics book club, but she got too busy, and none of her staff seemed to want to pick it up. Maybe she'll try again.

Also, and she can't believe she hadn't thought of this: what about a Jane Austen-themed book club where they'd read not just her work but also modern retellings of it? There are more of those than you can shake a stick at, and what a great excuse to reread one of her favourites: *Bridget Jones's Diary*? And then books about Jane Austen's life, too. Lexi can't believe she's never thought of that before. If they could corner the market on rabid Janeites, Pemberley Books would be unstoppable. Especially once they bring in all the cute themed merch that's out there. Wouldn't it be poetic justice if Jane Austen saved the bookshop?

And then, there's also nonfiction. Lexi never agreed to this whole division of labour, where Sam gets to be the Serious One and he gets the wealthy customers with Serious Jobs and Serious Incomes. And those aren't the only people who read about politics and history anyway. Does she feel a slight pinch at the idea of trying to win over some of his customers through this judicious book club scheme? Yes, but she shouldn't, no matter how hot a kisser he is. She was here first. Those people would be coming to her anyway, if it wasn't for him. And besides, all's fair in love in business. *You've Got Mail* taught Lexi that. (It also tried to teach her that it's okay to lose your bookshop if you find love in the process, but she is ignoring that.)

All right. So she has a plan. It's not like she's achieved *nothing*. She also hasn't walked into a wall or jammed her fingers in a door, which does seem like an achievement today. And she counted the concerned *you okay?* questions from her staff, and there were only three. It could definitely be worse, all things considered.

Chapter Twenty-Nine

Lexi gets home that day with a lot to process. In the times before John, she could always rely on Erin to help her make sense of the world. One of them would pick out a Hello Fresh recipe from the box and they'd peel carrots and caramelise onions as they talked. Sometimes Erin would have wisdom and ideas to share; sometimes, she'd just make the sympathetic noises that Lexi needed.

These days, Erin is often not home. She'll be on a date with John, or they'll be out scoping out venues or whatever the heck it is that wedmin actually consists of. Lexi seriously thinks that wedding leave should be a right, the way that parental leave is because she's not honestly sure how anyone holds down a job on top of planning a wedding. There should probably also be bridesmaid leave, but since America hasn't yet, in the year of our Lord 2024, managed maternity leave as a right, she's not holding her breath.

The thing is, though, being a bridesmaid in the US is something else: first of all, she is expected to pay for her own dress, a dress she doesn't get to choose and may never wear again. Then, she has to help organise not one but two hen do equivalents: a bridal shower and a bachelorette party. It's never entirely been made clear to her what the difference is between the two of them or why you need both. And then – she had seen this in films, but assumed it was just for dramatic effect (alas, it is not) – at the wedding itself, bridesmaids have to walk in first, and then stand in a line in their uncomfortable shoes at the front of the church, presumably so they can be gawked at by all the guests for the entirety of the ceremony. She isn't sure why this is necessary, either.

Lexi will do all of this for Erin, and do it gladly, since Erin is her best friend and has done far stranger favours for Lexi over the years, from going back to the flat to check the hob was definitely off to crawling under Lexi's bed to see if the spider she'd whacked with a shoe was definitely dead. Lexi will do anything to ward off the feeling that she's losing her best friend. She misses hanging out in front of Hallmark movies and Erin chiding her for not being able to recognise any celebrities. She misses those occasional Sunday afternoons when they used to sit at opposite ends of the sofa with their respective books. And, yes, Lexi also misses her sounding board, her amateur therapist. Staring into a Zoom screen for fifty-five minutes every couple of weeks and then parting with $120 isn't quite the same as putting on Taylor Swift and dancing around the kitchen after an hour of railing against DC men over creamy chicken and pasta, the homely smells of garlic and dill still hanging in the air. She really needs her best friend right now.

'Hi,' Lexi calls out hopefully as she pushes the door open, and she's surprised and delighted to hear a *hi* echoed back to her. And only one *hi*, which means that John isn't here. Which means real, proper conversation. Today of all days, Lexi is thankful, even if that gratefulness comes with a pinch to the heart, a reminder of how much she'll miss Erin when she's gone for good.

'How was your day?' Lexi asks.

'Uneventful.' She shrugs. 'You?'

'It definitely wasn't uneventful.'

'Ah.'

There's something in Erin's eyes that Lexi hadn't seen much of until recently, but now she sees it there quite often. Reluctant resignation, maybe? A *here we go* kind of vibe. A *Lexi being Lexi, brace yourself* kind of vibe. As if the things she used to find endearing about Lexi have become exhausting.

'The accountant came by and it's not good news,' Lexi says, not embroidering, not dramatising, just stating facts. 'But also, I came up with some ideas that will maybe bring in some cash, and some more customers.'

'That sounds hopeful.'

'Yeah.' Lexi takes a deep breath. 'Also, Sam kissed me today.'

Technically, Lexi kissed him. She's not sure of the reason for this tiny white lie, except maybe it's to hide the fact that she's pursuing the plan her best friend disapproves of. If she was just the passive victim of an ill-intentioned kiss, she can't be blamed for anything.

Erin's eyes widen in what seems like interest. Or maybe shock. 'Okay, tell me more.'

Lexi hasn't told Erin about the piano lessons; if she's noticed that Lexi leaves suspiciously early on Wednesday mornings, she hasn't said anything.

'He's a very good kisser.'

'So says half of DC.'

And even though it was likely playfully meant, and even though Lexi had that exact thought as she was kissing Sam, she's still a little bit annoyed.

'But, like, how did it happen?'

'Um.' Lexi thinks back to the moment. She can feel her pulse accelerating. 'It all started with me being mad at him.'

She's suddenly not sure she wants to process this with Erin after all. Because Erin wants Lexi to stay mad at Sam. She wants them to be enemies, holding each other at arm's length, and certainly not close enough for him to be her plus-one. Lexi, however, fantasises about a gorgeous, deep red dress she could be wearing at the wedding. The chance to dance with him, the whole room fading away like it's just the two of them. She won't bring him against Erin's wishes, though. She'll have to get her to approve of him first.

This will be easier to process once they're chopping vegetables together.

'What shall we eat tonight?' Lexi asks, eager to get settled into their usual pattern. Nobody knows Lexi better than Erin does. At this point, three years into them living together, she's not even sure that her sister does. Certainly nobody knows the version of her that exists in her American life better than Erin does.

'Oh,' she says. 'I'm not eating at home. John's picking me up any moment now.'

Lexi's heart sinks. 'Oh.'

'But tell me more about this kiss. Because you're all twinkly-eyed. Like you might be in love.'

Wait, Lexi thinks, *what? Not in love. Just a little bit flustered by all the kissing is all.*

Erin's phone lights up with a text from John. 'I should go,' she says, and she at least has the decency to sound regretful. 'But I want to hear more later.'

'Okay,' she says. 'Have fun!' But what she really wants to

say is, *Okay, when? When do you want to hear more? We never get to hang out properly anymore.*

It's too late for her to call her sister: it's 1 a.m. over in England. So Lexi is left with all this raw, unprocessed emotion. So when Erin is gone and the door is firmly closed, Lexi does the only sensible thing she can do with all of today's frustrations. She switches her vibrator onto its most vigorous setting.

Chapter Thirty

Lexi feels less frustrated the next morning, less of a tightly coiled bundle of nerves, but she's not any closer to having actually processed anything. Sometimes, in her life, it feels like things are just plodding along with not much to report beyond a great book she's read, a supplier being unreliable, or the wholesaler being careless with packing books so that the shop has to return more damaged goods than usual. Or, in her personal life: a new Taylor Swift album to learn the lyrics for, another terrible date with an entitled man, a meal she's offered to a family who's just welcomed a new baby.

Lately, though, there's been a *lot* happening, all at once. It's discombobulating. It's exhausting. Lexi's friendship with Erin feels like it's changing, and not in a good way. Things at the bookshop are fraught and uncertain, and she doesn't want to worry her staff with any of it, but she's also never been good at hiding how she's feeling. Usually, she'd say authenticity is a virtue, and in fact she considers it one of her best qualities. But it turns out that sometimes, it could be useful to be able to hide some things.

She picks up coffee at Peregrine and even Alli notices that Lexi isn't as bubbly as she could be.

'Uh-oh,' she says. 'Everything okay?'

If there wasn't a queue, if there weren't prying ears all over Capitol Hill, she might tell Alli some of it. Maybe even all of it. But there is, and there are, so instead Lexi offers up a platitude.

'I've just got a lot on my mind.'

Alli nods. 'Understood.'

'Thank you for asking, though. It's lonely being the boss sometimes.'

'Oh yeah,' she says, disappearing behind the coffee machine. 'I know.'

Lexi gets out her phone to pay, just as it lights up with an incoming text.

Emergency piano lesson sometime soon?

Her stomach somersaults. *Under what circumstances can a piano lesson possibly be an emergency?*

I have to stay late at work the next few nights.

Which constitutes a piano emergency . . . how?

She suspects she knows what he's getting at, but she's going to make him say it, or at least type it. To make him put into words how much he wants to see her, so that she can stop wondering if the desire she felt in his kiss was all in her head.

She watches the dots appear and disappear. She imagines he's trying to think of a witty comeback. She can also feel the brain cogs whirring from half an hour's walk away.

It's more of a you *emergency, I guess. I want to see you.*

She sends him the raised-eyebrow emoji.

Need, he corrects himself. *I need to see you.*

In Lexi's defence, it's hard to resist that kind of compliment.

Ah. Emergency understood. Tomorrow?

* * *

Lexi gets through the day, somehow. She chats to Hazel about the Jane Austen club, to Marcus about a queer reads club, to Debbie about a nonfiction club. Hazel is delighted to be asked; the other two need some time to process. Lexi reminds herself that this isn't necessarily bad news, just the way of the introvert who's often attracted to work with books, even in a customer-facing role.

A few of the staff are off sick this week, so she takes her turn behind the till, beaming smiles and positivity and cheerfully thanking everyone for shopping indie. She lingers by the romance section, checking the alphabetical order and tidying up the face-outs, and, because she's got it bad, noticing which of the men on the cartoon covers look most like Sam. She recommends books to customers, and generally waits for the day to be over so that she can go home, get under her duvet, and then it'll be time to get up and see him.

Lexi doesn't sleep well, of course, so even with the adrenaline it's a struggle to get up. She's going to be late. And that's the thing with people like her: their lateness isn't necessarily any indicator of their enthusiasm, or lack thereof. Their timekeeping has its own mind. It's like a wild animal they're constantly fighting against and struggling to tame. Much, it has to be said, like her libido these days.

I'm late, she texts Sam, so he doesn't think she's forgotten – as if she ever could have. *I'm sorry. Struggled to get up.*

I did not struggle to get up, he says, and it's hard to tell if he means the innuendo. She isn't even totally sure that is one that's used in the US. *But I won't take it personally.* Then, *Skip the coffee if it's easier?*

Wow. He really *is* impatient for her to get there. And that impatience is contagious. *You don't want to be around me before 9 a.m. if I haven't had coffee, believe me.*

When she gets to his building, he is waiting outside. Lexi is taken aback, maybe a little freaked out.

'Hi?' she says, the question mark in her voice obvious. 'Is this a passive-aggressive *you're so late I guess I should come down and meet you* situation?'

She sees it: the smile, just barely there and over before she's blinked. She's not entirely wrong, but he denies it anyway.

'No.'

'You just couldn't wait one more second to see me?'

'Something like that.'

Say what you like, Lexi thinks, you've got to admire a man who knows what he wants.

He motions with his hand for the coffee, and she hands it over. Their hands touch, as always, but this time there's no mistaking it's deliberate. The electricity feels so strong that Lexi almost expects to be able to see it.

They share the lift with a bunch of a strangers on the way up, which is probably just as well, or Lexi might be tempted to make use of the emergency stop button. But once they're in his flat, she feels suddenly shy. In her head, she's pinning him against the door and kissing him till he can't breathe. But, in reality, she's standing there, immobile, in all her British awkwardness.

'So,' he says, gulping down the coffee he apparently didn't want. 'You're sure this isn't a *sorry I'm late, I didn't want to come* situation?'

Lexi stifles a giggle, like a sixteen-year-old. 'Oh no, I

definitely wanted to come. You're the one who put a stop to that kind of behaviour last time, remember?'

Sam laughs, through his nose. Nobody ever completely grows out of being a teenager.

'All in good time,' he says. 'In good, good time.'

He looks her slowly up and down. She loves the way he looks at her hungrily, and she's also frustrated that he's making her wait. Love and frustration: it seems like they'll coexist forever when it comes to the two of them. If it's not too soon to start thinking about forever. Or, come to that, about love.

Out of habit, and maybe to tease him a little, Lexi sits on the piano stool and finds middle C with her thumb. She plays a C major scale with her right hand. And, out of habit, Sam walks over to stand next to her.

'Nice job,' he says. 'Want to try F major?'

They'd learned that one in the previous lesson. She remembers it being different from the other scales because instead of crossing your thumb under the rest of your hand after the third note, you do it after the fourth, so that you're not playing a black note with your thumb, because that's a little awkward. She does it seamlessly: F-G-A-B flat, thumb cross, C-D-E-F, and then back down again, without the clunky pause of beginners in the middle when she has to reposition her hand.

'I'm impressed,' he says.

This gives her more pleasure than maybe it should. It's only an F major scale. 'Thank you.' She beams up at him.

'Have you been practising?'

He eyes her suspiciously, as if practice would be a bad thing. Or at least a bad thing to keep from him.

Lexi shakes her head. 'Only in my thoughts.'

And it's true: it's contagious, his love of piano. She finds herself wanting to do well, wanting to learn. She can see why the ladies of Jane Austen's time got so into it: they didn't get to study much, and this is a great way to stretch your mind, and feel like you're accomplishing something. Often, at her desk, she finds herself practising the movements of the different scales instead of drumming her fingers, as she used to.

'Oh really? What else have you been practising in your thoughts?'

Lexi swallows the wrong way and coughs, which buys her a distraction and time as Sam fetches her a glass of water. The truth is, she and her fingers have become good friends over the last few weeks, and not just for piano playing.

She takes a long sip of water and eventually manages to get a coherent sentence out. 'Wouldn't you like to know?'

'I'm hoping you'll show me.'

She looks down at her fingers: her left hand resting on her lap, her right hand on the keyboard. Much as she's excited to learn D major today, she could be persuaded to spend their time together differently.

'Right now?'

Sam laughs. It's his turn to tease her. 'No. Dinner first, remember?'

'What is this obsession with dinner?'

'I'm a gentleman. I like to do things the right way.'

'Sure.'

'I'm taking lessons.' He walks over to his coffee table and picks up a book. An actual physical book, and not just any one: it's a clothbound edition of *Pride and Prejudice*. 'I don't think Mr Darcy could go straight to bed before a real date, do you?'

'Well, no. But then I doubt that Mr Darcy went to bed at all before marriage.'

Damn it. She's broken the golden rule. Never, *ever*, pronounce or hint at the M word before a man does, lest you scare him off. Especially don't let it leave your lips before you've even been on an actual date.

Lexi looks up at Sam from the piano stool, cringing. She's probably ruined it all forever now, and she'll have to go and live in Australia to get away from the embarrassment. But, to her shock, Sam is smiling, taking it all in his stride. 'Well, if that's what you want.'

He's kidding. Lexi is pretty sure he's kidding, but still. 'Nope,' she says, to put this notion to bed, even though they aren't heading there themselves. 'I mean . . .'

She's realised too late that maybe it sounds like she doesn't want marriage. And she does. It's way too soon to say if she wants it with *him*, of course, despite her frequent practice of their joint monograms.

He's smiling wider now, knowing she has tied herself up in knots, knowing it's going to be hard to untangle herself without saying some things that are definitely illegal to say to a guy you haven't been on a date with, no matter how much you fancy the pants off him.

'Marriage would be fine,' she says. 'I mean, potentially. Not necessarily to you.' He raises an eyebrow. 'Not necessarily – *not* to you . . .'

'This enthusiasm is truly heart-warming.'

'Oh, c'mon. Like Mr Womaniser over here is really into the idea of tying himself down.'

It was self-defence, really, bringing that accusation out. But Lexi feels bad about it now. It was unnecessarily mean. Still, even that doesn't seem to faze him.

'I've seen the error of my ways.'

Now that she thinks about it, it's been a few weeks since Lexi last witnessed a break-up scene or a woman deservedly whacking him with her handbag. Could this be true? Could he be a Reformed Character?

'Okay,' she says, but she knows she sounds a little suspicious.

'It's true.'

Lexi doesn't know what to say to that, so she plays F major again.

'Excellent,' Sam says. 'Time to move on to D major.'

And then, instead of just telling her to find D, going through music theory and helping her work it out, he moves to stand behind her.

'Let's try a different approach,' he says, the *chhhh* whistling in her ear, his breath grazing her face. He puts his arms out to either side of her and shows her the scale by playing it himself. Lexi isn't remotely concentrating, of course. Not on how many sharps are in the scale, not on where his thumb crosses under. She's trying to hold herself together as the warmth of him radiates out and onto her. They're not touching, but at the same time, they're embracing.

Sam kisses the top of her head, almost *fondly*, almost chastely. Almost in the manner of someone who doesn't go to bed till after marriage, or at least after dinner. The silence stretches out, and Lexi wants to stay in it, leaning on him, safe. Then he leans down and brushes her cheek with his lips. She spins around on the piano stool, and he touches her lips with his. There's nothing chaste about *this* kiss. It's tender and full of promise.

'Seriously,' he says. They're both a little breathless, like they've just engaged in a mammoth snogging session rather than exchanged one lovely kiss. 'I don't want to mess this up.'

'Me neither,' she says. She's desperate for another kiss, a deeper one. Her whole body is making that much very clear.

'Good,' he says. 'Then let's do this the Darcy-approved way.'

'Marriage first?' That seems a little extreme. Lexi is panicking.

Sam laughs with just his breath. 'No. But definitely dinner.'

'Okay,' she says, and she can hear the reluctance in her own voice. He does, too – it makes him laugh harder.

'It'll be worth the wait.'

'I don't doubt that,' she says, and this time he lets her kiss him, another lingering meeting of their lips. Nothing more, and it doesn't feel like anything close to enough. But it will have to be, for now.

Chapter Thirty-One

On the walk to their bookshops, Sam reaches for Lexi's hand. It takes her by surprise, but she's into it. *People will talk if they see us,* she thinks vaguely, and around the Hill there's always someone who is going to see you. Lexi doubts that she and Sam are important enough to end up on the Overheard in DC Instagram account, but you never know. In a quiet week . . .

Right now, though, she is too giddy to care. She's too giddy to have her guard up when he asks how things are at the shop, too. All the shop worries are right there at the top of her mind and on the tip of her tongue, her thoughts oscillating wildly between the butterflies of being deep in a crush, the sickening worry of those two lines on the graph, the frustration that those two things are not, in fact, unrelated, and her anger at The Owner of the Other Bookshop, who in her head she keeps separate from her lovely boyfriend. (*Boyfriend?* Is that what he is? Is that what he's becoming?) It's easier that way, easier than acknowledging the reality that they are the same person. It's a lot to keep track of. No wonder Lexi isn't sleeping well these days.

'Actually,' she tells him, 'they've been better.'

Sam's hand squeezes hers. 'How so?'

Lexi almost laughs at his formal phrasing, but she's learned to restrain herself over the years and accept that this is just how some Americans speak. It's not all the *'sup, dudes* of TV shows. It's also *luncheon* instead of lunch and always replying *you're welcome* or at least *mm hmm* when someone says thank you, even it's just someone you're holding the door open for.

'The numbers. They're not looking good. Like I said before, one of my best booksellers wants a pay rise, and she deserves one, too. They all do. But my accountant has basically told me that if I start going there, I'm screwed. That the bookshop's future is hanging in the balance as it is. I'm worried she'll leave, and I'm sad I can't do more for her.'

'That sucks.'

'Yeah. It really does.' She looks at him, trying to decide how honest to be. It's hard to break the habit of suspicion. 'With a good bookseller – it's not just their job, you know? It's their whole identity. Their friends stop by to visit and walk away from the shop with tote bags full of books they've recommended. They preach the virtues of independent bookshops far and wide and spread the word about how important it is not to shop at the Bad Place.'

'The bad place, as in my shop?'

Lexi laughs. He's several rungs down on the ladder of evil. 'No. The Bad Online Place.'

'Ah.' A pause, and then: 'You don't think it's a little much to ask booksellers for their whole identities in exchange for not much more than the minimum wage?'

She's pleasantly surprised that a cut-throat businessman would think of it this way. 'I do. But that's just it. I *don't* ask for that. A really good bookseller pours so much passion into the job that it just kind of *happens*. Of course, that kind of good will is what the entire publishing industry is built on.

Which is how people end up getting taken advantage of. I definitely don't want to be that kind of boss.'

Another squeeze of his hand. 'I bet you're a great boss.'

'I hope I am. Sometimes I think I care about people too much to be the hard-nosed businesswoman the shop needs to stay afloat, you know?'

He's quiet. Lexi wonders if this stuff has ever occurred to him. Because evidence suggests that being a hard-nosed businessman is his top priority. Should that make her like him less? Probably, but it's too hard to tell with his warm hand in hers, his index finger drawing circles at the base of her thumb.

'My booksellers are so fiercely loyal that it comes naturally to want to be fiercely loyal back.' Lexi feels herself getting choked up, a lump forming at the base of her throat.

Sam drops her hand and she panics briefly that she's lost him, that she's too emotional, that she's scared him off, but if a lump in the throat is too much for him, it's probably best that she finds out now. Because there's plenty more where that came from and she needs to be with someone who's going to be okay with a little emotion, or maybe a lot of it.

It turns out, though, that he was only letting go of her hand to put his arm around her shoulder: a side hug of sorts.

'You're lovely – you know that?'

Lexi is glad Sam is steadying her with his arm around her, because she'd be knocked sideways otherwise. She's never been good at taking a compliment, but she's learning.

'Thank you,' she forces out.

'You're welcome,' he says. 'Thank you for telling me that. I know you're basically sleeping with the enemy at this point.'

He runs his hand down Lexi's arm and takes her hand

back. She likes that he seems to feel the need to be attached to her. It's very much mutual. She is pretty sure it's going to feel like she has a phantom limb when she has to turn left and he has to turn right at the corner of 7th and Penn.

'I'm very much *not* sleeping with the enemy,' she reminds him. 'Dinner first, remember?'

'Ah, yes. *Hoping* to sleep with the enemy, then.'

'That might be worse, actually.'

They're at a crossroads. They watch the light turn red, then white, then red again. They're still standing there.

'You're right,' Sam says. 'Sleeping with someone can just be a foolish mistake. But *hoping* to sleep with someone . . . that's more than a temporary lapse of judgement. That's serious.'

He searches Lexi's eyes, wanting her, probably, to say that yes, this *is* serious, she *is* serious, her heart is seriously in peril if any of this goes wrong.

And, of course, it will go wrong, won't it? How can it not? He *is* the enemy. Or at least the friendly rival.

Lexi looks up at him and meets his eyes. 'Yes. It is.'

She wants to kiss him, but also she's afraid to. The *let people talk, I don't care* bravado of twenty minutes earlier has faded now that they're within sight of their respective streets. Lexi can almost see curtains twitching, Capitol Hill moms sipping coffee post-school drop-off and wondering if the two of them are planning world domination with a book empire or if they're about to stab each other in the back in order to assert dominance over this particular patch of the nation's capital. If it weren't for their linked hands, Lexi doubts it would cross their minds that they're currently fighting very different impulses, but one kiss seen by one mom would soon disabuse the whole neighbourhood of that notion.

'Is this whole thing a really bad idea?' Sam asks, as if reading Lexi's thoughts. The answer is obvious.

'Probably. But I don't want it to be. Do you?'

He shakes his head, and takes her other hand too, so now they're standing opposite each other, joined, potential Capitol Hill gossip be damned. 'No,' he says. 'I don't.'

They walk in silence the rest of the way, the kind of companiable silence that Lexi has read about but never really believed existed. If you love someone, she'd always thought, wouldn't you want to talk to them non-stop? Getting to know Sam, though, is teaching her other ways to be. Maybe silence is okay. Maybe fierce loyalty to one shop doesn't mean you have to hate another one. Maybe hard-nosed businessmen have hearts, too.

'You've got this,' he tells her on their corner before they go their separate ways and it's time to test the phantom limb theory. 'Go save that bookshop.'

Lexi squeezes his hand before she leaves him. She tries not to think about the fact that he's the one it needs saving from.

Chapter Thirty-Two

Lexi leaves the shop early, to go shopping for something to wear on her Official Date with Sam. She doesn't want to wear her usual tops, tainted with the disappointment of first dates with guys who won't shut up about themselves. In this case, she actually *wants* Sam to talk about himself. He's still a mystery, and while that's definitely part of the allure, the curiosity is also burning Lexi up inside. She's ready to cave and ask the questions. She wants to know why he opened a bookstore when he doesn't even seem to love books that much. She wants to know why he's still in DC if New York is so much better (which it isn't). She wants to know what the ex-girlfriend did to him, exactly, that left him broken and unable to hold down a relationship. (A little online stalking has revealed her name to be Amanda, but that's all the information she has managed to glean.) She also wants to know what his gym routine is, because those arms . . . Now that it's properly summer, she gets to see a lot of them. A definite perk.

She also wonders where he's going to take her. So to speak.

In Clothes Encounters on 7th Street, she looks through the tops in her size, picking out a few to try on. She thinks about *The Hating Game* and Joshua Templeton's obsession with Lucy's eye colour. Borderline creepy? Maybe, but also very romantic. Should she pick out something blue to highlight her own eyes? Or should she choose something that doesn't look that well thought out, something that will look like she just threw it on without trying too hard? Something that will make Sam think this isn't a big deal for her and he's going to have to work hard to win her over?

It might be too late for that. She might have shown her hand, what with her clear desperation that he throw her onto his bed straight away, even before the formality of a real date. She *could* try to insinuate that her heart will be harder to capture than her body, but she doesn't think she'd be fooling anyone. She thinks about *Friends*, how Joey can allegedly look at a woman's bra and have it pop open. That's the way someone can look at Lexi and have her heart pop open for them. Or not just *someone*. But the right person. Or sometimes, as is very possibly the case here, the wrong one.

On the changing room chair, Lexi's phone lights up with a text.

Hey. Above it, in bold, the name of the sender: Sam. Lexi's heart, traitor that it is, does a little flutter. There's no way it's staying safely tucked in her chest, is there? She'll have to be careful. Just in case this whole thing is an elaborate ploy to distract her so he can swoop in and take over the literary world in this part of town. It probably isn't, but you never know.

She waits for him to say something else, but there's nothing. *Hey* is so lazy. He's expecting her to carry the conversation when he's the one who started it. She's not letting him get away with that. It takes a lot of energy to resist the urge to write back, but she does. Lexi curses herself for enabling read receipts – she wants him to think she has better things to do than stare at her phone, even if staring at it is exactly what she's doing.

What are you up to? He writes eventually, and she mentally congratulates herself for the tiny victory.

She considers saying, *Nothing*. But the prospect of teasing him is too enticing to resist.

Buying something to wear for our date. So you won't be able to take your eyes off me.

That won't be necessary.

Most restaurants do tend to prefer you to wear clothes. At least, I assume so. I haven't actually asked.

See, that's where you've been going wrong with all those DC dudes.

I imagine most of them would have preferred we skip the chat and just get naked, yes.

A pause, then he sends a blushing emoji, Lexi is all out of banter.

I don't blame them.

She coughs, right there in the shop, holding a red off-the-shoulder top that she could wear with her laciest bra straps showing, just to tease and distract him. It may not be the most efficient way to get the answers about his life that she's looking for, but in this moment, it feels worth it.

We could've got naked a long time ago. You're the one who wants to do dinner. And that requires clothes.

As God and Jane Austen intended.

It feels weird and borderline blasphemous to put both God and Jane Austen in the same text chain as the word *naked*.

Indeed.

She's not quite ready to let the conversation go.

Should I get the top that shows my lacy bra off just a little bit?

She thinks about him behind the counter at his bookshop, trying to keep on his Serious Face, the face for Very Serious Customers who want to discuss Very Serious Books.

You're killing me here.

You've got nobody to blame but yourself on that one.

In that moment, Lexi wishes she had a flip phone like on American TV shows from the early 2000s. It feels like a suitable moment to snap a phone shut. Mic drop. End of conversation.

So she does the next best thing: she throws her phone in her bag, leaving Sam to type into the void.

Leaving him to think about her bra.

Chapter Thirty-Three

In the end, Lexi decides against the lacy bra strap scenario. Jane Austen likely wouldn't approve, and anyway, she doesn't actually want Sam to be too distracted. Much as part of her would like to jump into bed with him and get the sexual frustration well and truly dealt with, she also wants to know what makes him tick, why he seems like a different person when he's teaching the piano from what he does when he's being Mr hard-nosed Businessman. She wants to know which one is the real Sam.

They're both attractive, in their own ways. She likes sparring with the snarky business owner. She also doesn't hate getting to feel slightly superior, more of the expert. And as for pianist Sam, it goes without saying, doesn't it? Deft, elegant fingers. The way his body turns almost liquid with emotion when he plays, like he's putting his whole self into it. The smoothness of the music that results from all this. And then the way he looks at Lexi so kindly when she does something as deeply impressive as playing a C major scale with both hands at once.

Which Sam will show up at dinner?

Which one will show up in bed?

If they get there, that is. Lexi knows she shouldn't assume.

But she's shaved above the knee and all other relevant body parts and moisturised all over; she's got a couple of condoms in her bag on the off chance he's not prepared. (The chances of that are less than zero, but it doesn't hurt to make doubly sure.) She sang 'The Sexy Getting Ready Song' from *Crazy Ex-Girlfriend* as she did her make-up, bleached the not-quite-light-enough hair on her top lip, and carefully picked out her perfume (Armani Sì Passione seems appropriate).

So, yes, she's pretty much assuming.

In the end, Lexi decided not to reinvent the wheel for her first date attire. Instead, she's wearing a trusty favourite: one of her best sundresses, with pockets and a sweetheart neckline and blocks of colour that from a distance look like books on shelves. She likes both the illusion and the allusion, and of course, on this occasion, the appropriateness of it.

Walking down 8th Street to Belga, she finds Sam outside in what Americans call a button-down shirt, in blue and white plaid, and not that interesting, and yet somehow, on him, classy and smart. She gives him a little wave, wiggling her fingers when he catches her eye, and resists the temptation to speed up her steps. Casual. Nonchalant. But she flashes him her happiest smile, because that is just what her face spontaneously does at this point when she sees him, the delight at being here with him, her mortal enemy just three months ago. And possibly still her mortal enemy now. She'll have to see how the evening goes, and if his intentions are honourable. Or, preferably, slightly dishonourable.

'Hi,' she says, and then, babbling to fill the silence. 'Sorry I'm late.'

Sam looks at his watch – an actual watch! Why is that so attractive? Is it just the impression it gives of his being a real grown-up, not like the boys on Capitol Hill who play at being Adult and Important? 'Only two minutes. Didn't you say that your people consider that to be on time?'

She nods. 'We do.'

'Anyway,' he says. 'Hi.' He leans in and kisses her cheek. Chastely, but also lingering there slightly longer than, say, the French seem to when they're genuinely just saying hello. His lips on Lexi's skin feel like a promise, and he smells clean and bright and earthy. All of which might be more gallant and classy than a giveaway sight of, say, a lacy bra strap, but she's guessing the impact of it is similar to what the bra strap would have had on him. The hairs on Lexi's arms stand to attention in a way they never have during a Hinge date. The promise of the evening lingers in the air along with his clean and sexy scent.

'Thank you for making time for me in your busy schedule.' Once upon a time, all of three months ago, her sentence would have been dripping with contempt. Today, though, it's playful and flirtatious.

'Likewise,' he says. Then: 'Shall we?'

Sam leads Lexi to the hostess stand, his hand on the small of her back. He does it lightly, and yet he might as well be plugging her into an electric current. They have a window seat: her favourite for watching the world and the great and the good of Capitol Hill go by, though she has a feeling she won't be doing that tonight.

She notices now that he's had a haircut. He looks so smart and suave. She would happily just stare at him all night. But she's also hungry, so she tears her eyes away and fixes them on the menu. Her heart needs a little break from the view, anyway, so that it doesn't explode.

'You look lovely tonight,' he says, his hand over hers as she tries desperately to care about what she'll be eating. She looks up.

'Thank you.' She resists, for now, the cheesiness of a *You don't look so bad yourself*; she resists *I like to make an effort now and then*. She just takes the compliment and enjoys this romantic moment. 'I'm glad we're doing this.' She looks down at the menu. She's hungry, yes, but she's also feeling shy, suddenly, and awkward. They've mostly had two modes, she and Sam: snarky and sparring, and friendly and flirtatious; and with the second of those, there's usually a bed in the corner of the room, adding that edge of titillation and invitation to further adventure. There's a metaphorical bed in the corner of the room now too, of course.

Lexi usually likes to indulge at Belga. Mussels and *frites*, maybe a steak, a chocolate dessert. This isn't a place she comes for a quick weeknight dinner with friends to catch up or a post-shift drink with her staff. This is a treat-yourself place, and so she usually goes all in on the treating herself. But there's that metaphorical bed, and the very real one too, and she can't be so stuffed that all she can do is lie very still for an hour or two after dinner.

She looks longingly at the bread they bring. *It's bread or frites*, she tells herself. *You can't have both, or you'll regret it later.*

'I'm glad we're doing this too,' Sam says. 'I can't resist the fries here. You don't think mayo is going to be the right thing to go with them, and yet.'

'I meant you and me.'

'I know. My failed attempt at humour. I'm not so good with the jokes when I'm nervous.'

Lexi flips her hand over in Sam's, so that she can hold it. 'You're nervous?'

'Of course,' he says softly.

'I know I talk a tough game. But I promise you I'm not scary.' She could swear she's told him this before.

'I'm a little scared of how I feel about you.'

Is it possible to feel punched in the gut but in a pleasant way? It must be, because that's what Lexi is feeling right now. 'Oh?'

'You could really hurt me if you wanted to.'

They've barely taken a sip or two of their pre-dinner cocktails. It's a little early for deep and vulnerable. But Lexi rolls with it nonetheless.

'Do I seem like I want to?'

'No. But they never do seem like they do at first.' He says it lightly, but it doesn't take a genius to work out that there's real hurt and feeling behind those words, real lived experience.

Lexi will need a glass or two more before she goes there. Instead, she matches the lightness of his tone. 'I mean, I obviously wanted to kill you before.'

'Before?'

'But now I know how you kiss. I could never do that. It would be a real waste. I'd be depriving womankind of a great asset.'

'Fair.'

The waiter comes over to take their order, but Lexi has only glanced down at the menu to steady her nerves; she hasn't actually studied it. She asks for a minute from the server and tries to concentrate on the swimming words. She's never been here on a date; she's never looked at the options with those eyes before. Like, for example, she loves mussels, but is there any way to eat them elegantly, without the buttery goodness of the garlic sauce dripping down her chin? No, there is not. And speaking of garlic: in this kind of situation, either you both have it or neither of you does. Unless something goes horribly wrong in the next hour or so, they both know how the dinner is going to end. And if it *does* go horribly wrong – which is certainly not out of the question – Lexi will have bigger things to worry about than whether she was too overt with her garlic calculations.

'Speaking of which?' she says. 'If we're going to be, say, kissing . . .'

'Garlic?' he asks. She's relieved he's read her mind. 'I think we can assume there's garlic in everything here. I wouldn't worry about it.'

'And it won't kill the vampire in you?'

He laughs. 'No.'

The server is back, and they still haven't chosen. He only rolls his eyes a little bit when they tell him so, but they should probably get a move on.

'Want to share some mussels to start with?'

Lexi is stuck. Because she doesn't want the mess but she loves mussels, and for some reason, it seems important in this moment that Sam know this about her, and that he also knows she won't let a bit of mess and effort spoil her enjoyment of a good evening.

'Thought you'd never ask,' she tells him. 'They're messy, but so worth it.'

'Much like myself,' he jokes. At least Lexi hopes it's a joke. She'll ask him once they've decided on their order, because she can't risk the waiter coming back for a third time without their having an answer for him. You don't want to irritate the people handling your food, after all.

Lexi and Sam get through the mussels, with no choice but to laugh about their sticky hands and the juice dripping down their chins. If Lexi had wondered whether sharing mussels is similar to sharing popcorn at the cinema – hands accidentally, or maybe not so accidentally, touching, the delicate thrill of it all, she is quickly disabused of that notion. There's far too much going on for those kinds of shenanigans. And, unlike the cinema, where the darkness lets you retain some mystery, eating mussels in front of someone feels strangely intimate. Once you've seen someone dip their hands into garlicky sauce, retrieve a shell and inspect its contents, then use half of that shell to dig out the flesh and then pop it in their mouth, it kind of feels like you know everything about them.

The one saving grace when you're sharing is that you're usually too busy with your own mussels, never mind attempting to keep flirtatious conversation going, that there's not really the brain space to also analyse what the other person is doing with their mussels. So maybe not exactly ideal first date food, but not as bad as it could be, either.

And anyway, this isn't exactly your run-of-the-mill first date, the kind where all you know of each other is your carefully curated picture, your witty messages helped along by having time to figure out what to say, and a description making you seem far more fun or stable or interesting than you actually are. Lexi and Sam know each other's jobs – have first-hand experience of them, in fact – have encountered each other at both their snarkiest and their most vulnerable, and (eyes on the prize) also know how each other kisses. The promise of that hangs over this whole dinner. Maybe that's the real reason their hands don't touch in the mussel bowl. They don't need to test chemistry or manufacture it. They know where this is going.

Their hands *do* touch in the *frites* when they arrive with the steak, but not out of any kind of romantic impulse: it's just the impatience of dipping one of these sticks of goodness into mayonnaise and tasting at its hottest and crispiest.

'Stick of goodness, huh?' Sam says when Lexi voices this. 'That sounds like a euphemism if ever I heard one.'

'One-track mind,' Lexi says, like she's not the one who's been pushing them down this particular track.

He gestures vaguely towards her and her undone top button. 'Can you blame me?'

She puts a *frite* in her mouth and slowly sucks the rest in. He watches her, and a strange, soft animal sound escapes him.

'I guess not,' she says.

She lets the silence stretch out. She enjoys him looking at her, notes with pleasure his dilated pupils. They're drunk enough now that she could ask him about his past and he would probably tell her. In fact, alcohol or not, she is pretty sure she could ask him for anything right now and he'd give it to her.

'I feel like we should skip this steak and the dessert,' she tells him. 'And go straight—'

Sam cuts her off. 'Nice try,' he says in his *come to bed* tone. 'We are doing this the right way. Getting to know each other over food, like grown-ups.'

Lexi takes a sip of her wine. 'All right,' she says. 'Go on. What would you like to know?'

He thinks about it as he cuts a piece of his steak. Lexi is relieved to see that he does it the proper way, holding his fork between his thumb and his index finger and not gripped in a fist the way some Americans do. But the longer she waits, the more nervous she gets. He lifts the piece of steak to his lips, and then, right before he pops it in his mouth, he says, 'What is it about the bookshop that means so much to you?'

'Wow. We're going there?'

She waits for him to finish his mouthful. There are downsides to eating with a civilised person, after all.

'I'm not asking as your business rival. I'm asking because I want to know what makes you tick.'

'Fair enough.' She sees now that she shouldn't have been so defensive, but really, who can blame her?

She takes a deep breath and tells him about her happy childhood summers in the bookshop with her grandmother, learning the trade and the love of books and the art of talking to people about them. She tells him that it feels like a sacred trust her grandmother left to her, that she wants to honour it and her place in the Capitol Hill community. And then she tells him the thing she only tells her most trusted friends.

'I guess, being a little bit American in the UK, I never felt like I totally belonged. And with the red hair, and the Austen surname . . . But this bookshop is mine, you know? It's my little kingdom, filled with the things I love, where I make the rules. It's where I belong.'

'That makes sense,' he says. 'It explains why you're so

protective over it. It's not just, like, a business venture you've poured all your time and money into.'

'It's that, too,' she says quickly. She doesn't want Sam to think she's anything less than professional. But all the professional stuff she does, she does because of what the bookshop represents.

'Yes, of course it's that too,' he replies. 'But, first and foremost, I guess it's home.'

'Exactly.' She felt so vulnerable laying that out on the table, and for someone to understand so readily, to name it himself, feels like a gift. And for that someone to be the person she happens to have a raging crush on – and a hard-nosed businessman, no less – feels like a miracle. 'You get it,' she tells him, catching his hand, which is heading for the *frites* and grabbing it, squeezing it. She intertwines her fingers with his. She feels safe and cared for suddenly, like maybe she belongs with Sam. Like maybe, even more than the bookshop, *he's* the home she's been looking for.

It feels tricky and awkward to bring up something difficult after this lovely moment, this moment when Lexi feels like Sam *gets* her. But she wants to *get* him, too, and she's missing a piece of the puzzle.

She takes an on-ramp onto the conversation about the ex-girlfriend who dragged him to DC. 'Can I ask you something?'

'Anything.' He's still holding her hand, his thumb stroking hers. That's fine for one-handed *frite* eating, but Lexi is guessing he's going to need both his hands to eat the rest of this steak. As, come to think of it, is she. But sitting like this is so nice that she's reluctant to let go.

'What exactly happened with Amanda?'

'Ah.' He's noticed, suddenly, that he needs his hand back.

197

Cutting the next piece of her steak, Lexi is glad to have something to do with hers, too – and somewhere to look beside directly at Sam. If she's caused him pain by asking this question, she is afraid to see it in his eyes. And if he's feeling guilty and sheepish . . . she isn't sure she wants to see that, either.

'I told you that she wasn't as interested in me as she was in my family, right?'

Lexi nods, but stays silent, allowing space for him to keep speaking if he wants to.

'She kept wanting us to go home to meet my family. At first, I found it kind of touching, you know? She wanted to know more about me and my background. But I also didn't really want to take her home, because my parents – well, let's just say I don't have the easiest relationship with them.'

When Amanda contacted him about the shop being up for sale, it felt like an escape from proximity to his parents and a miraculous way out of his miserable job. *Besides*, she said, *I can earn enough for both of us, if necessary.* It seemed like a generous, supportive offer. But when they made it to his house for Thanksgiving – because, no matter how much you dislike your family, you can't miss Thanksgiving – it was obvious just how she intended to make that money: by weaselling her way into the family business herself.

'And right there, between turkey and pecan pie, I realised what an idiot I'd been. She was between jobs when we met. She knew my last name; she saw an opportunity. It didn't hurt that she found me attractive, I guess.'

'I mean, who wouldn't?' Lexi is trying to lighten the mood a little, to get him to smile. It works.

'I'm quite the catch.'

Lexi wants Sam to feel hugged and understood, the way he made her feel just now. But she also likes this lighter mood. It's a delicate balance, this first-date business, actually, even and especially when you already know how the other person kisses. When you really, *really* don't want to mess it up. But she's got dessert to get him to laugh. She says what she really wants to.

'I'm sorry she treated you that way. You deserve to be loved for who you are.' And then, because she's had just enough wine, she keeps going. 'Not for who your family is, and not for what you can achieve.' She hasn't, though, had quite enough wine to add that she'll love him like that if he'll let her. She hopes he can read it between the lines.

'Thank you,' he says, putting his cutlery into the 'I'm done' position on his plate. 'She really broke my heart, you know?' Sam looks up and right at Lexi, into her eyes. There might be an implication here, too: *You better not do that to me. I'm not sure I'd ever recover.* 'That's why I struggled afterwards. I wanted to find someone else, but I was hurting, so I self-sabotaged. Hence my reputation around DC, you know?'

Lexi nods. She does know. She just didn't know that *he* knew. She reaches for the last remaining *frite* and waits for more.

'This thing . . .' He points at her, then at himself. 'It's not a rebound thing. I really—'

And that, of course, is when the waiter comes to ask them if they want dessert.

'We'll take a look at the menu,' Lexi says quickly, more to get him out of the way than anything else.

'I got some therapy,' Sam says, taking another tack, obviously not quite ready to say what he'd been about to say.

Admitting he'd had therapy might be an even bigger deal for this hard-ass businessman, who, Lexi is realising, is actually a soft-hearted creative type who's had to build a shell around himself. 'That's how much I want this to work.'

'Thank you for telling me that,' she says, taking his hand across the table again. 'I know it takes a lot to make yourself vulnerable like this.'

Emotions and vulnerability spill out of Lexi every chance she gets, but she knows it's not like that for everyone. Especially Sam. She's touched.

'You're welcome,' he replies. 'Now what do you say we skip dessert and get out of here?'

Lexi thinks briefly and with a tinge of regret about the Belgian chocolate fondant, the way the homemade ice cream melts into it, creating a puddle of deliciousness. But even so, it's a no-brainer.

'I would like that very much,' she tells Sam.

Chapter Thirty-Four

Is there any walk like the walk back after a date, when you both know exactly what's about to happen? Despite Lexi's preference for all things Capitol Hill over all things Navy Yard, she finds herself wishing that they'd chosen a restaurant closer to Sam's apartment.

On the one hand, the twenty-minute walk gives her a little time for her dinner to go down. She's eaten more than she normally would before a session of what she's hoping will be vigorous exercise: another reason Belga maybe wasn't the best choice. Her self-control needs some work all around, and, in her defence, she knows it.

She finds herself wishing, for example, that she had been a little more mysterious, a little less obvious. Still, it doesn't seem to have put Sam off. Lexi is quiet now, though: the walk is more than long enough for her to say something stupid and ruin the moment. And if she has to go one more night without consummating this not-quite-relationship, she's in danger of destroying her vibrator from overuse.

'You okay?' he asks her as they walk down 8th Street hand in hand.

She's enjoying the night, and she's also really nervous. 'Of course,' she tells him.

'Because it's totally fine if you don't want to come back to my apartment.'

Maybe he's teasing; maybe he's joking. But his tone, tender and low, tells her otherwise; he's being a gentleman. Making sure he has not just her tacit consent, but her explicit, enthusiastic approval.

'Oh, I definitely do.'

'That's a relief.' He laughs, maybe nervously. It's good that they're both nervous, Lexi hopes. It shows that this means something to both of them.

'I'm just making sure I don't say something stupid to scare you off me in the next few minutes.'

'You haven't been able to do that for the last few months. I think you're safe for the next fourteen minutes.'

'Well, except you hated me a few months ago, Lexi points out.'

'No, I didn't. I never hated you.'

'Next you'll be telling me that you only opened a bookshop on Capitol Hill to get my attention.'

'It worked, didn't it?'

'Despite myself.'

They're at a crossing now. They'll be there for at least fifteen seconds. Lexi really wants to kiss him. She can't take it anymore. She turns to look at Sam, but with a glint in his eye, he shakes his head.

'What?' she asks, trying the innocent approach.

'Nope. Not yet. You've got your *kiss me* face on, and I am not starting this in the middle of I street.'

She wiggles her eyebrows. 'Starting what, exactly?'

'Our night together. Don't make me start and stop again. That's just cruel.'

Lexi huffs a little but has to admit he is right. Her body is primed, ready. If she gives it the go signal, things might get a little graphic even for Overheard in DC.

202

'Not long now,' he says.

'Wait,' she deadpans. 'We're not waiting until we're married?'

'Don't even joke about that.' And then, after a pause: 'People don't actually do that, right? That's, like, an urban myth?'

Lexi pictures her group of Christian friends. 'I think they do, yeah.'

'I can't decide if they deserve respect or mockery.'

'It's a little bit impressive, I think.'

'It's a little bit *something*, that's for sure.'

They're crossing New Jersey Avenue now; she can see his building from here, its name emblazoned on the front.

'I can't believe you live at The Novel. So appropriate.'

'I'm glad you approve.'

Somehow, they make it, stumbling through the doors to the building and into the lift. It's just them in there and Sam stares resolutely ahead so that Lexi doesn't go getting any ideas. But the second they're through his door, all that self-control is a distant memory. He leans her against the wall and kisses her deeply, hungrily, before she's even had a chance to drop her bag. It lands with a thud. It's possible her phone breaks. She doesn't even care.

'Hi,' she says, when they break to catch their breaths. She doesn't know why. It just seems like the thing to say.

'Hi,' he says back, breathing hard. 'Might I enquire whether you are having a pleasant evening?'

It's impressive to string together this many words at this kind of moment, let alone engage in some light Austenite role play. *This one's a keeper*, Lexi thinks.

'Exceedingly pleasant, thank you.'

'Perhaps you might find yourself more at ease with fewer garments?'

It's a sign of Lexi's twisted brain that the correct use of *fewer* is the hottest thing about this moment.

'I should like that,' she tells him, impressed with her own use of *should* and mildly disappointed in herself for caring right now.

She turns and scrunches up her hair with one hand so he can unzip her dress, then she lifts up her arms. He pulls it over her head, then spins her back to face him in one swift motion.

'No corset,' he notes. He's trying to be smooth, but his voice sounds a little strangled. 'Very daring.'

He kisses her neck and makes his way down her body.

'Perhaps—' Lexi can barely get the words out. 'You might also feel at your leisure with fewer garments?'

Lexi's legs are jelly. She can barely stand. She's thankful for this wall she's leaning on, taking all her weight. She runs one hand under Sam's shirt from the top to the bottom, undoing each button as she goes.

'I see you are also wearing no corset,' she says. 'I approve.'

He's tanned and toned, obviously spends time in the gym without overdoing it. Probably gets some laps in at his rooftop pool at the crack of dawn before anyone else has thought about it. Lexi could stare at him forever, but mostly, she wants his skin on her skin. She pulls him towards her, his warmth on hers.

'May I assist,' he gasps, his hand reaching behind her for her bra strap.

'You may,' she tells him, and miraculously, he finds it. Slowly, he slides a finger under each strap on her shoulders.

The bra falls away and she's in front of him, almost completely naked, vulnerable. There's no coming back from this now.

'Wow,' he says. She can feel herself responding to his hungry look. 'May I—?'

'Anything.'

He looks deep into his eyes, then his mouth trails down, teasing her with kisses.

Somehow, they manage to make it the few steps to his bed, which, is ready and primed. He wasn't messing around with keeping it as a sofa she notes vaguely. He was prepared.

His own fingers play under the elastic of her pants. She shivers.

'Is this okay?' he to asks, a note of desperation in his voice.

'It's incredibly okay.'

'That's a relief,' he says.

He's not wrong, there's no relief quite like it. It feels like coming home.

* * *

'Well,' Lexi says, when she's caught her breath. 'That was certainly worth the wait.'

A grin spreads over Sam's face. 'I'm glad you think so.'

She looks at him, waiting for the *too*.

'*I* just always knew it would be,' he says.

'You're awfully sure of yourself.'

She wants to joke about his having had plenty of practice, but now doesn't seem like the time.

'The anticipation is half the pleasure,' he says.

'The anticipation nearly killed me, though.' And it nearly killed her vibrator. Those things, it turns out, are sturdy.

Did the inventor get a Nobel Peace Prize? Because it seems like they should have. She nuzzles into him, her head in the crook between his neck and his shoulder. 'I can't believe I ever hated you.'

'You never hated me.' His voice hums through her bones, like she's part of the same body.

'Didn't I?'

'You were just jealous of my business prowess.'

'Yep.' 'Lexi rolls her eyes. Definitely jealous of all those precise right angles and uncluttered warehouse vibes.'

'I mean, who wouldn't be?'

'And the constant stream of Important DC Events with Serious People who think a little too much of themselves. The kind of people I used to go on dates with.'

She shudders, imagining a whole shop full of them. Imagining them being regular customers. Imagining not being able to just walk away and block their numbers.

But Lexi has shown her hand. '*Used to* go on dates with, huh?'

'I mean . . . before I gave up on terrible DC men.'

'And dated a terrible New York man instead?' Sam makes a fist with his spare hand, miming a microphone under his chin. 'Ladies and gentlemen, she has officially given up on other men.'

Lexi rolls her eyes, but she can't stop smiling. He's not wrong. She's smitten.

She doesn't know what it means for the shop. She doesn't know what any of her staff are going to say when they inevitably find out, though she can take a guess. But, right now, at this very moment, she doesn't care. Or, no, it's not that she doesn't care, exactly. More that it's a problem for Lexi the Businesswoman. Lexi the Infatuated is a different part of her. She resides in a different part of her brain, or perhaps her body, and she'd like to stay there for as long as humanly possible. For as long as inhumanly possible, too.

'We'll see,' she tells Sam. 'Don't count your chickens yet, mister.'

'But that was some of my best work just then.'

Lexi can well believe that. 'I am definitely not complaining about the quality of the work.'

'Good,' he says. ''Cause then I'd have to prove I can do more.' He kisses the top of her head. Rolls her gently away so he can free his hand. 'And we wouldn't want that, right?'

'No,' she says, and she shivers as he touches her again. 'We definitely . . .' Her breathing quickens. '. . . wouldn't want . . .'

'Wouldn't want . . . ?' Sam prompts her. Seeing, no doubt, if Lexi has lost the power of speech.

Which, it turns out, she has.

Chapter Thirty-Five

Lexi sleeps better than she might've imagined that night. If you'd asked her six months ago how relaxed she would be in Sam's bed after amazing sex . . . well, first of all, she would have said, *I'm sorry – what now?* And then, once she'd cleared up the tea she'd splattered down her top, she would have said that she'd probably lie awake all night, tossing, turning, puzzling over her mistake and what it meant not just for her heart but also for her bookshop. She never sleeps well on the first night in any bed – let alone the bed of her (former?) mortal enemy.

But then, the truth is that good sex is tiring. And the other truth is that, after sex with Sam, she feels more relaxed than she's felt in . . . months? Years? It's not just the release of what she now realises to have been long-building tension; it's also like her whole body knows that this is what she's supposed to be doing, this is where she's meant to be, this is who she's meant to be with. It could, to be fair, also be the release of oxytocin, but, as always, Lexi prefers the more romantic version.

It's hard to tell if Sam is actually asleep, or just letting her watch him, but there's a smile playing at the corner of his lips, so she suspects the latter. She's enjoying the undistracted view of his ruffled hair – usually so tidy – and the contours of his jawline. Without his eyes, though, the picture isn't complete. His eyes are what she likes best about him, the most mesmerising part of him. Luckily, she doesn't have to wait too long to see them. He stretches, and they ping open.

'Good morning,' she says.

He smiles in response, and reaches out to smooth her hair. 'Hi.'

It's awkward, this part. Because all Lexi wants to say is: *We did it! Can you believe it?* But it seems like that might not quite strike the right tone.

She's been thinking a lot lately about the alternative ending to the 2005 *Pride and Prejudice* film, the ending that was made for the American market and that, in the UK, she only discovered by fumbling around with the DVD extras, since DVDs were actually a thing back then, in the dinosaur age of her pre-teen years. In that ending, which totally wouldn't have worked for a British audience sceptical of too much gushing, or, for that matter, for any Austen purists, who'd note her understated restraint as well as the fact that her books always end pretty much straight after the wedding, Mr Darcy and Elizabeth kiss and embrace, seemingly amazed that they've actually made it.

And that tone *would* be fitting here. Lexi isn't exactly worried about scaring Sam off with her enthusiasm: if that was going to happen, last night would have done the trick. She was certainly very enthusiastic, three times over. But she goes for playful and detached instead of earnest because she is, after all, still British.

'What does a girl have to do to get a coffee around here?'

It's tea that she actually wants, of course. Tea is her straight-out-of-bed drink. But she knows better than to expect an

American to have a kettle, let alone PG Tips. She'll train him one day. But this is not that day. One thing at a time.

'Patience, my love.'

While Lexi hates being told to be patient, her stomach lurches – if pleasant lurching is a thing – at *my love*. Sam might be back in eighteenth-century-England character, but still, it's a nice thing to hear. If nothing else because you can't call someone that and then refuse them a coffee.

She wants to kiss him, but she's acutely aware of morning breath. The coffee isn't just for waking up; it's good for masking that. And when it comes to another kiss, she's not sure that she *can* be patient.

Still, she chooses to be gracious.

'Of course.' She settles back down under the covers. 'Your sheets are very soft.'

'I'm glad you like them.'

She has a brief fantasy of him picking them out, thinking about her as he did so. They're purple: her favourite colour.

'I'm sure you bought them with me in mind.'

Lexi should know by now that Americans don't always understand the nuances of British humour – that when bantering Brits start a sentence with *I'm sure* there's a strong chance the rest of the sentence will be preposterous. But old habits and ways of speaking die hard, and sometimes don't die at all.

'I did, actually.'

He says it with a straight face. There's no reason to doubt him. And now that she thinks about it, they did have the feel of newness about them last night. He really went and bought new sheets for their first night together? That's almost unbearably romantic.

'I'm so glad I was right about you,' she says.

'That sounds ominous. Right in what way?'

'I knew that under that gruff façade was a Mr Darcy, just dying to get out. There was a good heart hidden under . . .' She almost says, *under that arrogant exterior*, but she catches herself.

'Under . . . ?'

'Well, you know. Under all the *not-handsome-enough-to-tempt-me* stuff. It was nothing a piano recital and a walk in the park couldn't fix.'

Sam shuffles onto his side and props his chin against his fist, like he's expecting Lexi to say a whole lot more. 'You . . . tried to fix me?' he prompts.

'I tried to see if Jane Austen's tricks would work.'

Sam is frowning. Lexi doesn't love the turn this conversation is taking. She hasn't even told him about the *real* reason she used those tricks at first, but she's already said too much.

'So I was a project to you? Some kind of game?'

His frown deepens. Nobody in their early thirties should have frown lines this deep.

'Unbelievable.' Sam sounds disgusted.

Lexi feels her heart start to pound. She's made a terrible mistake. She's messed this up.

'But it didn't matter in the end! I didn't need the project. Because you're a great guy, and I saw that pretty quickly. Jane Austen taught me to look beneath the surface, that's all. And when I did, I liked what I saw.'

Talking doesn't seem to be getting her anywhere, so she stops. She waits for what seem like interminable minutes for Sam to fill the silence.

'I really fell for you, Lexi. I let my guard down and I fell for you. And now to find out I was just some project to you—'

'That's not—'

'I was a project to Amanda, too. My parents, as well. I've been someone's project all my life, it feels like. People trying to fit me into what they've decided I should be. I'm not doing that anymore.'

More silence. It's hard to know how to respond. It might help for Lexi to say how much she likes him, that she even thinks she might love him. But it's terrifying to lay that down and know he could still kick her out. Those aren't cheap, easy words to throw around. She won't say them until she knows he'll say them back, and that doesn't seem likely right now.

'I think you should go,' he says, quietly.

She lets a beat pass, lets him hear himself so that he can take it back. But he doesn't.

'Really?' she asks, her voice breaking.

He nods. This is where a Brit would say, 'I'm sorry,' even if they didn't mean it, just to defuse the tension. But that's not the American way, and it certainly isn't Sam's.

'But I—'

'Please,' he says. 'Just go.'

Lexi doesn't want to leave this comfortable, purple-sheeted bed. She doesn't want to leave this beautiful man. And yet here he is, watching her as she pulls the sheets back and gets up, naked, exposed and vulnerable, retrieving bits of clothing from the floor, and gradually dressing. She gives him a long, hard stare before she opens the door, a *you're hurting me* stare, a *this is a waste* stare, a *you're being an idiot* stare.

He stares back at her, evenly, a stare that gives nothing away but a cold, hard, proud exterior. Mr-Darcy-at-the-ball is back. She isn't handsome enough to tempt him, after all, or at least not perfect enough.

Lexi finds her shoes and clicks the door closed and it's not until she's in the lift that she finally lets herself cry.

Chapter Thirty-Six

In the fantasies Lexi has entertained of what life would be like after she and Sam had finally slept together, she'd imagined them hand in hand, walking to their respective bookshops in a post-coital haze. But instead, this morning, she's walking alone, and instead of pausing every few steps to kiss her hot boyfriend, she's pausing every now and then to wipe an accumulation of tears off her face and, after checking to see that nobody who'd judge her is within view, wipe her nose with the back of her hand.

You might think that she wouldn't care about being dignified at a time like this, that all that would matter to her is her aching heart. But the thing is, as a small business owner who lives in the community she serves, she never can let her guard down. Lexi, Lexi's shop, Lexi's brand: they're all one and the same. She can't afford to fall apart, even if all she wants to do is go home, burrow under her quilt with a tub of Ben and Jerry's, and cry till her eyes are red raw and the entire contents of a box of aloe-vera-enriched tissues is lying crumpled all around her. And sure, yes, maybe she could call in sick, give herself a day to wallow before she attacks all the shop's challenges head-on. But she's afraid that if she stops, if she allows herself a day to fall apart, she might not make it out of her room and her house ever again, and definitely not quickly enough to be able to put in place these new book clubs, come up with new ideas, and amp up revenue before the graph of doom becomes even more doomful.

The shop can't afford the kind of time Lexi suspects it will take her to get over this. Every day that income flatlines is a day closer to its demise. She's never let herself think of it that way before, never wanted to believe that demise could be in the shop's future, but now, with everything going wrong, suddenly it seems like a very real possibility. And if Sam is as angry as he seemed just now, she worries that he'll actually *want* to put her out of business. Rather than that being an unfortunate by-product of his success, it'll be the whole point. Revenge.

On top of everything else, Lexi feels like an idiot, because her staff could be out of a job soon, and it'll be because she couldn't control her sex drive. Because she let herself be tempted by a handsome face. What a ridiculous thing to gamble everything on. What a fool she's been.

She somehow makes it through the blur of the day, thankful that after six years in the job she can do most things on autopilot, including summoning enthusiasm when a customer asks her for a recommendation. Today, though, she mostly leaves that to Marcus and Tessa and ensconces herself in her office, enforcing cuddling time with Pippin whether or not it fits into his schedule. He seems to get it, though, making himself comfortable in her lap and purring away, her own personal ASMR, calming her heartbeat and the unpleasant fluttering in her stomach.

Lexi leaves before closing time and trudges home through the sweaty DC summer swamp. It's only a fifteen-minute walk, but she needs a shower by the time she gets home, and not just because she wants to wash Sam and the horribleness of this day off her. Not even just because it's the best place to cry when you want to be subtle. Worse luck though, or maybe best luck: Erin is home by the time she's out of the shower, and Erin is not so easily thrown off the scent. Lexi has never been great at hiding her emotions. Her body language screams defeat: she's shuffling her feet close to the floor and making no effort to stand up straight.

Lexi doesn't mind, usually, wearing her heart on her sleeve; it's her default mode. She's also never minded Erin knowing exactly what she's thinking, how she's feeling. But this time, it's tricky. Erin would never say *I told you so*, but she's only human, so she'll definitely be thinking it. And then there's the ickiness of dampening Erin's loved-up joy with her own sadness. Plus the fact that, really, she can't actually blame all of this on Sam. True, there's an argument to be made that he overreacted. But there's another argument to be made, too: that she was, in a sense, playing games with him, like a reporter in a Nineties romcom trying to prove something for an article, and that maybe if she'd been a bit more of an adult, a bit more sensible – a bit more like Erin – about the whole thing, she wouldn't be in this mess.

Lexi flicks the kettle on, because obviously what she needs right now is a cup of tea – the millionth of the day she has drunk in order to self-soothe – and she half-hopes and half-dreads that Erin will ask how she is. She is feeling the change in their friendship especially acutely. She doesn't know how Erin will react, exactly, and she also doesn't know how she *wants* Erin to react.

'Are things okay at the shop?' she asks.

Lexi is almost relieved to be able to deflect. And, after all, she *does* need to process this part of her life. She can't talk to her staff about it, and talking to Sam probably wasn't ever the wisest course of action. What if he uses some of what she told him against her now? She tries to remember what that might be, any insider secrets he could steal, but it feels like poking at a live wound to recall all those conversations they had holding hands or in bed.

'Things at the shop could definitely be better,' she says, trying to control her voice.

'You've weathered storms before, though, right? You'll be okay.'

Lexi nods. It's been an eventful few years – that's for sure – and Pemberley Books is still standing. She thinks, for some reason, of Jacinda Ardern's resignation speech back in 2023. 'There's nothing left in the tank,' she said. That phrase had stuck with Lexi then. She thought she knew how it felt, but now she *really* knows.

But she needs to dig deep. Scrape something up from the bottom of that tank. And she's got to use all her pent-up Sam energy somehow. Work could be the thing that prevents her from slipping into a bottomless pit of lethargy and depression.

Lexi takes a deep breath. 'Yeah.'

Erin looks at her intently. It feels to Lexi like she's looking straight into her soul. It's a superpower of Erin's – a big reason they've been so close. To be known deeply and accepted is a powerful thing. 'There's something else, though, right? Something is bothering you besides work?'

No point trying to hide it; for better or worse, Erin knows her too well. 'Yeah.'

'Sam?'

'Yeah.'

'What happened?'

'We broke up.'

'I – didn't realise you were together?' Her tone is level, judgement-free.

'I'm not sure we were, exactly. But we're definitely not now.'

Lexi weighs up how much she wants to tell her best friend. The amazing sex. The conversation afterwards. All of it? None of it?

'I guess I let slip that he was my Austen experiment,' she says finally. 'He didn't love that.'

'Yeah, I can see why that might feel weird to him. But it seems a little harsh to break up with you because of it.' Lexi is grateful that Erin hasn't said *I told you so*. She'd certainly be well within her rights to.

'I guess he thought I was playing games, and he was serious about me, so . . .' Lexi trails off. Her voice is seriously cracking now.

'Ah.'

Erin is holding out on Lexi, and she can tell. There are things she wants to say.

'C'mon,' Lexi tells her. 'Out with it.'

'Well, just that it sounds like self-sabotage to me,' Erin says. 'He sounds like someone who's not ready to be in a relationship and is coming up with excuses not to be. I'm sorry you got caught up in the middle of that. It sucks, and you deserve better.'

Lexi thinks, for the thousandth time that day, about how it felt to be in bed with Sam. That it seemed like he was ready to commit, ready to risk his heart, and she shattered it. She feels sad and angry that he's hurt her, and she feels like an idiot for going after a lost cause, but she also feels really, really bad for hurting him when he was taking that risk for the first time in so long. When he was trying to do things right.

'Did you sleep with him?'

Lexi knows that Erin isn't judging. Erin knows she's in the minority with the whole waiting for marriage thing. But she also really believes that sex is some kind of magical glue that binds you to someone irreparably and makes any break-up devastating. Lexi doesn't know if she believes that – but in this case, maybe she does. He'd waited; he'd wanted do things right, to get to know each other first. How she feels with him is not necessarily a reliable indicator of a soulmate, but certainly a sign that points in that direction.

'Yeah.'

'Oh, Lexi.' Erin comes over to her and hugs her. Lexi takes it in the spirit it's meant: compassion, empathy. Erin knows it's been a long time for Lexi, knows that for, ugh, eighteen months now – how depressing – she's never made it into bed with a guy from the apps, because by date three (on the rare occasion they got that far) something had always revealed itself to be wrong. Erin knows Lexi was hoping for someone halfway decent to break the long drought with.

'It was pretty damn great, actually,' she tells her through her tears.

Erin laughs. 'Well, good. At least there's that.'

'I feel like such an idiot.'

'We've all been there,' Erin says. 'We've all been bad judges of character.'

Lexi nods, sniffling, pulling away from the hug to find a tissue. Inside her, a small voice argues that in fact she hasn't been a bad judge of character, that she got it right, that Sam lashed out because she hurt him. But she tamps the voice down. She was right when she swore off men. When she swore off falling in love. She doesn't have time to fall apart. She's got a bookshop to rescue, in part thanks to him.

'Screw him,' she says. 'You're right. He's not worth wasting any more energy over.'

'You know what you need? An emergency karaoke session. I'll text the others.'

Beyond a shadow of a doubt, Lexi knows that Erin is right. Short of being with Sam, that is exactly what she needs.

Chapter Thirty-Seven

'I Will Survive' has always been Lexi's go-to karaoke song, and it's never been more apt than this evening. Her friends whoop and clap in all the right places. They haven't said *I told you so*; they seem to just be glad she's seen the light. They're all convinced Sam is the bad one, the one who broke Lexi's heart, the one who can't hold down a relationship, and it's easier to let them believe it. She yells the lyrics, and yells them even louder when Erin joins her. She feels like she's on her way to having her best friend back – maybe it's worth the trade?

It probably isn't worth the hangover she wakes up with, though. Lexi winces when her alarm clock goes off, but luckily she's anticipated this and laid out some bedside paracetamol for this very purpose. And by the time it kicks in, she feels better, and the catharsis of last night has kicked in, too. Screw him, she thinks. Who needs him? She's got her shop, and her shop needs her. That's where she should be putting her energy right now. She's disgusted with herself for ever having let herself get distracted by a guy, and especially by a guy who's the very reason her shop is struggling in the first place.

She stops at Peregrine for her much-needed latte, gathering her strength rather than grabbing that strength to go as she usually does.

'I've never seen you not in motion,' Alli says.

Thankfully, Sam isn't there. Not that she's thinking about him. And not that she's worried about bumping into him. She is a strong, independent woman. She's got this. It's just that it's maybe a little bit easier to be strong and independent and to have this when he's not around to look deep into her soul with those green eyes of his.

Lexi takes several deep breaths as she leaves Peregrine, crosses the road, and pushes the door to the bookshop open. She has seen the light: no more men, no matter how good the sex. She is strong. She is focused. She grins with all her yellowing British teeth at her colleagues tidying books and dusting shelves, getting the place ready for their first customers of the day.

'Morning,' she says brightly.

Hazel and Natalie exchange a look that seems confused. It's brief, and Lexi is pretty sure she isn't meant to have seen it.

'I know I've seemed confused lately,' she tells them. She might as well address the elephant in the room head-on, even though she refuses to give the elephant a name. If she did, they'd – rightly – question her loyalty, her judgement, her sanity. 'But I'm back now. Head in the game. One hundred per cent focused. Ready to hear all your ideas. Ready to take on the world, and especially rival bookshops.'

They exchange another look. One that could be implying that Lexi is coming across as a little unhinged. *Is* she sounding unhinged? Or are they just feeling whiplashed by the sudden gear shift?

In her office, she checks on a sleeping Pippin and starts brainstorming her Jane-themed ideas. She could waste hours down the Pinterest wormhole, and oh, look at that, before she knows it, she *has* wasted hours down the Pinterest wormhole. In her defence, she's found some good merch to sell, and some inspiration for ideas. They could have an annual Jane Austen Day: discounts on her books, panels by authors who've written retellings, giveaways on cute merch. It's unhelpful that Jane Austen was born in December, the busiest time of the year, but *Pride and Prejudice* was published in January, a time of year we can all agree needs some joy injected into it. Not only that, but it's the *end* of the month: by this time, everyone is ready to concede defeat on New Year's resolutions about spending less and admit out loud that they've given up on Dry January. It's a while away, but that will give them time to really plan it out, something to focus on and work towards.

She emails Megan to ensure they have an appropriate stock of relevant books, possibly even exceeding the usual amount. She also contacts Debbie, the merchandiser, so she can start looking for the really good stuff, from socks to mugs to notebooks. And then finally, Tessa, so she can begin assembling assets for announcing and promoting the event. By the time Pippin stretches, emerging from his mid-morning nap, Lexi is emerging too: a new woman, full of energy and ideas. It's all going to be okay. She's got an amazing team. They've got this.

Chapter Thirty-Eight

Without thinking, Lexi lets her steps lead her past Sam's bookshop on the way home from hers. If pressed, she'd have to admit it's only really on the way home if you're willing to make a slight detour. But she wants to stick her tongue out at it (probably just internally, but she isn't sure). She wants Sam to see how put together and not at all falling apart she is. And also . . . maybe she just wants to be near him because she misses him? No, it's definitely not that.

But she pauses, her tongue midway out of her mouth. Because there, in the window, are bright, cheerful, eye-catching covers. Which can only mean one thing. Romance novels.

What. The. Dickens.

This makes no sense. These books make no sense here, in his angular Apple Store of a bookshop, surrounded by Boring But Important Hardbacks. It's not what his Serious Customers come to him for. He's doing this to bait her. To irritate her. To threaten her with increased competition.

Well, it's not going to work. She's not going to let it rankle her. Except that maybe, first, before she rises above it, she's going to tell him what she thinks of this little scheme of his. The last of her post-karaoke hangover has dissipated, and she's got all this adrenaline from her flowing ideas.

Lexi pushes open the door and a buzzer rings out. Not a twinkly, pretty sound like in Pemberley Books – an industrial, joyless one, as is warranted by this shop's image. Sam looks up from behind the till and immediately rearranges his features into a frown. Lexi would have sworn she saw a smile first, but she's probably imagining that.

'Hi,' she says, and then she stops, because she hasn't thought through what she's going to say. Also because she needs a minute to compose herself at his hotness. She somehow forgot how those green eyes make her forget to breathe.

'Alexandra,' he says. Curtly – if anything with four syllables can be curt. Her full name in his mouth has no effect whatsoever. It's purely coincidence that her legs feel a little weaker than they did five minutes ago. 'To what do I owe the pleasure?'

He's mocking her. Repeating back to her what she said to him way back before anything happened, that day he brought the boxes to her and she first had the pleasure of seeing his toned abs. Before she knew what his mouth could do. But it's also a common enough phrase that it would be easy for him to gaslight her if she picked him up on it, so she chooses to let it go. She's got bigger fish to fry right now.

'I was wondering if you stocked any romance novels at all?' she says.

Lexi realises that there might be customers around who might overhear, and discover the collegial bookshop owner thing is all a lie if they hear them fighting. She looks around, but the shop's empty, as she expected: it's technically after closing time, after all. He just hadn't got around to locking the door.

Sam plays the game. 'Yes,' he says. 'We just started stocking them. Can I interest you in enemies-to-lovers, or—'

'Actually, I was looking for something more in the lovers-to-enemies vein.'

'Now, now,' he says, playful, distant. 'There's no need for that.'

But Lexi doesn't feel like playing. 'I think there is.' She's done with nice, with even trying to smile while she talks – that American skill she's never quite mastered, the one that makes you seem polite even while complaining. She's not in the mood to be polite, or even to seem it. 'Romance novels? Really?'

'They're a thriving and growing part of the publishing market,' he says, like she's new at this. Like she hasn't told him this herself.

'I'm aware.'

They stand there, scowling at each other. Then Lexi remembers her argument.

'It's not really very on brand for you, though.'

He shrugs. 'I'm still new around here. Ever evolving. Always looking for ways to bring in more customers.'

'Customers who usually go elsewhere for their romance novels?'

'If that's what it takes, yes.'

She will not cry. She won't.

'Come on,' he says. 'Do you really think people can't be interested in politics and also like romance?'

'Of course not. The intersection of that particular Venn diagram is what produced the most rabid *West Wing* fans.'

'Many of whom live within a one-mile radius of this shop.'

'I'm aware,' she repeats. This patronising parroting of her

226

own marketing strategies is beginning to wear a little thin. She doesn't really have any good arguments. She just hoped that by pointing out facts, by letting him know she's noticed what he's doing, he'd be shamed into standing down. But of course he's not ashamed. He's shameless.

'You're not the only one who can play games, you know,' he says.

Unbidden and very much unwelcome, tears spring to Lexi's eyes.

'I wasn't playing games.'

'You were doing weird Jane Austen role play. I got caught up in the middle of it.'

He's not entirely wrong, so she doesn't bother arguing. 'I really liked you. But now I see you're just a callous and cold-hearted businessman after all, I realise I was wrong.'

Sam winces. He tries to cover it up, but it's too late. Lexi's seen it.

'Is that really what you think of me?'

It isn't. She's a hurt person, hurting another person. She knows that.

'It didn't used to be.' She pauses. 'But now I see I was wrong.'

It unnerves her, how he can just stand there and let silence just – be.

'Okay,' he says eventually. 'If there's nothing else, we're actually closed for business for the evening, so . . .'

Lexi bites her lip to stop from yelling, *Why are you like this?* To stop from yelling, *Get off my patch!* To stop from yelling, *Using romance novels to hurt someone is a new low – you know that?* She swallows all those things down.

'All right,' she says instead. 'Bye.'

Her hand is on the door, and she's almost gone, when he calls out to her.

'Oh, and Lexi?'

She turns to look at him, and her heart does an unhelpful somersault.

'You should probably see someone about that Jane Austen obsession. It's not healthy.'

If this was a film, she would leap across the counter and slap him hard. Instead, she tries not to visibly wince from the blow and she keeps it together just long enough to get around the corner and away from his line of sight.

How could she have got it so wrong? How could she ever have thought that they could coexist on Capitol Hill, not just as booksellers but as human beings? How can she hope to keep her shop alive when it seems like Sam's made it his mission to put her out of business?

So much for her new-found vim and vigour, her great ideas, her Jane Austen Day. Thanks to a rabid and callous capitalist who now hates her for breaking his heart, she doesn't stand a chance.

And how could anyone *not* be obsessed with Jane Austen, anyway? Maybe it's the people who aren't who should see someone.

Chapter Thirty-Nine

Erin's not home when Lexi gets back, so she has no choice but to stuff down her feelings, rewatch an episode of *Derry Girls* to cheer herself up, and then get her laptop out to do more work, because now more than ever, she needs to get her act together. She won't let Sam and his stupid bookshop win. She brings up a list of most anticipated romance novels for the next few months and drafts an email asking Natalie to contact the publishers of as many of them as possible for events. Pemberley Books needs to cement their reputation as The Most Romance-Friendly Bookshop in DC, so that nobody thinks of Sam's shop first when they need their latest fix of Talia Hibbert or they're putting in a pre-order of the just announced new Emily Henry.

She brainstorms ideas for romance-themed merch, but being full of rage isn't exactly conducive to this kind of creativity. The best she can come up with is I♥Pemberley Books, and while she is pretty sure that many of her customers would wear that proudly around DC, it doesn't seem very original.

She drafts an all-staff email asking for romance-themed ideas: merch, competitions, displays, anything. She knows some people will roll their eyes, and not just because she forgot to hit *schedule* and so she's sent this email out at 10 p.m.

Romance never used to be this much of a big deal in the shop, but the section has grown and grown, and Tessa and Natalie are big fans, always making sure there aren't gaps on the bookshelves. Restocking, putting books face out, and lovingly tending to what they see as their patch.

But there are still plenty of Pemberley Books staff with other preferences, and those who like to remind Lexi of the importance of being a general bookstore, and not just a place to hang out for young professionals in need of good vibes and light relief.

And Lexi wants that too! Of course she does. She loves all books (except, perhaps, for the Very Important Nonfiction beloved by Washingtonians and sold by the truckload by Sam). Also, to be very practical about it, there's a bigger profit margin on literary fiction in hardback than on paperback romance novels. It's just, romance is more . . . fun? Lexi has been out with some of the shop's regulars to bemoan the state of DC dating and mentally cast their favourite actors in theoretical adaptations of the novels they've enjoyed. She also loves the aesthetic vibe of romance novels: the bright colours, the fun covers, but also, crucially, the fact that they're all the same size so they look great on the shelves together.

Some of her staff are impatient with her increasing emphasis on romance novels. But needs must: she's taught them that particular British expression. This isn't just about her predilection for happy endings or the genre her perhaps-distant-relative arguably invented; it's also about survival. She includes a line in the email to that effect, because she doesn't want them to think that she hasn't heard their concerns or doesn't care about them. A happy bookseller is a good bookseller, because enthusiasm is about eighty per cent of the job.

Not just that, but she values them as human beings. Bookish people really are the best people, and meeting one always feels a little like coming home. Lexi isn't naïve enough to buy into the notion of workplaces being like families, but still, her booksellers feel like a little bit more than just employees: kindred spirits, at least. And that might not be family, or it might be more like distant cousins than brothers and sisters, but it's pretty damn valuable all the same.

Lexi is still at the dining-room table with her laptop when Erin comes home, but she mutters hi and walks straight past her, wanting, probably to stay in her loved-up bubble.

Two hours later, Lexi hasn't moved. Is she filling every minute with work so that she doesn't have to think about Sam and how much she misses what they so briefly had? Obviously, yes. But also, because of him, she *needs* to work every hour God sends so the shop can stay afloat, running not to get ahead but instead not to fall too far behind.

Six hours after she flops into bed, her alarm goes off again, and she rubs her eyes, discombobulated, before she realises it's Wednesday morning and the alarm is so early because it would normally be time for a piano lesson. She wiggles her fingers, vaguely scale-like, in tribute to that particular dream, dead in the water. Or maybe not. Maybe she'll find another teacher. She was quite enjoying getting to know music theory and bashing out the odd tune. Okay, so a large part of the enjoyment was Sam's breath on her neck, his general proximity, the beckoning of that sofa bed.

But without those distractions, maybe she'll stand a chance of actually becoming a better piano player rather than a constantly distracted one.

She's awake now; she might as well get up. She's not going to get back to sleep after the screeching of her alarm and now, of course, intruding thoughts of Sam. She reaches for her phone and opens her email app. There's an email from Tessa, ostensibly a reply to hers – she was up late too, replied at midnight – full of enthusiasm. But it's an unmistakable compliment sandwich, the universally recognised tool of the emotionally intelligent who have bad news to deliver. *Love these brilliant ideas!* it starts and *So great to see the enthusiasm for romance!* it ends, and in between: *If you've got a chance to talk today, I have something I need to tell you.*

Lexi's stomach drops. This isn't good. She's lost her, probably: her fifty-cent pay rise, ill-advised and forbidden by her accountant, definitely wasn't enough to cover the increase in Tessa's rent, even with the extra hours. She's been doing extra marketing, spending ages battling algorithms and making TikTok and Instagram reels. Engagement stats are up and looking good. The shop can't afford to lose her. But the shop couldn't afford to keep her, either, and now look.

Sure, she writes. *I'll be in early today. 10 a.m., before your shift starts?*

Lexi lies back down, snuggles under the covers. She's so tempted to stay there for a while. But she channels her grandmother, her endless energy that kept the shop going for forty years.

Needs must.

Chapter Forty

When Lexi walks into the shop and locks eyes with Tessa, her suspicions are confirmed. Tessa looks sad and guilty, and is already pulling on the ends of her cardigan sleeves. *Here we go*, Lexi thinks. *Be kind*, she tells herself. Tessa loves working here; she's only leaving because she has no choice, and she gave Lexi forewarning. *Be a good boss to the end*, she tells herself. *Be nice.*

'Do you want to do this in the office?' Lexi asks Tessa. 'Or we could go and grab a coffee?'

Tessa's eyes light up a little. Understandably, the prospect of good coffee is hard to resist. But she swallows and says, 'Your office is fine. It won't take long anyway.'

Lexi's heart is in her throat as she walks down the steps ahead of her. When they get to the office, close the door, and sit down, she decides to save Tessa the trouble of saying the words.

'So, Tessa, what's up? Are you leaving us?'

She bites her upper lip and nods. The tears come immediately. 'I'm sorry. I love this place. But ...'

'Capitalism,' Lexi says gently. 'Love of a job doesn't pay the bills.'

She nods again.

'So is this your two weeks' notice?' Lexi tries to swallow her panic. Her sadness, too.

'Yes.'

'Okay.' Lexi reaches out and squeezes her shoulder. 'It's okay, you know. I understand. I just wish I could have done more to keep you. You've been a real asset to the shop.'

'Thank you for saying that,' Tessa replies, studying her sandals, her fresh pedicure, the kind you get done for an interview.

'Did you find a good new job at least?'

'Yes.'

Lexi waits. Does Tessa not want to tell her? Is there a reason she doesn't want to tell her?

Oh.

Oh no.

'Is it another bookshop?'

'Yes,' she says. 'I'm sorry.'

'It's okay,' Lexi tells her. But of course it isn't. And of course – of *course* – she doesn't need to ask which other bookshop.

She is going to kill him.

She is going to kill him with her own bare hands, if that's what it takes.

Chapter Forty-One

Lexi can't believe that for the second time in two days she's about to march into Sam's shop to yell at him, but here she is. This time, she doesn't wait for the end of the day, when she might happen to be walking past his shop. This time, she barges straight out of Pemberley Books five minutes after Tessa's gone upstairs and heads straight there, full of purpose, not a whiff of hesitancy about her.

When she pushes open the door, she's devastated to see that Great Expectations is full of people, and some of them are even paging through romance novels. And is that Daniela in the corner? Daniela who always – always – comes to Lexi for book recommendations? It's probably not the best time to conduct a cold-blooded, bare-handed murder of a rival. Maybe not even a good time to yell, but she can overlook that.

In the corner, a workman is measuring up a wall in a way that looks suspiciously like New Developments are being planned. The employee behind the counter looks nervously at Lexi, knowing exactly who she is and what's at stake.

'Hello,' Lexi says, keeping her voice as neutral as possible. 'Is Sam here?'

He exchanges a look with a colleague who's shelving books. Lexi suspects they may have been warned to look out for her, to keep her at bay. She's certainly not about to let that stop her.

'He's in the back,' he says eventually.

Luckily, Lexi knows where the back is and how to get there, through a doorway behind the measuring workman.

'It's private back there,' the shelving bookseller says, a note of panic in her voice. Perfect for a murder, then.

'I won't be a minute,' she tells her. Honestly, Lexi is kind of impressed at her own boldness. She can imagine the booksellers exchanging another look. It makes her smile.

The back is tiny in this shop, so Sam is right there in front of her when she walks in.

'Hello,' she says.

'H-i?' He's startled. She's thrown him off by coming back here, into his sacred space. Good. For once, he's the one on the back foot, standing awkwardly behind his desk. 'You're not meant to be back here.'

'I know that. But I needed to yell at you, and this seems like an appropriate place to do that.'

He sighs, poor put-upon Sam. She can't believe she ever thought he was hot, with his stupid green eyes and his stupid square jawline. 'What have I done this time?'

'Don't get cute with me. You stole my marketing person.'

'Ah.'

'That's all you've got to say for yourself? *Ah?*'

'All's fair in love and capitalism.'

'I hope you're paying her well at least.' Lexi has come as close to him as she can, with just the desk between them, not a hair's width more. She can feel his breath on her face. She tries not think of how it felt on her neck. Or on the rest of her body.

'I am, actually.'

'Good. She deserves it.'

They're standing facing each other, breathing hard. There's all this anger, all this competitiveness, but also . . . something else. The hairs on Lexi's arms are standing up in what she assumes is anger, though the dampness between her legs doesn't feel much like anger. And, of course, she remembers the last time they were breathing this hard. She remembers it being under slightly more pleasant circumstances, with less dust and considerably fewer clothes. Sam's face is increasingly pink; dollars to doughnuts he's remembering it too. Lexi wonders what it says about her that as well as wanting to kill him, she also wants to rip his clothes off?

This is all very confusing for her. It must be the stress of worrying about the shop.

'We're really doing this, huh?' he asks.

'Doing what?'

'This.'

Then he leans in and – what the heck? – kisses her.

Her body responds before her mind gets a chance to, guttural noises in the back of her throat betraying her, letting him know that as much as she's tried to ignore it, she's thought about him way too much in the last couple of days. Her vibrator, recently upgraded to one with several extra speeds, hasn't come close to making up for the lack of him. The desk between them digs into her hips as she presses herself as close to him as she can get. They could so easily do the movie thing, sweep the paper off it, and put it to other uses.

But then the door behind them creaks, someone clears their throat, and they fall apart, caught like two schoolkids, breathing hard still, looking at each other as if daring each other to . . . what? Admit they missed each other? Admit the stupidity of this war?

But it's not stupid. Sam knows how much the shop means to her. He knows how hard she's worked to keep it not only afloat but thriving. And still he's determined to wrest all this from her because . . . why? Because she used a few time-honoured tricks to get him to fall in love with her?

She must be out of her mind to let her guard down like this. To cheapen what she feels about the shop and what Sam is doing to it.

'Bye,' she says, vaguely in his direction, scurrying out of there like the rat she feels she is.

Lexi trudges back to the shop, defeated, her body on high alert – because: that kiss! – and also experiencing the whiplash of an unfulfilled promise. Her mind, however, is going in a thousand different directions. She has to find someone who's as good at social media and marketing as Tessa is. She has to beat Sam at this game, not only to keep the shop going but to salvage what's left of her dignity. What if the kiss was some misguided attempt to distract her, to throw her off course, to stop her minding about Tessa? It hasn't worked, obviously, but she has to *prove* to him that it hasn't worked, and prove it to herself, too. After all: what are men compared to books and bookshops?

In her office, Lexi plots last month's expenses and income onto the graph of doom. Somehow, it's getting worse: the lines are converging. Admittedly, she's spent some money on marketing this month that will only pay off at a later stage, but right now it looks scary. Once those lines meet, the shop will be in the red, otherwise known, in polite society at least, as up the creek without a paddle.

All this drama, and it's not even eleven o'clock yet. Lexi is emotionally spent and physically exhausted from her shortened night and the earlier rush of adrenaline. She picks up her phone: it's early back in London, but she needs her sister. She feels so alone on this side of the Atlantic, carrying the weight of this bookshop without either a romantic or a business partner, and more or less without a flatmate to bounce ideas off. It feels crushing, all of a sudden: these people's jobs, the vibrant centre of the community, all dependent on her being able to keep two lines apart on a graph.

She looks over at Pippin, purring away, his morning snooze still well underway, oblivious to the fact that she could really do with the soft weight of him in her lap. She types her sister's name into her phone, and she doesn't even know what she's going to write until the words appear, fully formed under her thumb.

I want to come home.

It's been ages, she types back, almost immediately. *It would be nice to see you.*

But Lexi doesn't just want to *see* her sister. She doesn't just want to visit. If everything is falling apart here, she can't stay in this town, in this country. She needs to go home to Monster Munch, apple Tango, and greasy caffs with proper bacon and no threat of Sam walking in.

No, I mean come home *come home.*

She watches the dots on her screen as her sister no doubt struggles to think of something wise and compassionate to say.

What's happened?

Everything's going wrong. Bookshop accounts aren't adding up. Erin's moving out soon. DC men are terrible.

DC men in general, or . . . ?

Okay, well, one particular man at the moment.

Ah.

More dots, doing their dance. And then:

Remember what the Reverend Mother always says.

She smiles at the reference to their many, many childhood afternoons watching *The Sound of Music* – something that, despite their age gap, they would both enjoy: Stephanie would relate to Liesl or aspire to be Maria, and Lexi would cycle through Gretl, Marta, Brigitta, Louisa. They could both recite the entire film verbatim at this point, and Lexi knew what Stephanie meant. The Reverend Mother was a big fan of not running away from your problems but facing them head-on: hence the glass-shattering rendition of 'Climb Every Mountain'.

Yeah, Lexi writes. *I know.*

But you should definitely come and visit soon.

Lexi's finger hovers over the British Airways app. In this moment, she's very tempted to book a one-way ticket, warbling Reverend Mother or not. It's definitely been too long since she visited home; since she had any kind of break. No wonder she's losing it slightly, or maybe more than slightly.

Book me a table at the India Grill. It's been too long since I had a peshwari naan.

No problem. Call me later?

Lexi sends Stephanie a thumbs up and takes a deep breath. Even just the thought of speaking to her sister, of going home before too long – that should be enough to get her through the day. Providing, of course, that nothing else goes wrong. Which, these days, seems like a big thing to ask of the universe. It's not even midday yet. There's still plenty of time for bad news.

Chapter Forty-Two

Lexi is no good to anyone at the shop today, so she leaves early to catch her sister before it's too late in the UK. And also a little bit to escape the weird vibe today: Tessa is putting on a brave and cheerful face for the customers and the other staff are being kind to her, but they all know what she's doing is treachery of sorts. Lexi gets it, and the person she's maddest at in all of this is unquestionably Sam, but it's still a little icky and awkward – not least because she herself has been far more treacherous than Tessa has.

'So,' Stephanie says. 'Spill. What's up? You love DC. Something bad must be happening if you want to leave it all behind.'

'Somethings, plural.'

Lexi can barely get through those two words without her voice cracking. It's a good thing she foresaw this and brought a loo roll into her room for this call to wipe her eyes: more efficient than tissues, quite honestly, even if it's somehow ten times more pathetic. She fills her sister in on pretty much everything, except for this morning's weirdly charged confrontation: she's not sure how to explain it, even to herself. She tells Stephanie about Sam, and the bookshop, and Erin, and how everything she loved about her life here is unravelling at once, pretty much like the loo roll she is clutching.

'Why do you think Sam is acting this way?' she asks her sister, always eager for her wisdom.

'Hurting people hurt people,' she says. 'I think it's as simple as that. He's lashing out.'

'Do you think it's revenge?'

'It could be a little bit of that too.'

'I didn't mean to hurt him. I didn't even think it *would* hurt him to know that this all started as a bit of a challenge. I *wanted* us to fall in love. That's no different to going on the apps, necessarily.'

'Nobody likes to feel manipulated.'

They talk about everything else: Tessa and the shop, those pesky lines on the graph, how Lexi never sees Erin anymore, how she still doesn't have a plus-one to the wedding. But all along she's thinking about that phrase: *hurting people hurt people*. Wondering if there's a clue to stopping the pain in there. Wondering if they can stop hurting each other long enough to keep both bookshops alive (or at least hers; truth be told, she's less bothered about his).

Then they talk about Stephanie's kids, their dance recitals and football matches and school mishaps. Lexi feels a weird tug in her gut, like she always does when they talk about her niece and nephew: she wishes she could be there, part of their daily lives, the little ups and downs of childhood, the scraped knees and stories at bedtime. When life was good in DC, Lexi could quieten those feelings with the knowledge that she was doing the right thing with her life. But now it feels like too high a price, to be this sad and this far away from her family.

She wants to honour her grandmother's legacy, to keep her alive through this shop. But it's more important to be there for living people than for those who've passed away, and not even books can fill the ache in Lexi's hearts for human connection. As she puts down the phone reluctantly – bedtime for Stephanie – Lexi is less sure than ever that she's in the right place.

Chapter Forty-Three

As luck would have it, this is the week of the monthly staff meeting: pizzas from down the road, leftover wine from the various book clubs, and a recap of upcoming events and buzzy book releases. Lexi always loves gathering her staff in one place – like a reunion of cousins who rarely see each other but have that one important thing in common, whether that's a long-lost great-grandparent or, in their case, a love of books and particular takes on book-related neuroses. It gives Lexi energy, hope and pride to see all her lovely and enthusiastic staff in a room together.

This week, though, they're sharing that room with a couple of rather large elephants: Tessa's tearful defection and Lexi's recent demeanour. She wouldn't blame anyone for feeling a bit sick from the roller-coaster: some days she's borderline manic, whipping herself into a frenzy over all the potentially great new initiatives they can try, in order to get that graph moving in the right direction. Other days, she moves slowly and sadly, projecting an air of resignation. She knows that if she was working with a boss like her, she'd be whispering with her colleagues, speculating.

Elijah and Debbie cast what seem like furtive glances at her as she sits herself down with a big box of cupcakes – not usually a feature of these meetings, but Lexi knows what Mary Poppins says about a spoonful of sugar.

They get into it: the books, the events, the new initiatives related to romance, and why they matter.

'As I said in my email, Sam at Great Expectations has decided, in his infinite wisdom, that his customers want romance novels too. We're losing ground to him as it is, and I refuse to concede this one.'

There's some vigorous nodding around the room. Lexi isn't the only one who finds it more than mildly annoying that Sam is increasingly encroaching on their patch.

And then Lexi unfurls a large copy of the graph of doom and Blu-Tacks it to the wall.

'I need to show you all this, just so you can see how things are going. Just to stress, this is nobody's fault. You are all working very hard and very well. There are circumstances beyond our control, like the rising price of books and competition from up the road. I've been wanting to give you all a raise for a long time—' Lexi can almost feel the room run out of air as everyone takes in a breath '—but until these lines diverge a little bit more, I'm afraid that won't be possible. I'm so sorry. You lot are the best team anyone could ask for. You've given so much to this shop, and I'm so grateful. But we're all going to have to work even harder for a while.'

There's silence. Nobody knows what to say to this. Lexi imagines they're thinking of plenty of responses, none of them appropriate to say to a boss: *Are you kidding me? We've worked our asses off for years!* And maybe, just maybe: *So sleeping with the enemy wasn't really worth it, huh?*

In the end, Natalie breaks the silence, and with it the tension.

'This calls for a cupcake,' she says, and nervous laughter ripples around the circle.

The box is passed around and people fill their faces with sugar, grateful not to have to think of anything to say for a while.

Lexi is just glad to have made it through the meeting without crying. Honestly, that might be her greatest achievement yet.

Chapter Forty-Four

The shop is short-staffed the next day, so Lexi jumps on the till for a couple of hours. She likes getting to do that. Honestly, she wishes she did it more. She doesn't particularly like being squirrelled away in the office as much as she has been lately, especially when it means looking at cheerless graphs. Give her direct contact with customers any day.

The control freak in her is glad to be in charge, glad to be the one to make the final decisions and sign off on things, and, of course, glad to make the shop her little kingdom, the place where she gets to decide what's what. But sometimes, she wonders if she wouldn't be happier as a bookseller, recommending great books and striking up conversations at the till: *Ooh, yes, I read her last one, she's great, isn't she?* Or *I stayed up till 2 just to find out how it ended.* Or *Did you know the sequel comes out next year?* She likes pulling faces at cute babies, watching customers interact with Pippin, and offering sweets from the treat jar to well-behaved children. (The less well-behaved ones take them without asking.)

She likes it, too, when she gets to tell people they've spent enough to earn a free book, thanks to the shop's loyalty scheme – who doesn't love a free book? There's no card needed or anything like that; their name alone unlocks the magic. And today, the third name Lexi asks for makes her do a double take.

'Amanda Delarue,' says the blonde.

Lexi manages not to vocalise the sharp intake of breath she's done on the inside or mention that Sam never said just how beautiful she was. She glances at the address that is showing for Amanda on the computer screen: looks like she's living in Chicago these days.

'Visiting from out of town?' Lexi asks her, making seemingly polite chit-chat. 'I'm not sure I've seen you around before.'

'Yep,' she says, her phone hovering over the credit card reader. 'I used to live in DC, but I left when I broke up with my ex. Coming back to see if I can rekindle the flame.'

People really will tell their booksellers anything.

'Rekindle the flame with DC?'

Amanda pockets her phone and laughs. 'No, I think that's a lost cause. With my ex.'

Lexi hopes it isn't obvious how hard she is swallowing.

'Oh, wow.' She hands Amanda's books over to her in a white paper bag, stickered with the shop's logo. 'Well, good luck.'

Lexi's hand itches to grab her phone and text Sam. *I think I just met your ex?* Or *Did you know your ex is in town?* Or *Amanda is prowling the neighbourhood!* But, of course, he probably knows already. Probably invited her himself. Probably told her to come to the shop on a reconnaissance mission and to further punish or discombobulate her.

Well, joke's on him: she's already at maximum discombobulation.

Lexi is so discombobulated, in fact, that when she heads back down to the office she doesn't notice straight away that Pippin isn't in his basket. To be fair, it's around midday, and sometime around now is when he usually rouses himself from his slumber, has a big stretch, which Lexi, of course, narrates – *Biiig stretch!* – and he either jumps onto her lap or has a wander around the shop, looking for a patch of sun to enjoy, or rubbing against the legs of friendly-looking bookshop browsers.

Sometimes, he'll retreat immediately to the office after the trauma of being manhandled by an overly enthusiastic child, but mostly he happily wanders among the bookshelves for a while before taking a break on the sofa in the young adult section, snoozing but ever alert to the constant possibility of those overly enthusiastic children. *Yes,* she imagines him thinking, *I do have beautiful patches of ginger and black and white. Thank you for noticing. Yes, I am special: only one in 3,000 tortoiseshell cats are male, and yet here I am.*

Pippin's getting old now: twelve years old and serious, no longer the playful kitten he was when her grandmother first got him. Lexi had her best DC trip that summer: not only did she have the shop to roam in, she also had a kitten to cuddle with when she got tired of talking to customers or, more likely, when they got tired of talking to her, an over-enthusiastic twenty-year-old who didn't yet know she was a bookstore-owner-in-training.

Like Pippin, and like Lexi, the shop has matured and evolved. Along with the redecoration when she took over, Lexi rearranged the sections a little, making more space for romance and for non-book merch like socks and tote bags and puzzles and journals – fun things beloved of bookworms but that also happen to have a higher profit margin, helping to keep the bookshop thriving.

Socks aren't enough, now, though: they need something more drastic. And because Lexi is thinking about that all day, it takes her until closing time to realise she hasn't seen Pippin since the night before. She tries not to panic: there's a million places he could be, places he probably explores endlessly after everyone else has gone home: the overstock cupboard, the staff kitchen, the gap under the stairs.

Lexi walks around shaking his dry food and making kissing sounds with her mouth: '*Pippin! Pippin! You're not in trouble, I just want to know where you are.*' But when he doesn't appear, Lexi's panic rises, and so do her tears. As if it wasn't enough that she's sinking her grandmother's beloved shop, now she's lost her beloved cat, too?

More shaking, more crying out: nothing.

He's not on or under the sofa.

He's not crawled below the shelves in the room of advance review copies.

He's not hiding from any overly enthusiastic children in the stockroom.

He's nowhere.

Crap.

Lexi texts Erin: *If you were a bookstore cat and you'd decided to have an adventure, where would you go?*

She texts her sister, a little less light-heartedly: *Help! I've lost Pippin!*

But it's 1 a.m. back home, and her sister is asleep, and it's date night here and Erin's out with John. So Lexi does the only reasonable thing: she sits on the bottom steps and cries. Then, when it turns out that hasn't really helped either, she does the whole calling/shaking/kissing noises routine again.

Still nothing.

Defeated, she locks up and leaves. It's not exactly as if she can sleep here on the off chance Pippin decides to materialise overnight. He's always been an indoor cat, but after twelve years of that maybe he's decided to go and see the big wide world. Lexi wishes he'd asked her first, given her a chance to warn him about the dangers of that world and to let her talk him out of that.

Firstly, there are cars. Cars! Lexi isn't sure that Pippin has ever seen a car before, and certainly not in recent months. What if he doesn't know to get out of the way? Her heart is thumping now. She's too scared to look at the pavement or the road. What if she finds her little furry companion squashed? She can't bear it. The only acceptable way for Pippin to die is peacefully in his sleep after a long and happy life. But it would be preferable if he didn't die at all, and certainly not in the midst of the bookshop falling apart and Lexi's heart being broken by the man responsible for that.

Unless it's an omen. What if it's an omen? An omen that no matter what Lexi does, the shop is doomed? Ugh.

Lexi feels so lonely, walking home to an empty house, after dark. She thinks again about England, her sister, her niece and nephew. Her sister has a spare room. She could land there, sort herself out.

And then she feels bad for even thinking of herself when Pippin is out here, all alone and no doubt terrified . . . or at least hopefully, because the alternative is unthinkable.

Usually, Lexi listens to a podcast on her way home, but today she has her ears open to anything that might alert her to him. When she gets home, she'll post on social media and ask for help from the local blogs: a bookshop cat is an institution, after all, and a tortoiseshell is pretty recognisable. But, in the meantime, she tries to stay alert.

And then she hears it: a scratching sound in one of the trees. She looks up, and there he is, stuck and scared. Lexi laughs, relieved: '*Pippin! What are you doing up there?*' He's alive. But elation quickly turns to dismay as she realises she has no immediate way of getting him down from the tree. She has two options: walk back to the shop, head down to the basement, retrieve her ladder, and lug it all the way here. Or, go round the corner, mere feet away, and see if Sam has a ladder she can borrow. Either way, she's going to have to go up a ladder, and she feels woozy just at the thought of it. Anything for this cat, though, right?

The thought of trekking all the way back to the basement of Pemberley Books seems too much to Lexi right now, after this exhausting day. As does having to interact with Sam, but . . . marginally less so? Lexi decides that she'll see if the light is still on in his shop, and if not, she'll have to resort to another plan. Maybe one involving a hot fireman? She's heard they're good at rescuing cats – that they spend way too much of their time doing it, in fact.

But Sam's light is on, so Plan A it is.

Lexi knocks, quietly. Because if Sam doesn't hear her, that's another reason to go for the fireman plan.

But he does.

'Hi,' he says, with something like tenderness in his voice. But then he remembers they're fighting. 'Did you come to yell at me some more?'

Ah, yes. Asking him for a favour after the way they left it last time – Lexi scurrying away after an ill-advised moment of hate-fuelled passion – is perhaps not her classiest move. But what can she say? She's desperate.

'No. I have come to you in my hour of need.' She's trying to charm him with her wit and with Austen-style dialogue, but really she just wants to fall into his arms and have him hug her.

'What's up?' His face is softer than she remembers from their last encounter.

'My cat, Pippin—'

'The bookstore cat?'

She nods. 'Yep. He escaped somehow, and now he's stuck up a tree. That tree over there in fact,' she says, pointing in its vague direction. She pauses, hoping he'll fill in the gaps. But he doesn't say anything. 'I know you probably hate me, but I was hoping that you might have a ladder I can borrow and that if you do, you might be able to be the bigger person here and help me out.'

Despite himself, maybe, he breaks into a smile. And oh, Lexi has missed that smile. 'Sure.'

Sam disappears into the shop and comes back with a metal ladder. Lexi swallows hard. She hates those things. As if in sympathy, Pippin, watching on from his perch, gives a plaintive meow.

'I'm coming,' she shouts towards him. Trying to sound soothing while shouting is definitely a challenge. Lexi isn't really sure she's managed it. Then she swallows hard, preparing to ask Sam a favour. 'Would you mind holding the ladder while I climb it?'

Sam smiles again, amused. But not mocking. At least Lexi doesn't think so. 'Sure,' he says again.

He locks the shop door behind him and she leads him to the tree. Sam leans the ladder against it and Lexi looks at it, willing herself to be the kind of fearless woman who isn't remotely fazed by the prospect of climbing up a ladder.

But, in fact, she *is* fazed. Very fazed indeed.

Still, in an effort of bravado, she makes it up the first five rungs. Pippin sees her, his eyes flashing dark, mirroring her own fear.

'It's okay, little one,' Lexi says, as much to her inner child as to the cat. And then she realises that in order to grab hold of Pippin, she's going to have to let go of the ladder, and she freezes to the spot, her legs jelly-like at the prospect.

'You okay?' Sam asks. His tone is kind. For a second, she lets herself believe he is a safe place.

'I don't like heights,' she tells him.

'Here,' he says, without hesitating. 'Let me.'

Feminism be damned, she doesn't need to be told twice. Any excuse to get off that ladder. She is not above being rescued if it means not having to deal with heights.

Lexi clings to the ladder until her legs feel steady again and the nausea recedes. 'Please don't judge me,' she says. 'There are lots of things I'm good at. Heights just don't happen to fall into that category.'

'I know that,' he says. 'It's okay.'

Going down the ladder is somehow even worse than going up it. On a day like today, in a week like this one, it's a miracle she's still standing, quite frankly. She has to take it very slowly. She can feel her cheeks burning from the embarrassment. She is a strong and capable women, and yet.

'I'll catch you if you fall,' Sam says. 'I'm right here.'

Something about that sentence makes her woozy, and this time it's not the height. It's the fact that he hasn't made fun of her or made her feel ridiculous. He's acknowledged her very real fear and let her know that he's here for her in the midst of it. She'd want to kiss him, if she didn't hate him so much. Gah – maybe she should have just called a hot fireman instead?

She has a flashback to her first memory of Stephanie grabbing her hand and pulling her back from the road she was getting ready to run across. In her mind now, there were thousands of cars rushing towards them. But memory is a funny thing; maybe that wasn't the case at all. Maybe the risk, then as now, was in fact minimal. And still, she was kept safe by someone she loved.

Lexi controls her jelly legs and makes it down to the safety of the pavement. She reaches out to Sam to steady herself, and he lets her put the palm of her hand on his chest. Instantly, that treacherous spark of something like electricity is back. She wants to lean against him with her full weight and have him hold her, let the rhythmic beating of his heart steady her. But she hates him. So she doesn't.

'I know it's pathetic,' she tells him, by way of apology, reluctantly removing her hand.

'It's not pathetic,' he says, in a soft voice. 'We all have things we're afraid of. Fears that make us do irrational things.'

'You're not afraid of anything, though.'

Sam snorts. 'I'm afraid of plenty.'

'Like what?'

She wonders if he might be on the brink of telling her, but then Pippin resumes his meowing, as if to remind Sam and Lexi why they're there. It's not for a heart-to-heart about their inner lives. It's to get his silly little self out of that silly big tree.

'Cats,' Sam says. 'I'm afraid of cats.'

Lexi laughs. 'This one's nice,' she tells him. 'I promise.'

'Okay.'

She reluctantly lets go of Sam and holds the ladder instead.

As if it were nothing, as if he were on firm ground, Sam climbs up one, two, four, eight steps.

'Here, little kitty,' he says tenderly. He makes the kissing cat calling noises and Pippin meows uncertainly. 'I'm not going to hurt you,' he says. 'I'm nice, I promise.'

Unless you own a bookshop, Lexi wants to clarify. *Then he might*. But it doesn't quite seem like the right moment to bring that up.

Chapter Forty-Five

Sam's up there for what seems like an interminably long time, both he and Lexi coaxing Pippin down. And then, finally, Pippin caves, and lets Sam pick him up. By the light of the street lamp, Lexi watches him painstakingly climb down, with one arm around her cat and one arm to steady himself on the ladder. It's a relief when they both make it down.

'Pippin,' she says, taking him from Sam. 'You silly goose. What's with all this adventuring all of a sudden?'

He strains against her, wanting to be let down onto firm ground. Frankly, she doesn't blame him. She puts him down and he stays put, probably enjoying the feeling of solid ground. It must be nice. It's been a while since Lexi had that experience. He brushes against her legs, over and over, and she bends down to stroke him, reassure him.

Sam leans the ladder against the tree and exhales. 'Anything else you need me for?'

Standing in the moonlight on this quiet Capitol Hill street, she can think of a few things she needs him for. But she swallows hard and restrains herself. He's most likely back with his ex-girlfriend, after all. He's decided that Lexi is playing games and he refuses to believe her when she tells him otherwise. She has no business thinking the thoughts currently running through her mind.

'No more cats stuck up trees,' she tells him. 'So I think we're good.'

'Okay.'

'But seriously.' She waits for him to meet her gaze. 'That was pretty heroic. Thank you.'

'All part of the service,' he says. 'We like to provide a holistic experience at Great Expectations. If that includes rescuing pets, well . . . that's what we do.'

'Even pets belonging to rival bookstores?'

She wishes she hadn't said that – reminded him how much they hate each other and all the reasons why. Because right here in the moonlight, with him having just rescued her grandmother's cat, she doesn't particularly want to hate him. Or for him to hate her.

'We don't discriminate,' he says finally, after way too long a pause. 'All cats matter.'

Lexi wants to hug him, but she's scared to. She doesn't trust herself.

'I better be going, I guess,' he says. 'If you're sure about the *no more cats up trees* thing.'

'I'm sure,' she says regretfully.

Sam nods and wipes his forehead with the back of his hand.

Lexi catches sight of something on his arm. 'Wait. What's that?'

'What?'

'That red thing on your arm.' It looked like a scratch, but she only caught sight of it briefly, so she can't be sure.

Sam turns his arm over to look at it, as if noticing it for the first time. 'Oh, that? It's nothing.'

Lexi grabs his arm – and there's that static again. 'It's not nothing. That looks like a really bad scratch. It looks like it could hurt a lot.'

He shrugs, but she looks closely at his moonlit face, and he does seem a little pale.

'C'mon,' she says, 'let's get you cleaned up. I've got a first-aid kit in my shop basement.'

'I'm okay. Really.'

'Listen,' she tells him. 'You just rescued my cat and the ungrateful little sod attacked you. The least I can do is disinfect your wound.'

He laughs. '*Wound* makes it sounds like I've been at war.'

Lexi lets the words hang in the air because, yes, they have been at war. And this is just a temporary truce.

'I need you at your best so I can fight you properly,' she tells him. 'Otherwise it's just too easy, and where's the fun in that?'

Sam smiles, more at ease now he knows Lexi isn't setting some kind of love trap for him. 'Fair enough,' he says. 'Okay.'

It takes longer than usual to make it down the street and round the corner, stopping every few feet to check Pippin is still following them. Then she has to unroll the metal grate at the entrance to the alley, open the door, and disable the alarm. It probably would have made more sense to do this at his shop, if he has a first-aid kit, which if he's following the law, he should. But Lexi has tea that she can make for him – very important after a battle wound, if underrated by Americans. And it's time for Pippin to go home, anyway. Despite how tired he must be after his ordeal, he gallops down the stairs as soon as Lexi opens the door, and when she and Sam make it to the office, she sees he's made a dash straight for his basket. Poor little guy. First things first: she fills his food bowl and gives him reassuring strokes until he starts to purr. Then she turns her attention fully back to Sam.

'Right,' she tells him. 'Sit. First, I'm going to make you a cup of tea.'

'Oh,' he says, getting ready to politely decline. Lexi has seen that look in American eyes before. She knows what it means.

'Non-negotiable,' she says, and bizarrely, this shuts him up.

She goes to the staff kitchen and flicks on the kettle, then fishes around for antiseptic cream and bandages. She winces at the thought of antiseptic on the cut, but Sam is a big strong man. He can take it.

'This might sting a little,' she says, in her best kindergarten teacher voice, as she sits down opposite him. 'But I know you can be brave.'

In response, he sticks his tongue out at her. Lexi is enjoying the playfulness. It feels flirting-adjacent, and that will have to be enough.

He nods. 'I can be brave.'

But there's still a sharp intake of breath when she gently dabs at his cut with cotton wool.

'Sorry.' She says it softly because the moment feels strangely intimate, and she doesn't want to scare that intimacy away.

'It's not your fault,' he says, a standard American response to her too-frequent need to apologise. Only, in this case, it's not quite true. Holding his arm with one hand, wiping his cut with the other, Lexi points out as much.

'Well, it kind of is a little. I asked for help with my cat, and that's how you got injured, so . . .'

'Fair point.'

His skin is warm to the touch and feels good under hers.

And, up close, despite the antiseptic, she can still make out his distinctive scent: clean laundry, salty skin, a hint of cedar and musk. Up close to Sam, Lexi hopes her breath doesn't smell too much of stale coffee; she wishes she had Tic Tacs in her bag and that she'd bothered with perfume this morning. Truth be told, she's not even totally sure she bothered with under-eye depuffing cream, and she knows the bags must be spectacular. And as for her hair . . . who knows what *that's* doing. Which is fine, because this isn't a date. This is her putting her cat's rescuer back together.

'He was afraid,' Sam says softly. 'He was afraid, so he lashed out.'

He searches Lexi's eyes with his. He clearly wants to know if what he's said has registered, that she knows he's not just talking about Pippin now.

'A common response, I think,' she says, making herself look straight at Sam.

He gives her a smile, sad and barely noticeable. 'Yeah.'

Lexi unwraps the bandage and gently wraps it around Sam's arm. She has this weird, unexpected thought: she wants to take him home and mend other broken parts of him. But it's too late for that. They've moved from enemies to lovers and back to enemies. This is just a temporary reprieve.

'There,' she says, when it's done. 'You're all set. But before you go, I need you to drink the tea.' It has sat, cooling, on the table while she's been cleaning and bandaging. Five minutes or five hours, who can say? It's like time has stopped in there.

Sam looks at Lexi sceptically.

'Tea cures all ills,' she tells him. 'If you were British, you would know that.'

'Good thing you're here to teach me, in that case.' He takes a sip from her Book Nerd mug. 'Huh. It actually tastes better when you put milk in it.'

'Well, yes. Obviously. We do know what we're doing across the pond.'

Lexi is getting tea envy. She was so focused on Sam that she didn't think to make herself one. Which, now that she thinks about it, is a metaphor for all kinds of things. Sam is both a great distraction, and the bane of her existence.

The silence between them stretches. There's nowhere to go from that comment except for dangerous discussions about monarchy and colonialism, and neither of them are in the mood to debate the relative merits of their countries of origin. They both know what they could do to break the silence, and they both know it's a bad idea, what with the fact that they hate each other and also his ex-girlfriend is both back in town now and possibly not his ex anymore.

'It's getting late,' Sam says in the end, saving them both. 'I should go.'

'Yep. I think we've both had quite enough excitement for one night.'

Pippin opens an eye, as if to ask: *You're still here? Let me sleep already.*

Sam watches her as she flips the light switches in turn, then sets the alarm and locks up.

'Am I going to have to change my alarm code now?'

He laughs. 'Breaking in isn't really my thing.'

'Which, of course, is exactly what a habitual breaker-inner *would* say.'

'Touché.'

On the corner, they pause awkwardly. This still feels very

unfinished, but short of snogging him right there in the street, Lexi isn't really sure what she can do to address that.

'Well, thank you for rescuing my cat,' she says.

'Thank you for taking care of my war wound,' he says.

And then they just keep standing there. The tension is intolerable. In the end, Lexi opens her arms for a hug, and Sam gratefully moves in for one. They stand there, on the corner of 7th and Penn, hugging for what seems like far too long, so long that it feels like the sun might come up and they'd still be standing there. Is he smelling her hair? Does she even want him to? She doubts her strawberry shampoo is perceptible beneath the day's panic-fuelled sweat. *Always wear perfume*, Lexi mentally chastises herself. *You never know when you'll want to be smelling nice.*

'Any time,' she says eventually, into his chest. 'You know where to come if you need a cup of tea and some antibacterial cream.'

'I'll remember that,' he says. He pulls away, and she immediately starts to miss him, like part of her skin has come unpeeled and stayed attached to him. She watches Sam walk away, and she reminds herself that she hates him. But somehow, it doesn't quite feel true.

Chapter Forty-Six

On her way to work the next day, Lexi picks up an extra latte. It's the least she can do for a person who's been mauled by her feral cat, particularly when they've been mauled while doing her the favour of rescuing said cat.

Although, Pippin would no doubt object to this characterisation. And fair enough: he's far from feral. He's usually no trouble at all. If Lexi didn't know better, in fact, she might think that Pippin chose the tree outside Sam's bookshop on purpose, that getting her speaking to him again was his plan along. If he's read *The Hundred and One Dalmatians* – and he is, after all, a bookshop cat, so maybe he has! – then he'll know this is a feasible plan. Maybe the scratch was a test: would Sam give up? Or would he see past the fear, overlook his own pain, and keep going? Is all of this a metaphor? Is Lexi losing her mind? She's not slept much lately; it's not impossible that she's delirious.

Anyway, it's Wednesday, and getting an extra latte is what she does on Wednesdays. She misses her piano lessons, though – and not just for the tantalising sofa bed in the corner of the room or the hot teacher who eventually flung her there. She enjoyed learning something from scratch, creating a melody from seemingly nothing in response to what were, only a few weeks ago, just meaningless blobs of ink impaled on indecipherable lines. She can see how music could be addictive. As can Sam.

But Lexi isn't addicted.

She can stop whenever she wants.

It's just polite to bring latte and check on a cat-inflicted wound, that's all.

She pushes the door to Great Expectations open, and the not-particularly-romantic buzzer sounds.

'Hi,' says the woman behind the counter, and Lexi clocks it straight away: it's Amanda. And then, she adds, 'Aren't you in the wrong bookstore?' She says it light-heartedly, but Lexi isn't fooled. She knows how to recognise the tell-tale signs of a woman being territorial. What is this woman who hurt Sam so badly doing back in his life? In his bookshop?

'I just came to bring a latte to Sam,' she says. She knows there's something about the way you say the name of the guy you like, something about the intonation or the emphasis or the false lightness of it, that instantly gives away how you feel. She hopes she hasn't just done that. Not that she *does* like him, anyway. It's simply that the way she said his name just then? It made it seem like maybe she did.

'He's in the back,' Amanda says, and Lexi's stomach drops like she's on a roller-coaster. The back. The place where unexpected things happen. Unexpected and very, very hot things. She hopes she's not blushing, not giving anything away.

She doesn't know why she cares what Amanda thinks of her. Maybe it's her flawless make-up, or her American teeth, or her unchipped nails. Maybe it's the humiliation of bringing coffee to someone who is clearly already taken – by a woman with flawless make-up, American teeth and unchipped nails.

'I'll take it to him,' Amanda says, doing that smiling-while-talking thing.

Lexi smiles back, then she speaks, because she's British and she can't do both at the same time. 'No, no, that's okay. You're busy.' She isn't. 'I don't mind taking it.'

Amanda looks Lexi up and down, clearly weighing up if it's worth the argument and how important it is to keep her away from Sam. 'Fine,' she says. 'I'll get him.' She must have come to the conclusion that Lexi isn't much of a threat with her imperfect make-up, British teeth, and slightly chipped manicure. Lexi doesn't blame her for coming to that particular conclusion. She's frazzled, and she probably looks it. Did she even brush her hair before she left the house this morning? It's likely. But she also wouldn't rule out having forgotten.

Amanda disappears behind a door, but Lexi hears her unmistakably. 'Someone's here to see you. I think it's the owner of that other bookstore?'

That other bookstore. Ha. If anything, Sam's is *the other one*.

He pokes his head around the office door. Lexi is relieved to see that he looks less pale than yesterday. 'Hey,' he says. Something about the *hey* sounds kind. Intimate, even. Lexi is tempted to look at Amanda, to see if she's noticed, but she keeps her eyes firmly on Sam (which, to be fair, isn't much of a hardship).

'Hi.' It takes her a moment to remember why she's here. 'I brought you coffee.'

'A Peregrine latte?'

'Of course.'

'Thank you.'

'It's the least I could do after last night.'

Lexi feels rather than sees Amanda's head swivelling towards her. She can feel her interrogating her with her eyes. Sam shuffles on his feet, so maybe he can feel it too. Or maybe he knows that the interrogation is really for him.

'I wanted to see how you're doing, too. How's the arm?'

Amanda stacks some papers that don't need stacking, then types some emails that don't need typing, if in fact they are emails at all. But Lexi isn't fooled: Amanda isn't missing a word of this.

'It's doing okay,' he says, lifting it as if to prove it's still there. 'Hasn't fallen off yet, at least, so I'm taking that as a good sign.'

'It's definitely not a *bad* sign.'

'Right? I'll be sure to put it in my gratitude journal tonight.'

Amanda's stopped pretending to be busy. She's watching Sam and Lexi. She's putting two and two together and getting 853.

'So it wasn't just a random cat,' she says.

'No,' Sam says, still looking at Lexi. 'It wasn't.'

'In fairness, though,' Lexi says, 'you'd have rescued a random cat. I know you would have done.'

Amanda narrows her eyes and looks from Lexi to Sam and Sam to Lexi. Because Lexi is right about him, and Amanda knows she is right about him, and maybe, just maybe, is wondering how she knows him so well. Will Lexi be the cause of an argument later? She can but hope.

'He would,' Amanda says. 'He's kind-hearted like that. 'Course, sometimes it means he gets taken advantage of.'

Lexi bites back a laugh. Sam is the last person on earth who'd allow himself to be taken advantage of. If he doesn't want to do something, he doesn't. 'Does it?'

Sam looks at Amanda. Amanda looks at Lexi. Lexi looks at Sam.

'Enjoy the latte,' she tells him. 'I'm glad you're doing better.'

She can't help but feel strangely victorious as she leaves.

Chapter Forty-Seven

The last thing Lexi has time for is more piano lessons, but she misses them. Her whole life right now is about the bookshop and Sam and how Sam affects the bookshop. She needs something else in her life. Something unrelated to Sam.

Not that the piano is entirely that. Her head swivels every time she hears a piano note, when she thinks he might be nearby. But she needs an outlet. Something *fun*. Something she can't monetise. And if it means she gets to think wistful thoughts about Sam while she's doing it, well . . . she'd call that a partial win.

She pushes open to the door to Music on the Hill and calls out cheerfully, 'Hello?'

At the counter, the same man as before greets her back. Greg, says his name badge. She didn't notice it last time. 'Hi. How are the piano lessons going?'

Honestly, she's surprised he remembers. She's only been there once before, and that was a couple of months ago. But Lexi always somehow forgets that she's something of a local celebrity: people remember she's the bookshop lady, and so they're always waving at her across the street like in some kind of Disney film even when she has no idea who they are. That, and there's her British accent, of course.

'They were going well, I think. But I need to find

somewhere to practise. And I need a new teacher. That's actually what I've come here to ask for your advice about.'

He raises an eyebrow. Lexi wonders, not for the first time in her life, if she is the only one who can't do that. If there's a school she can go to so that she can learn. But maybe she'll stick with the piano. Jane Austen's heroines got by fine without the eyebrow thing.

'Did things not work out with Sam?'

Lexi takes a beat. 'We'll call it creative differences.'

'I see.' He peers into her face, trying to read something there, though she can't figure out what that would be. 'I thought I'd seen you both around town together. You're not . . . friends?'

His little pause triggers a weird physical reaction in Lexi. Her stomach roils. If a random music shop man knows they are . . . friends, then who else does? This is Capitol Hill, where news travels fast. If he told his wife and she told her book club and they happened to mention it to one friend each and one of those knows someone who writes for one of the DC gossip sites . . . Honestly, she's lucky it hasn't been on the front page of the *Hill Rag* yet.

Also, how to answer this question? Are they friends, even without the ominous pause?

'It's complicated,' she tells him. Her mind is racing. She's trying to remember if they've kissed on the street. They've definitely held hands, and at the time, she didn't care. If anything, she wanted to flaunt it. She should have been more careful. What if her customers start to think their loyalty doesn't matter, because they'll be pooling resources soon anyway?

Worse: do her booksellers know?

She hopes not: imagine the betrayal. Sam and his shop are an existential threat to them, and she's cavorting with him? In theory, and often in practice, indie bookstore owners are all friends with each other. But, also, indie bookshops are usually respectful about not treading on each other's ground. There's a reason why *You've Got Mail* isn't about two lovely indies. They stand together against the behemoths, and one of the ways in which they stand together is by standing a suitable distance apart.

Second-hand bookshops are different; shops like Lexi's can partner with them, send over customers who ask for older or out-of-print books that are difficult for them to get. But a shop increasingly doing the same as Pemberley Books? Lexi isn't sure that her sofas and cosy vibes are enough to differentiate them. They'll lean in to the Jane Austen thing; they'll lean in to the romance and continue doing it better and more thoroughly than Sam, because their enthusiasm and their knowledge aren't cynical business decisions: they're heartfelt and genuine. Pemberley Books will always be the bookshop of choice for the Instagrammers, the people who prefer a certain kind of aesthetic.

But long term? Lexi isn't sure she's got the stomach for constant, cut-throat competition. The only adrenaline rush she got into this job for was the joy of finding someone just the right book, and the jolt of pleasure when someone tells her they love what she's done with the shop. She's not in it to win it; she's in it for a happy shop, happy customers, happy staff. And she has to admit that lately she's been anything *but* happy. She doesn't want to live like that, and she resents Sam for making it this way. She's not afraid of hard work, but there's a difference between hard and thankless.

The music man is studying her face. 'Complicated, huh?'

Lexi visualises the word snaking its way through the networks of the Hill. Who knows what conclusion the fifth person down the chain will draw? And does it matter anyway?

She nods, and he slides over a piece of paper.

'Here's a list of teachers I recommend.' He circles a couple with his green-inked pen.

'Thank you,' Lexi says, and turns for the door.

'I'd recommend sticking with Sam, though.'

Because Lexi is the bookshop lady, she has to be unfailingly polite. So she turns and says, 'Thank you. I'll bear that in mind.'

But, really, she wants to slam the door and scream.

Chapter Forty-Eight

It's not that Lexi walks past Sam's shop on purpose on the way to her own. There are, admittedly, several routes she could take if she wanted to avoid it. But his stretch of street is the prettiest, with a row of identical houses in different colours, a DC specialty that helps make this neighbourhood so lovely to walk around.

Lexi doesn't know for sure that any of those things are the actual reason her feet so often seem to take her past Great Expectations, but for the purposes of retaining some internal dignity, that is what she tells herself. There is also, though, the nosiness factor: she wants to know what the workers were measuring for the other day. Somehow, she didn't get a chance to ask Sam when she was busy bandaging his arm and fighting off her own lustful impulses, or when Amanda was there giving her side-eye.

It *could* just be a new bookshelf, of course, something as straightforward and harmless as that – although perhaps she shouldn't make assumptions on the harmless part, because who knows what he's planning next: a shelf of Jane-Austen-themed merch, maybe? A bookcase in Sam's hands could spell doom for her.

She slows down as she rounds the corner leading to Great Expectations. She's hoping to look in without having to stop and press her face against the window like some kind of desperate competitor, or worse, a jilted lover seeking any glimpse of the one who broke her heart and whom she can't stop thinking about. Because that would be pathetic, right? And she is not pathetic. She is a strong and independent woman, businesswoman and entrepreneur. And, as luck would have it, someone's pushing the door open as she walks past, so no pressing her face against the window is needed.

And she hates to say it, but . . . what she sees is a genius idea. Ugh. Why does he have to be so good at this? It's a bar. He's going to sell wine, which is genius for two reasons. The mark-up on wine is much higher than on books; it's easier to make money fast. But also, as she well knows from the tipsy book clubs that meet in her own shop, a tipsy browser is an uninhibited browser. A few sips in, all the resolve to read the books you had at home before you let yourself be tempted by a new one – let's face it, a flimsy resolve to begin with – has vanished as if it never existed. So the wine pays for itself twice. More sales of books on top of the sale of the wine.

It's a genius idea. It's also *her* idea. She's told him about this, told him that tipsy browsing is the best browsing and that, in fact, if she didn't have the whole Austen thing going on, she'd probably have called her shop Tipsy Browsing. She'd probably sell wine. She told him that. She can't believe he has taken her idea, and yet, of course, she also can. Because this is Sam: ruthless. He makes her so angry, and she really wishes this anger wasn't also a turn-on. Never mind the Jane Austen obsession: this seems like a way more harmful personality quirk.

She's wound up and steaming by the time she's made it to Pemberley Books. It must show on her face, because Natalie visibly recoils.

'You okay?' she asks Lexi, looking mildly panicked.

Lexi tries to rearrange her face into a reassuring smile, though she's not entirely convinced it works. 'Yes. Hi. Did I scare you with my thunderous face?'

'A little, yes.'

'It's okay,' Lexi tells her. 'It's not you. It's not anyone here.'

'Great Expectations?' she guesses.

Lexi nods in unnecessary confirmation.

'What have they done now?'

'They're getting a wine bar.'

'Oh.' Natalie's tone is the tone of someone who was expecting worse news, is relieved it wasn't, but also is concerned her delusional boss might be overreacting. But then she gets it. '*Oh*. That's kind of genius.'

'Exactly.'

'Is there any reason we can't do that, too?'

That . . . is an excellent point. One that Lexi will certainly consider.

'I guess not. Beyond being a copycat.'

'There's an argument to be made that he copied us first.'

There certainly is.

There's no monopoly on the bookshop idea, Sam told Lexi once. As far as she knows, there's no monopoly on wine bars either. He took romance; she can take back the wine idea. What was it he said to her the other day? All's fair in love and capitalism.

The cogs in Natalie's brain are whirring. 'We'd have to get a liquor licence, though,' she says. 'I don't know what that process is like. But I can find out.'

'Would you? That would be great.'

'I don't think you need a liquor licence to *give* wine away, though.'

Lexi wants to hug her, to kiss her on the cheek. 'Natalie, *you* are the genius here. I can picture it now: free wine on Saturday nights. *Sure, you could go and buy wine at Sam's. Or you could come and get it here, for free.*'

'I love it.' But Natalie's face clouds over, and Lexi can see another practical objection forming. 'Could get pricey, though.'

'Maybe we should do a pilot evening. Test it against purchases. Draw up some graphs.' Although the very thought of graphs makes Lexi's stomach roil.

'If we wanted to be really mean, we could trial it the weekend that Sam's wine bar opens.'

Lexi isn't sure she's quite ready for that kind of all-out war. But it's certainly an idea. She can definitely see it working once, as a novelty. But a regular thing? Who knows? She should speak to her accountant, though she's pretty sure she can guess his opinion.

'It's not going to be a problem, competing with Sam like this?'

Lexi's stomach drops. Is Natalie asking what she thinks she's asking?

'In what way?'

She doesn't answer. She lets Lexi stew. It's easier to let Natalie say the words herself.

'Well . . .' Natalie had seemed so self-assured, so willing to be direct in that very American way, but now she looks at her shoes. They're pretty great shoes: yellow Mary Janes, with a pink flower on the strap, but Lexi is fairly sure Natalie has seen them before. 'There are rumours.'

Ah. There it is. 'Rumours about Sam and me?'

'Listen, nobody would blame you. It's no secret that it's slim pickings in the DC dating world.'

'Are you *sure* nobody would blame me?'

Another silence that speaks volumes.

'I'm pretty sure *some* of you would blame me.'

'He's very attractive. And book people are kindred spirits.'

'True.'

It's always bugged Lexi that it's socially acceptable for people to give their opinions about a single person's dating life. If she felt petty, if she didn't know that Natalie meant well, if she wasn't trying her best to be a dignified, professional boss, she could shut down this conversation pretty quickly, just by asking: *How's your sex life?* Or *Do you still find your husband interesting after all these years?* But she knows Natalie isn't just being nosy here. It's fair enough to want to know if Lexi is sleeping with the enemy, because that would impact the shop and all the staff.

Lexi squirms, but she decides that Natalie deserves an answer, so she tells her.

'I had a temporary lapse in judgement. But that's over now.'

Natalie knows how to wield silence as a weapon. She waits.

'His ex-girlfriend is back in town, anyway.'

'Ah.'

Natalie is still looking at her. How much detail is she expecting from Lexi? How much does Lexi want to give her? In this moment, Lexi is really feeling the oddness of being a boss younger than most of her staff. Their instinct is to look after her and hers is to go to them for advice, but instead she's supposed to tell them what to do, and they're meant to believe that she's doing what's best for the business. Given her questionable romantic decisions of late, she wouldn't blame them for finding that difficult.

'I don't really have time for a boyfriend, anyway.'

She's floundering here. That has never crossed her mind as a reason not to date Sam. As a reason not to date in general, maybe. But with Sam, she could make it work. If nothing else because they both have similar pressures on their time.

'You're a young woman,' Natalie says gently. 'You have needs. It's okay not to pour every part of your heart and soul into the shop.'

Lexi chooses to take this in the kind spirit it's intended. She swallows hard. 'Thank you.'

'It does seem like dating your most serious competition might not be the greatest idea. But if it's meant to be, it'll work out. I'm a big believer in that. You've got to do what's right for you.'

Lexi has a little bit of whiplash. Natalie is swinging between telling her not to date Sam and also telling her to ignore her advice not to date him. It's very confusing.

'Just think about what's most important in your life, and go after that with your whole heart,' she says.

'It's not that simple.'

'If it isn't, then maybe you haven't found that one thing yet. How about while I look into liquor licences, you look into that?'

Seems fair enough. And incredibly kind of her to take on yet another task. Everyone in this shop is already working so hard.

'Deal,' Lexi says. 'Thank you.'

If there's one thing Lexi can do, it's make lists. So down in her office, where she could and maybe should be doing countless other things – consulting with her accountant about the latest idea, for example, or maybe making an appointment with a therapist – she writes some lists. The problem is that when she wants something, she always wants it with her whole heart. She doesn't know how to be any other way. And the list, as it always does, comes down to this:

Lexi Austen's wish list:

- *The bookshop to be a success*
- *A boyfriend/eventually husband*
- *A life: time for friendships; time for hobbies (like the piano!).*

Realistically, out of this list, she can only pick two at any given time. Hence her goal, what feels like a million years ago now, to go full pelt at the bookshop so she can employ a manager, delegate a lot of responsibility to them, and then, just maybe, have time for brunches and karaoke nights and – shudder – re-entering the world of DC dating.

There's no way that's happening in time for Erin's wedding, but that's okay. Lexi doesn't really *need* a plus-one. She'll be busy with bridesmaid duties. Looking at her list, though, something nags at her – this idea of 'a' boyfriend, like any boyfriend will do, like she can pluck one out of the ether, almost at random. But what's *really* bugging her, if she's honest, is this: she knows who she wants, and there's nothing random about it.

Chapter Forty-Nine

Lexi's feet, traitors that they are, also take her past Great Expectations on the way home that night. It's after closing time, but the light's still on: nothing unusual there; Sam often works late like she does. But as she gets closer, she sees it's not just one man scribbling at his desk. It's hopping in there, with people milling, glasses in hand. A soft launch of the wine bar, it seems, and a successful one at that.

She tries to look away before Sam catches her eye through the window, but it's too late. He's seen her, and he makes his way to the door and cracks it open. 'Lexi!' he calls. His face is pink and he's more relaxed than she's ever seen him. Clearly he's taking testing the wine bar very seriously. 'Join us!'

'Oh, I . . .'

She can't think of an excuse quickly enough. The combination of Lexi plus Sam plus alcohol seems like a bad idea, especially in public. Especially when she's trying to be clear-headed about What She Really Wants, and especially when, despite her tiny victory the other day, Amanda is very much back on the scene. In fact: yep, there she is, in the corner, topping up someone's wine glass. But none of that seems appropriate to say, and Sam looks so hopeful and happy that she can't bring herself to disappoint him.

'C'mon,' he says. 'You know what they say about all work and no play.'

Ah. Yes. Touché. That does sound a lot like her life lately.

'And *you* know what they say about sleeping with the enemy.'

'No sleeping,' he says, bumping her arm with his. 'Just drinking. And I prefer the term *rival*, don't you?'

He extends his hand and drags her in. Not much dragging required, really. Honestly, a glass of wine or two sounds like just what she needs. Especially free wine. And especially wine that's free because it's paid for by said rival slash enemy, cutting into his bottom line. Besides, Sam's hand is warm and Lexi is already drunk on that; she wants to keep hold of it, even if it's just until they get to the door. Some of these people might be journalists or bloggers, TikTokkers or just plain gossips, and she probably shouldn't give them anything to talk about, even though part of her wants to. All publicity is good publicity, after all, right? Or is she clearly drunk already despite not having had a sip of wine?

'Red or white?' a familiar voice asks cheerfully as Lexi walks in. Sam has evaporated from by her side, dispersed no doubt into the adoring crowd.

'Red please, Tessa.'

She shuffles on her feet, but to her credit, Tessa stays professional, handing her the glass with a smile that Lexi only knows to be tight because she knows her so well.

'It's nice to see you,' Lexi says, making deliberate eye contact. It's only been three weeks, but Pemberley Books feels emptier without her, and Lexi more alone in her Britishness. 'I'm glad you've found something that suits you and pays better.'

Tessa visibly relaxes. Her shoulders drop into a more natural position.

'Thanks,' she says.

'And you like it here?' Lexi focuses every bit of energy on keeping a level, neutral voice.

'I like the wine,' she says, which tells Lexi all she needs to know.

'Understood.'

Lexi braces herself for small talk with strangers; the wine will definitely help with that, as will the fact her face is well known around town: no painful *and what do* you *do* to answer; they can just jump straight into talk of books and bookstores. Ah yes, there's Greg from Music on the Hill, coming towards her, raising that eyebrow. Echoes of *complicated* float unvoiced between them.

'Come to support your piano teacher?'

'Something like that.'

'Well, that's nice.'

Thankfully, Greg is heading for the wine table, so he doesn't pause for too long. If Lexi doesn't know what's going on in her own heart, how can she playfully banter with a stranger about it?

Lexi casts her eye around the shop to find someone to chat with, someone she knows a little and won't have to do the worst of small talk with. She notices little touches as she looks around. It's less square, with fewer rough edges and parallel lines. Maybe it's the dim lighting; maybe it's the wine; maybe she's feeling more charitable than usual, but it seems a little friendlier, a little more inviting. She's feeling all kinds of ways about that: friendly and inviting is *her* brand after all. But she also believes it should be the brand of all bookshops, so she has to award Sam a few brownie points for that.

She blinks to attention; a wine bottle is being waved in her face.

'Refill?'

She's somehow managed to drink most of her glass in the few minutes she's been standing here. She must be more nervous than she realised. So Lexi nods, and remembers her manners and says, 'Please,' and forces herself to make eye contact with the person brandishing the wine: Amanda.

'Thank you,' she forces out, and brings out her customer-service smile.

'You're welcome,' she says, with the unnerving, unfailing politeness of Americans.

'So what do you think of our little wine bar idea?'

Our. Our idea. Suddenly it all becomes sickeningly clear. The hard turn into the trendier genres; what Lexi now recognises as the feminine touches; the idea of a soft launch like this, fairy lights and branded napkins, free tote bags and piles of free review copies. Amanda's becoming part of the shop, part of Sam's life. And she's very clearly ensuring Lexi knows it.

She swallows. 'I think it's genius. And it looks great in here.'

Amanda smiles, pleased with herself. 'Thank you,' she says. 'We think so.'

We.

Having made her point, Amanda is circulating now, making friends as only the bearer of top-up wine can, making sure everyone knows her face and acknowledges that she's part of this too.

Lexi finds herself alone again, wondering whether to down her wine and slip out unnoticed or find someone else to talk to. Across the room, Sam is chatting to Polina Boskova, the DC Instagram Queen of news and events, and he makes eye contact with Lexi and nods slightly, as if to say, again, *Join us?* She's thankful for his thoughtfulness, that he's seen her alone and wanted her to feel welcome, and not like an awkward spare part.

'You know each other, right?' Sam says.

'I'm not sure we've met in person,' Lexi tells Polina, 'but of course I follow you on Instagram. Always so impressed by the work you put in and how much you've got your ear to the ground for everything that's happening in this town.'

'Thank you,' she says. 'And, of course, you're Lexi Austen of Pemberley Books.' After all these years, it still gives her a little shiver of pleasure to be referred to that way. 'I love your shop.'

'Thank you.'

These may be bland pleasantries, but they're bland pleasantries that mean the world.

'Not tempted to copy the wine idea?' she asks. Possibly innocently, possibly not.

'Don't you dare,' Sam says, through what could be a cheeky grin or could be bared teeth.

Lexi laughs nervously. 'That's me told,' she says in Polina's direction, wriggling her eyebrows in a *so isn't this all jolly good fun* kind of way.

'Do I detect some friendly rivalry?'

There's something bloodhound-like about Polina's demeanour, which puts Lexi on her guard. 'It's inevitable,' she says. 'What with us being so close.'

Sam coughs, and she cringes inwardly.

'Geographically!' she adds a bit too quickly, a bit too emphatically.

'Ah, yes. It must be weird having another shop that sells new books on your doorstep.'

Lexi can't help wondering if Polina is trying to stir up trouble – a little argument to write or gossip about. Or does she really have no idea she's pushing all their buttons?

'We have slightly different emphases, slightly different markets,' Sam says. 'And besides, we each draw readers to the other, which can only help us both.'

These, of course, are the things they told themselves back when it was all going to be fine. Back when it *was* fine, really.

'But you each stay in your lanes,' Polina presses.

'Yes,' Sam says.

Lexi catches the romance novel display. 'That's the theory, anyway.'

The vibe has shifted so many times tonight, from friendly to awkward to fun, and now they're back in awkward territory, something like tension filling the air.

Polina clears her throat. 'Well, this has been fun,' she says. She has got all she needs from this conversation. 'But I should get going. Love what you've done with the place.'

'Thank you,' Sam says.

Circulating with wine, hovering just within earshot, Amanda's caught the compliment too and chimes in with a *thank you* of her own. Now the vibe feels more chilly than anything, ice in Lexi's veins as Polina looks from her to Amanda and back again. Wondering, no doubt, about some of the things Lexi has wondered about too. Is Amanda sticking around? Are she and Sam going into business together? What happened to her career ambitions? And, most importantly to Lexi: if Sam is able to forgive Amanda

285

for using him, then why can't he forgive Lexi the (surely) smaller sin of role-playing from Jane Austen to get him to fall in love with her? She might have been careless with his heart; she was maybe a little misguided, maybe a bit ridiculous, but it was because she liked him.

And now he and Lexi and Amanda stand there, and Lexi doesn't have the upper hand or the quick banter. Instead, she feels like she's shrinking, like she's surplus to requirements. It's not a nice feeling.

'Well,' she says, clearing her throat and, unable to think of a better *I'm leaving in a not-at-all-awkward-way* phrase than Polina's: 'This has been fun.'

'So soon?' Amanda is baring those white teeth again – that polite smile that belies the catty words.

'You know how it is. Places to be.' Those places are mostly in the kitchen making tea and in bed with a book to block out how awkward she feels. So that's two places. Plural. No word of a lie.

Amanda seems doubtful. 'Places more fun than this?'

Lexi looks around at the admittedly now thinning crowd, still chattering and laughing and downing wine. Fun, yes, at least in theory. But the amount of fun that can be had when standing around with a guy she both loves and hates and his ex and perhaps current girlfriend is . . . limited.

'Depends how you look at it, I guess.'

Sam raises an eyebrow. Lexi shrugs . . . enigmatically? Or perhaps just sadly, pathetically.

'Okay,' he says. 'Well, thanks for coming.'

'Thank you for inviting me.'

Inviting is a stretch. Grabbing her as she walked past, was more like it. But if Amanda has control of the guest list, perhaps that's the best he could do. Maybe he was even incurring her wrath by doing that.

Suddenly grateful, Lexi surprises herself by kissing him on the cheek. And then, just as suddenly self-conscious, she turns to kiss Amanda, too, to demonstrate that she's the kind of person who kisses everyone, no big deal, nothing to read into it. Then Lexi hoists her bag back onto her shoulder and turns to leave.

But then her bag catches on something and she stops, frozen.

A gasp.

A crashing of glass.

A few drunken cheers and claps from across the room.

Oh, no.

In a film, Lexi turning round to face the damage she's wrought would be in slow-mo. In reality, it happens super-fast: the grimace on Amanda's face, the passing of the napkins, the frantic dabbing at the deep red wine splashes on her pink blouse, the rushing in of Tessa with a dustpan and brush retrieving the glass from the floor.

All Lexi wants to do is what she's been *trying* to do – to get the heck out of there – but now she has to stay, apologise, offer to clean up.

'I'm so sorry,' she repeats over and over.

'It's fine,' Amanda says, with that same polite American smile she's had on all night, the one that says, *I want to kill you*. Only now it says, *I want to kill you with a set of blunt knives so that it's as slow and torturous as possible.*

Lexi searches out Sam's eyes for some reassurance that he doesn't hate her, that he knows it was an accident.

Did Lexi feel like throwing red wine at Amanda's

expensive, probably dry-clean-only top at several points during the evening? Of course. But would she actually have done it by choice? No, of course not. Not because she's nice – though she likes to think she is – but because she's a wimp. And also because she's a little bit afraid of what Sam would think of her. And now he's stone-faced, his eyes refusing to meet hers.

'I'll pay for your dry cleaning, of course,' she says, desperate to make it right, to stop the panic rising in her throat.

'It's *fine*,' Amanda says again. And in case there was any doubt over whether she means it, she adds, 'I don't know how much dry cleaning can really do with a red wine stain anyway.'

This awkward moment, standing opposite each other not saying anything, seems to stretch on into infinity.

'Anyway,' Amanda says, breaking the silence, 'weren't you just leaving?'

'I was.'

Lexi is still hoping for Sam's gaze to meet hers, for some kind of absolution in his eyes. But he won't look at her. The whole thing is so humiliating, but at least Lexi makes it round the corner before she starts crying.

Chapter Fifty

Surprisingly, miraculously, Erin is both home and still awake when Lexi gets back. She's humming to herself and looking a little flushed; John has probably just left after a particularly satisfying snogging session, made somehow all the more satisfying by the knowledge they're a day closer to consummating their union.

Lexi can't really imagine what any part of that is like. Would it be better if she didn't know how good sex with Sam is, or what an expert he is with his tongue? Would she be less confused about what she wants? Or would the desperation to know what he's like in bed and to feel every part of his skin on every part of her skin drive her to even more ridiculous measures?

She clears her throat as she walks into the living room, and Erin startles.

'Oh, hey,' she says. Then she takes a look at Lexi's face and her smile turns into a frown. Lexi accidentally wore her non-waterproof mascara today, which has turned out to be a disaster. 'What happened?'

Erin says it kindly, but because Lexi knows her so well, she can hear the faint note of controlled impatience in her voice. She probably wanted to go to bed full of loved-up fluffy feelings. For most of the time Erin's been engaged, Lexi has been having drama of some sort or another, and she feels bad about it. This time should be all about Erin. She should get to bask in her happiness. She deserves no less.

To be fair, Lexi doesn't do the drama on purpose. She would actually love it if her life would stop being ridiculous for just a few minutes. She would love to stop focusing on her own drama, preferably because in this scenario there would be no drama to focus on.

'I accidentally got invited to the soft launch of Sam's wine bar.'

'Wine bar? What happened to his bookshop?'

'It's a wine bar in a bookshop, which is actually a great idea. The mark-up on wine is bigger than on books, and when people are a bit sozzled they buy more books. So. Win-win.'

'Too bad you didn't think of it first.'

'I did.'

'Oh.'

'Yeah. Anyway. I was walking past, and they were having a party. And he saw me and dragged me in there.'

'Sounds like maybe he's still into you, no?'

Lexi shakes her head. It is all so confusing. 'Maybe. Or maybe he just wanted to show off.'

'Because your opinion matters to him?'

'Or because he wanted to unveil his great plan for beating me in the Great Bookshop Wars. Or maybe because his ex-girlfriend-and-maybe-also-current-girlfriend was there too and he wanted to show me how totally fine he is without me.'

'And they're definitely back together?'

'Sounds like Amanda basically designed the wine bar. She's been hanging around for at least a week.'

'A whole week!' Erin rolls her eyes. 'Sounds like they might as well be married.'

Lexi punches her playfully on the arm. She's missed this. 'Shut up.'

'And that's why you've been crying? Because Amanda was there?'

'He's obviously got it in him to forgive and start again when someone really matters to him.' Lexi is trying to keep things light, but her voice is cracking. Erin squeezes her shoulder. 'But no. It was going okay. I was holding my own. And then, just as I left, I turned and my handbag somehow caught Amanda's wine and it spilled on her top. A full glass of red wine on her pale pink top.'

Erin snorts.

'What? It's not funny.'

And then, just like that, Lexi gets it, the funny side of it. She snorts too. 'All right,' she tells Erin. 'Maybe it is a little funny.'

'I think it calls for a high five, actually.' Erin holds up her hand, but because Lexi is laughing, she somehow misses, and that makes her snort, and then they're both laughing uncontrollably, in that ridiculous way you do when something isn't really that funny but it's like alien joy has taken over your body.

Lexi struggles to catch her breath. She clutches her stomach in delightful pain. It feels good to laugh like this: everything has been so serious and so hard lately, and this is like medicine. It feels good to laugh with Erin, specifically, too: they've both been so busy, and Lexi hates that they're drifting apart. The thought of that deflates Lexi's mood just a little bit, which is actually a welcome relief, because it means a chance to catch her breath, and for the sharp pain in her belly to subside. She doesn't meet Erin's gaze. She can't, because if she does, they'll be off again.

'It's not like you to laugh at someone else's misfortune,' Lexi says, still avoiding eye contact. Erin would be mortified if she was the one to spill red wine on someone's top. She'd probably already be online, googling where she can buy a new one, or looking up miracle remedies to clean the stain. But another thing about Erin is also true: that she is fiercely loyal.

'You know what they say. The enemy of my friend . . .'

Lexi hadn't thought about Amanda as an enemy, exactly. More an inconvenience or an irritation. Maybe even a rival, hypothetically, if she wanted Sam, which clearly she doesn't, because who would want to be with a ruthless capitalist who can't forgive a small flight of fancy, even if he is kind and thoughtful and hot, a sensitive pianist type with talented finger skills in multiple arenas? Nobody, that's who. And certainly not Lexi.

'Well, I appreciate you being on my side.'

'Of course. And I appreciate the amusing visual image.'

Lexi and Erin pause to savour it, and giggles rise up in Lexi's throat again. 'If I'd been trying to do it, I probably would have failed. My bag had to catch the glass in just the right way, you know?'

'Exactly,' Erin says. 'That's what makes it so delicious. The unintentionality. And yet somehow your subconscious also played a part.'

'It took over my handbag, like some kind of ghost.'

'Exactly. Way to go, Lexi's subconscious.' Erin holds her hand up again for another high five, and this time Lexi's lands on hers with a satisfying clap.

It's late, and they should both go to bed, but this is the most fun, the most bonding, that Lexi and Erin have had in a while, and neither of them quite wants to let the moment go.

'So . . . I take it you really like him then?'

If Lexi did, this would be the moment to admit that. But she doesn't. She was crying because she was embarrassed; that's all.

'What's the point if he's back with his girlfriend already?'

'That isn't really what I'm asking,' Erin says gently, but, of course, Lexi knew that.

She shrugs, because she doesn't want to admit her feelings out loud, even to herself. But she can see in Erin's eyes that she's drawn her own conclusions.

'You don't like him,' Lexi reminds her.

'But it doesn't matter if *I* like him,' she says, which is infuriatingly sensible of her. 'It only matters if *you* do.'

'None of it matters if he has a girlfriend.'

'Who he dumped once before.'

'C'mon, Erin. You've never heard of second-chance romance?'

'Of course I have. I've read *Persuasion* like everybody else I respect. But that's exactly why I'm rooting for you and him.'

Lexi rolls her eyes, but she's touched. And a little confused. 'What happened to him being a womaniser?'

'I guess I'm hoping that he likes you enough to reform his ways.'

'That makes two of us. But Amanda really broke him, I think.' Lexi fills Erin in on the backstory, Sam giving up everything including his beloved New York City to come and live in DC with her, only to find out she was using him all along.

'Yeah,' Erin says. 'That's why I wouldn't be so quick to assume they're getting back together. It doesn't exactly sound like a match made in heaven.'

Lexi shrugs again. 'I should probably focus on the bookshop right now anyway. I don't really have time for romantic shenanigans.'

'Any bright new ideas?' Erin sounds so hopeful. Always rooting for Lexi.

Lexi tells her about wine night. She knows Erin will get it; after all, they'd enjoyed tipsy browsing together on that Galentine's Day night out in North West DC a few months ago. After dinner, still buzzed from the wine, they'd wandered around Kramers and picked up armfuls of novels, lured by pretty covers and recommendations from staff and each other. The next morning, they'd counted their new books in awe and looked at their receipts in horror.

'Tipsy browsing is the best browsing,' Erin says now.

Lexi pictures a mural of a girl reading with a glass of wine. A cute new logo featuring a bottle.

Sam would kill her. And right at this moment, giddy and exhausted, that seems like reason enough to do it.

Chapter Fifty-One

Lexi's fingers feel like they're starting to ache from not playing the piano. Only a few months ago, she'd never touched one, and it's not like she was playing every day even when she was learning. Still, while she should be looking up the rules for serving wine in a bookshop, she finds herself looking up pianos instead: how much they cost, how heavy they are, how much of a headache it is to move them.

If she's going to be looking up anything that isn't wine rules, she should probably be trying to figure out what she is going to do when Erin moves out. Despite how much fun they had together last night, it was also a reminder that Erin will be leaving soon. Lexi has put off even thinking about what that means for her (to be fair, she has had one or two other things to think about). She doesn't want to live with a random, haggling about dirty dishes and whether they're best left in the sink or next to it if you don't have time to do them right then and there. At thirty-two, she also feels like she's too old for all of that.

Which explains, in part, why she's assumed the ostrich pose and gone down the piano rabbit hole. She tries to picture a lovely flat with a piano in the corner of the living room, but here's the thing: the picture is incomplete, because a piano without Sam to play it feels wrong.

'Numbers not adding up?' Natalie asks, setting a cup

of tea on Lexi's desk, and she realises she's sighed out loud and not just in her mind. And that, for people to make her tea without her even having to ask, she must be radiating anxiety and the need for some TLC.

Lexi clicks out of the music shop tab. 'Something like that.'

'Well,' Natalie says, 'I come bearing good news.'

'Good news *and* a cup of tea? Things are looking up.'

'The good news is that we don't need a liquor licence to give wine out for free. And the other good news is that wholesale wine is cheaper than I thought.'

She's made a very organised and informative spreadsheet detailing exactly how many books they'd need to sell to make up for the price of the wine, and it's very doable – essentially just a couple of books for each bottle, which seems eminently possible, with the added buzz of a full and happy shop and a few less inhibitors when it comes to spending money. She goes through it together with Natalie, and it almost seems too good to be true. But Natalie is nothing if not thorough, and a tiny bubble of hope forms in Lexi's stomach, fluttering, light, like the first signs of a crush.

So it's full steam ahead for the first wine night. Lexi's accountant pulled an unconvinced face when she told him about giving away wine for free, but when she showed him the calculations, he relented a little. It's possible that she forgot to mention the extra expenses for the first night: napkins with the shop's logo and tote bags that say *Tipsy browsing is the best browsing*. They were designed for free by her friend Imani, though, and they're also for sale online, so Lexi is crossing her fingers that they'll soon make their money back on them. Imani also designed a logo for wine nights, so they have something new and interesting to post to the social media that has been slightly sleepy since Tessa left.

Lexi is nervous to press *post* though. Until now, it has been all internal discussions and brainstorming with her supportive friends, but once it's out there, once people see it, then what? And by *people*, she specifically means Sam. She knows you can't copyright an idea, and she knows that technically it was hers first, but she also knows that if she were him, she'd be mad, and she doesn't know what, exactly, that is going to look like.

Her fingers hover over her phone and she takes a deep breath. It's too late to back out now, anyway. The wine has been paid for and the tote bags have been ordered. Like most things in life, if this is worth doing, then it's worth doing whole-heartedly.

She closes her eyes as she taps *post*, looking away from the potential car crash, the collision with Sam, but also feeling the kind of excitement in the pit of her belly that she hasn't felt in a while: the high of a creative idea that might actually work, might mean the shop doesn't just survive but thrives, when just a few weeks ago even survival seemed barely attainable.

The best thing about having her own bookshop, Lexi sometimes thinks, is exactly this: these creative ideas she's free to dream up and go with the flow on. Over the years, she's often talked to authors about how it feels to be in *the zone*, where nothing except them and their book are present and they don't notice time passing. Lexi has had brainstorming sessions that have felt that way, like a shot of adrenaline injected into her veins.

So what if Sam is mad? She was here first, on this patch, and he's broken her heart and deserves a little revenge, even if Lexi isn't proud of herself for seeing it that way. But when she opens her eyes and sees he's already texted her, a message that simply says *WTF*, all her bravado leaks out of her. The happy adrenaline and the creative high desert her as quickly as they arrived, replaced by a fight-or-flight response, her legs jelly-like and an inability to form coherent sentences even in her own brain.

She stares at the three letters, unsure how to respond or if she even needs to. She doesn't have the stomach for out-and-out war. She's just trying to keep her bookshop alive. And in the end, that's what she tells him. The fight for her bookshop has both everything and nothing to do with him. She wants to win; she's determined to win. But if it was something else threatening its survival – a rent increase, say, or a global pandemic – she'd be fighting every bit as hard.

Nobody's going to buy wine at my shop when they can get it at yours for free. Sam writes.

Sure they will. Mine is bog standard; yours is carefully selected and curated.

But yours is free. He points out.

And therefore I'm making no money on it.

Which makes me think that the only reason you're doing this is to undercut me. A leaf straight out of the capitalist playbook.

I thought you liked capitalism?

It's like Sam has been waiting to have this argument, like he's been practising this exchange in his head for months. He leaves no time at all between their texts.

I just didn't think that you of all people would want to play that game.

Me of all people?

You know what I mean.

Lexi does know – and she takes it as a compliment, actually – but that doesn't mean she's going to make it easy for him.

No. Enlighten me.

Sam makes Lexi wait for his response. Maybe he's serving a customer. Maybe he's formulating a cutting and winning argument. But Lexi waits and waits; she replies to an email or two; she feeds Pippin; she waits some more, and nothing.

All day, she has an uneasy feeling. She should be pleased to have had the last word. But that's not what it feels like. Like so many things between them, it feels unfinished. And that makes her a little queasy with unease.

Chapter Fifty-Two

It feels like opening day all over again on the first Tipsy Friday. Lexi's staff have actively embraced it and put as much energy into the day as they do with the annual birthday celebration or Independent Bookstore Day. There are balloons tied to the chalkboard outside: *Tipsy Browsing is the Best Browsing*, Megan has written in swirly letters, surrounded by bottles with smiley faces. The Washingtonian and CityCast DC are sending people to report, and this is not just a good sign, but a sign that before the evening has even started, people are talking about Pemberley Books again. The shop is not just a beloved, long-established local business, but it's also innovative and cool, and that most precious commodity of all: newsworthy.

For that, Lexi supposes she has Sam to thank, in a way. They were chugging along, doing okay – doing well, even – but not really challenging themselves. Now they've got Jane-Austen-themed celebrations and new book clubs in the pipeline as well as Tipsy Browsing, on top of all the reasons why people already loved them. They're somehow both diversifying and staying firmly within their niche. Plus, Pippin's a great asset, and it's thanks to Sam that Lexi still has him. So, all in all, Sam does have his uses.

And just as Lexi is thinking this, it's like she's conjured him: there he is, walking through the door. She's behind the counter, because she loves to be in the thick of action on days like this, and he makes eye contact with her as he walks in. Her stomach lurches, not entirely unpleasantly, and she swallows hard.

'Thank you,' he says with his most flirtatious smile as he takes a glass of bubbly from one of the youngest staff members, whose cheeks instantly pinken. Lexi's protective instincts kick in and she wants to warn him away from charming her booksellers, especially given that he's already lured away one of her best. But she's determined to have good vibes only in this place today. She's also determined not to allow herself to get distracted, though she notes in passing that his shirt brings out the green in his eyes and that he's had his hair trimmed and it's looking tidy and smart in that clean-cut way she likes.

'Well,' she says to him as he approaches the counter. 'This is most unexpected. To what do I owe the pleasure?'

The smile doesn't leave his face, and the butterflies don't leave her stomach.

'I wanted to come experience tipsy browsing for myself,' he says.

For some inexplicable reason, she can't stop matching his smile with her own. 'Welcome to the party.'

And it does feel a lot like a party. The shop is filling up, slowly but steadily, laughter ringing out from various corners, the volume of chat increasing to a pleasant buzz. Lexi hasn't allowed herself anything to drink yet – she intends to stay as close to The Serious Professional as she can bear, even though she knows she'll cave eventually.

'Champagne,' Sam says, lifting his glass in her direction. 'Nice touch.'

This is torture for Lexi: she wants to be judged as richer and classier than she actually is and let him believe it's actual Champagne, when in fact she's desperate to correct this common American misnomer. And she can't do it; she can't leave it unsaid.

'Actually . . .'

Sam's satisfied smirk tells her that he was goading her, poking the pedantic bear in her. 'Let me guess. Not actually Champagne, because it's not from the appropriate region of France?'

'Exactly.'

He shakes his head. 'You make me laugh.'

'I'll take that as a compliment.'

'Oh,' he says, smiling wider somehow, 'it is.'

And they stand there, in this crowded shop, looking at each other. It's only a few seconds, but Lexi's heart is thumping. She knows she's going to give in and have the non-Champagne Champagne much earlier than she'd planned – to steady her nerves, her shaky hands, and her treacherous heart.

Eventually, they tear their eyes away from each other's faces – hard to tell whether she's first, or whether he is, or if it's some kind of Mutually Assured Preservation. She watches as he and his glass of non-Champagne disappear into the increasingly large and lively group of customers-turned-revellers.

At least, Lexi hopes that they're customers and not just revellers. But just as she's beginning to question the wisdom of handing out free bubbly without any obligation to buy anything, a slightly flushed regular makes her way to the till with a pile of books, one of which Lexi has seen her pick up and regretfully put down several times over the last few weeks.

'I was trying to resist,' she says, sliding them towards Lexi so that she can scan them. 'But then I thought, what the heck, you're only young once.' Then she catches Hazel's eye and looks mortified, like she's said a terrible thing. 'Not that old people can't enjoy romance novels. Not that age has anything to do with it. I just—'

Beside Lexi, Hazel laughs. 'We know what you mean,' she says. 'Nobody's offended. Not even the less young among us.'

'Thank you,' she says, grabbing her bag of books from the counter and stifling a hiccup.

Lexi watches her pull the wrong door before remembering it's the left one that opens. This customer has been to the shop approximately eight hundred times. She knows which door opens just as she knows that she has a teetering stack of unread romance novels with cartoon covers at home and certainly doesn't need another five right now.

'Tipsy browsing is the best browsing,' Lexi says to Hazel, not-so-subtle code for *This bet is paying off*, and she nods vigorously and enthusiastically. 'Speaking of which . . .'

Lexi walks around the counter and helps herself to a glass, then takes one over to Hazel. She looks at Lexi quizzically, unsure: ah yes, Americans and their careful attitude to drinking.

'Tipsy working is also the best working,' she tells Hazel, winking, and she takes the glass. Lexi is enjoying the festive atmosphere and she wants her staff to enjoy it too. It's been heavy lately, a little black cloud of stress hovering over her head and following here everywhere she goes. It's high time the atmosphere lightened up. Besides, Hazel is sensible, conscientious and careful enough on the till not to make mistakes even after a few sips. It's just scanning and bagging and handing over receipts, anyway, not like in England where booksellers have to manually input the total into the credit card terminal. Lexi would never trust herself to get that right, even sober. And she'd certainly miss the very subtle *Not Authorised* message when a contactless payment doesn't go through; she'd end up having to chase the customer down the street like in a meet-cute of a predictable but very enjoyable Nineties romcom. Here in the US, the terminal buzzes angrily when there's a problem, and there's no mistaking that kind of thing.

As for customer orders – one of the trickier things to master with the not-entirely-intuitive computer system – Lexi doubts there'll be much of that tonight. This is a night for impulse buying and browsing, for catching up with friends from around the Hill you bump into unexpectedly, for standing next to the cosy mysteries and recommending your favourite to strangers. It's not a night for admin tasks.

And that goes for Lexi, too: this evening is everything she loves about bookselling, all the reasons this shop charmed her when she was little even though she couldn't have put it into words back then, beyond *I love the way books smell*. She had to stifle a cheer when she found out she'd inherited the place, because she didn't want it to seem like she was cheering her grandmother's death instead of this exciting way to keep her alive along with her legacy to the community. She anticipated moments just like this: when people share the joy of books, when that joy is amplified *because* it's being shared. Books, after all, bring people together and give them something to talk about when they think they have nothing in common.

Lexi is buzzing, and it's (mostly) not the Champagne, and it's (mostly) not Sam, or the fact that he seems to have come at best in peace as a supportive friend and at worst curiosity. Those things don't hurt, admittedly, but the buzz is about the full shop, the emptying shelves, the sheepish but delighted demeanour of shoppers giving in to their impulses, the excited conversation, and the anticipation of so many of these readers coming back next week or next month to tell Lexi that they loved the book, to find the bookseller who recommended just the right thing and ask them for more titles they should try. She's encouraged her booksellers to be even more enthusiastic, even more liberal with their suggestions tonight, and it's working. When she circulates amongst them, she can tell there's nothing forced about it. The energy in the room is feeding itself, vibrating and ricocheting off each bookseller and each satisfied customer.

She hasn't felt like this at work in a long time, and she's guessing her staff haven't either. Lost in the moment, standing in the centre of her bookshop – her beloved grandmother's beloved bookshop – it takes her a while to notice that Sam is standing right in front of her.

'Hey.' He says it gently, but the interruption makes her jump. Part of her wants to be mad at him for interrupting her moment, but he's so handsome and he smells so good that she can't be. She's glad he's here, seeing this, and not in a weird, vindictive kind of way: she's glad because she's proud of herself and her staff and what they've built here. The happy, successful bookshop owner feels like the truest part of her, and Lexi wants Sam to see that, to really see *her*.

Not that it matters, or not that it should.

'Hey,' she says back.

'So this seems like a roaring success.'

Living in the US has made Lexi less bashful, better able to take a compliment. In England, she might have said something self-deprecating like *Oh, there's probably nothing else to do on a Friday night in DC* or *Yeah, free wine will do that.* But instead, she says, 'Yeah, it is, isn't it?' And she lets herself grin as widely as she feels like grinning, so widely her cheeks ache, so widely that Sam has no choice but to mirror it. Not that it's a choice, exactly – more of an unconscious reflex, like a shared yawn at the end of a long shift the week before Christmas. They stand there, grinning, like earlier, but with added verve and enthusiasm, and Lexi's cheeks are burning now and suddenly, much as she loves everyone being in her shop, she wants them all to leave so that she can kiss Sam. Instead, she takes a deep breath, trying to rid herself of what is clearly a ridiculous thought, but her cheeks only burn hotter.

'You're in your element,' Sam says. 'It's so great to see. It's like – you're alive in a whole different way.'

It occurs to Lexi to ask if he feels that way in his shop, ever – alive in a whole different way – but she doesn't want to ruin her enjoyment of the night by reminding him that they're rivals, by reminding him that this evening is part of her fight for survival – a night made necessary in large part because of him.

Her internal buzz fizzles a little. Her cheeks start to relax out of their grin. She tries not to focus on those things; she tries not to resent him, to cling to the joy. Because, in this moment, it's clear that Sam means his comment kindly: his voice is tender, and even sexy.

'Thank you,' she says. She lets herself appreciate that he's seeing her, just as she wanted him to. And he's still standing there, looking like there's so much more he wants to say. Out of the corner of Lexi's eye, she's aware of a raised phone in their direction. She pictures a hashtag: #bookstorebabes, and stifles a giggle. She wonders vaguely if anyone will send a tip to one of the DC blogs, implying that Sam and Lexi's rivalry may be rooted in sexual tension as much as their own drives for success and survival.

'Busted,' she wants to say to him, but then what if she has to explain to Sam what it is the phone-wielding photographer might be seeing, might be busting them for? Instead, she pulls her eyes away from him, looking for a customer who might need a recommendation, a legitimate way out of a moment she'd actually be perfectly happy to stay in forever: she and Sam looking at each other in the centre of her successful bookshop buzzing with satisfied customers.

She finds a gap on a shelf that needs filling with a face-out. She turns to do it, but first she can't resist gently touching Sam's arm, saying, 'Thank you for coming,' then adding, embarrassingly, 'It really means a lot,' because it does, this coming in peace, this coming to support her, this pride in her that she feels coming off him in waves.

Maybe it wasn't his intention, but she's almost sure it's why he's still here, and she barely cares whether anyone will notice as she walks over to the shelf, rearranges the books and Sam follows her and says, 'You're so good at this.'

Lexi barely cares who sees what or what conclusions they might draw because she's drunk on the buzz of the bookshop, and the non-Champagne Champagne, and maybe a little bit on falling in love, even though it's stupid and it makes no sense and they're mortal enemies and he maybe even has a girlfriend. Alcohol doesn't just lower resistance to buying books; it lowers Lexi's resistance to caring about DC gossip, and to the blatantly obvious truth.

And tipsy flirting, it turns out, is the best flirting.

Chapter Fifty-Three

On Monday morning, the shop feels filled with hope. It's like breathing in fresh air – like getting off the train in the Lake District on a camping weekend with her uni friends years ago, when she'd got on among the stress and crowds and pollution of London Euston. She'd stepped off and immediately her blood pressure had lowered, settling at a healthier level than usual, and her lungs had filled with something they had forgotten existed, had forgotten to crave. Pure, fresh air that almost hurt when it entered her London-scarred lungs.

That's how it feels walking into the shop today. Natalie and Hazel are chatting, their shoulders – is Lexi imagining it? – visibly more relaxed, as if a rucksack full of hardbacks has been removed from them. Debbie and Marcus are smiling as they dust shelves, replace an old staff pick with a new one, or pull out some face-outs to fill gaps on the biography shelf. All of them greet Lexi with friendly, open faces, all traces of false cheer and resignation erased, and that feeds her own relief, the spring in her own step as she wanders downstairs to greet the books and check her email, to crunch the numbers from Saturday night and see just what they've done to the curve on the graph of doom. It turns out she doesn't hate maths quite as much when it's cheerful maths.

Downstairs, trolleys are full of books for shelving. Even in their wildest dreams of what Saturday could be, they hadn't ordered enough to replenish the many gaps left by happy shoppers. But that's okay: gaps mean more space for face-outs, and face-outs often mean sales, so it's a win-win, and the new stock will be here from the warehouses in Pennsylvania and Tennessee in just a couple of days. Apart from anything else, Tipsy Browsing was a way to get rid of books that have sat around unbought for a long time, and that is space that can now be filled with books that they know (or at least hope) will fly straight off them again. It feels exciting. And now she's got a bit of distance, the panic over the online gossip has receded, too.

It feels like those first few weeks of rebranding, when Lexi was fresh and full of ideas and enthusiasm. She'd gradually forgotten what it was like to be a new bookshop owner, a new bookseller, hungry to share her love of reading and eager to keep building community in her grandmother's footsteps. She'd allowed herself to get more and more submerged by the admin and the maths and the worries about the graph, so that unconsciously she had become used to survival as the goal, rather than growth and innovation and, above all, joy. But Friday night had been like filling her lungs with that long-forgotten joy, and Lexi intends to cling to this feeling for dear life.

Pippin stirs as she creaks open the door to her office. He opens one eye, just to check that it's just Lexi today, and not hordes of not-entirely-sober twenty-somethings. He wandered out at the beginning of the evening on Friday, just to see what all the commotion was about, and consented to being fussed over by a few people before running back to the safety of his basket. Lexi is pretty sure that could he have slammed the door behind him to keep the world out, he would have. Satisfied that it's just harmless little Lexi, he closes the one eye he opened and burrows back into his morning snooze position, curled in on himself.

Humming the last song she'd listened to on the way to the shop – something by Ed Sheeran – Lexi turns to her desk. First mistake: she's in such a hurry to get to work that she doesn't make tea first. The first rule of office work is to always make tea before you start.

In an attempt to salvage a modicum of work-life balance, Lexi doesn't have her work email on her phone. She doesn't want her thumb to absent-mindedly go there when she's at karaoke or scrolling through her sister's messages for the latest pictures of Chloe and Peter. She only wants to work when she chooses to work, which, admittedly, *is* most of the time.

Today, she wanted to be at the shop as soon as she could. She could hear her email calling her. She was thinking there might be Google Alerts leading her to rave reviews of Tipsy Browsing or messages from journalists requesting an interview or a quote for their latest article on the resurgence of independent bookshops, a favourite topic of lifestyle sections during slow news weeks. In her giddiness, she'd even imagined a request to speak on local TV about great business ideas.

But, instead, while those emails may well be sitting there in Lexi's inbox, her eye is drawn immediately to a subject line marked *Rent*. The brakes slam on her good mood. The wobbly-leg feeling she's learned to recognise as adrenaline-fuelled fight-or-flight surfaces. *It could be good news*, she tries to tell herself. Free rent for a year! Special offer if you sign a long-term lease! A reward for being the Best Tenants Ever, always paying on time no matter what global catastrophe comes their way.

Of course, that's not what it is.

In the history of the world, when has an email with the subject line *rent* ever been good news?

Certainly not today.

Lexi swallows hard as she scans down the message. *I'm sure you understand . . . increased cost of living . . . we wish we didn't have to . . .* She slams her laptop shut and rests her head on the desk. Beside her, Pippin purrs, absolutely oblivious about his imminent ejection from the office.

Because this is it.

Lexi poured her last ounce of energy and enthusiasm into Tipsy Browsing. She's got nothing left. Jane-Austen-themed tote bags won't save the shop from a massive rent increase. Three per cent – sure. But that pesky zero after the 3 won't disappear no matter how hard she looks at it. The graph of doom, which once upon a time was a graph of delight, used to predict they'd be able to weather a storm like this. They'd been on track for a forty per cent increase in turnover when they signed the lease. But not anymore. Friday night now seems like it was the last hurrah, a closing-down extravaganza rather than the ushering in of a new era.

She thinks of her staff, newly relieved, newly happy, newly energised; she thinks about telling them that all their hard work ended up being for nothing. Breaking bad news is by far the worst thing about being a boss, especially when it's undeserved bad news. Lexi feels so lonely in this moment, carrying the weight of all of it on her own two shoulders. The weight of those rucksacks full of hardbacks now rests on her.

Lexi closes her eyes, thinking of what a relief it would be

to have a business partner or a manager put a hand on her shoulder and gently ask, *Would you like me to tell them?* By rights, Sam should have that honour. Or her accountant. Or her landlord. Anybody but Lexi.

This feels like too much, after they've all worked so hard, after they've achieved the results they wanted and even beyond, to somehow still have failed. Lexi would like a trapdoor. She'd like to disappear. She'd give absolutely anything not to have to deal with this.

Chapter Fifty-Four

Lexi calls her accountant and uses the classic 'want the good news or the bad news?' tactic, but he asks for the bad news first, so she never gets to tell him about how well the first, and likely now last, Tipsy Browsing Friday went. Then she calls the landlord, determined to be strong and business-like and convincing, but, of course, that doesn't work; of course, it only takes three minutes before she's full-on sobbing down the phone at him.

Because she's been so determined not to cry, she hadn't thought to grab her tissues from the staffroom, so she's reduced to wiping snot from her face with the sleeve of her cardigan: not exactly the image of the hard-ass businesswoman she intended to project – thank goodness it's not a Zoom call – and that she's sure her grandmother would have projected at such a moment. But maybe it's not all bad, because the landlord's voice softens. As landlords go, he's actually pretty decent; he likes that one of his buildings houses a bookshop: not overly lucrative, even in the glory days, but so wholesome. It makes him look good, possibly even makes him feel good. Lexi can imagine him at dinner parties among the Capitol Hill set, casually dropping in his contribution to the literary world. And it's not all talk, either: he's always offered very generous rates, which is how the bookshop has been able to survive this long.

For a long time, she waited for the other shoe to drop. She was certain that when it was time to sign a new lease in 2022, he'd hike the price, as everyone else seemed to be doing around then. Instead, he told her he knew it had been a rough couple of years and he wasn't going to do that. His kindness made Lexi feel what she now realises was a deceptive level of security. And even though she'd circled in red the date of the next lease renewal and seen it coming towards her, it just didn't *feel* like it had been two years. She wasn't ready for this negotiation. But capitalism, as she well knows, doesn't wait for you to be ready.

'I'm sorry,' the landlord says, and, in his defence, he really sounds like he means it. 'I wish I didn't have to. But it's that, or sell up. And if I sell, well . . .' He pauses, maybe waiting for Lexi to fill in the gap herself, but she's too busy wiping her nose on her increasingly soggy sleeve. 'That could be even worse for you.'

A tiny part of her wants to be mean and say, 'I'm willing to take my chances on that.' But he sounds genuinely stricken, and after all, in some ways, they're both victims of the same system.

'Look,' he says, when the silence has stretched out past the point of discomfort. 'I can give you another three months, if that would help. But it's the best I can do.'

'I appreciate that.' Lexi holds in a hiccup, her voice wet and snotty. And she really does appreciate it: it takes the pressure off for now; it means she doesn't have to burst her staff's bubble right this very second. That's not nothing: they deserve this moment. They've more than earned it. But in three months, she'll be right back here. Tipsy Browsing is enough to reverse the graph of doom, but it's not enough to increase turnover, let alone profit, by thirty per cent.

The bookshop's landlord owns all the small businesses in their little section of Capitol Hill, and it's not as if the toy shop or the frame shop or the shoe repair shop can afford the increase in rent either. No wonder the landlord sounded miserable. They'll all be out of business soon, and this little cluster of shops will either become a ghost town or a whole load of banks and mid-range chain restaurants. And honestly, Lexi isn't sure which one of those is worse for the heart of the community, never mind its aesthetic.

She looks up at the wall, at the *Nevertheless She Persisted* cross-stitch that Erin made for her unironically when she officially took over the shop.

'There are going to be some tough times,' she'd said, 'and when there are, I want you to remember that you're strong. You've got this, okay?'

Lexi has done what Erin and her cross-stitch have told her to: she has spent six years persisting in the face of sometimes unimaginable difficulty.

But she's out.

Of energy.

Of ideas.

Of creative mathematical solutions.

She'll take the three months, and take them gladly. It will give her time to wind things down, sell her stock at half price, help her staff find other jobs. It'll give her time to pack up her stuff and get ready to move back to London.

It's time. She misses her sister; she misses her niblings. She misses real bacon and ready salted Hula Hoops. She misses being able to make references to childhood TV and other people understanding them. She misses making plans with friends who end their emails with *xx* rather than *best*. And she can't stay when the shop shuts: it will break her heart every time she walks past its shell, every time she bumps into one of her former team, which she's bound to, because Capitol Hill is a village.

Sure, she'll miss the pastel houses and the tiny parks; she'll miss air conditioning in summer and the occasional real, proper knee-deep snow in winter. She'll miss living in a city where being a nerd makes you cool and she'll miss being thought of as smart and charming because of her bog-standard British accent. She'll miss the octopus salad from her favourite Puerto Rican restaurant and the duck fried rice from Chiko and the Mexican food from just about anywhere but especially Santa Rosa, just down the road from the shop, and getting pleasantly sozzled on their happy-hour margaritas. And every time she goes back to London, she really tries to find good coffee, and every time it's disappointing; she knows she'll miss Peregrine most of all.

And, of course, irritatingly, she'll miss stupid Sam and his stupid green eyes.

Without thinking, she grabs her phone and scrolls to their latest text thread. She doesn't know, exactly, why she wants to tell him what's happening. To guilt him? Maybe. To give him a chance to tell her not to leave? It's possible. Or just so that he hears it from her first. Or, most frighteningly of all, maybe it's the biological need for a consolatory snog, even though all rational thought warns her that won't be possible, what with the girlfriend, et cetera, and is certainly not wise.

Finding their last chat, she notices something she hadn't seen before: amid the flurry of activity on her phone after Tipsy Browsing, she's missed a message from him. It says, simply: *Proud of you xo*

She taps the heart so that he knows she's thankful, that his words mean something. And then, through her tears, she adds: *Thank you xo*

And then: *But it isn't enough.*

Lexi stares at her phone, willing Sam to respond. He's probably busy, serving customers who used to come here but now go to him instead. He'll probably ignore her message for two days the same way it looks like she's ignored his.

But no: his response lights up her phone almost straight away.

What do you mean?

Just heard my rent is going up 30%. It's over. You've won.

Then she deletes that last bit, because even though she feels like it's amply deserved, it seems harsh, and right now what she needs is a friend. And maybe also that consolatory snog.

Oh no. That's really rough.

Dots, no dots, dots again.

I don't know what to say.

Lol I can see that.

I'm sorry.

Thanks.

Come over tonight?

Lexi should say no. She should say, *I don't think that's wise.* She should say, *Haven't you got a girlfriend?* But tonight is date night for Erin and John. Lexi will be alone with her dark thoughts, too stunned to cook. So what if it's not the wisest thing? She'll be gone in a few weeks anyway and she'll never have to see him again. She won't have to worry about whether he'll dump her for Amanda, or dump Amanda for her. He'll be in the past, all of this will be, and she can forget all about how he destroyed her business and ruined all other men for her. It'll be like none of this ever happened.

Chapter Fifty-Five

If she's honest, Lexi would have to say that what she wants is for Sam to rip her clothes off as soon as she walks in the door. She doesn't want to think. She doesn't want to talk. She just wants mindless distraction. She's a little feral with desire.

She's missed him.

And he's so hot.

Lexi has all this pent-up rage and frustration energising her, and that energy has to go somewhere. And she knows it's ugly, but she's also kind of relieved that she won't be here to face the consequences when it inevitably goes horribly wrong. She can walk away. And she will.

But Lexi's animal thoughts are halted when Sam opens the door. He stands there in the checked shirt that she loves because it brings out the colour in his eyes, brow furrowed in worry and empathy. And he doesn't, as she'd hoped, and as she'd pictured all the way to his apartment, kiss her and immediately find some buttons to undo, a zip to rip downwards, a bra to unclasp in one deft movement.

Instead, he opens his arms wide to her, offering a hug, and the animal in Lexi is gone, replaced by a young woman in need of comfort, in need of being looked after. Embarrassingly, she starts to cry, and not the pretty kind of tears you see in movies, either: snotty, ugly tears that she's grateful he can't see with her face smushed into the gorgeous shirt she's currently ruining.

'It's laundry day tomorrow,' he says softly, into her hair, as if reading her thoughts. 'Go as hard as you like on this shirt.'

That makes her laugh, for some reason – laugh through her nose so that more snot comes out, which makes her laugh a little more, mostly at herself and how pathetic she is. This is definitely not the animal seduction she'd pictured on the way over. When she pulls away, which she'll have to eventually, there'll be snot and tears on his shirt and her eyes will be – already are; she can feel it – red and puffy and swollen. The death knell, surely, to any attraction Sam might feel towards her.

'I think it should probably be laundry day *today*,' she says, pulling back and admiring the mess she's made. It feels like a weird kind of revenge to ruin his best shirt, his most attractive shirt, the shirt that makes him irresistible to women. Unless it's just her who feels that way; in which case, it's not so much revenge as an own goal.

Sam looks down and, to his credit, does not seem particularly horrified.

'I have other shirts,' he says. He unbuttons it, and takes it off, and then Lexi's face is against his bare chest. Something primal awakens in her, in the hair on her arms. How is it possible to be this sad, exhausted, frustrated, and also this turned on at the same time?

'Would you like some water?' he asks softly, and no, what she wants is to stay pressed up against him, but also yes, she is thirsty, and she can't put off his seeing her puffy face forever.

She nods against him. 'Yes. Please. Thank you.' So polite, so well brought up, like the nice girl she is, the kind of nice girl who definitely doesn't jump her mortal enemy who might have a girlfriend just because she's having a bad day, a bad month, a bad year.

Sam gently takes her arms and peels them away from him. 'Make yourself comfortable,' he says. 'You know where the couch is.'

Lexi would know where the couch was even if she had never been here before. In a studio apartment, it's hard to miss it. But it's not just a couch – it's a couch loaded with meaning and memories.

She sits up against the arm, her legs pulled up next to her, and she watches as this shirtless hottie pours her a glass from his Brita filter. Nobody in their right mind drinks DC water unfiltered, so this shouldn't be a big deal, and yet still, the domesticity of it, the intimacy of this everyday moment – pouring water from a filter jug, shirtless – it does something to Lexi's insides. It feels like safety, as if she never has to experience the sensation of having nowhere to go.

'Here,' he says, handing the glass to her. 'No ice, just like you British like it.'

It's possible, of course, that Sam has just run out of ice. But it's also possible that he's overridden his natural impulses, paused to think about it, and indeed done it just the way Lexi likes it. Maybe, if she was staying, she could even train him to make tea the right way: not just the basics of kettle use, but also the little things: not too much milk, the squeezing of the teabag until the tea is just the right colour.

But she's not staying, and he'll never learn. She'll be on a plane soon, her bookshop shattered and her heart broken. Lexi thought she'd cried herself dry, but her eyes start leaking again. How has everything gone so wrong?

'Hey,' Sam says, sitting next to her. 'It's okay. You're okay. I'm here.'

She wishes she could relax into his kindness and his reassurance. She wishes there wasn't always the niggling response lurking behind the unsaid: that his being here is precisely the problem, or rather the source of many of the problems. Still, weirdly, there's nowhere she'd rather be than on this couch with this not-quite-cold-enough water and this handsome shirtless man next to her.

Horizontal might be preferable, but all in good time.

It's not like she's got the energy right now, anyway. She needs to draw breath after all that crying.

Lexi shuffles closer to Sam and rests her head on his shoulder. *Rest* being the operative word: she's exhausted. Not just from the crying, but from the last few months of running to stand still, the last few years of carrying the weight of a business she loves through the challenges of twenty-first-century life. She'd like to share that weight with someone. To be able to put it down for a while, and have them carry it for the next bit of the road. But instead, here they both are, carrying their competing weights, each of them in their own corner.

'The bookshop isn't okay, though,' she says. 'My staff's jobs aren't okay. My grandmother's legacy . . .' Her voice cracks.

'Your grandmother's legacy isn't just about the physical bookshop,' he says gently, his voice vibrating pleasantly through Lexi. 'I bet there are adults walking around now who love books and it all started when they were read to at story time in the shop. And maybe those adults have kids now, and they passed on their love of books to them, and those kids will go on to write books of their own, or maybe even open bookshops. Your grandmother's name is legend around here. That won't go away if the shop shuts.'

The *if* is weirdly comforting. The shop shutting seems like a certainty to Lexi, but the fact that someone else can have a little hope on her behalf makes things feel a little better. And the rest: it's beautiful. It takes some of the weight off Lexi's shoulders, because it's not only up to her to preserve her grandmother's legacy. She's ensured that herself. Lexi feels at peace. More relaxed. Lighter.

'Thank you,' she tells Sam, lifting her head and turning towards him. The air feels like it's crackling. They look at each other, Sam probably wondering the same things as Lexi: don't they really want this? Is it a good idea? Does *she* really want this?

'I'm glad you're here,' he says.

She closes her eyes and waits, for what feels like forever but is perhaps all of a quarter of a second, and then his lips are on hers, pausing, lingering, as if to say, *Is this okay?* And because it's very much okay, Lexi leans in to him and deepens the kiss until she hears a sound at the back of his throat, animal-like, pleasure and pain at the same time.

He pulls back just long enough to say, 'I missed you.'

'I missed you so much,' Lexi says, 'even though sometimes I want to kill you.'

'This feels like more fun than that.'

'It's a worthy substitute.'

Then his hands are in her hair, and then up her shirt, and then somehow, they find her breasts.

'Is this okay?' he asks, out of breath. 'I mean, you're sad. I don't want to take advantage.'

'This is very much helping,' she tells him, 'with the whole being sad thing.'

He laughs, relieved. 'Pleased to hear it.'

Lexi doesn't want to interrupt. Everything is going so well, but she has to know. The fact that she's leaving doesn't just suddenly make everything okay. 'But what about Amanda?'

'What about her?'

'Aren't you guys together?'

'No.' He pauses. 'She wanted to be. She came back to DC to try to win me back over. But it's too late. Too much water under the bridge. And, well. You.'

Lexi can feel a grin overtaking her face. 'Is it bad that I'm not sorry?'

Sam laughs into her hair. 'No.'

'And is it also bad that I'm not sorry I spilled wine on her that time?'

'Not at all,' he says. 'I couldn't look at you, or I knew I'd laugh.'

Lexi flashes back to his stony face; she'd read it entirely wrong. She needs to learn not to make assumptions. But for now, it's time to focus on the task in hand.

'It seems unfair that you're the only one who's topless.' Sam says.

'I couldn't agree more.'

As he deftly unbuttoned her blouse, the air between them cracked with anticipation. The lingering touch of his fingers sent shivers down her spine, and she found herself lost in the moment.

* * *

Later, with his arm wrapped around her, she nestled closer, the warmth of his embrace enveloping her like a comforting blanket. 'I could stay here like this forever,' she whispered as his face turned towards her.

'Then do.' His eyes say, *I mean it.*

'I can't. The bookshop . . .'

'We'll figure it out.'

'I'm leaving, Sam.'

He freezes for a second, like Netflix buffering in the middle of a key scene. 'I'm sorry – you're *what*?'

'I'm going back to England. Everything is too difficult here. I miss home. I miss my sister.'

'You weren't going to ask me what I thought first?' There's no mistaking the shock in his voice. 'If I wanted to try to make this work?'

'You're the reason I'm leaving,' she blurts out, defensive, trapped. And doing a very bad job of explaining her thoughts, much less her feelings.

'I see,' he says, sitting up, fumbling for his shirt. 'Then leave, I guess.'

'Wait,' she says, a pathetic note of pleading in her voice. 'No. That's not what I mean. This is all so confusing.'

'It's confusing for me too,' he says. 'I miss you when we're not together. Our bodies feel like they were made for each other. But I can't keep doing this. I can't keep thinking I might love you, only for it to turn out that you're just using me. So leave. Give us both the chance to get over this.'

Lexi feels slapped. Shocked.

He loves her?

Her body is still sending her pleasure signals. Her mind is struggling to make sense of what's happening.

'Seriously,' he says. 'This is all a game to you, and my heart can't take it. So go. Drink all the iceless water England has to offer. And have a nice life.'

The finality of his tone leaves no room for doubt.

There's nothing for Lexi to do now but get dressed and leave.

Chapter Fifty-Six

Lexi doesn't usually text her sister this late, but she's not sure what else to do, where else to turn. The flat is dark and empty, and Lexi's sensible American friends are probably all tucked up in bed ready for their 5 a.m. wake-ups for a run or a visit to the gym before their world-changing days at the office.

Any chance you're up?

I am now.

Lexi refuses to feel guilty about this. If people don't want to be woken up by text messages, they should have their phones on silent.

You okay?

. . .

Give me five secs, okay? I'll call you.

It's 6 a.m. over there, the sun barely rising, if the sun can ever be said to fully rise in England. Stephanie's house is probably still, for at least another half an hour or so, before the routine of getting ready for school and work starts up again. In solidarity with what her sister is probably doing at this very moment, Lexi makes herself a cup of tea. She's just putting the milk back in the fridge when the phone rings.

'So, what's up?'

In the brief pause before Lexi speaks, she hears the tell-tale sound of raindrops on an umbrella. Stephanie is standing outside in the rain to talk to her, probably in the unlikely combination of wellies and pyjamas. This is love: for Lexi, and also for the family whom Stephanie doesn't want to wake up too soon (although possibly that is mostly self-preservation). Brits may not say *I love you* to each other as much as Americans do, but they can read the signs. Taking a call in wellies and pyjamas before weekday madness begins is certainly one of those signs, and it makes Lexi feel both grateful for her sister and sad that she's so far away.

'I've messed everything up,' she tells her. 'Sam, the bookshop, everything.'

'Wait,' Stephanie says. 'Slow down.'

Lexi tells her everything, or at least almost everything. Then, when she finally stops talking, Stephanie is quiet. If it weren't for the increasingly insistent drumming of the raindrops, Lexi would wonder if they'd been disconnected.

'How soon are you thinking of coming home?' Stephanie asks.

'Soon.'

Lexi feels guilty about how long it's been since her last visit. There were those years when travelling was difficult, and then, when they were back to more or less normal, it never seemed quite the right time to leave the shop.

'I miss you. All of you.' On the fridge, the latest picture of Chloe and Peter in their burgundy and grey school uniforms smiles down at her.

'We miss you too. It would be so nice to have you home.'

Usually, Lexi corrects people when they call London home. DC is home now: it's where she's built her life, built a community, survived a pandemic. It's where the coffee shop staff know her name and her order, where she can't go for a run without bumping into someone she knows. This tiny capital city, with its green spaces, its earnest twenty-somethings determined to make their mark, its quirky politicians who buy the most unexpected books, its Puerto Rican and Mexican and fusion restaurants.

This time, though, it hits different. Lexi thinks of her first term at uni, everything new and strange, how she'd called Stephanie, who'd come to pick her up. For one blissful weekend, Lexi had felt like her old self again. She thinks about how amazing it would be to feel that again. How she probably wouldn't want to come back to DC. She thinks about Chloe's dance recitals, her toes pointed inside her pale pink ballet slippers, her tutu making her look like the Disney princesses she loves. She thinks about letting Peter win at Connect Four. She thinks of cups of tea with her sister, taking the Tube into Central London for a spot of shopping. It all feels, suddenly, so comfortingly familiar. She'd be part of a family. Maybe she wouldn't even notice her singleness. She'd forget about Sam in an instant. And anyway, who needs sex when you've got easy access to peshwari naan?

The thought of being back in London is like a warm weighted blanket, like changing into dry clothes after getting caught in an unexpected downpour. When she falls asleep, she dreams of tube stations and afternoon scones, the ducks in St James's Park, and the international aisle at Sainsbury's, and she wakes up strangely rested, except for her still-puffy eyes reminding her of what's gone so wrong in DC.

Chapter Fifty-Seven

Lexi has no choice at this point but to call an emergency staff meeting. She's messed her booksellers around long enough, yanked them this way and that, and they deserve to know what's happening. She's ordered pizza and wine, and been organised enough to chill the white, to avoid the Bookshop Special of warm pinot grigio in a paper cup.

She watches Hazel and Debbie and Natalie and Megan trickle downstairs to the sofa area after closing time, having counted the money and wiped the surfaces and – oh the glamour! – cleaned the toilets. One by one, staff who weren't on the shift join them: Hazel, Elijah, Marcus. The buzz down there is a low-pitched one, a humming of stress in the atmosphere. Nobody expects an emergency meeting to be good news, after all. But Lexi also wouldn't blame them for thinking this was an exception, after Tipsy Browsing Friday and how well it went. They all thought they'd hit on a perfect formula. A way back from the graph of doom. Lexi had hoped the next meeting would be different from this – full of laughter, optimistic projections, ideas for new Tipsy Browsing merch. Instead, she watches her staff eat rapidly cooling, limp slices of pizza, and she takes a deep breath.

'Thank you all for coming at such short notice,' she says. 'I know I've always asked a lot of you, and that's never been truer than in the last few months. Tipsy Browsing was a roaring success, and I want to thank you for all your time and energy and enthusiasm and determination. You truly are the best—' her voice catches in her throat and she pauses to compose herself among the pin-drop silence '—the best team I could have ever asked for.'

There's no way out of this one now. Lexi is like a gymnast, who's let go of one of the uneven bars, and it's time to grab the other one before she face-plants.

'Unfortunately, our landlord has given me notice that he's raising our rent by thirty per cent. And there's just—' Her voice catches again, but this time it's less noticeable among the gasps and the whispered swear words. 'There's just no way I can make this work anymore. I'm sorry.'

There's a respectful pause, a moment of silence for the death of life as they've known it, and then everyone raises their hands and starts to speak all at once. It feels so desperately lonely in Lexi's chair. She finds herself wishing for a hand on the small of her back, or gently squeezing her own hand. She finds herself, weirdly, wishing for Sam, of all people, to be here. Maybe to take the blame. But also, maybe, because he gets her. He cares. Except not anymore, because she's ruined it. But she can't think about that right now, or she'll never hold it together. Chances are slim as it is.

Lexi waits for the hubbub to die down, for everyone's polite instincts of waiting for each other to speak to kick back in, and then she answers their most pressing concerns.

'We have three months' grace,' she tells them. 'I understand if anyone wants to leave before that. I'll help you all with jobs as much as I can.' In the six years of doing this job, Lexi has got to know a lot of people in the book world. There are marketing jobs in publishing companies, event planners in all kinds of industries, jobs selling books into bookshops that would suit her most chatty, most enthusiastic staff down to the ground. And, of course, there are other bookshops: several great ones in DC, many others across the region and the country. There is so much talent in this room; Lexi is confident they'll all be okay. But breaking up this team, this community: it will be so painful, and they all know it, even those who aren't scared of change, who even find it energising. She tells them all this, miraculously getting through it with only minimal tearing up.

'What if . . .' Natalie puts her hand up, timidly but with a determined look on her face. Lexi nods to encourage her to go on. 'What if we started a GoFundMe? Would we be able to raise enough money that way to keep going?'

Lexi's heart sinks, and she can't tell exactly why. Maybe it's because she recognises denial, famously the first stage of grief, and it hurts her all over again to be causing her team this pain. Maybe it's because she can foresee the disappointment for her, for all of them, when it doesn't work, when they fall short of their goal. And maybe it's also because when she spoke to her sister on the phone last night, Stephanie couldn't hide her excitement about Lexi coming home. Maybe because she misses Dairy Milk chocolate, and custard, and the particular smell of British paperbacks. But Lexi takes in Natalie's hopeful face, and she can't say no.

'You can certainly try,' she says, realising too late her mistake: she's said *you*. Not *we*. She hasn't included herself in this fight. It's obvious that she has surrendered herself to this fate. Lexi tries to justify her lack of enthusiasm with what she says next. 'The challenge with that is to raise enough money to make this work long term. We're not just talking about a temporary stopgap for a cash flow issue.'

'So maybe,' Natalie says, 'we raise enough to make up for the shortfall for a year. A year is a long time. Anything could happen in that time.'

There are murmurs of appreciation and approval. Lexi does the maths as quickly as she can in her head. They're talking about tens of thousands of dollars. Even if her heart was still in it, it seems highly improbable they could raise that kind of money in this current economy. Impossible, even.

'Let's try for a hundred thousand dollars,' Natalie continues. 'I bet we can do it. We tell the Washingtonian and CityCast and the DC blogs and our own social networks. I bet we can do it within a week.'

She's always been one of the most enthusiastic staff, one of those with slightly crazy ideas that sometimes work out and often don't.

Lexi looks around to see earnest nodding, murmurs rising this time, in hope this time. The hope lifts her, too, the cresting wave of it.

'You're very welcome to try,' she says.

Chapter Fifty-Eight

More as an act of support than because she thinks it will actually do anything, Lexi asks her friend Sofia to post the GoFundMe link on their virtual church noticeboard. Ten minutes later, a text pings up from Catherine: *I donated, and I sent the link to my friend who runs a Capitol Hill Facebook group.* Twenty minutes after *that*, the church places a huge order for books for their next Women's Conference and a whole load of Jesus Storybook Bibles that they give to families with new babies.

A sensation that Lexi recognises as hope starts to bubble up in her gut, but with it: dread. She'd resigned herself to the seemingly inevitable; she'd followed London accounts on Instagram; she'd written the dates of Chloe's next dance recital in her diary. And she'd started to feel something like relief at the thought of soon being far away from Sam and starting to get over him.

What if this works? What if she can stay? Does she even want to? She concludes that the important thing is that her staff's jobs will be saved, and that the bookshop will be saved – that she can own it without working there, be a hands-off boss. Surrendering control doesn't seem like something she could easily do, but there's a first time for everything. Lexi likes to think that she's growing as a person.

She hits refresh on the GoFundMe page and sees that the numbers have climbed vertiginously again. This can't be happening. Can it? Lexi feels slightly ridiculous for not having asked for help in the first place. She reads and rereads the paragraph that Natalie wrote as an introduction to the crowdfunding appeal: it's a love letter to the shop, to its place in the community, a reminder of what Pemberley Books means not just to her, but to others. It makes Lexi a little tearful.

Mindlessly, she refreshes the page again: another incredible increase. Mostly small amounts from people whose names she recognises: regular customers, friends of friends, local authors.

And $2,000 from one Sam Dickens.

Lexi gasps, her hand on her mouth.

Because she thought he hated her, never wanted to see her again, couldn't wait till she was on that plane back to London. And she'd assumed he'd be delighted to have the bibliophiles of the Hill all to himself.

She grabs her phone to text him, but she sees he's got there first.

Call me, he's written, like he doesn't know she's a millennial who will instantly assume someone is dead if texting isn't sufficient.

I saw your GoFundMe contribution. Thank you. That's really generous.

You're very welcome. But I still need you to call me.

Lexi's heart is racing, and not just at the thought of actually talking on the phone, like that's still a thing people do in the year of our Lord 2024.

Sam picks up on the first ring, and there's warmth in his voice that wasn't there last night.

'Hi.'

'Hi.'

So far, Lexi fails to see how this couldn't have been done by text. But she has to admit it's nice to hear Sam's voice, to feel him with her on the other end of the phone. To feel less alone.

'So listen. I have a proposal for you.'

Her blood turns instantly to ice. She isn't sure how she feels about proposals being made over the phone while surrounded by mountains of Post-its and a close-up of the graph of doom. She hasn't even had time for a manicure lately. The photos will be rubbish. 'Um . . .'

She hears him laugh, a jagged breath through his nose. 'Not that kind of proposal.'

'That's a relief.' She hears herself and quickly corrects her faux pas. 'Just that it's a little soon in our relationship, given that last night you said you never wanted to see me again. And also given that the phone is not exactly . . .' Lexi is babbling. She hears herself doing it. She decided there's no digging herself out of this hole and so she shuts up, to let Sam do the talking.

'My dad just called me,' he says. 'He was looking for properties to invest in.'

Lexi struggles to process what this has to do with her. 'And . . . ?'

'I told him about your rental plight. He's on board.'

'On board for . . . ?'

Lexi can almost feel Sam rolling his eyes at how slowly she is processing this.

'To buy the property the bookshop's in. That entire little row of shops.'

There's buzzing in Lexi's ears This is probably bad news. All she knows of Sam's dad is of a shadowy figure lurking threateningly in the background.

'He wants to clear his image as this big bad businessman. Do something for a local community. He wants to buy all the properties and rent them out at the current rates for the next five years. Thought I'd sound you out on it, see what you think.'

The buzzing in Lexi's ears intensifies. She doesn't know what she thinks.

How can she possibly know what she thinks?

'That sounds . . . I mean. Potentially great?'

Sam laughs. 'I love the enthusiasm.'

'I'm just a little shell-shocked, that's all.' A British understatement if ever there was one.

'That's fair.'

'And the GoFundMe? What happens with that money?'

'You can still use that for rent. Then you'd have extra funds for marketing. Or, you know, whatever you want to do. Whatever the bookshop needs.'

Lexi doesn't have to think to know the answer to this. 'Hire a manager.'

'Yes.'

'I could go on holiday. I could have time to see my friends. I could go on more dates with terrible DC men!' Lexi is suddenly, inexplicably, thrilled by this prospect.

'You could do that,' Sam says uncertainly. Lexi braces herself, because she somehow knows what's coming. 'Or you could date me.'

'The quintessential terrible DC man.'

'Hey.'

'Sorry. I guess technically you're a terrible New York man.'

It's a good sign that she is able to banter with him. It feels like she's the old Lexi again, for just a second. That she's climbed out of the pit of despair. But also: she's not sure about all this. Tying up her business interests with Sam's family feels a little risky. For her bookshop, but also for her heart. Things could get awkward, but, on the other hand, they already are.

'I mean,' Sam says. 'I'm not really calling for your permission, as such. If my dad's decided to do something, he's going to do it. I couldn't stop him even if I wanted to. But what I'm saying is, the option to stay in DC is there if you want it. Dating me is optional.'

'Good to know.' And it is. Not just the option to date Sam, but the option to stay here, to keep the shop, to hold on to her life.

She snaps out of banter mode and infuses all the gratitude she feels into her voice. This offer from Sam's dad surely didn't come out of nowhere. He talked him into it, despite her repeated trampling on his heart. She's floored and flabbergasted but also a little uneasy, even if she can't figure out exactly why. 'I'm so thankful,' she says. 'You can't even imagine. I wish I could hug you.'

'Well, that didn't work out so well last time.' He seems to be trying to keep his voice light, but Lexi can hear the regret behind it.

She thinks of the fight. But she also thinks of what happened before the fight. So, it depends a little on how they are defining 'ending'.

'I won't say stupid things next time,' she says.

'Don't make promises you can't keep,' he says, but she can hear the smile in his voice.

'Let me think about all this,' she says. There is so much to think about. Saying goodbye to London again, if only in her mind. Turning her back on a chance to start over, with a mess-free blank page. Now that Sam has a solution, where does that leave them, exactly? 'I just need a second to gather my thoughts.'

'Take as long as you need,' he says. 'I'll be waiting.'

Chapter Fifty-Nine

Lexi goes through the rest of the day in a bit of a daze. When all this is over – whatever that ends up looking like – she's going to have to take a week on a beach to lie very still for long periods of time. This roller-coaster has been exhausting. Elation, despair, frustration, satisfaction – and that's just the shop. The stuff with Sam has been bonkers too, and she hasn't had five seconds to process it. At least in Jane Austen's day, women basically just sat around waiting for letters from suitors, and then when the letters came, they could give them their full attention and spend all their time analysing them. Meanwhile, Lexi is supposed to somehow figure this out while saving a business.

Except that now, Sam's saved it for her . . . which she's not sure about. It's chivalrous and kind, and Lizzy Bennet would certainly approve, but she feels a bit weird about it all. She's a strong, independent woman, and this is 2024. It seems a little like conceding defeat to take his family's money. A little bit . . . anti-feminist?

Erin laughs when Lexi explains this to her. 'Seriously? You, the romantic? You're going to say no to possibly the most romantic gesture in the world because it's too . . . old-fashioned?'

'Well, when you put it like that . . .' She'd been trying to focus on the practicalities, not be distracted by romance (again). And yet her stomach does a little somersault at the thought of it, and the thought of what it means for her and Sam.

'Taking the money from a big bad businessman to save a local indie . . . That's like Robin Hood in reverse. *You've Got Mail* with a better ending.'

'Robin Hood in reverse,' she repeats. 'I like it.'

'Take it,' Erin says. 'I mean, I don't want to tell you what to do. But take it.'

Lexi breathes out, a long breath that feels like it's releasing the tension of the last few months. 'Okay.'

'Okay? You're taking it? You're staying?'

'I'm taking the money. I'm securing my grandmother's legacy. I'm making sure Pippin still has a roof over his head. But it doesn't have to be me who runs the shop. I could go home and watch its success from afar while also enjoying the British weather.'

Erin spits out her wine. 'I'm sorry, did you say *enjoying* or *enduring*?' She looks at Lexi, drilling into her soul with her eyes. 'It's not like you to run away. Your dream guy is standing right in front of you. He's yours for the taking. He saved your cat and he's saving your bookshop. He likes you despite the fact that you keep messing things up with him. And you're going to move back to England for – what, exactly?'

'To spend more time with my family,' Lexi says, and then she laughs a strangled laugh, because that's exactly what politicians say when they're leaving for an entirely different reason, and everyone sees right through it.

'You're running away,' Erin says again, shaking her head. 'Because the romantic part of the chase is over and now you're faced with the practicalities of actually making it work with Sam, and that's less fun.'

'I think it would be really fun, actually.' Lexi feels a blush creeping into her cheeks. She tries not to think of the way he touches her.

'There'll be some fun parts, yeah,' Erin agrees. 'But it's scary, your business tied with him like this. And the day-to-day of making a relationship work . . . well, Jane Austen never wrote about that, did she? And there's a reason for that. She was a hopeless romantic, like you.'

Lexi thinks about what it might look like, to live with Sam. To get to play the piano whenever she wants, but also maybe to have to pick up his socks sometimes. To get to know all his annoying habits, rather than just being irritated with him over the graph of doom. To be genuinely angry with him sometimes and not always be able to resolve it with well-timed sex or by walking away. To have to actually talk things through.

Erin's right. It *is* scary. And Lexi *is* tempted to run away. Under the grey skies of London, thousands of miles from here, drinking tea after her niece's dance recital, it would be so easy to feel like her life in DC never happened. That it was all some kind of illusion. That men like Sam don't exist in real life. She could get a job where she's not responsible for anything, where no burden lands on her shoulders. Move into her sister's spare room while she figures things out. Turn the page on this whole chapter.

Lexi tries to make herself want all of that. But deep down, in her gut, where it matters, where her decisions are made, she doesn't. She wants to see another DC spring and complain to her colleagues about not being able to get close enough to the cherry blossoms because of all the tourists. She wants to see the maple trees on A Street turn the most striking red under the bright blue DC skies of October. She wants another Thanksgiving with Erin's family, expressing gratitude for all she loves about her life here and then arguing loudly about politics over pecan pie. She wants to be right at the heart of her community, eavesdropping on book club conversations among her regulars, with Pippin in her lap. She wants to put her favourite books in the hands of her favourite customers.

And yes, she wants to be with Sam. She wants to get to know him, what really makes him tick, to help figure out what it is that he really wants, if business is it, or if he's just doing that to impress his dad and earn his love, when in fact maybe he does want to be a piano teacher. Or a wine expert. Or something else entirely. Or maybe he does want to be a bookseller, and maybe they could figure that out.

Maybe they can be partners, instead of enemies. Lexi likes the sound of that.

Chapter Sixty

It's a risk for Lexi to show up at Sam's place unannounced, but something about it feels right. She sneaks into his building behind someone else and knocks on his door.

'One moment,' she hears him shout. She pictures him wandering around with just a towel around his waist, frantically grabbing a T-shirt. She wants to say, *No worries, you can be naked for this*, but she also doesn't want to spoil the surprise. So she waits, patiently, the lattes in her hand growing more lukewarm by the second.

'Hey,' he says, opening the door, his voice surprised but soft.

'Hello. I've come for my piano lesson. And to deliver you a coffee?'

'Piano lesson?'

'It's Wednesday, right? Did I get the day wrong?'

Sam grabs the latte that Lexi is holding out to him and takes a sip before replying. 'You didn't get the day wrong. I just didn't know that we were still . . . doing that.' He smiles an uncertain smile.

'Oh, yeah. I know we got a bit off track. But maybe we could pick up where we left off?'

'With the piano lessons?' Sam looks no less confused as the minutes go on, and Lexi doesn't really blame him.

'Well, with the other stuff too. It all got a bit weird for a while there.'

'When I found out I was your project.'

This again? Sam really knows how to hold a grudge, apparently. But at least she knows she's not going to run off this time.

Lexi resists the almost overwhelming urge to justify herself. Her silence leaves Sam room to keep talking.

'I know. I was an idiot. You were the best thing to happen to me for a long time, and I messed it up because I was afraid. Afraid of getting hurt again, so I saw hurt where there was none intended. I'm sorry.'

'You are totally forgiven. But also, I'm impressed at this new-found self-awareness.'

'Thank you, I think.'

Lexi looks into his face and he lets her eyes meet his. She swallows hard.

'It's the therapy,' he says. 'It's also made me realise that I should stop selling books out of spite.'

'So now you're selling books out of . . . what? Love?'

'Yes.' Sam holds Lexi's gaze. 'Love.' They almost kiss then; Lexi can tell by a slight change in the atmosphere, even though neither of them has moved a centimetre. 'Except . . . I've actually decided I might do something different altogether.'

'Oh?'

'I'll go back to the piano,' he says. 'I'll teach, and I'll try to find gigs. Books are fine, but I can take or leave them. You've shown me what it's like to truly love them, and I think they deserve someone who is truly passionate about them.'

Lexi has so many feelings. Can she be with someone who only thinks books are *fine*? Does it matter, as long as he respects them enough to know what they deserve?

'But first, if you'll let me, I'll look after your bookstore while you fly home for a while. A week, a month, whatever you want.'

Lexi is surprised by the first thought that comes into her head and out of her mouth. 'I don't want to be away from you that long.'

Those magic words: they unlock something. His mouth is instantly on hers. They're both breathing hot and heavy.

'That,' he says, manoeuvring her to the bed between words, between kisses, 'is the correct answer. Let's not do this breaking-up thing anymore, okay? I want to be with you. I don't want to compete with you.'

'Even though making up is so fun?'

'I'm sure,' Sam says, his hand finding Lexi's bra clasp, 'that we can find adequate substitutes.'

'You know what I'd really love?' Sam says afterwards, both of them tucked under the duvet and grinning like cats with the cream.

'Let me guess.'

Sam snorts. 'No, not that. I'd really love if we could successfully talk. Or not talk, whatever. But just, like, I'd love to not kick you out of my bed this time.'

'I'd love that too.'

Chapter Sixty-One

Lexi picks up the phone to make the call she's been dreading. Stephanie had been so excited about her coming home; Chloe was thrilled that she was going to see her dance, and not just later on video, but actually there, in real time, in real life. And Peter had already planned a Big Library Day Out for them so that Lexi could help him pick out his books for the next few weeks, months, maybe his whole lifetime. Her heart breaks a little that she won't be able to do that for him because instead she's choosing to stay in DC and do it for other people. She resolves to write him letters, to send him books, to be a better auntie to him and Chloe all round.

'Hi,' Stephanie says, out of breath. There's a streak of mud on her cheek; she's been outside, finishing off the gardening, forgotten the time.

'Hey. Do you need a moment to catch your breath?'

'No, no, it's all good. Fitting this in before ballet. There's no time for things like breathing.'

Lexi swallows hard. If she was there, she could offer to drive Chloe to ballet. She could make life easier for her sister on so many levels.

'This can wait,' she tells her, to be helpful, and also, maybe, because she's chickening out. 'If it's a crazy day.'

'I don't think it can,' she says, looking directly into Lexi's soul the way that only big sisters can. 'You said you needed to talk. You don't say that unless it's for real.'

Stephanie watches Lexi pause to think how to start, and she decides to help out.

'Has something happened with Sam?'

'A few things.' Lexi decides to spare her some of the details. 'But the main thing is that his dad is buying the building, and not putting the rent up.'

'So the bookshop is safe?'

'The bookshop is safe.' Lexi fills Stephanie in on Tipsy Browsing, the GoFundMe, the support from the community.

'That's great,' Stephanie says, but Lexi can tell her enthusiasm is somehow forced.

She waits. Maybe Stephanie will save her from having to spell it out.

'So you're not coming home, are you?'

Inexplicably, Lexi starts to cry. Maybe it's the mention of the word *home*.

Maybe it's the relief of Stephanie having guessed. Maybe it's the exhaustion from the last few months, everything that's happened and not happened and almost not happened and then happened after all. Maybe it's the bittersweetness of having two places she calls home, knowing she'll always feel tugged between two cities, two cultures, two different kinds of paperback smells. That wherever she is, she'll always be missing someone.

'I'm sorry,' she gets out, finally, between sobs.

'It's okay,' Stephanie says. 'I want you to be happy, and if DC is where you're happy, then that's where I want you to be. It just doesn't seem like you've been all that happy there lately. That's why I wanted you to come home.

Well, and I suppose it would have been nice to have you around.'

'I know. I'm sorry.'

'Don't be. You've got to do what's right for you.' Lexi thinks of Stephanie pulling her back from the road, back when she was three. Pulling her out of harm's way. She's doing it again now, graciously giving Lexi a way out. 'We miss you, but we'll be okay. Just promise me that if he breaks your heart again, you'll be on the next plane out.'

'I promise.' It's an easy promise, because Lexi trusts Sam not to hurt her.

And also, because if he does, it'll be the final straw, the thing that breaks her. This year has left her fragile. She needs a trip home, some time in Stephanie's kitchen, some time being reluctantly dragged to the garden with her, the therapy of digging her hands into the earth, chatting while kneeling on sore knees, with the rumble of Heathrow-bound planes above and the distant thrum of the North Circular, the white noise that passes for silence in London.

'Can I come and visit soon?'

'Of course you can,' Stephanie says. 'Come often. Come for ages. Be in our lives more, if you'd like. There's a way to do that and still live in DC. And you'll have to bring Sam over, too.'

The thought makes Lexi smile. She can't wait to show off this handsome man she's somehow bagged.

'All in good time,' she tells her sister. 'I love you.'

'I love you too,' Stephanie says, a rare moment of effusiveness. Lexi says it more easily these days, because it comes easily to Americans, between friends and sisters. Brits, though, have to struggle a little to force it out, and it's all the

350

more meaningful when they do. 'Don't be a stranger, okay? I've got to run.'

And with that, the screen goes blank.

It's done.

Lexi is staying in DC.

She'll miss the butter chicken and the peshwari naan, cheering her nephew at football matches and beaming with auntie pride at ballet recitals. But this is home, this quirky city full of overachieving nerds. And Ṣam.

He's home for her, too.

Epilogue

January is a quiet time of the year in any bookshop. It's cold; it's dark; nobody wants to leave their heated home. Everyone has spent all their extra cash and then some in December. So it's lucky that *Pride and Prejudice* was published in January, a great excuse for Pemberley Books to put out press releases and invite influencers, and launch a new line of merch. Tipsy Browsing is still going strong, and bringing in a substantial amount of sales, but it's old news now, not enough to get people buzzing quite as much anymore. Jane Austen, though, will always be popular, and a Jane Austen Day is new and exciting. What, after all, is the point of sharing a name if you can't capitalise on it, just a little bit?

The balloons are back out; the chalkboard outside is newly decorated with a lesser-known Austen quote: *Oh! I am delighted with the book! I should like to spend my whole life reading it*; Pemberley Books is open late and there's a quiz at 8 p.m. with a gift card to be won. Debbie has scoured Etsy and all the shop's usual suppliers for Janeite tote bags and puzzles, stickers and mugs, and dotted them around the shop, as well as having a couple of tables dedicated solely to her and her books.

And then, of course, there's Lexi's very own Mr Darcy, sadly not dressed in a wet shirt, but looking very handsome nevertheless as he busies himself with handing out drinks and snacks. Lexi is even letting him play on the till today, though he had to prove to her that he knew how to use their system first. He offered to be on wrapping duty, but Debbie watched him do a dummy run and immediately removed him from his post.

Lexi looks around and holds back happy tears: the shop is thriving, the books are selling, there's talk of expanding into the shop next door, whose owners chose not to renew their lease despite the favourable rates that Sam's dad gave them.

Somehow, Lexi and Sam have mastered the art of having sex without immediately breaking up. When Erin moved out to get married, it didn't seem worth it to look for another place to rent when there's a Lexi-shaped space in Sam's bed, so she moved in with him – like the plot of *Persuasion* where nothing much happens until it suddenly all does, all in a rush at the end. He's hired a manager to run the shop as a second-hand bookshop again and started teaching the piano to actual students and picking up the odd gig here and there – including once a month at Lexi's shop, where they've squeezed in a fairly decent electronic piano.

Order has been restored to the Capitol Hill neighbourhood. Order has been restored to Lexi's heart. The bookshop is safe, and so is her grandmother's legacy.

And then, today, Jane Austen Day, after ringing through one customer's purchase, Lexi looks up to see the one thing – the one person – who she didn't even know she needed to complete the picture: of all people, her sister. Her mouth drops open.

Stephanie laughs her big, joyful laugh and shuffles her way to behind the counter, opening her arms wide for a hug.

'What are you doing here?' Lexi asks her sister, a rhetorical question.

'Celebrating Jane Austen, of course! What else?'

Lexi can't stop hugging her. Over her sister's shoulder, she watches Sam take out his phone to capture the moment.

'Did you know about this?' Lexi asks him, and Stephanie replies for her.

'He bought my ticket.'

'What?'

'Hate to say it, but he might be a keeper.'

Lexi agrees. She and Sam spent Christmas just the two of them, in what Erin calls their love bubble, having a lot of sex but also curling up in front of festive movies with bowls of ice cream and freshly made, still-warm popcorn. Lexi ordered Christmas pudding and brandy sauce and made Sam wear a paper crown from a cracker all day; she introduced him to the British pigs in blankets – as opposed to the American version, essentially glorified hotdogs, which are delicious but can't possibly hope to compare to chipolatas wrapped in streaky bacon. Lexi closed her shop between Christmas and New Year, to give herself and her staff space to decompress, with Debbie newly in charge as the manager. And then real life kicked back in, and she and Sam found their rhythm. Wednesday mornings are still for piano lessons, and then Lexi leaves so that Sam can teach other people and she can get her bookshop admin done.

And like all couples, they argue about whose turn it is to unload the dishwasher or take the bins out. Lexi is grumpy when Sam's alarm goes off way too early so he can get to the gym, even if she's grateful for the results. She'd be happy doing this for the rest of her life, or at least until children, not that she's thinking about that at all, obviously, or that she's occasionally thrown out some ideas for baby names. It's still the honeymoon phase, despite the occasional sock on the floor (mostly hers, it turns out), but life is good. Life is even better, though, with her sister here.

The hours roll on; the tills fill with credit card receipts and the merch piles begin to dwindle. Before the quiz starts, Lexi makes a speech, thanking everyone for their loyalty, for their custom, for sticking with her through the tough times and giving money to the GoFundMe; thanking her staff for their dogged and enthusiastic work. And she ends by thanking Sam, for bringing her sister, for inspiring her to be more creative and determined in the face of competition. And for being a much better partner than he is a competitor. *Ahhh*, says the crowd, and then Sam speaks up, too.

'Actually,' he says, 'I have something to say, too. It is a truth universally acknowledged that a single man in possession of a DC studio apartment must be in want of a wife.'

Gasps all round, including from Lexi. Her hand flies to her mouth as he kneels.

'My feelings will not be repressed,' he says, and she doesn't know if she is hearing properly over the thumping of her heart, or if she's just remembering the words. 'You must allow me to tell you how ardently I admire and love you. And to ask for your hand in marriage.'

Lexi is having trouble getting her thoughts in order, let alone getting them out in coherent sentences. But she's nodding furiously, and holding her hand out for the ring, and so her body must know before her brain does that she's saying yes.

'Am I given to understand that you accept?'

'Yes,' she says, finding her voice. 'A thousand times yes.'

Different sister, different proposal, someone murmurs, like exactly who says what in which adaptation really matters at a time like this.

And then there's whooping and cheering and confetti, bottles of actual Champagne that Lexi somehow hadn't noticed in the fridge. She mouths, *Did you know?* to her sister, who nods and laughs.

And in the midst of it all, in Lexi's saved and thriving bookshop, surrounded by books and her staff and her favourite customers, she kisses Sam as if nobody's watching.

Acknowledgements

Writing a book is truly the loneliest thing, and yet it takes a village. I'm grateful for mine. Thank you to everyone who believed I could do this (especially Becky Bennett), and everyone who had faith when I didn't (shout out to Andy T).

Thank you to everyone who has supported and nurtured my writing dreams – in some cases, for more than thirty-five years. Especially thank you to Paul, Arlette and Hélène Vandenbroeck who took my creativity seriously even when I was a child, and to my dad who has always actively encouraged it. Also to my mum, who never really got it but always faithfully posted her (totally unbiased, I'm sure) glowing reviews. To Brian and Chitra, for feeding me, listening to me, and giving me a lovely place to live during the painful editing parts of this book – and at so many other times in my life. To Rebecca Kabat – thank you for being the guy the guy counts on. And to Sandra Vanderbilt, Jaime Amrhein, Sonia Faletti – my DC ride or dies. I miss you and our beloved city.

Thank you to everyone who's ever answered a query on my random Facebook posts. Especially thank you to Allison Cunningham for naming Second Reading and Julia Mead for coming up with Great Expectations.

Thank you to Helen Cullen, who pointed me in the direction of this project in the first place, and to Thorne Ryan and Lucy Frederick for the opportunity. Elisha Lundin,

Jade Craddock and Helena Newton made this book funnier and more coherent – thank you!

To all booksellers and bookshop owners: I salute you! What you do is so important. Thank you to all my ECB colleagues for three lovely years at the most wonderful bookshop, and to Laurie Gillman and Cathy Landry for taking a chance on me and welcoming me into the fold.

And last but by no means least: thanks go to you, the reader. There are so many forms of entertainment out there and so many books to choose from. I'm grateful you picked mine!